DEATH'S DISCIPLE: BOOK TWO

TRAITOR'S TOME

EMMA L. ADAMS

DALATHAR
AMANAR
SETEMAR
YALA'S CABIN
SKY TOWER
ENCLAVES
OF YALETAR
SOUTHERN JUNGLE

Seven years ago, Captain Yala led a squad of six fellow soldiers and their armoured war drakes as part of Laria's army's flight division. During a clash with the rival nation of Rafragoria over possession of an unmanned island, King Tharen, Laria's monarch, called Yala's squad to claim the island before their rivals could gain a foothold there. Yala agreed to take on this secret mission before the watchful eyes of the king and his trusted allies the Disciples of the Flame, little suspecting that the island in question would contain an abandoned temple to the god of death, Mekan.

When Yala's squad landed on the island, they found Rafragoria's soldiers had already infiltrated the temple and had met their deaths at the claws and teeth of Mekan's monsters. Their actions ripped open an opening to Mekan's realm, otherwise known as the Void, and Yala and her squad found themselves fighting for their lives. Yala managed to slay the monstrous void drake and sustained a life-changing stab wound to her leg as a result, while her squad-mate Dalem begged the god of the flames to help them escape the island alive. As a former Disciple of the Flame, Dalem was able to gain the god's attention, but he paid the price for the destruction of the island with his own life.

When they returned to the mainland, Yala and her surviving squad-mates learned that King Tharen was assassinated by Rafragorian soldiers during their absence and that he told nobody else of the mission he gave her squad. While she'd hoped that her squad-mate's sacrifice would help her gain the sympathy of the Disciples of the Flame, their leader Superior Datriem refused to believe Yala's reports and warned her never to share the truth of what they saw on the island with anyone else. Shortly after, the new king disbanded the flight division of the army and Yala and her surviving squad members parted ways.

After years of living in seclusion in the deep jungle, Yala little expected anyone to disturb her early retirement, much less a war drake. The beast turned out to belong to a Disciple of Life called Niema who claimed to have been sent by her Superior to seek out Yala and to deliver a cryptic warning of danger. It emerged that Niema learned of her location from Vanat, Yala's former squad-mate with whom she'd had a brief romantic entanglement after the war, but Yala's refusal to leave her home came to an end with the arrival of a group of mercenaries who claimed to have been offered money to eliminate her.

Yala killed the mercenaries with the aid of a Disciple of the Sky, Kelan, who was pursuing them for his own reasons. As her house was destroyed in the process, Yala reluctantly joined forces with Niema to find Vanat and learn who was responsible for sending the mercenaries after her. Following Vanat's tail to the capital, Yala and Niema once again clashed with Kelan, who revealed that he was sent by his own Superior to investigate the rumours of someone meddling with death magic in the capital and that he discovered that the mercenaries were allegedly working for a mysterious group called the Successors. Suspecting that Niema was also aware of this, Kelan pushed her into revealing that Yala in fact appeared in a vision experienced by the Disciples of Life that convinced them she would be a powerful ally against the rise of Mekan, the god of death.

Shaken by this revelation and suspecting a connection with her experiences on the island, Yala explained to Niema that she and her squad members survived their clash with Mekan's beast through Dalem's sacrifice and not because Yala possessed any unique abilities. Niema's faith refused to relent, not even when they found Vanat's dead body on the road, murdered by the Successors. Furious at the loss of her friend, Yala parted ways with her companions upon reaching the capital and went to track down her surviving squad members. While Machit was willing to listen to her, Saren refused, while Viam was safely working within the royal palace and Temik's whereabouts were unknown. Yala warned Machit of the mercenaries' seeming intention of eliminating all the survivors from their squad and he agreed to help her find the truth about the Successors' motives.

Yala and the others soon discovered that the Successors had indeed been meddling with death magic, and in the ensuing confrontation, the Successors' leader Melian revealed her face. Claiming to be a Disciple of Death and a follower of Mekan, Melian attempted to sacrifice Yala and her friends to gain the favour of the god of death in order to overthrow the monarch and claim supremacy. While Machit was killed in the struggle, Yala managed to fend Melian off with the help of Niema, who called upon the war drake using her abilities as a Disciple of Life and ordered it to attack the mercenaries.

In the ensuing chaos, Melian escaped, while Kelan went to rejoin his fellow Disciples of the Sky and met with the unwelcome news that some of them believed Yala to be in league with the Successors herself. It soon transpired that the source of the rumours was none other than the Temple of the Flame, which Melian had infiltrated with the help of Yala's former squad member Temik. When Yala tried to tell him the truth, Superior Datriem attempted to have Yala captured and sentenced to death.

With two groups of Disciples pursuing them and Melian's whereabouts unknown, Yala was forced to accept Kelan's offer to seek out shelter with the Disciples of the Sky. While Superior Sietra believed Yala's innocence, she also revealed that Melian was right. Anyone who glimpsed Mekan's realm had the potential to become a Disciple of Death—which thanks to their experiences on the island, included Yala and her squad—whether they acted on that potential or not. As a result, Superior Sietra decided to imprison Yala as a risk factor and sent a team of her own Disciples to the capital to deal with Melian.

Kelan disagreed with his Superior's choice, but Niema's horror at Yala's connection to Mekan led to her turning her back on both of them. With help of some of his fellow Disciples of the Sky, Kelan helped Yala her escape captivity and returned to the capital, but they arrived too late. Temik, seeking revenge on the Disciples of the Flame for their role in his squad-mate's death on the island, already killed Superior Datriem and drugged the other Disciples of the Flame, leaving the path wide open for Melian to enact her plan to claim supremacy. With the dead swarming the city at her command, Melian was waiting to slay Yala's war drake and cut her throat in the city square.

Before Yala could bleed out, Niema returned, using the power of the god of life to rescue Yala from the brink of death. During her recovery, Yala reunited with her surviving squad-mates – including Viam, now working at the royal palace, who admitted that she was the one who found the books King Tharen used to learn of the island's existence and handed them to Temik in the hopes of revealing the truth of what their squad experienced there. After Temik gave the books to Melian instead and enabled her to learn how to contact Mekan, Viam wanted to make amends by helping Yala.

Accepting that the only way to beat Melian was to call upon Mekan herself, Yala followed Viam's instructions and raised the dead war drake that Melian slew, riding upon its back to interrupt Melian's attempt to break into the palace and assassinate the king. However, Melian had already opened Mekan's realm by slaughtering some of Kelan's fellow Disciples. While Yala managed to kill Melian, she was unable to close the Void and the god of death refused to listen to her. At the last moment, Temik reappeared and gave his own life to the god of the flame in the same way Dalem did, closing Mekan's realm and ending the slaughter.

As the city made its slow recovery from the devastation of Melian's attack, Yala decided to stay with her surviving squad-mates to make sure nobody else attempted to follow in Melian's footsteps. *Death's Disciple* ends with Kelan and Niema leaving the city to return to their homes – and with Niema encountering the unexpected sight of the undead war drake sitting at the roadside outside the capital, as if waiting for someone.

PROLOGUE

Niema's first vision from the god of life came on an ordinary afternoon in the rain-drenched jungle of southern Laria.

Dizziness struck, causing the basket she carried to slip from her hands. The supplies she'd gathered from the nearby village—fruits, nuts, and bread—scattered across the damp earthen path as a sudden clamour of emotions hit her like a thunderclap. Not from her five fellow enclave members and the invisible cord binding them together, but from a terrible fear that had no obvious source and which reminded her of the time she'd run into a wild drake and had simply frozen, unable to utter a sound.

Images of a tall stone building appeared in Niema's mind, blurred at first, as though washed out by the rain. When she closed her eyes, the stone construction became clearer, as did its surroundings. Thick jungle circled a platform of paving stones, upon which stood a wide stairway leading to the gaping hole in the building that might have once been a door. Everything was age-worn, overgrown, and utterly unfamiliar to her.

What is this place? A memory? Not hers. She'd never seen a building like it, or the worn, ancient staircase…

Or the woman, standing on the stairs, looking directly at her.

Niema's mouth parted in surprise, but before she could utter a word, the ground tore open, stones cracking as though wrenched apart by a being of impossible strength. From within came the shape of what she might have taken for a giant bird, but *wrong*, its features twisted and decaying. Feathers dripped from dead flesh, its skeletal wings oozed darkness with each beat, and viscous smoke ballooned outward from the gaping maw that covered the area in front of the stone construction. Revulsion rippled through Niema's very being. *What is that?*

Rain splashed down the back of Niema's tunic, shocking her back to the present. Gasping, she swayed. *Those memories weren't mine.* She'd never seen that building before. Nor had she seen that woman. Yet the images were as clear as if they belonged to her.

She gripped the basket reflexively, a possibility tickling at the edges of her mind. She'd heard of other Disciples receiving insight directly from Yalet Herself—a great honour, but a rare one. Rare enough to be unheard of in recent years, at least according to Superior Kralia, but what other explanation was there? Niema had sometimes seen her fellow Disciples' memories in her dreams, but she'd never seen such an apparition in the waking world.

"Yalet preserve me," Niema murmured.

Superior Kralia alone was most favoured by the god of life. If anyone would know the truth, it would be her. Pulling herself upright, Niema ran in a zigzagging path towards home, raindrops falling off the branches on either side of her like pebbles. It never occurred to her to doubt what she'd seen. Yalet's power manifested in every bird, every tree, every fragment of life in the sustaining forest in which Niema made her home—yet that terrible beast she'd seen in the vision had not been one of Yalet's creations.

Minutes blurred into a single breathless span, and soon, Niema came upon familiar ground and the houses nestled within the trees where her enclave made their homes. She dropped the basket of supplies in front of a startled Hachim and then took off like a bird shaken into flight. When she reached the Superior's clearing, she skidded to a halt. A monster looked down at her, its sharp teeth a mere finger span from her head.

The reptilian beast perched on claws that were each as long as one of Niema's forearms; its wings were folded against its back, and teeth protruded from its mouth, stained with dark blood.

Next to the beast stood a figure dressed in a robe woven from flowers and reeds with a simple crown atop her coiled hair. Superior Kralia watched Niema approach, her expression strained with the effort of keeping the beast from escaping her control. She whistled between her red-painted lips, and the war drake growled in response, its claw raking through the soil.

"Niema." Superior Kralia stepped forward to greet her Disciple. Belatedly Niema fell to her knees in the customary gesture of a Disciple to her Superior, but she found herself unable to drop her gaze from the monster standing at her side. Niema might hold reverence for all Yalet's creations, but that didn't mean she was unaware of how easily those claws might rip her open.

"Superior Kralia." Niema rose to her feet. "Why … why is that creature here?"

Niema had never used her abilities on a beast of that size before, and while its large wings were tucked against its back, its huge form was ill suited to the jungle. When her

Superior gave no answer, she asked, "Is … is it to do with that vision?"

Surprise flickered within Superior Kralia's eyes. "You saw, too?"

"Yes—didn't everyone?" She'd suspected otherwise, but a weight lifted from Niema's mind at the knowledge that she hadn't experienced those terrible images alone.

"No." Superior Kralia let a moment lapse before speaking again. "Then it has to be you, Niema."

Niema's heart skipped. "I don't understand."

"No, I don't expect you do." Superior Kralia's mouth pinched, an expression Niema had never seen before. It reminded her, with a jolt, of the way her mother had looked when she'd told Niema she didn't expect to survive the sickness that had ultimately taken her life.

"What did I see?" Niema whispered. "I-I've heard Yalet gifting some Disciples with visions, but I never thought…"

"That was indeed a vision from Yalet Herself." Superior Kralia extended a hand towards the still, formidable form of the war drake. "This beast was found wandering the eastern coast by another enclave leader. The vision he saw through its eyes caused him much distress, and he contacted the rest of the enclave leaders so that we might seek Yalet's guidance."

"You're saying that beast … showed us the vision?" Niema faltered. "I thought it came from Yalet."

"Do you forget that Yalet exists in all of nature, even a beast such as this?" Superior Kralia gestured to the war drake's scaled form. "She guided this creature to our people to warn us of a terrible threat."

Niema's throat went dry. Superior Kralia's gift enabled her to establish a bond with this beast, to see the images in its mind, but why had Yalet seen fit to bless Niema with the same vision?

"I didn't know." She swallowed, her heart racing. "That vision was a warning … of what?"

"This creature has seen Corruption."

Dread skittered up Niema's spine. *Corruption.* The very antithesis of the power she wielded with her own hands, like its originator: Mekan, the god of death.

That monster in the vision … she'd known instinctively that it was not of Yalet's creation, but to hear the truth from her Superior's lips sent a quake through her very bones.

"Where?" she asked. "Where is this…?" She couldn't speak the word. *Corruption.*

"Far away from here," Superior Kralia answered. "I do know that the beast witnessed the sight with its own eyes, and Yalet guided it here to share those images with our enclave."

Witnessed … but the beast hadn't been alone. "Who was that woman?"

"Whoever she is," said Superior Kralia, "we must find her."

Niema frowned in confusion. "I don't understand."

"Yalet must have shown her to us for a reason," the Superior went on. "She slew Mekan's agents with her own hand. I saw."

Tendrils of dread unfurled within Niema's chest. "Do you think Corruption is coming *here*?"

The very notion of Corruption infecting the forest was unthinkable, but if Yalet Herself had sent the vision, who was Niema to disbelieve?

"I think we must prepare for the possibility, yes," Superior Kralia said. "But first, we must gather information. We must find out who this woman is."

"She's not from the enclave." Niema had never left her small corner of the jungle in all her nineteen years of life. "The woman might be anywhere."

Niema's fellow Disciples had rarely ventured outside of

their enclaves, especially not to the large cities. Going by sheer numbers, the woman was more likely to be in one of those cities than elsewhere, but Niema couldn't begin to imagine finding a person amid the noise and chaos of Dalathar or Setemar.

"She might," said Superior Kralia. "However, we are not the only Disciples to have seen the vision, and I intend to convene with the other Superiors at this week's summit so that we can decide our course of action."

Niema inclined her head. "That … that sounds wise, Superior Kralia. What should I do until then?"

"Prepare." Superior Kralia allowed a moment to pass before she spoke again. "When the time is right, I would like you to seek out this woman yourself, Niema."

———

Superior Kralia gave Niema no clue as to how she expected her to complete this seemingly impossible task, nor did she update her on the situation until close to a week had passed. Mercifully, the war drake had departed the morning after the vision, but unease permeated the enclave. Niema saw grave faces everywhere she went, though she went about her routine as if nothing had changed. Whether she was fetching and preparing food, tending the gardens, sewing clothing, delivering supplies to the elderly Disciples, or taking part in the various rituals and ceremonies dedicated to Yalet, she remained on edge, prepared for another apparition to strike her at any moment.

None came, but the woman she'd seen in the vision haunted Niema's dreams. For the first time since she could remember, she had an experience that she didn't—couldn't—share with the other five members of the enclave to whom she was bonded. And she might yet have more to come; if

Yalet's will took her far away from the enclave, Niema was in no position to refuse.

Prathen, the oldest of their number, attempted to assuage her fears. "I won't lie, it'll be hard at first," he told her one evening as they sat around the cookfire for their evening meal. "You won't remember this, but when you were a child, when only Ekim and I were bonded, I spent some time in Setemar. I was shocked the first day when I woke up and I could no longer sense her."

"I didn't know you'd been to the city." Niema took the bowl of freshly prepared grains and vegetables Ekim had offered her. *I won't be able to sense them any longer.* She'd forgotten what life had been like before they'd been bonded —before she'd been able to feel five hearts beating alongside her own, and before she'd always known five sets of hands would be waiting to catch her should she fall.

"Oh, it was a long time ago, and she won't ever let me go that far away again." Prathen laid a fond hand on Ekim's arm, who smiled. "It'll be hard, but if you do this, it'll be an experience you'll never forget. And the stories you'll have!"

The younger members of the enclave had taken the news much less calmly. Diaman had begged her not to leave, while Threl demanded she bring back plenty of gifts.

Hachim, by contrast, had a more practical outlook. "It's more likely that this woman will be in a place with a large population, like Dalathar."

"You think I'm going to have to go to the capital?" To most enclave members, Dalathar was a distant hazy place, a mythical land of dense crowds and towering buildings.

"If you do, you have to bring back a war drake," Threl insisted. "They're *huge.*"

"Didn't you see the one Superior Kralia brought here a few days ago?" Niema suppressed a shiver at the memory.

"Ekim wouldn't let me." Threl stabbed his spoon into his food bowl.

"Wise of her," Prathen said. "Nasty creatures, those. Don't get too close to their teeth if you do see one, Niema."

Ekim tutted. "Niema isn't a child, Prathen. She's two years past taking her vows as a full Disciple."

"Three," Niema corrected. "I'm not going to Dalathar. I don't understand why I received the vision to begin with."

"Yalet chose you," Ekim said. "A wise choice on her part, to be sure."

"Exactly," Prathen said. "The Superior cannot leave her people, but you can."

"What if we don't want her to leave?" Diaman tugged at Niema's sleeve. "Niema, I'm scared you won't come back."

"Don't be ridiculous." Hachim put down his food bowl, curtains of dark hair falling to either side of his face as he reached to pry Diaman's hand from Niema's wrist. "It's Niema's choice, isn't it?"

"Yes…" Niema paused. Of all her enclave members, Hachim was closest to her age. They'd gone through their ceremony to become full Disciples together three summers prior. "I can ask Superior Kralia to let you come with me."

Hachim shook his head. "It's your task, not mine."

"It's not fair!" Diaman wailed. "Why her?"

"Sweet child, come here." Ekim held out her arms, folding the youngest member of the enclave into her generous embrace. "Niema has been given a great honour. It should be celebrated."

"Exactly." Prathen's expression brightened. "Ah—good fortune. Superior Kralia is back."

Niema's head snapped up, her gaze picking out two novices scurrying away from Superior Kralia's glade. She put down her food bowl, a flurry of unease whipping around her insides like a bloodfly trapped in a jar. Though she had not been summoned, she rose to her feet and walked the short distance to the glade.

From the abject fear in the novices' expressions, Niema was already prepared for the sight of the wild drake crouched beside the Superior. Warily, she knelt before the large altar. "I apologise for the intrusion, Superior Kralia."

"Rise, Niema," Superior Kralia responded. "I expect you've guessed the news I received from the other Superiors."

Niema straightened, her palms dampening with sweat. "The other enclaves were given the same warning?"

"Yes, and the other Superiors bore witness to the vision the two of us saw." Her gaze swept over the thick greenery fringing the glade and then pierced Niema. "They agreed that as the only non-Superior, it is clear that you were chosen for this task."

Niema's heart contracted. "The others ... they do not want me to leave."

"Understandable." Her tone was calm, yet firm. "This is not a journey I would ask you to take lightly, but I believe the threat of Corruption is imminent."

Once again, Niema flinched at the word, and her reaction was echoed back across her bond with the five others. "Where? Where is this..." The word *Corruption* stuck in her throat.

"We have found the location of the woman in the vision," said Superior Kralia. "According to my messenger, she was last seen in Setemar."

"You *found* her?"

"We did." Superior Kralia inclined her head. "It has been many years since the war, and I gather many soldiers took up residence in Setemar. It'll be easier for you to find her there than in Dalathar, to be sure."

"The war?" The war drake let out the faintest growl, and

Niema's breath lodged in her chest. "Oh… the woman was a soldier?"

Where else would this beast have seen her? War drakes were bred for battle, an affront against Yalet's will, and urged to take lives not for survival but for conquest. How could a soldier possibly be their saviour?

"I believe so." Superior Kralia's mouth turned downwards at the corners. "I am surprised that Yalet would choose a warrior, too, but to bring down such a terrible foe as Corruption requires skills that we do not have, and sacrifices that we are unable to make."

War. She couldn't imagine such a life. She and her fellow Disciples took vows against harming other living creatures and to break those commands was to experience visceral pain to the core of their very being.

Niema sucked in a breath. "You still want me to find her?"

"Yes," said Superior Kralia. "I do."

"Alone?"

Again, Superior Kralia dipped her head. "None of the other Superiors were willing to spare any of their enclave members, nor were they … *quite* as convinced of the urgency of the threat as I."

"I'm not ready for this." Dread thumped in her chest, and she could have sworn the beast in front of her reacted, its nostrils flaring, its eyes seeking the prey animal within easy reach.

"Yalet will protect you." Superior Kralia's steady gaze anchored Niema. Who was she to doubt her Superior—to doubt her deity? "See for yourself."

She gave a short whistle and the wild drake lowered its head at her command. Taking the implied order, Niema whispered her own prayer to the god of life, and the beast's gaze fixed on her. This time its eyes didn't contain any hint of a threat, but meek obedience.

A whistle flew from Niema's lips. The wild drake nudged one step closer, then another, and she placed a hand upon its scaled head. Sharp edges brushed Niema's soft palm, and the rustling trees seemed to whisper, *See, Niema? Yalet's will permeates even a wild beast such as this.*

Superior Kralia wore an approving expression. "Yalet rewards those who are faithful, and few are as devoted as you. Moreover, you're young, strong, and open-minded enough to walk amid the regular folk without losing your way."

Am I? The forest was a part of her blood and her bones, yet was the world outside not of Yalet's creation, too? Despite the confusion and fear of the past few days, she'd listened to Prathen's stories with just as much curiosity as the younger children had.

And as little as she could forget the beast she'd seen in the vision, the woman's face was also burned deep into her memory.

Niema bowed her head. "I accept the task you have given me, Superior. I have faith that Yalet will not lead me astray."

1

There were too many fucking stairs in Dalathar.

Yala Palathar descended into the undercity with a stream of curses, her cane smacking each step and her feet unsteady on the slick stones. While the past few days of heavy rain had washed away the stench of the corpses that had once clogged every entrance to the lower level of the city, the place looked even more desolate than it had during her last visit. Rivulets of water ran off roofs, and gaunt faces peered through windows in the shacks that flanked Yala on the way to the crossroads where she'd arranged to meet Nalen.

The broad, bearded man waiting for her cracked a grin. "Thought you'd be late."

"Blame those wretched stairs." Yala maintained a firm grip on her cane to avoid slipping on the rain-slick cobbles. "You know, I'd have much preferred to meet aboveground."

"This isn't a conversation I want to have within hearing distance of the city guards."

"Why?" Yala liked Nalen, who'd once fought in the army and now helped protect the people of the undercity against threats both living and dead, but his paranoid streak often grated on her nerves, justified or not. "Viam kept her word, didn't she?"

Yala had been under the impression that some of the ex-soldiers from the Undercity had found employment among the king's guards, after their ranks had suffered substantial losses during Melian's attack.

"She did," he grunted, "but that doesn't make me trust those scumbags, and people are often quick to discard their origins when offered a way out."

"True enough." In her day, the only way out of poverty had been through conscription into the army, but the new King had abolished that law when he'd taken the throne. Yala rarely thought of the orphanage in which she'd spent her formative years after her parents' deaths in a fire, but here among the dilapidated shacks, she could hardly blame anyone who seized on the first opportunity to escape.

"Not that I'm referring to you," added Nalen. "You're a special case, seeing as you saved our hides."

"Don't be absurd," she told him. "Didn't I tell you not to stick me on a pedestal? As far as I'm concerned, the last thing these people need is to attach false worship to someone who can't do a damned thing for them."

"You stopped the place being flooded with the dead, that's enough for some. Better than His Majesty managed."

That's true enough. King Daliel had inherited one hell of a mess to clean up and had done little to fix the many problems Laria had faced since the war. He hadn't so much as peered out of the palace complex since the battle that had shaken the upper city, perhaps fearing retaliation. Frankly, Yala considered it lucky that there hadn't been more revolts on the level of Melian's attempt to topple him from his throne some weeks prior.

Granted, most would-be rebels wouldn't have had the

audacity to seek the allegiance of Mekan, the god of death, to achieve their goals.

"Go on," Yala pressed Nalen. "Why exactly did you bring me down here? What is it?"

He glanced around, then whispered, "Corruption."

Yala's heart missed a beat. "How many times have you found Corruption in the last few weeks?"

"This time it's real." He drew closer, his face a grim mask. "In the river."

Of course it'd be in the fucking river. "Let's see, then."

He beckoned her past another row of shacks. Faces peered from the windows, brightening when they saw her, and some even cheered or shouted her name. She never knew how to respond to that kind of behaviour. The gods knew she was no saviour of theirs, but the undercity folk seemed to have designated her as one all the same.

Ducking between two of the small dwellings, Nalen lifted a misshapen sack tied with a rope that didn't quite hide the outline of what looked like a human foot. "Had to stash it somewhere … didn't find the rest of the body, mind."

"That's a severed leg, Nalen." There was a difference between an ordinary dead body and one that had been touched by Corruption—and Yala had a deeper understanding than most, being a Disciple of Death. Not that she'd chosen the title for herself. Her last encounter with the god of death hadn't ended on pleasant terms, and her heart sank with a familiar dread when Nalen opened the bag wider. She peered inside, wrinkling her nose at the smell, but its contents gave no signs of interference from Mekan or His followers.

"I swear it was twitching when I found it," Nalen pulled the rope taut, sealing the sack. "Creepy."

"Bodies do that sometimes," Yala said. "Besides, I'm fairly

sure a decaying one-legged body hopping around would have drawn attention."

Annoyance aside, she didn't blame Nalen for being on edge; she suspected the entire city had been haunted by a miasma of nightmares in recent weeks since the dead had infested the streets. Before then, she'd been able to count on one hand the number of people who'd seen such a sight aside from herself.

"What should I do with it, then?" He looked at the sack. "Bury it?"

"In my experience, burying things leads to them clawing their way out of the ground." The trouble was, the alternative would involve paying another visit to the Disciples of the Flame, and Yala had no desire whatsoever to meet whoever they'd chosen as their new leader.

Or to be more precise, whoever Dalathik, the god of the flame, had selected, and given that His last choice had let Corruption rise in the capital, she had little faith in the Disciples *or* their deity to make a good decision on the matter.

"I'm not tossing it back into the river to poison the water supply," Nalen growled. "I swear I was sick for a week the last time I drank from the undercity well."

Yala sighed inwardly. "I'll get rid of it."

After checking the ropes were secure enough to conceal her grisly prize, Yala left the alleyway. More pairs of eyes watched her walk to the stairs out of the undercity, and climbing was even more awkward with a severed limb in addition to her cane. *Why did I agree to this again?*

At the top of the stairs, she assessed her options. The limb wasn't infested with Mekan's power, but part of her expected to feel the chill of the void through the damp fabric of the sack, and to hear the chilling whisper that had haunted her dreams since the battle. Frequently she woke with the sensation of ghostly hands gripping her throat, and the grim knowledge that if she ever called upon Mekan's name again, the odds of her own survival were not favourable.

"Guess I'll have to get rid of you the old-fashioned way." Yala carried the sack across one of the bridges over the river. The gushing water below remained murky, but the guards had been thorough when they'd removed any dead bodies and handed them to the Disciples of the Flame.

Who, then, had been responsible for throwing a corpse into the river? Hadn't they worried it might come back to life? *Maybe that's why they cut off its legs,* Yala thought, then gave herself a mental shake. There were countless reasons someone might commit murder, and not everyone would consider the risks of leaving a body for the next would-be Disciple of Death to find.

For all she knew, there was no risk, as no Disciples of Death remained in the city aside from herself.

Yala carried the sack to an alley near a slaughterhouse, trusting the already foul smells to mask the stench of rot. Unease tugged at the pit of her stomach, but she could hardly haul the limb around the city asking people if they knew who it belonged to. Best to rid herself of the burden while she could.

With the sack gone, Yala made her weary way home. Yala and Saren had negotiated where to move their lodgings after the latter had been evicted from the pleasure house where he'd once resided, and they'd compromised by selecting a property close enough to the centre of Dalathar without venturing into the noisy and expensive upper city. The narrow tenement might not be as remote as her jungle cabin had been, but its location gave Yala some semblance of peace and quiet, most of the time.

Yala retrieved the key from a pocket and unlocked the door. She'd taken the lower floor as her own, but the furnishings remained sparse. Unlike Setemar, the capital was a haven for thievery, so her first act upon moving into their new home was to pry one of the floorboards loose and stash any valuables underneath, covering the hole with one of the battered armchairs she'd picked up from the market. The opposite side of the room contained some planks of wood she'd set up for target practise; over the past weeks, she'd began the gruelling process of trying to get back into fighting shape. Years of idleness had slowed her quick reflexes and her body ached as muscles she hadn't used in years protested at her carrying that accursed sack.

Saren was in an even worse state. When she called his name, his only response was a faint groan.

"Hey, Saren," she repeated. "You alive?"

After a short pause, he appeared in the stairway, his eyes bloodshot and his skin sallow. "Unfortunately."

"Have you been up there all day?" Since the battle, the owner of the pleasure house where Saren had once lived had refused to return his alcohol to him, claiming payment for damages. As a result, Yala had made three attempts to convince Saren to stop drinking liquor and all had ended in her finding him insensible in a tavern. Each of Yala's squad members had found a different way of coping with the burden of the horrors they'd witnessed on their last mission, but seeking oblivion held little appeal to Yala. Recent events had provided a new series of nightmares that no amount of liquor would dull.

"Define 'day'." He stumbled on his way downstairs, resting a hand against the wall for balance. "Where've you been? You smell horrible."

"The slaughterhouses."

"That would explain it." He wrinkled his nose. "What were you doing there? Wait. I don't want to know, do I?"

"Disposing of a severed limb." She made her way to one of the armchairs and sat. "Nalen found it in the river."

"Why's it always the river?" He fell into the other chair and produced a flask from a pocket. "Whose leg was it? That should've been my first question."

"No clue." She rested her cane against the chair and made a mental note to obtain a footstool during her next trip to the markets. "He claimed it was infected with Corruption, which turned out not to be true, but I took it off his hands anyway."

Familiar horror flickered over Saren's face. "Are you sure it *wasn't* infected?"

"Of course I'm sure." She suppressed a shiver. "I'm concerned about why someone would commit murder and dismember the body after the dead were walking around the city a few weeks ago."

Saren's head slumped to his chest. "Maybe that's *why* they dismembered it."

"Where's the rest of it, then?" Yala's mind refused to let the questions subside; curiosity gnawed at her like a wild animal. "Nalen was convinced the leg was twitching, but he's on edge, and I didn't *see* any … weirdness."

"What'd you do, toss it in an alley?"

"Did you want me to bring it in here?"

"Gods, no." Saren shuddered. "I thought… I thought you might have gone to *them.*"

The Disciples of the Flame, he meant. "Did you really?"

"Well… I suppose not." He chuckled. "I wonder if they've chosen a new leader?"

"I was wondering the same, but I don't see them inviting me for a visit soon, considering my role in the death of their last Superior."

"Their last Superior killed the damned *king.*"

Yala levelled him with a stare. "Please tell me you haven't been spreading that."

"I'm not an imbecile." He scowled at the flask. "This tastes abysmal."

"What is it?"

"Drake piss." He coughed. "Or it might as well be. Fuck that Giran for stealing my liquor."

"Considering the state we left his pleasure house in, we're lucky he didn't take every coin we had."

"He's a prick." Saren shrank further into his seat. "Why did you have to mention severed limbs? I didn't need that image in my head."

"It's just Nalen being paranoid, Saren. Trust me, I'd know if he was right."

"I guess you would." He let the flask fall from his hand. "This is doing nothing for me."

"Neither is drinking yourself into an early grave." She stretched out her good leg and trapped the fallen flask under the heel of her boot. "Now, I'm not your squad leader any longer—"

"Stop that sentence there."

"—but you're living with someone who nearly became a sacrifice to the god of death, so you might want to consider being more aware of your surroundings."

"As a walking sacrifice to the god of death, you've some nerve lecturing me about my life choices." He snatched the flask from underneath her foot and cradled it like an infant.

Yala huffed. Often, dealing with Saren's petulance reminded her of the times she'd been put in charge of supervising new army recruits, and while she'd had them muck out the war drake pens if they gave her grief, Saren was a friend. Besides, he'd never been the person to go to if one wanted a serious conversation. That role went to Viam, whose current job at the palace complex meant Yala rarely saw her, and Yala could hardly show up at the palace smelling like a slaughterhouse. Though Viam at least might have some suggestions about how to handle Nalen's paranoia that didn't involve personally disposing of every body part that crossed his path.

And what if he was right? The thought prodded her. Yala rose to her feet and nudged the armchair sideways to reveal the loose floorboard beneath.

"What're you doing?" Saren peered at her as she used her cane to prop the floorboard open and reached for the small bag in which she kept her one concession to the title of Disciple of Death—a curved claw that had once belonged to a beast from the void.

Saren sprang out of his chair as if he'd sat on a prickly groundfruit. "You *kept* that?"

"Obviously."

"No wonder there are bodies walking around." He backed across the room, waving his hands as though to swat a bloodfly. "Are you out of your mind?"

"There's one way to confirm if Nalen was right." She ran her fingertips over the end of the claw, the splashes of her own blood as red as rust against the black scales, and a tingling sensation whispered across her palm.

"You'll be the death of both of us."

"I did warn you when we signed the paperwork for the house." She'd also paid half his share, as he'd drank so much of the money her squad had received after the flight division had disbanded that his habit of sleeping his way around half the city had likely spared him from being rendered homeless. "I already have Mekan's eye on me, remember?"

The god of death hadn't spoken a word to her since she'd reneged on their bargain and seen Him banished from this realm, but the claw was the closest she'd have to a means of direct access. Destroyable only by Dalathik's holy fire, it was a piece of Mekan's realm and would surely react if anyone else in the region had been meddling with death.

Saren fell back into the armchair and covered his face with both hands. "Get that thing out of here."

"That's the plan." Yala pushed the floorboard back into place and hefted her cane. "I'm going to look for the rest of the body."

"If it's walking, please don't bring it back here," Saren mumbled into his palms. "I don't need the dead following me again."

Do you think I do? Someone had to take responsibility and somehow, the role always fell to her.

Yala left the house, tucking the claw into the belt that held up the loose trousers she'd chosen as the most comfortable clothing to wear in the heat. Drakeskin would offer more protection, but it was too damned hot, the air like thick soup when it wasn't raining. Saren had had a point about the lingering smell, too, though the general stench of the city was hard to shift at the best of times and it wasn't uncommon for her sweat to carry a layer of grime. Yet another aspect of living in the capital that she'd forgotten during her years in self-imposed exile in the jungle.

Yala's steps carried her back to the river and over the bridge. Nalen had found the body near the undercity, so she reached the other side and mentally mapped the route alongside the river. If the body had been dumped further upstream, it would certainly have floated this direction.

With the gushing river on one side, she reached into the pouch at her waist and traced the curved shape of the void drake's claw with her fingertips. A chill rippled up her palm, and she scented a familiar tang in the air, one that raised the hairs on her arms. A skittering noise echoed, and her gaze picked out a small animal crouched in the shadows above the swollen waters.

A skirrit, a small rodent, its fur plastered to its body with filthy water and dark blood. Shadows oozed around its paws, and its sightless eyes were like dull glass beads.

Someone had called upon Mekan. Nalen had been right.

2

Superior Sietra could not have possibly devised a worse punishment.

Kelan studied the open book, willing the letters to stop sliding about as if they wanted to escape the pages, and wishing that the Superior had assigned him a text that didn't make the subject of warring gods seem as dry as a drought-ridden field. He'd slept terribly the previous night, while the laborious process of reading the aged text made his head throb as though he was nursing a hangover. Rubbing his temples, he pushed the book aside. Nobody had come to check on him in a while, and the quiet library was a pleasant enough place for a nap; the daylight streaming through the wide windows urged him to put his head down and let the sunbeams lull him to sleep.

Seemingly a heartbeat later, a voice woke him. "Kelan?"

Laima peered over his shoulder and Kelan lifted his head from the book, rubbing his eyes with the back of his hand. "Yes?"

"You're supposed to be working," she reprimanded him. "Not sleeping."

"I know." Since the battle, he'd struggled to sleep at night without being revisited by nightmares of clawed beasts from the Void, and the dull work was more effective than any herbal remedy. "Did you come here for a book, or...?"

"Not me. Superior Sietra wants to talk to you."

"Oh." He stretched his stiff neck and rolled his shoulders. "I don't suppose she'd mind if I stopped to grab something to eat first?"

"It's your own fault for sleeping through dinner."

Sure enough, the sky outside had darkened since he'd last looked out the window. Kelan pushed to his feet and did his best to pull himself together before he headed out of the library to meet with his Superior. While he'd accepted the punishment for going against her direct orders, he couldn't help thinking she'd have been better off handing the task to someone more competent in academic matters. She rarely had to give a severe punishment to a full Disciple like him, and she'd already given him a temporary demotion in rank *before* he'd helped a prisoner escape from Skytower. Since the prisoner in question had saved the capital of Laria in the process, he was less disgraced than he would otherwise have been, and research wasn't supposed to be painful. In theory.

Laima picked up one of the books, flipping it open. "What's this?"

"A history book."

"Looks like a treatise on farming methods to me." She tossed him the book, which he caught in his left hand, stifling a grimace as the movement jarred his injured shoulder. The wound had healed over the past few weeks, but he'd been left with a scar across his upper arm that itched like an infected bloodfly bite.

Kelan placed the book back on the table. "Did you want to take some of these books off my hands?"

"It's your punishment, not mine."

"Sometimes I'd rather she'd assigned me to clean out the latrines."

"If not for you being incapacitated, she probably would have." Her attention lingered on his shoulder, and he wondered if he hadn't hidden the pain as well as he thought he had. "This is bound to have some purpose. Why history? Of what?"

"The Disciples."

A furrow formed in Laima's brow. "Doesn't the Superior already know it all?"

"I thought so, too."

Skytower had a more extensive collection of texts than anywhere in Laria except Dalathar. Some tomes even dated back to the nation's origin, back when the foundations of Skytower had been laid down alongside the Temple of the Flame and the Temple of the Earth. Texts from that era were mostly unreadable in their original language, but modern scholars with entirely too much time on their hands had translated some of them into modern Larian. That didn't make them any more comprehensible to Kelan, who was inclined to think that a nation that had never seen a Disciple of Death until a few weeks ago was highly unlikely to have any mentions of the subject in their history books.

"Unless..." Laima's eyes widened. "She wants you to research *Corruption*. She doesn't, does she?"

"There's so little information on the subject that I'm unlikely to be able to make an altar to Mekan here in the library." He spoke in jest; as far as he knew, it wasn't possible for a Disciple to change allegiances to another deity. At least, he'd never heard of anyone doing so.

"Don't *joke* about that, Kelan." She surveyed the stacked tomes as if they might sprout teeth and bite her. "Superior Sietra must have thought you'd find something."

Yes, but I'd sooner pull out my eyes than read every title in here. "Not in any of the Larian texts, and the others…"

The texts from the Parvan Empire were unlikely to help either, as their Hierarchs had outlawed Corruption some centuries prior. Rafragoria's Empress hadn't, but few Rafragorian texts were translated into Larian, and even fewer found their way to Skytower.

"She wouldn't set you an impossible task." Laima, not to be deterred, picked up a book and carefully cracked open its aged spine.

"Feel free to peruse the stacks." Kelan selected two titles to take with him to see the Superior, hoping Laima would develop a sudden interest in scholarly research and take the entire task off his hands.

Now to convince Superior Sietra of the same. He suspected Laima was correct that his injury had spared him from being assigned to perform menial chores that were usually designated to novices, but losing his rank meant being forced to sit with the novices at mealtimes and to wait at the back of the line, which inevitably meant being left with the cold scraps the ranked Disciples had left behind. That was better than nothing, though, and his stomach growled its displeasure when he contemplated having to scrounge whatever rations were left in the kitchens after his meeting with the Superior.

Gliding to the top floor of the tower, Kelan reached the Superior's office and rapped his knuckles on the wooden door.

"Come in," called a strong feminine voice.

Kelan entered, tucking the books under his arm, and knelt on the rug before her. Superior Sietra, dressed in the dark blue tones of a clear night sky, gave the impression of agelessness, her curly dark hair topped with a gold headdress that reflected the sun's dying rays as it slipped below the surrounding hills. Golden light glinted off the carved serpentine figures coiling around the chair in which she spent most of her time; as a child, Superior Sietra had lost the use of her legs after a severe illness.

"Have you been in the library all afternoon?" she asked as he rose to his feet. "I hope you've made decent progress on the task I assigned you."

Heat crept up his neck, as if she were reprimanding him as a novice for not completing his assignments to satisfaction.

"I've been working my way through the history section," he evaded. "I rather think King Larial's scribes could stand to be less verbose."

"Yes, they have a tendency to meander," she said. "I recall a whole volume on farming methods."

"You've read them already?" Had he spent the past few weeks giving himself a headache with no cause?

"I thought there was a chance there might be a reference I overlooked." She surveyed him. "I thought you'd appreciate the chance to recuperate. Has your injury healed?"

He stretched out his arm. "It has."

The injury had cost him a little mobility in that side, but he'd survived. The rest would heal in time, and it struck him that she'd been much less harsh on him than he'd deserved.

"Good," she said. "Aside from King Larial's treatises, did you find anything illuminating in our collection of texts?"

He held up the pair of books he'd brought with him. "Very little. Laria has no history with Corruption, and the few Rafragorian texts in our possession have little information on any of their Disciples."

"As one would expect," she said. "Were there no mentions of Mekan at all?"

"Only as a pejorative," he answered. "If any book with

more information exists, I imagine it'll be in the hands of the Disciples of the…"

"Flame?" she finished.

"They did invite a Disciple of Death into their midst." Unwittingly, but Kelan didn't know where else to search outside of Skytower. Laria might not have openly banned Corruption, but that didn't mean most other Disciples would be pleased to know Mekan's influence had taken root in the nation.

"I intend to send an envoy to talk to them soon," Superior Sietra said, "but I have a different assignment for you."

"Really?" He did his level best not to sound overeager, though he'd begun to think she'd intended to keep him confined to the tower to the year's end.

"Yes," she confirmed. "We have yet to hear from the Disciples of the Earth in Setemar, so I've chosen to send you and Laima to investigate."

"Setemar?" Wait. "Me… and Laima?"

"I can trust you to keep this matter between you two?"

"Yes, of course."

Not only did she trust them to keep silent, but she must also have faith in the pair of them not to murder one another during their mission. It didn't surprise him that she had yet to hear back from the Disciples of the Earth, who'd remained ensconced in their temple and hadn't deigned to answer the door to any visitors during his last visit to Setemar.

"Good," she said. "I'll restore your rank. I think you've learned your lesson."

"Thank you, Superior Sietra."

That could have gone worse. He cast a smile in the direction of the mural of Terethik on the wall, depicting the serpentine deity hovering above a contingent of humans at prayer; it seemed his god had not entirely forsaken him after all.

Laima wasn't waiting for him outside the office. Probably,

that was for the best; if she didn't already know about their upcoming mission, he would prefer not to be the one to break the news. Granted, she hadn't been nearly as snappish with him since the battle, and at least this mission would afford him a chance to make amends for the disastrous way in which he'd ended their romantic relationship several months prior.

Assuming he managed to avoid another encounter with the god of death.

———

Niema knew from the birds that she was almost home. After the weeks she'd spent away, she'd all but forgotten the particularities of the forest in which she'd spent almost her entire life, but the song that came from the trees around her formed a symphony as familiar as her own heartbeat.

"I'm nearly there." To stave off loneliness, she spoke to the animals around her, whispering her secrets into their unknowing ears. "Strange. I miss the city now, almost."

The capital of Laria had been a wondrous nightmare, and yet on the lonely nights of travelling through the deep jungle, she missed the raw energy of the city, the way it had quickened her heartbeat and made her feel as if she was part of something more than herself. Like being with her enclave members, but far vaster, far stranger. In the jungle, she might have been the only person left in the world.

At first, she'd been glad of the chance to drink fresh water out of the rivers rather than avoiding them as a health hazard; it'd taken days for the stench of the city to wash out of the clothes Yala had given her. Even her attire had changed from handmade garb to the proper trousers and shirt of a city dweller and hard-soled shoes that were much sturdier than the woven reeds that had simply fallen apart upon her entry to Setemar's cobbled streets.

Yala. Niema hadn't quite dared mention Yala's name in the message she'd sent to tell Superior Kralia of her imminent arrival, but she didn't have much longer to prepare. For weeks she'd wondered how to break the news that Yala wasn't their saviour, not in the way they'd assumed from the vision Yalet had imparted upon them. Everyone, even Superior Kralia, believed that Yala was supposed to help Niema defeat Corruption.

She wasn't supposed to be a Disciple of Death herself.

Niema had yet to unravel her complicated feelings on the matter, but it was impossible to give an honest account of the events in the capital without having to face the question of whether Corruption had successfully been vanquished. The notion of lying to her Superior repelled her, but what choice did she have? She looked to the trees for answers, listening to the chorus of birdsong, which soothed her misgivings. *I'm almost home.* Strange, that the notion could bring both pleasure and melancholy at the same time. She'd been gone close to two months, and she'd travelled further from the enclave than she'd ever believed possible.

Niema caught sight of a red-striped bird she recognised as the messenger she'd sent to tell her enclave of her return. She extended a hand, but instead of flying to her, the bird let out a sharp cry that hit her like a clenched fist ploughing into her stomach.

"What is it?" Chills raced down Niema's arms as the other birds fell to silence, the echoes of that single cry lingering in the air like a warning. "Please—take me to the others."

The bird let out a short noise of distress, and then took off into the surrounding forest.

Niema's pace quickened, her mind racing. While she'd been far enough from her enclave that she could no longer sense their emotions, had they been able to feel some of what she'd experienced in the capital? Niema had called upon the god of life's power to its fullest extent to save Yala's life, and she'd felt the aftermath ripple through their bond. That had been the last time she'd sensed them.

Between one breath and the next, they returned. Five extra heartbeats in her chest, five sets of discordant emotions battering her like a storm. She stumbled, a part of her wanting to run into their painful embrace, the other part of her wanting to flee, lest she lose all sense of herself amid the torrent of emotions.

What am I thinking? Sucking in quick breaths, she tried to pin down what she felt from the others. Pain, grief, and dread. Someone was hurt. Badly.

One of her enclave members—one of those bound to her soul—was dying.

3

Yala inhaled the scent of death and felt its chill settle into her bones. Her eyes tracked the skirrit's unsteady gait, until the rodent skittered out of sight, as though the shadows themselves had drawn the small creature into their embrace.

That'll poison the water supply, she thought, rubbing her chilled hand on her trouser leg. The creeping sensation of being watched by unseen eyes vanished when she removed her fingers from the claw concealed in the pouch at her waist, yet the clammy coldness on her skin remained.

"You're still here," she murmured, unsure if she was talking to the god of death or the person who'd been fool enough to draw His attention. "Now… where's the rest of the body?"

The city was drenched in enough other unpleasant scents that a rotting corpse wouldn't draw undue attention, but using Corruption had effects on the surrounding world. Corpses rose, stirred by Mekan's hand, and not necessarily under the control of the person who'd initially called the attention of the god of death. Unless they were cleansed by holy fire, but there wasn't much of that outside of the upper city.

Yala walked with careful steps, following the gushing river to where it ran behind the shacks of the undercity. Presumably it was around here that Nalen had found the severed leg, though if the rest of the body had been dumped in the river, it'd likely end up elsewhere.

Frustrated, Yala slowed, her hand seeking the knife she kept strapped to her waist, and she pressed her fingertip to the edge until blood beaded on the surface. Then she released the knife and slid her hand into the pouch containing the severed claw, letting her fresh blood smear onto its already stained edge.

Every shadow seemed to sharpen before her sight, and the scent of decay caught in her nostrils, carried on the faint breeze. Her steps carried her forward until her attention snagged on a tunnel into which the river disappeared, from which skittering noises issued. She peered inside and spied numerous small rodents, their rotting tails writhing like worms, their decaying fur peeling back from their bones. It was too narrow to crawl inside even if she'd been willing to suffer the indignity—not to mention the stench.

A second set of footsteps rang out on the cobbles. Yala stiffened, surprised to see a city guard approaching; she hadn't seen one this far from the city wall since they'd had to clean up the aftermath of Melian's attempted coup. He spied Yala watching him, his hand jumping to the shortsword strapped to his belt. *Expecting trouble, is he?*

Yala gave him a wary nod. "Morning."

"What're you doing?" he released the sword, letting it swing back to his side.

The king's guards were typically found on top of the wall

circling the upper city or outside the palace, but they must have altered their patrol schedule after having spent weeks carrying twitching corpses to the Disciples of the Flame before the god of death could claim them. *Should have asked them to burn the animal corpses, not just the human ones,* she thought.

"Grim question, but I wondered if any guards found a corpse earlier today?" Yala asked. "Nalen found a severed leg, but not the rest of the body. Figured I ought to check in case someone is dumping bodies in the river again."

The guard's mouth pulled down at the corners. "No corpses. Certainly not in the river."

"All right." Her skin prickled. "I imagine the body won't be hard to find, if it's missing a leg."

He grunted. "I'll let the others know to keep an eye out."

"Thanks." She assumed the city being flooded with walking corpses a few weeks ago had made the guards less inclined to ignore any reports that sounded suspicious.

The question was, who *had* been fool enough to meddle with Corruption? Only those who looked upon Mekan's realm had the potential to become Disciples of Death, but the Void had ripped open in plain view of half the city a few weeks ago. Even Viam wasn't certain on how it all worked, though Yala did know that calling upon Mekan's will required a piece of His realm like the claw in her pocket, a remnant of the monster to which she owed her injured leg. The Disciples of the Flame were supposed to have burned every trace of Mekan's monsters, but evidently, they'd missed one.

"Gods be damned," she growled. "Does it have to be them?"

Most of the Disciples of the Flame had been unconscious throughout the battle due to their would-be leader having drugged his fellow Disciples in order to enact his coup, but they alone dealt with cremating the recently dead. They also despised Disciples of Death … or they had. In truth, Yala didn't know how much of their prejudice remained after Melian had infiltrated their ranks. It'd been one of their people who'd assassinated their former leader and not Melian herself, but if their new Superior was anything like his predecessor, she'd be a fool to go to them for advice.

With a muttered curse, Yala turned her path towards the gates to the upper city. If she didn't at least *try* to stop whoever had raised the dead, it'd be just her luck to wake up to rotting skirrits on her doorstep next. Aside from the Disciples of the Flame, the only people she knew with the skills to counter Mekan's touch were the Disciples of Life, whose deity was opposed to the very notion of anyone forging an alliance with Mekan. The one she'd met—Niema —had been frustratingly naïve, but her ability would certainly have come in handy today. Yala didn't expect to see Niema again for a long while, if at all. If her fellow Disciples learned that she'd saved the life of a Disciple of Death, she'd be lucky if her Superior forgave her the transgression, let alone allowed her to venture into the capital again.

After she'd stopped at a public fountain to wash the grime from her face, Yala made her way to the gates. The guards eyed her but let her pass; she sincerely hoped the man she'd run into hadn't passed on word to the others that she'd been asking after dismembered corpses. No, most likely it was her filthy clothes that earned undue attention; between those and the blood crusting her fingernails, she'd never be deemed presentable enough to enter the palace. No matter. Viam would be horrified if she did, and besides, this was not a discussion fit for a public place.

Yala crossed Ceremonial Square through bustling crowds that gave no signs of having been slowed by the battle a few weeks ago, though some traces lingered in the form of boarded-up windows, cracked flagstones, and even a visible dent in the side of the giant golden statue of King Larial. Halting outside the towering gates that separated the palace complex from the rest of the city, Yala caught the eye of one of the guards.

"Can you pass on a message for me? I need to talk to someone who works in the palace's administrative division. Viam Tiathar."

The guard—female, head shaved, even the hilt of her shortsword polished to a sheen—studied Yala. "You look familiar."

"I get that a lot." Either the guards knew her from the army, or they'd seen her fly into the palace complex on the back of a dead war drake. Neither subject was one she particularly wanted to discuss. "I'd appreciate it if you could let Viam Tiathar know I need to talk to her. Give the name Yala Palathar."

The guard's eyes widened. "Did you say *Yala—?*"

"Just pass on the message." She turned away, not in the mood to hear the inevitable exclamations as they realised she was the person who'd faced the Void inside the very palace they guarded and walked away alive.

Viam survived, too, and I doubt everyone gawks at her. Viam, though … she was unobtrusive. Yala, with her scarred face, her cane, and her habit of staring people dead in the eyes instead of hiding behind a book, drew notice. Yala's other surviving squad-mate had also been unwittingly responsible for Melian's acquisition of certain books containing instructions as to how to call upon Mekan, but Yala wasn't given to nurturing grudges for honest mistakes. Others were far more deserving of her ire.

As she crossed Ceremonial Square, the Temple of the Flame drew her gaze. Carefully angled to catch the sun no matter its position, the tower's wide windows drew in as much light as possible to create the effect of a beacon, a reminder of the god Dalathik who had given the city its name.

He's not the only god in this city, though. Her fingers strayed to the claw at her waist, but she curled her hand into a fist instead. She'd be courting death to walk near their temple with a piece of Mekan Himself on her person.

Other than the Disciples of the Flame … come to think of it, there was a striking lack of Disciples of the Sky present in the square. Given the losses they'd suffered during the battle, their absence was understandable, but if any were present, they'd be at the Disciples' Inn.

Yala had never been there, but she gathered that the inn was the favoured accommodation of any Disciples who visited the city and a hub for gossip from far afield. Kelan was unlikely to be around, given his role in helping her escape Skytower against his Superior's orders, but she veered in that direction, regardless.

Upon reaching the farmhouse-sized building, Yala rapped her knuckles on the wooden door, and a matronly woman answered. Her narrowed gaze took in Yala's plain, muddied clothing, and then her eyes went wide. "You…"

Shit. Please tell me she doesn't know my name too. She'd thought the Disciples of the Sky were aware of the dangers of letting word of Yala's Disciple of Death status spread outside of their ranks, but it might have been too much to expect the inn's staff not to gossip, considering they'd had to help clean up the aftermath of the battle.

"I'm Yala," she said. "I've met some of the Disciples who've stayed at your inn."

"Yes… I suppose you have." Unease flickered across the woman's face. "If you're looking for a room, I'm afraid they're all occupied."

"Are there any Disciples of the Sky currently staying here?" A challenging note that she hadn't intended entered Yala's voice. "Or did someone order you not to let me inside?"

"No, but we have to maintain friendly relations with all Disciples, and you're an unknown entity," she said. "Frankly, I'd be happy to take your money anyway, but I can't alienate the rest of our clients. I have a family to feed."

What in hells did they tell her? "I'm not here for a room, I'm looking for the Disciples."

"There aren't any—not at the moment," she amended. "We rarely go more than a few weeks without any guests, so I expect that won't last long."

"Really." Yala suspected that she'd have replied in the same way if there *had* been Disciples here, but that didn't seem to be the case, or she'd have caught a glimpse of one sooner. "Do you take messages?"

"I do, but I can't promise it'll get there in a timely manner without any Disciples in the city. They'll be back, I'm sure."

"Thanks anyway."

Yala caught sight of a robed figure out of the corner of her eye as the woman closed the door. Her spine stiffened at the sight of the familiar white cloak and the scent of smoke in the air like the aftermath of a pyre.

The Disciple of the Flame was female, her robe unadorned and her hair in an elegant knot, and her mouth formed a smile when she saw Yala watching her. "You're Yala Palathar."

"Do I know you?"

"My name is Mieren," she said. "High council member of the Disciples of the Flame."

Yala's instincts itched to reach for a weapon, but even a Disciple would be a fool to attack her in broad daylight. "Were you looking to speak to someone at the inn?"

"No." Her searching gaze travelled over Yala's face. "Not yet, but our new Superior would very much like to meet with you."

"Send your new Superior my regards, but I have to decline." Despite her curiosity, Yala would not easily forget that their former leader had tried to have her burned for heresy, nor that his people had gone as far as to have the last monarch assassinated to stop the rise of Corruption—only to remain oblivious when a Disciple of Death had infiltrated their own ranks.

"I hope you'll reconsider." Mieren inclined her head, and Yala could have sworn her attention lingered on the pouch at her waist. "Superior Shralin is most anxious to meet you, and he has an offer to make."

An offer? If the Disciples of the Flame had returned to their previous stance on Corruption as worthy only of being burned out of existence, it was laughable that they'd expect her to willingly set foot into their midst. If *not,* though…

"Like I said, I'm not interested." Yala walked away, her cane hitting the pavement with each step. Despite the growing ache in her leg, she didn't stop until she reached the gates out of the upper city.

She could have sworn even the guards patrolling atop the city walls watched her walk through the gates. Would she have to resort to a disguise if she ever wanted to avoid attention? Being a nameless soldier had suited her just fine, once, but anonymity seemed to slip further away with each passing day.

How, she thought, *do I always end up getting caught in the Disciples' web?*

———

"What the *fuck*, Yala," said Saren. "You called Mekan again? You *spoke* to Him?"

"I didn't." Yala removed the pouch from her belt, fingers clumsy due to the unnatural chill from the claw inside and the sting of the wounds she'd sliced with her dagger. "If He'd been listening, I'd know."

Saren leaned forward in his armchair. "You're supposed to keep the rest of us out of trouble, not walk into it yourself."

"Supposed to?" She swallowed angrier words—that she wasn't responsible for her squad any longer, that most of them were dead—but the light dimmed in Saren's eyes as if he'd picked up on her thoughts.

"If the dead attack again, who else is going to stop them?" he challenged. "Those fiery fuckers who'd happily burn the rest of us along with the dead?"

"They have a new Superior," Yala informed him. "I'd like to think he won't make the same mistakes as his predecessor, though his high-ranked council members seem more concerned with telling the staff at the Disciples' Inn not to let me rent a room."

"Really?" Saren lifted his head. "Yielen doesn't usually turn people away. I bet she remembers you were responsible for her having to carry half-dead Disciples off the battlefield a few weeks ago."

"Like Kelan." Yala frowned. "How do you know who the inn's owner is?"

"I may have stayed there once."

"I didn't know you'd slept with a Disciple." When Saren made a noise of disbelief, she added, "They don't let anyone else stay there, I know."

He glowered at her. "Does it matter? Or do you still hate every Disciple in existence?"

"What—no." She gave a wry smile. "I think it's too late for that now I'm effectively one myself."

And you are, too, she added silently, but that wasn't strictly true; unlike Viam, Saren hadn't dabbled in Corruption, and he certainly hadn't conversed with Mekan directly as Yala had. To the Disciples of the Flame, though, that distinction might not matter.

"You aren't," Saren said. "You don't spend all your time kneeling at an altar until you shrivel to a husk."

"No." She drew in a breath. "The Disciples of the Flame's new leader wants to meet me."

Saren groaned. "Please tell me you didn't say yes."

"Of course I didn't," she replied. "Allegedly, he wants to make me an offer."

"An *offer.*" He snorted. "That sounds like he's readying himself to blackmail you like Superior Datriem did."

Yes ... it does. "I wasn't going to say yes, considering I have a piece of Mekan's realm on my person."

He jabbed a finger at the pouch. "If I were you, I'd burn that thing."

"Regular fire won't leave a mark on it." She'd tried, once, when she'd been bored during one of the long, empty nights in her jungle cabin. "And I'm not letting the Disciples of the Flame touch a piece of Mekan's realm after what Melian did."

She returned the claw to its place under the floorboards, while Saren watched with the air of someone handling a war drake without any protective gloves. "You'll be the death of both of us."

"Likely, yes." She straightened and nudged the floorboard back into place, then fixed Saren with a flat stare. "Is this going to be a problem? Will I wake up to you going through my possessions in the middle of the night?"

"No, I'm not fucking touching that thing."

"Good." She pointedly ignored the flickering shadows

that gathered around the edges of the floorboard, though it might be worth getting a secure box to keep the claw in, for peace of mind. She didn't *think* its power would leak out and raise any skirrits and birds that perished near the house, but that was yet another question to ask Viam whenever she was able to get away from the palace.

Either way, Yala had no intention of paying any more visits to the upper city that day.

4

Kelan had missed the sensation of soaring through the open sky during his confinement. He had not, however, missed the rain. The damp veil across his vision made navigating difficult, while rainwater crept through every gap in his cloak and cooled against his skin. His shoulder ached a little when he stretched out his arms, but it was a marked improvement to the weeks of pain he'd endured after the battle.

When his vision cleared, he glimpsed Laima watching him soar ahead of her. She'd reacted to the news that they were expected to work together with less recrimination than he'd expected and had been positively cordial towards him, but that didn't mean she'd forgotten her old grievances. Time would tell if they were able to work together to fulfil Superior Sietra's orders without ending up at one another's throats again.

Setemar came into view, first as a set of jagged cliffs that merged with the walls around the inner city, and then in the form of clusters of houses spreading outward from the walls like ripples on a pond. The city grew bigger with every wave of population growth, with new neighbourhoods springing up each year, but the inner city remained contained within the solid walls that had existed from its foundation, not built by human hands but shaped by the Disciples who'd founded the city and carved the Temple of the Earth into the very cliffs themselves.

Kelan and Laima landed just outside of the wall; generally, it was considered more courteous to enter the inner city on the ground rather than flying over the gates, though he doubted the Disciples paid attention to such matters.

Upon reaching the temple, Kelan surveyed the sheer cliffs that formed the walls. The Temple of the Earth might not be as impressive on the outside as Skytower, but they said the tunnels beneath extended deep into the earth to the mines on which the city of Setemar had initially been founded. The front steps of the temple were flanked by serpentine carvings of Setem, god of the earth, but otherwise there were few markers of divinity. The place didn't even have windows. Rather drab, Kelan thought—not to mention inconvenient for curious visitors.

Laima glided up the stone staircase to the door, while Kelan cleared his throat. "You do remember what I told you about my last visit here, didn't you? They wouldn't answer the door to anyone, not even a Disciple of Life."

"This is different," she replied. "Superior Sietra sent word of our coming."

"They never responded to her previous correspondence." The Disciples of the Earth had reacted to the news of a threat from Corruption by going underground, literally, and if reports of the events in the capital a few weeks ago had reached them, they might be even *less* inclined to leave the safety of their temple.

Laima wasn't to be deterred. Kelan glided to her side while she rapped on the door with her knuckles. When nobody answered, he rose into the air parallel to Setem's stern face in the hopes of finding a crack in the rock through which to see inside. One would think the Disciples would want to let in *some* daylight, but not so much as a crack disturbed the sheer cliff face.

"Kelan, get down from there," Laima hissed. "Superior Sietra told us to approach on the ground."

"I'm aware." He also knew that the instant he set foot inside the temple, his abilities would be cut off—and for all he knew, the same might occur if he strayed too close to the cliffs. Being stranded up in the air would not help their cause, so he was careful to remain several handspans from the cliff face as he rose higher.

"Kelan." He heard her swearing and stifled a grin. He'd been starting to worry that she'd keep up a pretence of stiff politeness towards him throughout their entire visit.

He found no hidden entrances to the temple, and if any secret passages or doors existed on the other side, he'd have to fly straight over the cliffs and leave the city to find them. Instead, he glided downward and found Laima had waylaid a passing guard.

"We can't get in there," the guard told Laima. "They closed the doors weeks ago, without any warning. Didn't even tell the city governor."

"Did you ever go inside?" asked Laima. "They must get supplies somehow."

"Once a week." The guard, whose grey hair was plastered to his forehead with rainwater, eyed Kelan as he descended to land beside Laima. "We have instructions to leave a supply cart outside the temple on market day, and it's always empty by the day's end."

"Our Superior sent a message," he ventured. "Several, in fact."

"Messages are taken in with the supplies," said the guard.

"Otherwise, we haven't had so much as a word from them. You're the first Disciples I've seen since that business in the capital a few weeks ago."

"You heard?" Kelan seized on the opportunity. "That's why we're here. We want to discuss those events with the Superior of the Disciples of the Earth."

"That's not possible," the guard said. "If you want to send another message, you can wait with the supply cart when the next delivery is left at the temple."

Market day... that's Setemos, Setem's day. "We can't wait until then."

"You haven't a choice." The guard angled himself as though to walk away. "Nobody can get into that tower if the Disciples don't want them to."

Likely true, but he didn't need to waste three days in Setemar with Laima's joyless company. There must be another way to get through to the Disciples that didn't involve hiding inside a supply cart.

As Laima thanked the departing guard, Kelan studied the stern faces of the statues carved into the cliff. A plan formed in his mind and with a smile, he turned to his companion. "Where do you want to start?"

"Start what?" she asked.

"Asking questions," he said. "I think it's safe to say we won't get anything from official sources."

"You want to ask unofficial ones." Her jaw twitched. "Meaning you want to drag me around every tavern in Setemar."

"Not *all* the taverns," he said. "Only the good ones."

Laima rolled her eyes. "That doesn't mean you need to spend all your coin on the first day."

"If we get the information fast, I won't need to." He arched a brow. "Of course, you're welcome to stay at the inn and leave me to do the questioning."

"And wait for you to get distracted by some pretty maid or wandering mercenary woman? Not a chance." She propped a hand on her hip. "I'm coming with you."

———

The skitter of dead rodents haunted Yala's dreams that night. Several times she woke, half convinced she'd heard a noise from the floorboard where she'd put the void drake's claw, but she refused to give into the impulse to check. In the end, the only real disturbance came from Saren staggering to the house after a night out in the pleasure district and vomiting on the doorstep. Having dealt with the same countless times during her years as squad leader, she helped him crawl upstairs and then returned to her sleeping mat.

When grey light seeped into her eyes through gaps in the thin curtain, Yala gave up on getting more rest and began her day's exercises. When her first dagger sank to the hilt into the wooden target, Saren banged on the floor and yelled at her to go back to sleep.

"I had years to do nothing but sleep," she called back. "We got up earlier in the army."

"Under duress." In daylight, her fears from the previous night seemed irrational. Was she afraid of rodents now? *Honestly.*

Yala's restless energy refused to abate, and after dressing, she walked to the market to buy supplies. The past weeks of heavy rain had noticeably swelled the river, making it doubly hard to tell if there were any more body parts in the murky waters, but she made a mental note to check in with Nalen after she took the packages home.

As she was leaving the market, a guard accosted her. "You."

Yala lifted her head, recognising the guard who'd found

her skulking around looking for traces of Corruption the previous day. "Yes?"

"Yala, is it?" he said. "You wanted to know about the rest of that body."

"Yes." Not a welcome development. She hadn't expected him to remember their encounter, much less seek her out with an update. *And he knows my name.* If word got out among the city guards that she'd been asking about dead bodies floating in the river, they'd likely soon suspect her of putting them there.

"We found who it belonged to," he went on. "The murderer came straight to us and confessed. A butcher's apprentice who turned on his master with his own cleaver, would you believe it?"

"Did he now?" At least he wasn't accusing her of committing the murder herself, but her wariness remained intact. "You found the rest of the body?"

"No," he said. "We didn't. I wondered if your friend Nalen had."

"Not that I'm aware of, no. Do you know Nalen?"

"We've spoken," he said. "He was asking about the missing corpse, too … seemed to think it'd walked off."

Damn you, Nalen. His paranoia was going to land her in trouble if she wasn't careful. "The undercity bore the brunt of the incident a few weeks ago. It'll be a while before he can look at a corpse without jumping. You said the culprit handed himself in?"

"Yes." The guard eyed her. "Oddly enough, he mentioned *your* name when he was sobbing his confession."

"Mine? What did he say?" Her heart plunged downward, as though she'd missed a step climbing into the undercity. "Where is he now?"

"Jail." He pointed over his shoulder. "I can take you there."

Bad idea. And yet… "Fine."

The jail turned out to be located near the guardhouse at the right-hand side of the city wall. Yala dropped off her packages at home on the way before following the guard to a somewhat dingy building that smelled of effluence and general neglect. One guard at the door attempted a glib comment while checking her for weapons, but the hard stare she offered in return prompted him to leave the daggers strapped at her waist alone. *At least I didn't bring that severed claw,* she thought.

The butcher's apprentice was a lanky boy of no more than sixteen, who cowered in the corner of his barred cell and watched Yala approach with the air of someone contemplating their executioner.

Yala peered at him through the bars. "You worked for the butcher, didn't you?"

He sniffed in response. "Y…yes."

"You mentioned my name," she went on. "Where'd you hear it?"

"I…" His eyes widened. "Who are you?"

"Yala Palathar." She moved closer, conscious that he wasn't the only prisoner crammed into the dirty cell and that the other occupants were eyeing her hopefully, perhaps thinking she'd come to haggle for their freedom. "You?"

"Ket," he mumbled. "That's my name. Ket."

"And mine's Yala." She lowered her voice. "I don't know you. We've never met. Who told you my name?"

He shook his head. "I … don't know."

"You don't know." He might be lying, but he was scared half to death, and while it wasn't hard to conjure up sympathy for the level of abuse that would cause an apprentice to crack and murder his master, the urge to know who'd spoken her name prompted her to continue. "There's no need for secrecy. You've confessed to murder, haven't you?"

"He promised to help," mumbled the boy, half to himself. "But … he couldn't."

"Who is 'he'?" *Help with what? What kind of trouble did this boy walk into?*

"He never shared his name," Ket said. "He offered to … to help me fix him."

"What does that mean?" Chills raced down her spine. *Fix him.* "Who offered to help you?"

He shook his head, violently. "I don't know who he is. I swear. I heard he could help, but he made it worse, and…"

"And what?" *Fix him.* The image of the man's severed leg flashed before her eyes. "Ket, what did you do with the rest of the body?"

He let out a quiet moan at her words. "I tried… I tried … but it was all wrong."

"Who took the body, Ket?" she asked, harshly, impatience pushing past her initial sympathy. "Who said my name?"

"I don't know, I don't know!" He rocked back on his heels, pressing his palms to his eyes. "I'm sorry. Sorry. I killed him. Please forgive me…"

Movement behind her. Yala spun, tensing when the guard loomed out of the darkness. "What?"

"You won't get any more sense out of him," he said. "You don't know him, do you?"

"No." If she had a sliver of sense remaining, she'd walk away rather than pursuing the line of questioning that inevitably led to someone who offered the impossible. Someone like—

She's dead. Melian is dead.

"Poor boy," said the guard. "He'll hang for this. No way around it."

"Can't I…?" Do what? Buy his freedom? She'd spent more than she'd anticipated when she and Saren had selected their property, and besides, if word got out that she was paying for criminals to walk away from jail, she could expect to find a knife in her back within the month. "Can't anyone speak for him?"

"No family's stepped forward." He ushered her outside. "Besides, he confessed. We can't go around letting murderers walk free, can we?"

Except those of us who killed for the king? Yala bit back the words and asked, "Isn't there leniency if he was defending his life?"

"That's not what he said in his confession." He waved her off. "Go on. Yala … Palathar, is it?"

"Yes." Palathar, of Palath—the last remnant of her family line. How easy a life, a name, a lineage, might be snuffed out. Like the poor wretches inside that cell. Would her name endure beyond her expiration, whispered by murderers or by those who sought to follow in Melian's footsteps?

And just where is the rest of that damned corpse? The question gnawed on her as she walked home, only for her thoughts to slam back into the present when she found the door slightly ajar and a robed figure visible through the window. Tensing, she reached for one of her daggers and stepped inside to confront the intruder.

The Disciple of the Flame held up his hands, placatingly, but his ability to conjure up fire to his palms at the whims of his deity meant that the gesture didn't reassure Yala in the least. "I'm here in peace."

Saren. Shit. Was he upstairs? If so, he must have slept through the break-in. She kept a firm grip on her knife, the memory of searing flames all too fresh in her memory. "Why are you in my house?"

"My Superior requested me to come and extend a second invitation to hear his offer."

"You mean your Superior didn't want me to avoid giving

the answer he wanted. You might remind him that his predecessor tried to have me killed."

His gaze darted to the door. "I... I'm sure there was a misunderstanding."

"A likely story." Saren appeared in the stairway. "Sneak into my house while you're sleeping, will you? Tell you what, if we throw you into the river, I'd like to see your god come to your rescue then."

"That's not necessary," the Disciple mumbled. "Please— we mean no harm. We simply wish to have a discussion with you, Yala Palathar."

"Tell me about your offer while you're here." She sidestepped him, leaving the way to the door clear. "If the Superior told you what it is, that shouldn't be a problem. If not..."

The Disciple's shoulders slumped. "I... I don't know, precisely."

She allowed herself a faint, mocking laugh. "The woman who spoke to me yesterday wasn't nearly as ignorant."

A flush crept across his cheeks. "Our Superior has a great many burdens on his shoulders. His predecessor died at a terrible time."

Due to his own ineptitude. "If your Superior is going to keep sending his followers to infiltrate my house, I can promise the next one will be delivered back to him in pieces."

The Disciple blanched. "I ... if you make such threats inside the temple, I cannot promise Dalathik would not strike you down."

"Now we're being honest with each other." She could see Saren trying to catch her eye and had little doubt he was trying to urge her not to follow the intruder, but she didn't trust this new Superior not to send more senior Disciples after her if she broke the man's kneecaps. "I'll meet him outside, in public, or not at all."

"You… I'll ask." The novice backed towards the door. "I'm sure he'll be amenable."

"As sure as I'm in line for the crown." She walked after him, her cane rapping on the floor, stifling a smirk as he flinched at each strike. "Fine. I'll see what he has to say for himself."

"Yala," Saren called from behind her. "Don't go with him. He'll have you tossed on the pyre."

"He wouldn't give me the honour." She closed the door to the house and turned to her unwelcome visitor. "How did you find out where I lived?"

"I asked the city guard."

Great. They know where my house is, do they? "Don't have any contacts amongst the local mercenaries?" Yala supposed they'd probably all been killed or fled the city, but she wouldn't easily forget that Superior Datriem had hired rogues to pursue her. If he'd applied the same attention to seeking out traitors under his own nose, they might not be in this mess.

The Disciple gave her a frightened look and didn't speak to her again until they reached the gates to the upper city. Even from here, Yala could see the temple's towering form catching the light of the sun as it climbed towards its highest point.

She'd sworn never to set foot in that temple again. *Fucking Disciples, turning my promises into naught.*

5

Niema followed the bird with increasing trepidation. Flashes of emotion hit her over and over like punches, causing her to bite her tongue lest she cry out in pain and attract one of the jungle's predators. It was only midafternoon, but Niema could have sworn the forest was darker than it should be, the shadows deeper and the trees quieter.

Finally, she reached a sight that was achingly familiar, a dirt track flanked by trees that bore the signs of having been coaxed to grow around the paths to make it easier for Disciples to see their way home after the sun set. Soon she'd reach the wooden huts where the enclave members lived, the source of the heartbeats crashing in her chest and a tumult of emotions cascading upon her like a waterfall.

"Niema!" The voice's owner tackled her around the middle like a rampaging raptor, driving both of them to the ground.

"Threl." She looked up at his crumpled face, streaked with tears. "Threl, it's all right, I'm back."

"It's not all right," he sobbed. "Prathen... He's dying."

Her heart spasmed. "No."

I knew something was wrong. She'd felt the ripples of sorrow and pain, interspersed with her own trepidation about her return, but she hadn't wanted to believe what terrible grief would have prompted those emotions.

Threl sobbed, and she hugged him, feeling his pain as acutely as her own. "Where are the others?"

"They're with him," he mumbled against her chest. "I came here because I—I sensed you were back."

"I don't understand." How could she have sensed nothing before her return to the forest? Yes, she'd known that the lack of closeness would dim her bond with the others, but such a tragedy shouldn't have escaped her notice. "How—how did this happen?"

"I don't know," Threl sobbed. "He just... He collapsed in the middle of the day, a few weeks ago. None of our healers have been able to figure out what was wrong. Superior Kralia told us that you—you must have been badly hurt on your mission."

It's my fault. The truth constricted around her heart like a serpent's coils. She'd known instinctively when she'd healed Yala from death that that her enclave members would surely have sensed some of what she felt, but she hadn't known her gamble would push one of her own enclave members to the brink of death.

She swallowed. "I did get hurt, but I'm fine now, and he'll be fine, too."

Please let it be true. Please, Yalet, let it be true.

Threl sniffed, releasing her. "I'll take you to him."

"I—I need to tell the Superior I'm back." If she went to the others first, if she let their emotions swallow her like the ocean, she might forget to be careful when she recollected the events in the capital in front of Superior Kralia. For Yala's sake ... she couldn't take the risk.

"I'll go with you."

"No—go back to the others," she told him. "You can manage without me for a few more minutes, can't you?"

"I'll tell them you're here." He ran down one of the branching paths, while Niema continued onward, her legs shaking as she walked down the familiar route to the clearing where her Superior was usually found.

Her nerves buzzed like a nest of bloodflies, and when she rounded the corner and locked eyes with Superior Kralia, her words fled. For the past few weeks, she'd rehearsed this conversation countless times, but all her preparation departed when she set eyes on the woman who she'd never been able to hide anything from. Not because they shared a bond like that between her and her enclave members, but because the Superior was Yalet's chosen, and was sharply attuned to any creature that lived in the forest, human or otherwise.

Niema fell to her knees and whispered to the ground. "I'm sorry."

"Rise." Superior Kralia's tone was uncharacteristically cold. "I confess, I never expected to see you again, Niema."

Her thoughts tumbling, Niema climbed to her feet. "You thought I'd never come back?"

"I would have expected you to make haste to return when your enclave member fell ill, and when you didn't... I feared you were lost."

Niema's eyes stung with tears. "I didn't—I didn't know. You were right when you said I wouldn't be able to sense the others from so far away. I had no idea."

Superior Kralia's expression softened. "I believe you," she said, "but a terrible wrong has occurred, and I would like you to tell me the full story."

How much does she know? At a guess, Superior Kralia would have suspected Niema had called upon the god of life for a miracle, but it was much harder for her to work out which details to share now that she knew the terrible consequences her decision had wrought. Starting from the moment she'd left the enclave, Niema began her story of her journey to the capital with Yala in search of an enemy known only as the Successors.

"The Successors…" Niema took in a shaky breath. "They were Disciples of Death. Their leader, Melian, tried to have Yala killed—that's when I called upon Yalet to heal her. I thought she was our only hope of survival."

"The woman from Yalet's vision," said Superior Kralia. "She saved us, yes? What did she do?"

"She…" Niema's throat went dry at the memory of Yala waking from apparent death. "She survived. I was weakened by the miracle I called upon and fell unconscious, but I learned later that Yala was able to kill Melian, the Successors' leader, and bring an end to the horror she unleashed."

"She single-handedly defeated Corruption?" Superior Kralia pursed her lips. "What manner of skills did she display?"

"The Disciples of the Flame were involved, too," Niema added, not wanting to make Yala sound as though she possessed abilities beyond any regular human. "One of Yala's friends was a novice in their order. When Melian opened the void, her friend gave his life to Dalathik to destroy all access to Mekan's realm."

She was aware that there were holes in her story, and that mentioning the Disciples of the Flame ran the risk of Superior Kralia realising the vision hadn't been accurate—but she didn't know how to explain that Superior Datriem had willingly let an agent of Corruption stay within the Temple of the Flame itself. Two, if one counted Yala's former friend who'd only turned against his former ally when he'd realised that Mekan had no intention of sparing any of them.

"I see." Superior Kralia gave a nod. "It seems we owe this Yala a debt. I only wish her victory had not come with such tragic consequences."

Niema inclined her head, and a spasm of pain shook her body, a reminder that the consequences had hit her own enclave members far worse than herself. Another reason to hold her tongue was that any punishment the Superior inflicted upon Niema would rebound upon the others, too, but what kind of punishment would fit a crime of this severity? She'd never heard of anyone unintentionally leading a fellow enclave member to the brink of death.

Superior Kralia pursed her lips. "I'll think on the matter. For now, you should go to the others."

Niema hadn't told her everything, but the pain lapping at the edges of her mind warned her that soon she'd lose all ability to think clearly. "I—thank you. I will."

She hurried from the clearing and followed the path to the wood-frame hut where her fellow enclave members lived. The beat of the others' hearts tugged her towards the door like a rope around her chest.

The hut consisted of one room, where Prathen lay upon a sleeping mat. The second eldest of their group sat by his side, while Threl had draped himself over the older man's feet. Hachim sat hunched in a corner, his eyes red-rimmed, and Diaman sprang to her feet when Niema entered. Hurrying to the door, Diaman raised her fist and struck Niema on the chin.

"How dare you leave us!" she screamed.

Niema stumbled back, one hand clutching her face. "I didn't—"

"You did this to him!" Diaman dropped to her knees with a wordless howl of despair. "It's your fault."

"I didn't mean to." It was hard to breathe through the others' pain. She'd never thought of their bond as stifling beforehand, but despite her desperation to put things right, part of her longed to run into the forest until her thoughts were her own again. "I want to help."

"Diaman, stop." Hachim rose upright. "Niema can help."

"I'll try." Niema lowered her hand, seeing her own devastation reflected on the others' faces. "If we pray to Yalet…"

But she'd already asked for one miracle. Did she have the right to call on the god of life for another?

I have to try. Crouching at the foot of Prathen's sleeping mat, she pressed her forehead to the ground.

"Yalet," she whispered. "Please help us."

The others whispered the prayer, a murmur that became a chorus of song, a plea to their deity to spare Prathen's life. Niema could barely feel him, his heartbeat far quieter than the others, and guilt curdled in her chest.

She'd brought him to this, and she'd have to live with the consequences of her choice.

———

Ceremonial Square was bustling at this hour, with crowds thronging the market stalls and a hum of noise in the background as they crossed the square to the Temple of the Flame. The novice Disciple didn't seem bothered that they were treading on ground that had been littered with corpses not so long ago, walking past the spot where Melian had cut Yala's throat and left her to bleed out on the stones. If a stain remained, Yala didn't linger long enough to look, nor did she hesitate to climb the stone stairs to the temple's front doors. The novice reached the door and pushed it inward, gesturing her to follow him inside.

Yala didn't move. "I said I'd meet your Superior outside, and I stand by that request."

"I… I'll fetch him." As he fled, Yala pushed her cane

through the door to keep it from closing, her gaze roving over the inside of the temple. The gilt-framed windows afforded a view of the cavernous hall with its marble floors and pillars and balconies, with most of its light centred on the altar in front of the largest statue of the god of the flames.

Her grip tightened on her cane at the memory of being condemned to death upon that very altar. Had they added Superior Datriem to the portraits of past Disciples? Did his aged, cruel face forever watch anyone who entered his domain?

Yala shook off the thoughts as the novice returned, followed by a man dressed in gold-threaded white robes. The new Superior was much younger than she'd expected, maybe forty at most. His receding dark hair was covered by a head-dress that the old Superior had never worn, decorated with gold embroidery that matched his robes. How he and the others could stand to walk around in thick layers under the blazing sunlight, she hadn't the faintest clue. Likely they viewed the constant discomfort as a test of their piety and devotion to Dalathik.

Yala watched the Superior approach. His gaze flickered to the ground as though he expected her to kneel, but her leg already ached enough from climbing the stairs, and besides, she owed this man nothing.

Superior Shralin halted in the doorway. "Yala Palathar. I've heard a lot about you."

"You must be Superior Shralin." She indicated the novice who stood behind him. "There was no need to send one of your people into my home to ask for a meeting with me."

"Novice Yachin is … somewhat overcurious. My apolo-gies." He swept the novice aside with a dismissive hand. "*You,* though… I've been curious to meet you. I'm told you were instrumental in preserving us from certain ruin."

Which part? When I was flying a dead war drake to certain

doom, or when I was bleeding to death in Ceremonial Square? "I rather think the honour goes to Novice Temik, not me."

Her chest tightened when she spoke the name of her previous squadmate, who'd died to save the city. She preferred not to think on whether he'd have made the same choice if she hadn't been there to remind him what they stood to lose if Melian's plan succeeded. Had Melian walked away victorious, none of them would be here to debate the matter.

"Yes," said Superior Shralin. "Novice Temik was honoured with a funeral surpassed only by that given to my predecessor, may Dalathik preserve his soul."

Did he not realise Superior Datriem had condemned her to death on this very spot—or that he'd died at Temik's own hand? *I hope you afforded the same rites to those murdered by the enemy you let into their ranks.* With difficulty, Yala bit back the unfair comment; he was far from the only Disciple to have spent the battle for the city unconscious due to being drugged by his supposed allies, and he'd likely not had the faintest idea of the role Temik had played in the near down-fall of the Disciples of the Flame.

That did not make her any more inclined to *like* the new Superior, especially given the way she'd been coerced into meeting him.

"You had a request for me," she said. "Might you tell me what it is?"

"Yes." The Superior wore a hint of discomfort in his expression. "Something was stolen from us ... an item with dangerous properties. I'm told you might have come into contact with it."

"With what?" *An item with dangerous properties?* What in the gods' names was he talking about? "I've never stolen anything from you."

"No... I'm not accusing you of thievery," he amended.

"You are aware, I assume, that the one who called herself the leader of the Successors was self-taught in the art of Corruption."

"Melian?" Self-taught or not, she'd learned from books that she'd obtained from the palace, due to Viam's assumption that Temik intended to use them to expose the king's murder.

"Correct," said Superior Shralin. "One particular book hasn't been seen since her death. It's quite distinctive … bound in drakeskin, with no title imprinted on its cover."

Yala's mouth parted. "The book Melian used to learn Corruption is *missing?*"

Her mind jumped to the severed leg, to the terrified apprentice rocking in his cell. If the book had found its way into another would-be Disciple's hands…

"So it would seem," said Superior Shralin. "We've searched the temple thoroughly."

"Are you sure someone didn't burn it?" If Melian had been carrying the book with her when she'd died, the Disciples had burned her to ashes. Yet she'd also met her end inside the palace, where the books had been hidden before Melian had obtained them.

Yala had never been clear on how many Disciples of the Flame had been aware of the previous monarch's interest in Corruption, but she assumed Superior Datriem had told as few people as possible. Did this man know?

"I'm quite sure," said the Superior. "The book is too valuable to burn. As far as we know, it's one of the few volumes on Corruption in existence, and I don't need to tell you what might happen if someone else attempts to gain mastery over Mekan's will."

Was this some kind of elaborate trap? "The book might not even be inside the city."

"I believe it is." His searching gaze bored into her. "I also believe you're in the best position to find it."

She forced a laugh. "What position would that be?"

"You have contacts and friends among Disciples and non-Disciples alike."

Is that the only reason? Admittedly, if someone had indeed learned to use Corruption, it was unlikely to impact the Disciples of the Flame unless an intruder infiltrated their ranks again. No, the common people would be the first to suffer, and with her own name already spoken by someone condemned for murder...

"Your predecessor had me sentenced to death for crimes I never committed," she found herself saying. "How do I know you won't do the same?"

For an instant she wondered if she'd pushed too far, but Superior Shralin's expression showed more sadness than anger. "Superior Datriem made mistakes, but his intentions were honest, and I have little doubt that he would have pardoned you when the truth of Melian's deception arose."

No. He wouldn't. Yala was a convenient substitute, someone to blame for his mistakes, and if she wasn't careful, Superior Shralin would cast her in the same role. "If you were to swear on your deity's name that I won't be harmed by any Disciple in your ranks, I'd feel more secure about putting my neck on the line for you."

Plainly not all the Disciples trusted her, if the woman she'd run into the previous day at the Disciples' Inn was any indication. Moreover, if Superior Shralin believed her to be a Disciple in her own right, then giving orders to a Disciple of another deity set a dangerous precedent.

"I see," he said. "It is not within my power to speak for every Disciple in my ranks, but I can promise you I will not allow you to come to any harm inside our temple."

And outside of it? Maybe it was too much to expect, but she would have much preferred for the Disciples to ignore her existence altogether. "And if I were to refuse your offer? What then?"

"If you refuse?" he repeated. "Why … it would be a shame for all your sacrifices to be rendered pointless by someone with delusions of following Melian's lead, wouldn't it?"

Was that a threat? She couldn't tell, and she'd be the first to admit that her experience with Superior Datriem had coloured her perception of the one who'd taken his place. He didn't seem to think *she* intended to use the book, at any rate.

"I wouldn't expect this individual to escape your attention for long," she said. "Maybe you won't need my help."

"Perhaps." His eyes simmered with the faintest hint of a flame. "However, given your history with Melian, the thief is more likely to show themselves to you first. If they do, I hope you'll make the right decision, Yala Palathar."

6

Kelan drummed his fingers on the table, habitually angling himself towards the door to listen to the conversations of each new group of people who entered the room. So far, he'd picked up little of use, but being outside of Skytower for the first time in weeks made him disinclined to complain at the simple pleasure of sitting in a tavern over a meal and some drinks.

Laima glowered at him over the rim of her mug of ale, as if it was his fault that the people of Setemar were so reticent to offer useful information. That, or she disapproved of his choice of tavern. Setemar had fewer options than the capital did, with the result that he'd picked out the same place where he'd encountered a group of mercenaries while hunting for Yala. The dingy lanterns and grimy tables were admittedly less than appealing, but they hadn't been given a great deal of coin to last throughout the duration of their mission.

"This is a waste of time." Laima pushed her plate away. "The tavern owner is a grump, and I don't know what kind of foulness they put in this ale. It tastes like a gutter."

"You've never been to the Drake's Eye tavern in Dalathar,

have you?" He already knew the answer. Laima preferred more high-class establishments. "I'm told this is a favoured haunt of the city guards, and I imagine a few mugs of this ale might lead them to be more talkative on the subject of the Disciples."

Laima made a sceptical noise, while Kelan tilted his head when a new group of individuals walked into the tavern. *There they are.* Four city guards—off duty, due to their lack of uniform, but recognisable as such by the shortswords they carried at their waists.

"Expecting an attack, are they?" he murmured to Laima, who made no response.

Kelan watched them sit down, ears pricked, but at this busy hour, the collective noise of the other patrons made it difficult to catch more than a few words in a row.

"…I'm out on Setemos *again*, had enough of those fucking tunnels…"

Tunnels? Such as the tunnels that belonged to the Disciples? He tried to catch the rest of the man's sentence, but a group of rowdy locals walked past, and Laima gave him a pointed look as if reprimanding him for eavesdropping. Kelan shrugged and rose to his feet instead. If she wanted them to make any progress, there was only one way forward.

He approached the guards, who eyed his cloak with suspicion, falling into silence.

"Apologies for disturbing you," he said. "We're Disciples from Skytower, and we were sent to talk to the Superior of the Temple of the Earth. I understand that they aren't taking visitors, but I wondered if any of you had any contact with them."

"You're the ones who kept asking all the questions," said a grey-haired male guard with a nose that looked as if it'd been broken a few times. "No, we haven't had contact with them.

If you want to send a message, wait until the next supply delivery."

"And you're in charge of those?" Out of the corner of his eye, he saw Laima rise to her feet with a resigned air. "Our Superior already sent several messages but has received no response and we're here to follow up."

"If you didn't receive a reply, you should have concluded the Superior didn't want to talk to you," the guard responded. "Harsh, maybe, but true."

"That's not how our Superior interpreted it," Kelan said. "She was more concerned that the Disciples of the Earth might be in trouble."

That was stretching the truth a little, but he couldn't think of any good reason for an entire order of Disciples to close themselves off from the outside world indefinitely, and with no explanation.

The guards exchanged glances, and the older one spoke again. "I suggest you stay out of this."

"I find it hard to believe nobody has set eyes on a single Disciple in weeks," he added, unable to help himself. "Have they all been struck down by a contagious disease?"

Laima gave him an exasperated look, which he ignored, as the first guard rose to his feet. He had a head's height on Kelan, but that meant little when he lacked the ability to hover a handspan above the ground.

"I told you," the guard said, "to stay out of this, Disciples."

"Out of what, exactly?" he said. "It seems to me that Superior Dovial is intent on repelling our own Superior's kind offer of help, unless he isn't aware that you're driving away any other Disciples who arrive in Setemar. Did he give you the order, I wonder?"

The guard took a step forward, one hand on his shortsword.

"Don't start a fight on my property," the tavern owner

called across the room. "If you're going to beat each other bloody, do it outside."

"We're here on the authority of our Superior." Kelan raised his voice so that the tavern owner could hear, too. "We're not here to start a fight. Trust me, that's the last thing I want."

Laima elbowed him in the spine. "What Kelan means to say is that we have orders, and we're also concerned for our fellow Disciples." She addressed the guards in a placating tone. "You might have heard about the events in the capital a few weeks ago. We witnessed it for ourselves, and we have reason to believe that the Superior would wish to be informed—in person."

"He's not your Superior," said the guard. "He makes the decisions, not you."

"I think he'll want to know we fought a Disciple of Death." Kelan hissed out a breath when Laima caught his arm, unintentionally jostling the shoulder where the void drake had stabbed him. She let go swiftly, but the guards' expressions of awed horror told him he'd hit a nerve. "Have any of *you* seen the god of death?"

"I can send you one step closer to Him if you say another word." The grey-haired guard's voice held less heat than before, though his hand hovered near the hilt of his blade.

"Fair." Kelan forced a smile despite the unpleasant memories his words had stirred. "If you'd heard Mekan's voice, you'd understand the nature of the threat we wish to report. You'd also know why we want to speak to Superior Dovial in person, not through an emissary."

"What did you see in the capital?" asked a younger male guard, shrinking away when the older one glowered at him. "I heard the rumours… I heard the city was under attack by *monsters.*"

"You heard correctly," Kelan told him. "The rest, we've

come to tell the Disciples in confidence, but I'll gladly share the story with you later, after we've spoken to them."

Laima elbowed him again, and he sidestepped. *What?* He'd have thought she'd approve of him prompting the guards' curiosity, but the older man remained unimpressed. "You think you can bribe us, do you?"

"I never mentioned bribery," said Kelan. "Only that there's some information which should be shared with Superior Dovial first, and that I'd prefer to tell him directly."

Another guard, who'd remained seated, spoke up. "Fine."

"Huh?" Kelan turned to the younger man. "What's fine?"

"I'll pass a message on to the Superior." The guard took a hefty swig of his ale. "See if he'll be willing to talk to you tomorrow."

Tomorrow. Laima's back stiffened in surprise, while the older guard glowered at his companion. "That's not your choice to make."

"It's not yours either," the seated guard retaliated. "If they survived the dead, I don't want to get on their bad side, do you?"

Now they were getting somewhere. "Good choice."

"Kelan," Laima hissed out of the corner of her mouth. "Our Superior didn't give us permission to recount the events in the capital to the city guard."

"I didn't plan to." He returned to the table alongside her. "Plainly they've heard rumours, though. I think Superior Sietra would rather they had accurate information, don't you?"

Laima sat down, pressing her lips together. "I suppose."

"I do think my decisions through occasionally." He lifted his ale mug. "Now, tomorrow we'll find out why the Disciples closed their doors."

———

Hours passed while Niema and the others prayed for Prathen's recovery. Time ceased to matter, and she remained oblivious to the world outside of her five fellow Disciples until a newcomer appeared at the edge of her consciousness. Superior Kralia stood in the hut's doorway, looking gravely upon the prone form of Prathen on the sleeping mat. Ordinarily, they would have all knelt before her, but Niema, Hachim and Ekim were already on their knees, while Threl and Diaman lay on each side of Prathen. Baskets of supplies from fellow enclave members sat in the corner, mostly untouched.

"There's been no change," Ekim told the Superior. "With Niema here, I thought he might improve."

"He's very weak," said Superior Kralia. "I fear faith alone will not be enough to save him."

"Is there nothing we can do?" Niema's voice cracked, her throat dry from lack of use. "Yalet's blessing can revive someone from the brink of death. Can we not do the same for him?"

Superior Kralia's gaze sharpened. "Prathen would never want you to harm the forest to save him, nor to risk your lives."

I deserve it. The truth was bitter on Niema's tongue. She'd unwittingly taken Prathen's life to save Yala's; maybe it was only right that she gave her own life to return his. "I'm willing."

Superior Kralia surveyed her. "I will talk to you alone first."

Niema rose to her feet. She knew her enclave members would be able to sense her fear, but she hoped their pain and grief would dim any suspicions they might have had as to her intentions. Heart jangling in her chest, Niema followed Superior Kralia out of the hut and through the darkening forest until they reached the clearing.

"Now," said Superior Kralia, halting before the altar. "I want you to tell me more of what occurred while you were in the capital."

"I told you everything." Her pulse thrummed, sweat trickling down her spine. "What … what else do you want to know?"

"If you plan to attempt to heal Prathen by calling upon Yalet's blessing, I need to know precisely how he was damaged to begin with."

"I… Melian cut Yala's throat," Niema said. "I prayed to Yalet to spare her, but there was little energy to draw upon in the city. There were few plants, few animals, and we were surrounded by the dead. I gave my own life force instead, and somehow … I must have drawn on the others, through our bond."

Superior Kralia was silent for a long moment. "It's rare for anyone to call Yalet to save someone from certain death. You must have known the risk."

"I thought my life alone would be forfeit." Niema swallowed. "We were desperate. Melian had killed so many, and … and even Superior Datriem was dead."

"He's dead?"

"He was killed by one of his own novices who had allied with Melian." She'd left that part out of her report, too intent on ensuring none of the blame fell upon Yala. "I left the city before they chose a replacement."

"That is grave news," she said. "It explains the reports I'm receiving from the other enclaves … that the threat has yet to be vanquished."

"The threat of Corruption?" The word brought a shiver of dread to her limbs, even amid her own grief and terror. "Melian is dead. She's gone."

"I fear Mekan has a foothold here now that He has

accessed this realm," Superior Kralia murmured. "He will tempt any person willing to listen to His lies."

Even a king? The question rose unbidden, spoken by a voice in the back of her head that might have belonged to Yala. After all, she had told Niema that the former monarch had dabbled in Corruption—or had at least been interested enough to send Yala's squad to an island containing an abandoned temple dedicated to Mekan, and to set in motion the events that had seen to Niema's arrival in the capital.

Strange, how close she felt to Yala despite the chasm separating their lives. She'd never sensed her emotions the way she had her closest enclave members, and yet she'd raised Yala from death, and that was bound to have left a mark on both of them.

If she died now, if she gave her life to save Prathen … what if she'd been wrong, and Corruption *had* endured? Who would step in to help Yala when she ceased to exist? Maybe she deserved to share in Prathen's fate, but a part of her whispered that she didn't want to die—and that Prathen wouldn't want her to either. Prathen would have understood her choice to save Yala, unequivocally. He'd supported her mission. He'd believed in Yalet, believed in Superior Kralia, and believed in Niema.

And if he knew Yala was a Disciple of Death? What then?

That, she could not answer.

Superior Kralia's searching gaze compelled her to speak, to offer more details that none but her could give. "He… Mekan even fooled the Disciples of the Flame. Melian infiltrated their ranks with the help of a novice, who went on to murder their leader."

"As I feared," she said. "Even other Disciples are not immune to being corrupted. I hope Dalathik picks a worthy successor who will be strong enough to endure temptation."

"I do, too." More terrible truths warred in her mind. The

former Superior had murdered the king, or at least had someone do it, and Mekan hadn't been responsible for his choice. Superior Datriem had committed the crime with his own hands, and he'd condemned Yala to death. What was to stop his successor from doing the same?

Stop that. Niema willed her mind to stop conjuring up terrible thoughts, but they came like a river bursting its dam, pushed by the tide of emotions from her enclave. If she died, who would help Yala against any future threats? None of the others would understand why Niema had befriended a Disciple of Death; she knew in her heart that it would take an event as tumultuous as the one she'd witnessed herself to change their minds.

Superior Kralia gave no sign that she sensed Niema's internal war, but very little escaped her; Niema hoped fervently that she put her behaviour down to grief alone.

"I will inform the other Superiors and enclave leaders of what we have discussed," said the Superior. "I might have asked you to come with me to our next meeting, but I understand why you need to stay with the others."

Niema understood: if she left again, Prathen would surely die. "I want Prathen to survive. Is there no other way?"

"Other than to give your own life in exchange?" Superior Kralia exhaled. "It is a terrible decision to make, Niema, but I pray that Yalet gives you strength to endure."

It's my choice. I have to do this. "I hope so."

Superior Kralia gestured to the altar draped in greenery and the bright trees flanking the glade. "Here is the best place to perform the ritual. Ask the others to bring him here."

Niema ran out of the clearing and straight to the hut. The others waited for her, and after she'd repeated Superior Kralia's orders, Hachim and Ekim carefully lifted Prathen off the sleeping mat to carry him to the clearing. The two youngest, red-eyed and serious, followed Niema's lead.

They don't deserve this. Ten years she'd been bonded to Prathen and Ekim, who'd welcomed her with open arms into their home. Hachim, her friend and confidant, had shared her grief over her mother's sickness, and she his joy when he'd knelt before Yalet's shrine and asked to retake his oaths as a man instead of a woman and had felt the goddess's acceptance blossom through their bond. Diaman and Threl, young enough that they slept curled around one another like wild kekins, had joined the four of them not three years ago, but their suffering would be no less should Niema breathe her last in Prathen's place.

Regret writhed serpent-like in Niema's chest as she helped the others place Prathen upon the altar, which had been forged from the stump of a tree felled in a thunderstorm. Flowers adorned its surface, sprouting out of the dead wood, and Yalet's power thrummed like a beating heart.

Niema knelt, next to the others, and pressed her forehead to the earth.

"Yalet," she whispered, to quieten the doubt in her heart. "Yalet, please spare Prathen. Take my life and give it to him."

Niema whispered the words and a green glow ignited below her forehead, filling her vision with Yalet's vibrancy. Niema couldn't hear Her voice as she had Mekan's, but the warm rush of energy in her veins and the sense of being part of something bigger than herself were as familiar as breathing.

Sudden weakness gripped her. She fought the dizziness, trying to keep her focus on Yalet, on her deity, but darkness encroached on the edges of her vision. Thoughts crept in, unwelcome. How could a god of life allow someone to die to save another? How could She allow Niema to bring a member of her own enclave to the brink of death? As Niema wrestled those thoughts, the darkness spread, masking the gentle glow of Yalet's magic.

Then, a cold whisper. *"No ... this one is mine."*

Fear slapped her, sharp as an icy waterfall. Her eyes jerked open, focusing on Prathen, and then on the others. They remained kneeling, unmoving, not reacting to the voice that had cut through to her very soul.

Mekan ... she'd heard *Him.*

Niema toppled forward into a dead faint.

7

"Those underhanded fuckers," Saren growled. "They tried to blackmail you."

"I'm aware of that," Yala said, pacing the room. She'd returned from the Temple of the Flame in a foul temper that burned like one of the candles at Dalathik's altar. "If I ignore him, I'm setting myself up to be framed for whatever Melian's would-be follower does next."

"And if you don't, one of his people will leave you as a pile of ashes in an alleyway," he said. "He specified that you're safe in the temple, but outside of it?"

"Wouldn't you rather the book was in our hands instead of with someone who wants to bargain with Mekan?" Yala rapped her cane on the floorboards, her frustration spiking. They'd argued in circles for long enough and always came back to the same place. If Yala ignored the Superior's offer, she'd risk a repeat of Melian's coup or worse. Given how many people had seen Yala ride on the back of a dead war drake, she'd have no recourse to argue when she inevitably found the blame laid at her feet.

"There's got to be another way," Saren said. "What if

they're trying to trick you? They might have burned the book for all we know."

"I don't see the Disciples calling on me for help unless they genuinely need it." Superior Shralin hadn't invited her for a demonstration to show that the Disciples of the Flame retained their dominance. He'd admitted that they'd lost a dangerous object, and when she pushed her own grievances aside, the stark facts remained.

Saren scowled. "You're playing into their hands whether you help them or not. They aren't going to leave you alone."

"Don't I know it." Yala sighed. "I already left a message for Viam. She's the last one who handled that book and she'll at least know what it looks like."

Saren made a sceptical noise. "She's more likely to look the other way than help us."

"What would give you that idea?" Yes, Viam had gone straight back to her job after the dust of the battle had fallen on the palace, but unlike Yala, she'd already had a life here in Dalathar prior to Melian's scheme.

He shrugged. "I don't know, maybe she doesn't want to talk to the Disciples. *I* don't want to talk to them either."

No ... and she might not want to risk them realising she has the same potential to become a Disciple of Death as me. Though since neither Viam nor Saren had flown a dead war drake over Ceremonial Square, there was a fair chance they'd escape notice—unless they spent too much time around Yala.

"It's that or go into the palace grounds myself, since that's the last place Melian's body was seen," Yala replied. "If she had the book with her when she died, someone else might have stolen—"

Rapping on the front door silenced her. "That'd better not be another Disciple."

Yala marched to the door and yanked it open. Viam startled, one hand jumping to the elaborate knot of hair piled atop her head. Curls spilled out, framing her round face. Her gaze darted from Yala to Saren.

"Is this a bad time?" she asked.

Saren gave a short laugh. "Is there ever a good time?"

"No … come in." Yala beckoned, shooting Saren a warning look.

Instead of sitting, Viam shuffled to the side of the room, fiddling with one of her puffy sleeves. Viam had adopted the attire of the nobility so expertly in the years since the war that one would never have known she'd once been a soldier if they hadn't seen the transformation with their own eyes. As a former noble who'd fled her controlling parents to join Yala's squad, Viam looked far more at home clothed in finery than she ever had in uniform.

Yala picked up one of her daggers, idly taking aim at the wooden targets across the room. "We have a problem. The Disciples of the Flame have informed me that someone has stolen Melian's book."

"Melian's…" The colour drained from Viam's face. "Not one of *those* books."

"The very same."

Viam flinched as the dagger struck the wooden target with a rattling thud. "Who? If someone was—using the book, there'd be signs."

"There are." Yala hefted another dagger. "Nalen found a severed leg in the river, and the boy who got arrested for murdering its owner was muttering nonsense about someone helping to 'fix' his dead boss. Oh, and there are dead skirrits sniffing around the undercity."

Viam swayed on her feet. "No … that's impossible."

"Trust me." The knife thwacked into the target. "It isn't."

"She's dead." Viam folded her arms across her chest as if to hold herself together. "Melian is dead, and the books… I thought she had them with her when the Disciples of the Flame burned her body."

"Did anyone check?" Yala had been half-dead at the time and hadn't been in any position to see if Melian might have left any material possessions behind. "I don't think so."

"Unless His Majesty has taken up his father's old hobby," Saren added. "Dabbling in Corruption might run in the family."

Viam blanched. "No. He wouldn't."

"How do you know that?" Saren tilted his head. "You don't know the king personally. Or do you?"

"He isn't anything like his father," she said defensively. "You must have guessed from what he did to the army. He doesn't want Laria to be embroiled in any more conflict, and he's never set eyes on the books."

"How is that possible?" Scepticism leaked into Yala's voice. "He and his dad might not have had much in common, but surely they *talked* to one another."

"King Tharen kept the books hidden in a corner of the library," Viam mumbled. "It took me long enough to find them."

"You were looking on purpose?" Saren cut in. "Why? I thought you wanted to forget everything we saw in the army."

"Of course I did." Her hands clenched at her sides. "I— wanted to check the new king didn't have any aspirations to follow in his father's lead, so when I found the books, I removed them from the library myself."

"And handed them straight to the enemy," Saren added.

"I already said I made a mistake." Angry tears gleamed in her eyes. "What more do you want from me?"

"Enough," Yala said. "We've already been through this, Saren. Viam—according to the new leader of the Disciples of the Flame, the missing book is bound in drakeskin. Does that sound familiar?"

"Oh." Viam frowned. "Did they mention the title?"

Saren barked a laugh. "What's it called, *A guide to liaising with the god of death?* Too obvious?"

"According to the Superior, there isn't a title on its cover."

"The Superior?" Viam's eyes grew wide. "Wait, they already chose a replacement?"

"What do you think?" Saren scoffed. "And no, they didn't pick someone better than Superior Datriem. They're all the same."

"It's not them who makes the choice, it's Dalathik," said Viam. "The god of the flames doesn't want Mekan to gain access to the human world."

Saren grunted. "Dalathik doesn't make choices based on what's best for anyone else, I guarantee it. Anyway, the new Superior only gave the task to Yala because he didn't have anyone else to blackmail."

"Actually, it was more to do with my contacts in the undercity," Yala put in. "I get the impression most of the mercenaries they hired ran away when things got out of hand—or were taken down by the dead."

"Serves them right." Saren swivelled to Viam. "Well? Are you going to help us?"

"I… I don't know what I can do," Viam said. "If I let any information slip at the palace, I'd lose my job at best, and at worst…"

"At worst the king would figure out that you betrayed them."

"Saren." Yala thwacked him in the shins with her cane, causing him to yelp and fall out of the armchair. "At worst, we *all* get burned on a pyre."

"Right." Viam's jaw tensed, her eyes glittering with

unshed tears. "If I ask too many questions, the king will find out the Disciples of the Flame killed … killed his father."

"Doesn't he deserve the truth?" Saren gasped, crawling back into his seat. "Fucking *gods*, Yala, there was no need for that."

"There's no need for you to act like a petulant novice either," she retaliated. "If you'd been this much of a pain in the arse when we were in the army, I'd have fed you to the war drakes."

"You don't mean that."

Exasperated, she turned back to Viam. "Can you at least keep your eyes open?"

"I will, but … you're really going to look for the book yourself?"

"The new Superior implied that if I don't, there's a fair chance *I'll* get blamed for whatever goes wrong next."

Saren sighed. "I'm not going to be able to talk you out of this, am I?"

"No." She levelled Viam with a stare. "I don't need to ask you not to drop my name in front of anyone in the palace, do I? Half the city guards already know who I am."

A flush darkened Viam's cheeks. "No, of course not. I didn't give anyone your name."

"No … that was unfair of me." She rubbed her forehead. "Nalen's talk has me on edge, and the Disciples…"

"Wouldn't Niema help?" asked Viam. "Or Kelan?"

"Niema isn't likely to be able to leave her enclave again for a while, if at all," said Yala. "Kelan's people haven't been in the city for ages, and getting a message to Skytower is even less likely than me being granted an audience with the king."

Either she'd have to go through the Disciples' Inn or a private courier that would cost her the remnants of her savings, and the message would still take weeks to arrive at its destination.

"Also, I wouldn't count on the Disciples of the Sky to help," Saren added. "Last time, they left you stuck on a roof."

Yala inclined her head. "There's that, too."

"I'll look around the palace," said Viam, "but I don't think the missing book is in there. Someone would have known."

Yes. Melian left enough dead bodies behind that someone would have noticed if they got up and started walking.

Yala didn't believe the king had taken the book himself, but neither did she believe he was in any way prepared for any further incursions from the dead. If she wanted to prevent another Disciple of Death from rising in Melian's place, Yala might have no choice but to fulfil the Superior's request.

———

Viam's steps took her through the palace gates, into the sprawling complex where the tiered form of the palace overshadowed the smaller buildings clustered on either side. The grounds were too vast for her to see the walls circling its edges, but the sensation of being enclosed tightened in her chest as she crossed the rain-wet stones where she'd watched Yala face the dead.

Where the Void had ripped open, spewing a nightmare into the middle of the capital.

Every day she knew how lucky they all were that the king had gone into hiding before Melian had made it through the palace gates, and that Yala had managed to stop her from breaching the palace itself. Most of the staff had survived, and those who hadn't had been glad to give their lives in defence of their king.

And yet Viam didn't need Saren's taunts for guilt to wake her in the night, struggling to breathe as if she were drowning. Like the others, she'd been haunted by the island, despite the years that had elapsed since their return, but her recent memories were far worse. The Void had been *here,* and every time she crossed the flagstones outside the palace, she found herself sprinting as if the Void itself clawed at her heels.

Viam slowed her pace when she reached the squat building that housed the various administrators who kept the palace functioning. She opened the door and the familiar scents of paper and ink wrapped around her, soothing her nerves. Composing herself, Viam sought out the large room which held the palace's library and walked under three golden archways until she found the section she needed.

Rationally, she knew the books weren't here, but Viam trod down the row of shelves with her eyes open for a spine without a title written upon it, a drakeskin-bound tome that she'd unthinkingly handed to Temik in the hopes of exposing the former monarch's misdeeds. It sickened her to remember how relieved she'd been that she no longer had to worry about someone finding the books she'd hidden inside her trunk and having to explain herself—without admitting that the king's own father had delved into a power nobody should know existed…

"Viam."

She startled to hear her name, then relaxed when the speaker came into view. "Oh, it's you, Brenat. You surprised me."

Brenat was one of the first people Viam had met when she'd taken up employment in the palace. Her towering stature and muscles that were more suited to a dockworker than a scribe had initially intimidated Viam, but her habit of taking newcomers under her wing like juvenile drakes made her difficult to dislike.

"Your head was in the clouds," Brenat remarked. "Something wrong?"

"No." The lie was obvious, but deception had never been Viam's strong point. "Looking for anything?"

"Yes—you." Brenat's mouth curved into its customary grin. "You left the palace. Where'd you go?"

"To see an old friend." The ornate clock affixed to the wall chimed with a reminder that it was nearly time to go back to work. "We should leave."

"Didn't you want one of these?" Brenat pulled a book off the shelf at random. "The journal of the fourth monarch of Laria, dictated to his long-suffering scribe. Why don't they ever write their *own* journals?"

Viam shrugged, though she'd wondered the same. Brenat's habit of saying exactly what was on her mind was refreshing compared to the nobles' tendency to do the opposite, and not for the first time, Viam wished for some of Yala's bluntness. Even now she trod carefully with every interaction, governed by propriety and fear in equal measures.

"You're talkative today." Brenat pushed the book back into place. "I get it, the rain makes me melancholy as well."

Viam bit back a laugh. "If it did, I'd have to check you hadn't been replaced by an imposter."

"Nobody can imitate me that easily." Brenat's grin froze, her gaze fixed on a point behind Viam.

King Daliel stood in the library's entryway.

Viam's mouth went dry. King Daliel was dressed in his customary robes of red silk and gold thread, and a gold-embroidered headdress topped his carefully combed hair. He looked more of a scholar than the soldier his father had been, yet her old instincts drove her to kneel upon the soft carpet. At her side, Brenat did the same, but the king smiled at the pair of them.

"Rise," he said. "You need not kneel here. This is your home."

Viam rose to her feet, hiding her shaking hands behind her back. *It might be my home, but for how much longer?* She ducked her head, sensing his attention lingering on her, as if he could see through her skin to the lies hidden beneath.

Don't be absurd, she chided herself. He didn't know the first thing about her, nor she him. Unlike his father, he wasn't given to public displays, and she could count on one hand the number of times she'd seen him in her place of work.

"Are you here to see the records, Your Majesty?" Brenat asked in a breathy voice.

"Yes—it's been some time since I last visited." He strode into the library, seemingly oblivious to the trail of dazed-looking staff members he'd left behind him. "Good day to you both. May Dalathik's light shine upon you."

Viam forced a smile, her heart thumping like a drumbeat. *Calm down.* Yet again she wished she had a small fragment of Yala's courage, but if anything, she'd lost her nerve alongside her military training. Her legs shook as she walked out of the library, though she told herself the king's sense of timing was nothing more than a coincidence. He hadn't witnessed the battle, hadn't seen her crouching in the shadows while Yala had faced Melian's dead army...

Abruptly, Viam realised Brenat had been talking for at least a minute and she hadn't heard a word. "Ah—sorry. What was that?"

Brenat eyed her with concern. "Are you sure you're all right?"

"Yes, I'm fine," she said, glad she had an excuse this time. "I didn't expect His Majesty to show up *here.*"

"Me neither." Brenat glanced behind her at the open door to the library. "If he wanted a book, he could have asked someone to bring it to him."

True ... unless it was a book that he didn't want anyone else to see.

No. He'd had no awareness of his father's interest in Corruption, nor the true reasons for the last war with Rafragoria. To him, the attack on the palace would have come out of nowhere.

"I haven't seen him outside the palace in months," Viam said.

"No, he often takes walks in his private gardens, but I assumed he was too busy to check on the likes of us." Brenat headed for the stairs to the upper floor where they both worked. "The last time he dropped in here, he was discussing the proposal that we offer some crops to the Parven Empire in trade. Of course, that was before this year's harvest failed."

"He wanted to trade with the Parvens?" Better than Rafragoria, she supposed; while the war might be over, the Rafragorians and Larians would forever be bitter enemies. "What do we have to offer?"

"Very little, and I expect the rumours around recent events have only made things worse."

Recent events. "You think word made it overseas?"

"Of course I do." Brenat gave a slight laugh. "Really, do you not think hordes of *dead bodies* wandering the streets of Dalathar wouldn't have been the talk of every sailor who came within hearing distance of the docks? To say nothing of that monster that attacked the palace?"

"There weren't many surviving witnesses, though." Inwardly she winced; she'd been trying to *avoid* drawing attention to her own involvement in the catastrophe. "Distance distorts truth into rumour."

"Well, obviously." The curiosity in Brenat's expression urged Viam to steer the conversation into safer waters, especially when she asked, "Where'd you hide, anyway? You weren't in the dormitories."

"The library," Viam lied, wishing she'd said nothing at all. "First place I could get to."

Brenat peered at her. "Sorry. I shouldn't talk about it. I know you've been having those nightmares since the attack on the palace."

"What?" Viam's spine stiffened. Had she been talking in her sleep?

"Don't worry, you didn't wake me up," Brenat added. "You weren't screaming, more … moaning. I heard a name, though. Yala."

Heat rushed to her face. *Gods. Even in my dreams, I can't do anything without her being there to give me orders.* "Did you?"

Brenat tilted her head. "Who is she? Old lover?"

"My squad leader." Simple words weren't enough to convey what Yala was to her, nor the other members of her squad, even the ones who were dead.

"Oh." Brenat's curiosity shifted to alarm. "Shit. Is she…?"

"She's alive." It'd taken a miracle—in the literal sense, directly from the god of life—but she'd survived. "She got me through the war in one piece."

And how had Viam repaid her? She'd given the books on Corruption straight to the enemy, which Yala was tasked with recovering lest they all suffer the consequences.

Gods but she had to do something to help Yala.

The following morning, Kelan and Laima left the inn where they'd spent the night and made their way to the Temple of the Earth. They'd argued over breakfast about whether it was wise to disturb the Disciples first thing in the morning, with Laima expressing her misgivings over their choice to enter the temple at all.

"If they're in trouble, they didn't ask for our help," she said as they left the inn. "They'll think we're interfering."

"We're hardly the worst people who might have offered to come and help," he commented. "Imagine waking up to the Disciples of the Flame on your doorstep."

"Superior Sietra said that Superior Dovial never got along with them." Laima glided ahead of him to the temple, where one guard waited at the foot of the stone staircase and a second stood beside the wooden door at the top.

"Did Superior Datriem get along with anyone?" He lowered his voice when the older guard they'd spoken to at the tavern the previous day strode to meet them.

"This is your last chance to change your mind," he told Kelan. "I can't promise the Superior will agree to talk to you."

"Ah, but you can't promise he *won't*." He eyed the second guard at the top of the stairs, who rapped on the door. "Can they see who's outside? Do they have a secret spyhole?"

The guard didn't answer, but when the door swung inward, Kelan glided upstairs. Darkness masked the view inside; the room on the other side might be the size of a cavern or a cupboard and he wouldn't have been able to tell the difference. As Laima ascended the stairs to join him, the younger guard emerged through the door. "Go on in. He's waiting for you."

"I have to say I prefer our temple," Kelan remarked to Laima in a low voice. "Superior Sietra is always courteous to guests … not that we get many of them."

Laima did not reply. Tension laced her features as her feet touched down outside the door. Maybe she'd realised their abilities would be cut off when they walked inside; in truth, he'd forgotten that inconvenience in the wake of his triumph at finally being granted an audience. No Disciple could access their powers within another deity's temple, so Kelan allowed his feet to touch the ground and crossed the threshold.

Silence and darkness awaited. Then a dim light shone, resolving into a lantern carried by a young man dressed in brown robes. Beyond, Kelan glimpsed the edges of a chamber that appeared to have been carved out of the inside of the cliff itself; its stone walls inset with sconces containing unlit lanterns below towering statues of robed figures. Past Superiors, he guessed, and he could imagine the chamber would look quite impressive if there'd been a source of light except for the lantern in the novice's wavering hand.

The man—a novice, he assumed—bowed to them. "You are from the Disciples of the Sky? Please, come with me."

The novice led them through the darkened chamber to a winding stairway that was carved from stone. The steps were uneven and steep enough that Kelan had to rest a hand on the wall to avoid tripping; without the god of the sky to catch him when he fell, he'd only embarrass himself. One would think the Disciples would have used their abilities to make their temple easier to navigate, unless they'd been trying to put off any visitors. *Well, they're doing a spectacular job.*

At the top of the stairs, the novice shone his lantern over a wooden door inset with gold. "The Disciples of the Sky are here. Superior Dovial, should I let them in?"

"Yes … let them in," said a weary voice.

The door nudged inward, revealing a smaller room. Almost every finger span of wall space was covered in carvings, some of Setem in His serpentine form and others more abstract. Blue light shone from within, as if the rock itself contained luminescence, but faded in a way that put Kelan in mind of a dying flame.

The man inside the room looked somewhat faded, too. His beard was threaded with grey, his headdress was lopsided, and he wore robes of a similar slate-black colour to the uncomfortable-looking chair he sat on. Kelan knelt, as did Laima, on the prayer mat in front of Superior Dovial of the Disciples of the Earth.

"Rise," said the Superior. "You're Superior Sietra's ambassadors, correct?"

"Yes," Kelan answered, conscious of the glance Laima cast in his direction as if to warn him not to make a mess of this. "You received her letters?"

"I did," he said. "The letters made no mention of the subject you raised to the city guards yesterday, however."

"Letters can be intercepted," Kelan answered. "Some subjects are best discussed in person."

"Yes, they are." He drew in a breath. "You were a direct witness to the events in the capital a few weeks ago, as I understand it."

He doesn't know? Kelan had been under the impression that the mere mention of the word *Corruption* had been the reason the Disciples of the Earth had closed their doors to all outsiders.

"Yes … I was." Superior Sietra hadn't given him precise instructions as to how much to tell the other Disciples, but it would hardly be sporting to obscure the truth from their Superior. "The short version of the story is that a group of aspiring revolutionaries dabbled in Corruption, and we ended up with dead people walking in the public library and a resurrected war drake running rampant around Ceremonial Square. I'm amazed that you've managed to avoid hearing about it so far."

Laima gave a quiet groan, but Superior Dovial's expression scarcely changed. "I heard the rumours, but they didn't specify *who* was behind the attack, except that they went by the name of the Successors."

"Their leader's dead," Kelan told him. "The Disciples of the Flame saw to that—ah, did you hear Superior Datriem was killed?"

"Yes, I was sorry to hear of his passing." His tone was neutral, but Kelan doubted he was remotely saddened by the death of his fellow Superior.

"He died fighting the dead," Kelan explained. "Our Superior was concerned you might have suffered the same fate."

Laima cleared her throat. "I apologise for my companion's bluntness. He means to say that our Superior was concerned for your well-being."

Kelan thought he'd been positively restrained; he hadn't mentioned that if the Disciples of the Earth had deigned to leave their temple during his last visit to Setemar, he and his allies might not have been left to face the dead alone.

Superior Dovial leaned forward in his seat. "Yes… Superior Sietra was always a friend of mine. It was ill-mannered of me to ignore her letters."

"Was there a reason?" Superior Dovial was undoubtedly alive, if a little worn, but where were the other Disciples? The temple was far too quiet. Upon realising he'd spoken again, Kelan added, "If there's anything we can do to help, we'd gladly do so."

"Thank you for the offer." He rose from his chair. "It's difficult to explain. It might be easier to show you."

Kelan and Laima exchanged raised eyebrows as Superior Dovial beckoned them through a narrow opening in the back of the chamber. The ceiling was low enough that they had to walk at a slight crouch through the tunnel that stretched before them.

"Can't you make the ceiling higher?" Kelan asked the second time he hit his head. "I thought that was within your powers."

"Kelan," Laima hissed from behind him. "Have you tried *thinking* before you speak?"

"Might have, once." He straightened with relief when they reached a smaller chamber, dominated by a towering serpentine statue of Setem above a large stone slab.

Kelan stepped into the chamber, rubbing his forehead. "This is … cosy. Is that supposed to be an altar?"

Laima ground her teeth, but Superior Dovial looked more anxious than insulted. "Yes … that's the problem."

Kelan blinked. "What do you mean?"

"Our prayers aren't being heard," replied the Superior. "As absurd as it might sound, it's almost as though something is preventing Setem from hearing us."

He approached the altar, murmuring a prayer, and knelt before the stone slab. Kelan watched, expectantly. He might not know how the precise details of how the Disciples of the Earth's rituals worked, but he was fairly sure the altar wasn't supposed to remain completely inert, as though it was nothing more than solid rock.

Superior Dovial lifted his head. "Our deity's power runs throughout these walls, yet he has given no response. Not for weeks."

"How can that be possible when we're inside your temple?" Laima's mouth parted in shock that mirrored Kelan's own. The Disciples of the Earth hadn't gone into hiding out of fear. They'd withdrawn because they had no access to their power—to their *deity*.

"What about outside?" Kelan asked. "Has anyone left the temple since this started?"

"Yes, and it's worse when we're outside of Setem's protection," said Superior Dovial. "The temple keeps us safe."

For the time being, Kelan couldn't help thinking. No force that could block a god's power was one he'd want to share a home with. How had the Disciples existed in this miserable state for weeks?

"Thank you for trusting us with this," Laima said to Superior Dovial. "We'll try to help. Do you know where or when the trouble started?"

"Yes." Superior Dovial turned his back on the altar and indicated for them to follow him out into the tunnel again. "It was sudden ... very sudden."

No wonder the temple was in such a state. From what he knew, the Disciples of the Earth were supposed to be able to move the very earth beneath their feet, which enabled them to create new tunnels and chambers as easily as drawing breath. If their abilities had vanished overnight, they were stuck with any inconveniences they might have built into their temple beforehand. That might account for its claustrophobic, closed-off feel, but the silence was what set Kelan's nerves on edge.

Superior Dovial didn't speak until they reached the room

with his slab-like chair. There, he paused, rested a hand upon the faintly glowing statue of Setem as though he was drawing what little solace he could from his deity's presence. "You were in the capital? You saw Corruption?"

"Yes … we did." Hadn't they already told him that? The Superior didn't reply, but when he released the statue, the faint light that had gleamed beneath the surface was gone.

"Come with me. This way." The Superior beckoned again, this time heading for the winding staircase that lead to the main chamber.

Someone had lit a couple of lanterns while they'd been gone, which provided enough light for Kelan to see that the chamber wasn't dissimilar to the layout of the Temple of the Flame, except with each floor hidden behind thick stone walls rather than exposed through balconies and wide windows. Here, numerous doors branched off the main chamber, and as Superior Dovial opened one of them, Kelan glimpsed several robed figures darting out of sight behind a statue.

"Novices." He tutted. "I knew your presence would cause a stir."

I was starting to think this place was deserted, Kelan thought, glimpsing more Disciples peering curiously through cracks in doorways. "I imagine they haven't had much excitement in a while. Has nobody left the temple at all?"

"No … rarely." He ducked through the door and into another tunnel. Picking up a lantern, he led the way downward, into darkness.

After a short time, Kelan realised they must have walked below the city. That thought, coupled by the unwelcome absence of his own deity, made the air seem tight, suffocating. It was little relief when they came to a pile of rocks stacked haphazardly in front of another wooden door.

"Had to close it somehow," Superior Dovial muttered,

seemingly to himself. "Can't have novices wandering down here."

It struck Kelan that the Superior might not be entirely in sound mind. Superior Dovial shifted the rocks one-handedly until Laima offered to hold the lantern for him, to which he reacted as if she'd offered to hit him on the head with a club.

When the way through the door was clear, Superior Dovial beckoned them into the room on the other side with a shaking hand.

The chamber contained another altar and nothing more. Shadows lingered upon the stone slab, and Superior Dovial's lantern cast its dim shine over the small bones of dead rodents and the shrivelled corpses of dead insects gathered around its edges. The stench of rot permeated the air, making Kelan want to gag.

"This…" He swallowed, hard. "This is Corruption."

———

Niema woke with a gasp. The last thing she remembered was hearing a voice she never should have heard in the forest.

Now … someone must have carried her back to the cabin. Breathing hard, she lifted her head, and her heart sank when she saw Prathen lying on his own sleeping mat surrounded by the others, as if they'd never tried to heal him at all.

Was it my fault? She'd willingly offered her life, and yet the god of life hadn't taken her offering. Had Yalet sensed Niema's misgivings? Or had that voice—had the voice of Mekan truly spoken in the heart of the god of life's domain?

"What…" She swallowed against her dry throat. "What happened?"

"Nothing," Ekim murmured from Prathen's side. "The ritual didn't work."

They didn't hear the voice? No… Niema had suspected from

the moment that the voice had spoken that the words had been for her alone.

"Where is Superior Kralia?" She addressed a solemn-eyed Hachim, who offered her a wooden mug of water. Taking it in shaking hands, she drank deep.

"She went to meet with the other enclave leaders," he replied. "She'll be back by dusk."

"How long have I been asleep?"

"Close to a day." He took the empty mug from her, his hands trembling as badly as hers.

"A day." Her gaze snapped over to Prathen. "Is he…?"

"No better, no worse," said Ekim. "I hoped Yalet might respond to our prayers, but even with all of us present…"

It's my fault. The truth burned inside her like poison. "I have to go."

"Niema, you aren't well," said Hachim. "Niema!"

Already on her feet, Niema stumbled towards the door and out into the forest. The sun was already sinking beyond the trees, a reminder of the time she'd lost. Superior Kralia surely couldn't have heard Mekan's voice herself, but she'd seen the ritual fail. She'd seen *Niema* fail. And when she found out why…

She heard Hachim shouting her name and quickened her pace, guilt and pain churning inside. Fear drove her onward, fear that being close to Prathen would only serve to hasten his doom. Hachim's calls faded, though his pangs of hurt and confusion continued to prick at Niema's heart.

They don't deserve this.

Niema stopped to catch her breath, resting a hand on a low-hanging branch. Only now did she realise that in her desperation to escape, she'd lost sight of the enclave. Thickening shadows seeped between the trees from the sinking sun, and dread settled in her nerves.

Niema knew the forest intimately, her senses attuned to

the sound of each animal, the shape of each plant, the scent of the rain on leaves and soil. And right now, the way the small hairs stood up on the back of her neck told her there was something deeply, profoundly wrong. A change in the wind brought a chill in the air, a stench that had haunted her nightmares for weeks.

A bird descended in a shower of leaves, flying at a crooked angle. Flesh sloughed from its bones, and its skeletal beak snapped at Niema as it tumbled downward. Niema gagged, raising her hands to shield her face.

The bird fell to the ground with a soft thump, and then sprang up, wings pumping, shedding viscera. Backing away, Niema reached for a fallen branch and held it up to keep the foul thing from touching her. Another revolting thud followed as the bird hit the ground; its broken wing jerked, unable to fly. Niema vomited into the bushes, heaving, but the bird kept twitching.

Swallowing bile, Niema extended a hand. "Yalet, help me. Lay the dead to rest."

Green light surged around the bird's small body and vanished just as quickly. Niema whispered another prayer to help the poor creature find peace, and this time she felt the forest respond and loan her its strength. Plants shrivelled, their leaves losing their shine as the light around the creature brightened, and at last, the dead bird stopped trying to rise.

Yalet was still with her … but Mekan had touched the god of life's domain.

Nowhere was safe.

9

Yala started with the undercity. She didn't know the capital's underworld as well as Machit had, but she did know her former comrades, and she knew that Nalen would be willing to talk.

"Find anymore body parts?" she asked by way of greeting when she found him at the undercity entrance.

"No." He raised a brow. "Should I have?"

"Maybe," she said. "Also, I'd appreciate it if you didn't go around mentioning walking corpses to the city guards."

His mouth parted. "Oh. Sorry. I didn't think."

Nobody ever does, that's the problem. "It's lucky they already caught the murderer. A butcher's apprentice, who cut his boss with a cleaver."

"Harsh," he commented. "They never found the rest of the body?"

"No, but…" She lowered her voice in case another guard happened to be nearby. "You were right about someone messing with the body. Can I trust you not to share this with anyone?"

Nalen's expression darkened. "Depends on if it endangers everyone else in the undercity."

"Telling them the truth would endanger everyone more efficiently than lying, let's put it that way."

"Fair." He gave a faint shudder. "I was right? Really?"

"Someone told the poor butcher's apprentice they could *fix* his master's body," Yala told him. "Also, one of the books Melian used to teach herself to use Corruption is missing."

"Fuck."

"Exactly." Yala gave him a measured stare. "I don't think anyone in the undercity would be foolish enough to try, but *someone* is certainly making use of her old tomes. Do you know where the local mercenaries are spending their time these days?"

"Shit, I don't know." He furrowed his brow. "I thought most of them left the city, or…"

"Or got torn to shreds," she finished. "I thought so, but there's not much in the way of honest work around here."

"You've got that right." Nalen glanced over his shoulder down the dingy stairway. "The guards offered me a job, did you know? I turned them down. I have better things to do than walk around on top of a wall in the rain when I could be helping people here."

"You sound like Machit."

He winced. "He was the best of us."

"Yes, he was." A sigh lodged in her throat. "Unfortunately, you're stuck with me now. Are you sure you haven't heard or seen anything recently? Is there anyone who had contact with the mercenaries?"

"Not a chance," said Nalen. "You might want to try the pleasure district. I know there's a gambling den that's popular with mercenaries from outside the capital, but the name escapes me."

"I'll ask around."

Leaving the undercity, Yala made for the jail. She doubted she'd get any more sense out of the poor butcher's apprentice, but the guards already knew her name, so she could hardly do any more damage to her ill-fated attempt at anonymity.

Unfortunately, the guard she'd spoken to the last time wasn't there when she arrived at the jail, and two hostile faces greeted her approach.

"What?" asked a lanky guard with a missing ear. "Yala what? Never heard of you."

That's something, I suppose. "I visited here yesterday to talk to one of the prisoners."

"Who's that?" He didn't sound like he much cared about her answer.

"The butcher's apprentice," she said. "Attacked his master and then handed himself in for murder."

"Him?" The guard scoffed. "He hanged himself overnight."

Yala's mouth went dry. "Is he—his body—still in there?"

"What kind of question is that?" he said. "The Disciples of the Flame came for the dead this morning, same as usual."

The Disciples. It would have been nice if Superior Shralin had mentioned that earlier, though it was possible he didn't care to ask questions about criminals whose bodies were handed in to be cremated. If the Disciples had already burned the dead, it'd be too late for her to look at his body to see if he carried any more traces of Mekan's meddling.

The guards' scowls urged her to leave, but she stood her ground and asked for directions to the butcher where the unfortunate apprentice had worked.

As she'd expected, the shop was closed, its windows boarded up. Most local businesses had seen better days, and while Yala scanned the street for any signs of Corruption, none emerged. *What did I expect? Mekan Himself to be crouching in an alleyway?*

Irked, she turned away, opting to walk home through the pleasure district in the hopes that she'd find the gambling den that was allegedly a favoured haunt for mercenaries. Not that it'd be open at this hour.

As she'd expected, the pleasure district was deserted, with one notable exception. Saren hovered on the corner of the street, looking decidedly shifty.

"What're you doing?" Her gaze swept over him and lingered on the closed door of the pleasure house above which he'd once lived. "You're trying to steal back your liquor, aren't you?"

"I'm trying to *ask* for it back," he corrected. "Also, Giran might remember someone mentioning the Successors."

"Right." Admittedly, it'd slipped her mind that this very building was where Melian had first tried to gain Mekan's favour. "Might be worth a look."

Yala knocked on the door, reminded of when she'd set eyes on Saren for the first time since her last visit to the capital. While some of her squad leader's instincts remained, if he wanted to hurl himself headfirst off a cliff, it was hardly within her power to stop him.

The door swung inward, revealing a long-haired man dressed in a glittering green robe. His face would have been startlingly handsome if he hadn't worn a scowl that resembled a war drake on a bad day. "No, you can't have the liquor back, Saren. We're done."

"That's not why I'm here." When Giran scoffed, he added, "Not the only reason I'm here. I'm with—"

"You." Giran's eyes widened at the sight of Yala. "Aren't you the one who terrorised my staff and caused a massacre?"

"That was the fault of the Successors." At the name, he startled. "You've heard of them, haven't you?"

"I've heard of them, yes," he said. "Revolutionaries?"

"Giran, they're the ones who gutted your business." Yala

gave a sweeping gesture at the pleasure house's exterior. "I thought none survived. Do you remember anyone mentioning where they usually held meetings?"

"No, but I distinctly recall a fucking *war drake* rampaging through the street, and Disciples brawling on my doorstep."

"That wasn't my doing." Yala held her ground. "I'm here to stop any future incidents, and I can only do that if I know where the Successors are hiding these days."

"Shit, I don't know." Fear flickered in his eyes. "More incidents? What the hell is going on?"

"Trouble," Saren put in. "Can I have—?"

"No." Giran closed the door in their faces.

"Great." Yala turned to Saren. "Are any of the staff who survived that night likely to remember where the Successors originally recruited them?"

Saren stepped back from the closed door. "I don't know. The library?"

The library. It'd slipped her mind that her own first encounter with the Successors had been in the abandoned public library, but nobody would be foolish enough to hold any future gatherings in such an obvious place. "No, if they have any sense, they'll want to avoid the upper city."

"Now the guards are actually paying attention." Saren gave the pleasure house a last glare before walking away, cursing Giran under his breath.

Yala gave him a moment to calm down before she spoke. "You and he were involved in more than a business arrangement, weren't you? He wasn't just your landlord; he was your lover."

Saren's head jerked up. "And?"

"Wasn't nice of him to kick you out over something that wasn't your fault." Saren was mercurial, yes, but she hadn't known him to ever live with any of his lovers, and it was further proof that her arrival in the city had certainly screwed up any veneer of normality Saren had managed to scrape together after the war.

In response, he walked ahead, signalling that he was done with the conversation. As Yala followed, a memory poked its way into the forefront of her mind. "The Successors took Machit to a warehouse to interrogate him. Then they let him go."

"Oh, shit, they did." Saren slowed enough for her to catch up. "There are warehouses over by the docks."

"Might be where they started." Yala continued walking, formulating a plan of sorts. In truth, she didn't know if the survivors from among the Successors had gone back to their old haunts, but she couldn't keep walking in circles. She needed a direction.

When they reached home, Yala made for the floorboard under which she'd concealed the void drake's claw. As she moved the armchair aside, Saren groaned. "Not that creepy thing again."

"This creepy thing is the only way for me to find Melian's surviving allies, Saren." She lifted the blood-streaked claw and slid it into the pouch at her waist. "It's too useful to destroy."

"Useful," Saren muttered. "Sometimes I wonder if you hear yourself, Yala."

"I might say the same for you." Picking up her cane, she made for the door again, intending to find the next merchant heading to the other side of the city who might be willing to give her a lift.

———

Twenty minutes later, Yala stood before a row of unfamiliar warehouses. Somewhere here, Melian's allies had tried to interrogate Machit, but the briny smell of the sea mingled with the less pleasant aroma of tanners and slaughterhouses making it impossible to tell if anyone had recently used Corruption in the area. Whatever Saren said, the void drake's claw had one key advantage, and when Yala's fingers brushed against the pouch at her waist, the familiar scent of death caught in her nostrils.

She ran her fingertips over the claw, breaking the skin of the partly healed cuts from the previous day. Fresh blood mingled with the shadows seeping out of its surface. A wordless whisper tickled her ears, a rasping echo like a stone dropped into a canyon. Despite the humid heat of the day, goosebumps sprang up on her arms, and she released the claw. *I'm close ... but where are Mekan's followers?*

Following her instinct, she walked along the row, and the chill grew more pronounced. Thickening shadows clustered between the large warehouses, and when she paused in the mouth of an alley, her ears picked up a sound like a fingernail tapping on a glass window. Peering into the alley, she spied a rain-soaked lump that at a closer glance turned out to be a sack. The material twitched, as though a small creature was trapped beneath, and through its open rim, she glimpsed a shape that resembled a human hand.

Her stomach turned. *There's the rest of the body. Or a different body, maybe.* How was she to tell? Dead men couldn't speak, despite the twitching, and when she nudged the sack with her cane, shadows seeped out like spilled ink.

It was then that she noticed a figure ahead of her in the alley. She lifted her head, and movement in the corner of her eye told her someone was behind her. *Damned fool.* She'd been so fixated on finding indicators of Corruption that she'd made the amateur mistake of not focusing on her immediate surroundings.

Yala brought up her cane in defence as her pursuers closed in from both sides.

———

This is going to be a problem, Kelan thought, watching the shadows oozing across the surface of the altar. As his eyes adjusted to the gloom, he glimpsed more shadows vanishing snakelike beneath a mass of rocks blocking another tunnel entrance at the altar's side.

"Corruption," Superior Dovial whispered. "I tried to seal all the gaps in the walls, but it … it's…" He choked on the words, gesturing at the altar with a trembling hand.

Cold dread raced down Kelan's spine, and despite the suffocating air, his skin chilled as though all warmth had been leached from the room. The inexpertly piled rocks in front of the opening didn't look stable enough to keep out a human intruder, let alone the god of death—but *how* had Mekan gained access to Setem's temple to begin with?

"Shouldn't the god of the earth's power have prevented this?" Laima asked, echoing his thoughts.

"It should have." The Superior gripped the lantern with both hands. "Our tunnels lead underneath Setemar and beyond, and I can only assume that it was through one of those passages that Mekan was able to gain entrance to our domain."

"Isn't He the god of death, not the god of underground tunnels?" Kelan bit back a wince when Laima pressed her heel onto his toes. "Ah—I was under the impression that Mekan is incapable of acting in this realm without the aid of a Disciple."

I think. In truth, Kelan didn't know how much Mekan had in common with the other five deities; now he understood, too late, why Superior Sietra had wanted him to research the subject.

"Nevertheless," said Superior Dovial, "this is our current dilemma."

It certainly is a dilemma. How Mekan had encroached on another deity's temple brought a flurry of questions that Kelan couldn't answer, not least concerning the effect it would have on the Disciples of the Earth. Yet Superior Dovial had sealed them inside their own temple regardless.

A scratching noise caught Kelan's ear. He lifted his head, tracking its direction to the sealed tunnel entrance, and Laima leaned over to him. "What is it?"

"Did you hear that?" Kelan pointed to the pile of stones heaped from floor to ceiling. "It sounded like—"

Dirt flew in all directions as the pile of rocks collapsed sideways. Superior Dovial let out a quiet moan, lost in the sound of stone thudding against packed earth. Then a dead man emerged from the tunnel. Skeletal, rotting flesh clinging to bones, feet unsteady on the uneven ground as he half-crawled through the gap created between the pile of rocks and the tunnel wall.

Kelan took a step back, drawing his blade and using his other arm to shield his face from the shower of soil. As the dead man staggered forward, Kelan swung the sword. His blade sliced through the dead flesh, and his gorge rose at the stench. While his blade plunged into the man's chest, the corpse's hands continued to scrabble, reaching for his throat.

Kelan shook the blade to dislodge its burden. Flung sideways, the man hit the ground in a twitching heap of limbs and rotting flesh. Laima slammed down her own sword, pinning one of the dead man's twitching hands.

"Persistent, isn't it?" Kelan stepped back when Superior Dovial reappeared with a rock and struck the squirming corpse in the sagging skin of its neck. With a second strike, the man's head detached from its body, rolling to a stop at Kelan's feet.

"I prefer using a sword to a rock, personally," Kelan remarked. "But whatever works."

"Kelan." Laima brought her blade down to sever the man's other arm. "Any idea how to stop this thing from moving?"

"Bury it." The Superior crouched and picked up the corpse's dismembered head, shuddering. "They usually stop twitching after a few hours."

Kelan eyed him. "Sounds to me like you've done this before."

"Correct." Superior Dovial's shoulders hunched, and he picked up a severed arm in his other hand. "The first one showed up at the same time as—that."

Kelan followed his gaze to the shadow-drenched altar. "Who was this man, one of your recently dead Disciples? Do you bury them?"

"Usually." The Superior's voice trembled. "The most devout, we render in stone, but everyone else is buried inside the temple itself."

The most devout. "Those statues in the main chamber … they were the former Superiors?"

"Correct."

Setem's tenets said that those who venerated the god of the earth would be returned to Him upon their deaths, but Kelan hadn't realised how literally the Disciples interpreted those commands.

Laima made a quiet noise of horror. "You mean—there are hundreds of corpses under our feet?"

"Apparently so." Kelan tried and failed to find a diplomatic way of saying 'you're fucked'. "I'd say it's good that most stone is too solid for the dead to dig through, but clearly they're persistent enough to keep trying."

"Kelan." Laima gagged. "We have to get that thing out of here."

"I know." Without access to his abilities, he was resigned to picking up the rest of the twitching corpse with his own hands. "Do your other Disciples know how bad the situation is? If you're finding dead people wandering around the temple every morning, I assume they do."

"Some of the others know," Superior Dovial walked through the door through which they'd entered the small chamber. "I tried to keep word from spreading to the novices, but it's affected three altars now."

"That seems inconvenient." Kelan kept his attention on the back of Superior Dovial's head to avoid looking at the twitching torso and legs he carried. "We're not likely to run into any novices and cause a panic on the way out?"

"No, most of the tunnels are out of bounds to everyone but me and the top-ranked Disciples," he said. "I had to find a way to keep the situation contained. Novices don't leave their dormitories, for the most part."

"Your Disciples have been stuck inside a cave for weeks without being able to go outside?" He'd thought the Disciples of the Flame were joyless disciplinarians, though Superior Dovial had good reasons for confining his people to their temple.

"Better than the alternative." Superior Dovial led them through a warren of tunnels until they came to a dark pit at the end of a short passage. "Here. Put the body in there."

Due to the absence of any lanterns, Kelan could only guess at how far belowground the hole in the ground extended, but he hoped it was deep enough that the bodies couldn't claw their way back up again. He watched Superior Dovial drop the man's head and arm into the darkness and then passed him the rest of the body. *Hardly a funeral worthy of the gods, but he'll retain a little dignity in death.*

As they walked back through the tunnels, Laima retained a grim silence, while Kelan racked his mind for possible solutions. "Is there anything we can do to help? We can ask our Superior for advice..."

His own people's abilities were of little use in this situation even if he'd been able to access them underground. The Disciples of the Flame had the power to stop the dead from walking, and while he'd seen Niema do something similar with her own abilities, her people were even further out of reach than the Disciples of the Flame were.

"If there's another incident on a larger scale, we might need assistance." Superior Dovial led the way through the tunnels back to the main chamber. "Otherwise, I fear there is little anyone can do to save us. Setem alone can forgive us."

It's not Setem who's the problem, it's Mekan, he thought. A Superior ought to be more trusting of his god, though he could hardly blame the man for being shaken by the dead infiltrating his temple.

When they reached the main chamber, Kelan found himself eyeing the statues of past Superiors as if they might move of their own accord. If they did, it would be Mekan's power commanding them and not Setem, but he was reasonably sure that even the god of death couldn't reach through solid stone. Mekan would have a harder time accessing Skytower, at the very least, but that knowledge didn't quell his profound unease at the notion of his fellow Disciples losing their connection to their deity.

When they left the temple behind, the sky god's power rushed back into Kelan's hands, washing over his sweat-damp skin. *Thank the gods for that.*

Superior Dovial might have already resigned himself to his fate, but Kelan would not so easily be deterred. He glided to a water fountain to wash the stench of the dead from his hands and then went looking for Laima. Nearby, he found her losing her breakfast in the gutter. His stomach turned, but he pulled himself together and passed her a handkerchief.

"Thanks," she mumbled. "I feel like that monster is crawling over my skin."

"It's an improvement on reading every book in Skytower's library."

Laima gave him a rude gesture over her shoulder. "How can you be so flippant when a dead man attacked us inside another god's temple?"

"Better than digging my own grave, like Superior Dovial seems intent on doing," he said. "Are you well enough to come back to Skytower?"

She wiped her mouth on the handkerchief. "Superior Sietra told us to stay here."

"She told us to find out what was going on, and we have," he said. "I think it's safe to say it's beyond our power to stop Mekan when we can't even access Terethik's power inside the temple, but Superior Sietra might have more ideas."

"That's true," she allowed. "Fine."

10

Yala spun the cane and knocked her first attacker's knife away, but the man in front moved faster than she'd anticipated. She hit out with the cane, knocking him to the ground, but the first man recovered, his hands wrapping around her throat from behind. She rammed her elbow backwards, and a masculine grunt answered, the grip on her neck lessening a little. Tilting her head, she slammed the back of her skull into the man's chin, and he released her with a howl of pain.

As the man she'd knocked down came at her again, Yala reached for her dagger and found herself gripping the void drake's claw instead. Upon seeing the flicker of shadow, the man stumbled away from her. "You … you're one of *them.*"

"Who did you think I was?" She released the claw and swept his legs out from under him with her cane. As she spun to her second attacker, she found that he'd backed away from her, too.

"Nobody," he said, blood dripping from his nose. "You looked like an easy mark."

Yala bit back a laugh. "You planned to rob me, is that all?"

How had she managed to attract a pair of clueless muggers who weren't Disciples at all? *I'm losing my touch,* she thought.

"Never mind." The second man rose upright, rubbing the back of his head where he'd hit the ground. "Never mind. We'll go—"

"Nice try." She slammed the end of her cane into his arm hard enough to hear bone crack, and he fell to the ground once again.

Behind, his companion turned tail and fled. Yala might have pursued him, but it wasn't worth the hassle, and she only needed one of them. Surveying her fallen victim, she bared her teeth at him. "You've seen someone like me before? Care to give me a name?"

He whimpered. "M… Melian."

"I know *that* name. She's dead."

"Still counts." He clutched his broken arm and tried to stand, but she hit him in the kneecaps this time. While he rolled on the ground, Yala reached into the pouch to reveal the bloodstained claw. Thick shadows swirled around its edges, as if it was some kind of lantern that shone with darkness and not light. *That's new.*

"Give me another name," she ordered the man. "Melian wasn't the only one."

"Trienan." He scrambled backwards, slipping in a puddle. "Lives at number seven, dockside, but you're wasting your time. He left the city ages ago. I don't know anything else, honest!"

"You know a lot for a simple mugger." He looked so pathetic, lying in shallow puddles of recent rainfall that Yala was inclined to leave him be, but not if her name ended up in the mouth of another murderer. "Sure I can't prompt your memory?"

"No." He fetched up against the wall, one arm hanging

limp and useless at his side. "Everyone with their ears open knows … knew … Melian."

"Do they now?" When he tried to stand, she hit him in the skull with her cane. He slumped against the wall, near the bloody sack that contained the twitching corpse. If this man ended up dying, it wasn't her problem… unless his body tried to stand up again.

That's going to be a nuisance. As she took a step back, a faint whispering reached her ears again. Her hand dropped to the claw, her gaze picking out shadows leaking out of its surface like blood. Heart racing, she pulled the claw out of the pouch, and the whispering grew louder. *Is it coming from … inside?*

Was that Mekan's voice? The claw was a remnant of His own realm, a direct link to the god of death Himself, but she hadn't thought to wonder if He could hear her, too. She hadn't handled the claw much since the battle, and before she'd moved back to the capital, she'd kept the sole reminder of the last mission under the floorboards of her jungle cabin.

Yala held the claw up to eye level, where it continued to ooze shadows onto her palms. "What are you?"

No reply came, though the faint whispering continued. She couldn't discern any individual words; the voice was not speaking Larian. Yala was also reasonably confident that if Mekan *could* hear her, He'd have found a way to inflict a grisly death upon her for cutting off His access to this realm. The whispering, though…

Damn him, Saren was right.

Unfortunately, there was no obvious way to dispose of the claw without it ending up in the hands of someone more easily manipulated. Even if she threw it off a pier, it'd probably end up in an unlucky fisherman's net or wash up on a beach further down the coast. Sliding the claw back into the pouch, Yala considered her options. If the mugger had told the truth, the seventh house at dockside was the home of someone who'd known Melian. This Trienan might not be in the city any longer, but she had to start somewhere.

Leaving the alley, Yala went to find someone to ask for directions. The first dockworker Yala spoke to reacted with confusion. "Nobody lives there."

"I know that." She frowned. "How do *you* know?"

"A noble family with too much money bought that whole row of houses for development last year."

Noble family? Yala had suspicions that Melian had come from an affluent background—somewhere that her delusions of self-importance wouldn't have been challenged, at any rate—and this further added to her impression. Certainly, one had to have substantial coin in hand to purchase a single property near the seafront, let alone several. "I need to know where it is."

The worker pointed. "That way."

Yala followed his directions to a row of narrow houses facing the docks. They weren't numbered, so she counted to find the seventh door and found it locked. As she'd expected, it was easy enough for her to force the door open with her shoulder.

Rubbing her upper arm, she entered a room laid out like a study. Books lined the shelves, while folded papers were stacked upon the ink-splattered desk. A close look at the topmost page showed a title, 'The Successors' Demands. She opened the page and found a painstakingly handwritten list detailing the ineptitude of the current government.

This must be how Melian had got the word out about her revolutionary activities, she thought. *I gather it doesn't mention anything about raising the dead.*

She flipped the folded page over to reveal a crudely drawn map of the dockside warehouses, one of which was marked with a circle. Yala committed the route to memory and then rolled up the paper and tucked it into the pouch where she kept the void drake's claw.

Melian's directions took Yala to the same stretch of warehouses where she'd encountered the thieves. *Coincidence? I doubt it.*

She pushed the warehouse door open and darkness greeted her on the other side. Softly she trod past rows of boxes, sharp eyes alert for danger. Whoever stored their goods in here clearly didn't care about Melian using the warehouse to host illegal meetings. That or she'd paid them off. Why would she need a space this large? She must have been more popular than Yala had realised, which only increased the likelihood that some of her supporters had survived the massacre.

A growling, masculine voice spoke from nearby. "I thought I heard someone creeping around."

Then a solid body slammed into Yala, tackling her off her feet. She fell, thrusting her elbow out at the last minute to catch her weight. Pain tore through her forearm and wrenched her shoulder, splintering her already dim vision.

"Fuck." Yala grabbed for her cane, which mercifully hadn't fallen too far away, and rolled onto her back to face her attacker. She jabbed his ankles, once, twice, rewarded by the satisfying thud of his body hitting the floor.

Yala pushed upright, leaning on her cane, but he moved faster despite his size. As he clambered to his feet, she reached for the dagger at her waist and stabbed. His lunge brought a gush of blood and a gasp as his body hit the ground again. This time he didn't rise.

"Who are you?" She straightened upright, leaving her knife buried in his broad chest. "Do you know Melian?"

He broke out in a fit of coughing, blood gleaming at the corners of his mouth. "You … you're Yala Palathar."

At least this one knows my name. "Were you the one who

promised the butcher's apprentice that you could 'fix' the master he murdered?"

More coughing. "Who told you that?"

"He knew my name, you prick." Yala peered down at his face, which was drawn tight with pain. "How well did you know Melian? Did she teach you?"

"Wouldn't," he rasped. "Had to teach … myself."

Who was this man? Not someone important to Melian. At a guess, he was one of the mercenaries who'd fled during the battle and had therefore avoided being turned into one of Mekan's puppets. That or he'd never shown up at all.

"Harsh of her." Yala dropped to a crouch with her weight on her good leg, hearing the rattle of his breath. "Tell me. Did Melian own a book containing instructions on how to use Corruption?"

When he didn't reply, she pushed her cane against the knife in his chest. He choked, spraying blood. "She gave all the books to Trienan, before he … left."

Yala reached to pull out the knife, her hand stopping a finger span from the hilt. Something other than blood seeped out of the wound, dark and thick and viscous. Shadows, coiling upward, towards her.

Quickly Yala wrenched the knife out of his chest. The dying man's gasps followed her out of the warehouse, into the light, where the shadows dispersed as if they'd never existed.

This is going to be a big fucking problem.

———

"You're bleeding," Saren said when Yala walked into the house. "Who did that to you?"

"Not my blood." She dabbed her face with a sleeve, cursing herself for not checking her reflection before she'd found a wagon driver willing to take her back home. The gods knew what stories would be spreading about her now. "One of Melian's allies got a little too close."

"I didn't know any of them were alive." Saren leaned of the armchair to pick up the folded paper she'd dropped on the floor. "What in Mekan's rotting hell is this?"

"Possibly instructions directly *into* Mekan's rotting hell," she said. "Melian wasn't just preaching to the lower classes. That was in her old hideout up by the dockside."

"How'd you find her hideout?"

"Luck, mostly," she said. "And the fact that she was flaunting her coin for the entire seafront to see."

"Did one of her people ambush you?" He sucked in a breath when she pushed up her sleeve to reveal the raw skin beneath. "Let me look at that."

"Amateurs." She let him examine her skinned arm and wrenched shoulder, though she'd already concluded the injuries weren't serious. "I got the name of someone who was close to Melian. This Trienan is allegedly the person who had the books."

"Her lover, you think?" He wrinkled his nose. "I don't want to imagine her fucking anyone. It probably involved corpses."

"I don't care who he is, but he left the city ages ago."

"Maybe he and the book left the country." Saren dabbed at her elbow with a damp cloth. "Then they'd be someone else's problem."

"Wouldn't that be nice." Either way, Yala had no intention of leaving the city. "Wherever they went, I'm not chasing them."

For one, she didn't have a Disciple of the Sky's ability to traverse the country in the space of mere minutes. Nor did she have access to a war drake any longer; the dead one she'd raised using Mekan's power had vanished after the battle, and she'd made no effort to hunt it down.

"Good." Saren balled up the cloth and tossed it across the room. "I won't say I told you it was a bad idea, but I did."

"Not quite." She reached for the void drake's claw. "This thing did something odd."

"Aside from being fucking creepy?" Saren backed away. "I swear that thing is bad luck. You shouldn't keep it in the house."

"If it's bad luck, so am I." In daylight, it was easier to tell the difference between the claw's glossy black scales and the shadows clinging to its curved edges. "I didn't consciously draw upon its power, but I swear I heard … whispering. Not in any language I know."

Saren knocked the claw out of her hand with a surprisingly coordinated swipe. "If it's whispering in your ear, how long until it starts trying to puppeteer you?"

"Mekan can't do that to the living, Saren." When she reached down to pick up the claw, Saren kicked it aside and yelped when its sharp point snagged on his bare foot.

"That was your own damned fault." She scooped up the claw and carried it across the room. "Look, it's better here than in someone else's hands, and for all I know it was trying to point me in the right direction."

"Trying to help you." Saren hopped on one foot, while she returned the claw to its place under the floorboards. "You're losing your wits. Mekan doesn't *help* anyone. He's the opposite of the other gods."

"Says who?" She nudged her armchair back into place to cover the floorboard. "Did Dalem tell you that?"

"No, it was probably Viam." He fell into an armchair, rubbing his toes. "She's the book smart one. Why does it matter?"

Yala shrugged. "Just strikes me that I'd be better prepared if I'd known more about the gods before all this."

"Nah, Mekan's an unknown. He doesn't have temples, or books … well, all right, maybe He does have books."

"Exactly." To her own annoyance, the thought came with the slightest twinge of curiosity. "It'd be nice to have some direction so I can be prepared for whatever Melian's allies try next."

"I thought you only wanted to find the book to give it to the Disciples of the Flame." Saren groaned. "Oh, no. You want to collect *another* of the god of death's creepy possessions?"

"I'd sooner it was in my hands than with Melian's allies." Not to mention the Disciples of the Flame—and they hadn't said anything about her not being allowed to *read* the book before handing it back to them. "I'll ask Superior Shralin if he's aware that the book might have left the city."

It wouldn't be the first time they'd tried to send her directly into a trap. *Let's see if the new Superior is as scheming as the old one.*

———

Superior Kralia wasn't due to return to the enclave until the evening, so Niema had little choice but to return to the cabin. While she'd washed away all traces of the dead bird, the memory of its twitching refused to leave her mind, and her dread only grew worse when she returned to the suffocating death-scented heat of the hut where Prathen was dying.

How can Mekan be in the forest? She didn't want to lay another burden on the others' shoulders by confessing what she'd seen, but she couldn't shake the suspicion that her failure to save Prathen's life had somehow been responsible for this. The god of death had spoken to Niema, and now His rotting touch had infected the forest itself.

With the others' grief muddling her thoughts, it was all but impossible to think clearly. Pain constricted her throat and gripped her chest, as if the threads joining her and the others had turned to serpents' coils.

She looked out the window and saw Superior Kralia striding down the path towards her clearing and Niema rushed outside at once.

"Niema." Superior Kralia slowed her pace to allow Niema to catch up. "I thought you were unconscious. Are you well?"

"I…" Niema glanced over her shoulder at the hut. "I have to talk to you. I saw something … in the forest."

"I think I know what you saw." She beckoned Niema to follow her into the clearing. When they were alone, Superior Kralia faced her. "You saw the dead."

Niema's blood chilled. "How?"

"The other enclaves have given similar reports," said Superior Kralia. "Stories of a beast wandering the forest, changed in such a way that suggested Mekan's hand had lain upon it."

"A … a beast?"

"A wild drake."

Abruptly Niema's mind went to Yala, and the war drake she'd raised from death to fight Melian. *It can't be the same one … can it?* "I didn't see a wild drake, but I saw a bird infected with Corruption."

"It's spreading." Superior Kralia's mouth turned down at the corners. "I feared this might happen."

"Why?" Niema's heart jangled. "How can Mekan be *here*? The jungle is Yalet's domain, isn't it?"

Unlike the other Disciples, Yalet's followers had no need for a temple, nor any of the extravagant altars and prayer mats that Niema had seen in the Temple of the Flame. Yalet existed everywhere that life did, abundant and endless.

"Mekan is crafty," said Superior Kralia. "He must have sent His beasts beyond the capital, intending to sink His claws into our realm."

That doesn't explain how He got in here. Unless … wait. Mekan had no altars, nor any temples. Life existed everywhere, but so did death. She'd never considered that before, but if Mekan was like Yalet and could take root anywhere…

"I… I didn't see any others." Niema faltered. "Where was the beast last seen?"

The war drake. If *that* was what had started it all, and if the Superiors probed too deeply into what had caused it to rise from death, the trail would lead them straight to Yala.

Superior Kralia surveyed her. "The beast has been spotted in several places, but nobody has been able to catch it."

Niema tried to calm her breathing. "I was able to call upon Yalet to lay the dead to rest who walked in the capital. Perhaps I might do the same to this beast."

If I were to find the war drake myself, I can use Yalet's power to return it to death. Nobody needs to know Yala was the one who raised it.

"Did you?" Superior Kralia pursed her lips. "Its exact location is unknown. It seems to be roaming at will."

Looking for Yala? Surely not. Yala likely didn't even know the beast had survived, or existed, endured, whatever the word was for a force that lingered in a state beyond life and death both.

Sudden pain lanced through Niema's chest. Her vision blurred, and her knees buckled under the weight of agony that sprouted like a bitter bloom.

Prathen.

Superior Kralia took a step forward, her face a mask of concern. "Niema…"

"Prathen!" Niema pushed upright. Every step burned like fire, but so did each moment she spent apart from the others when their own torment ripped her heart out at the roots.

Inside the hut, she found the others kneeling around Prathen. Mutual grief racked their bodies with silent sobs.

Niema dropped to her knees, too. "Prathen ... no."

"He's in Yalet's hands now," whispered Ekim.

Threl let out a wordless howl, which Diaman echoed. Hachim threw his arms around Niema. The others' pain washed over her like a river, and in the moment before the currents swept her away, the image of the dead bird rose in the back of her mind.

We have to bury Prathen immediately. If they didn't, Mekan might try to claim him.

Grief washed away the thought, carrying her into its embrace.

11

The flight back to Skytower was uneventful. Laima spoke little, though Kelan had the impression that she was as relieved as he to feel the air cooling against their skin and washing off the stifling heat of the underground tunnels. With a little luck, Mekan wouldn't make another attack on the Temple of the Earth in their absence.

We didn't make that much of a difference, he reminded himself. *We had no more access to our deity than the Disciples of the Earth did.*

When Skytower came into view, the two flew up to the second highest floor where Superior Sietra's office was located.

After knocking, he and Laima entered, finding the Superior seated at her desk with a book laid open in front of her.

"Superior Sietra." He knelt, as did Laima. "We have news from Setemar."

"I gathered," she said. "Speak."

"We gained access to the Temple of the Earth," said Kelan, rising to his feet. "Superior Dovial greeted us with the news that he and his fellow Disciples are unable to leave their temple due to interference from the god of death. Their altar has been … corrupted."

Superior Sietra's gaze sharpened. "Explain."

He did so in as few words as possible, conscious that they needed to return to Setemar before nightfall but also aware that he and Laima were in no position to help without guidance. Laima added a few comments of her own but otherwise didn't contradict him; she too must be conscious of their lack of time.

"That is quite the predicament," said Superior Sietra, when they'd finished. "I suspected the Disciples of the Earth were having difficulties of some kind, but not this. Not a single Disciple is able to contact Setem?"

"None of them can access their power inside their own temple, let alone outside of it," Kelan confirmed.

"They can be excused for not answering any correspondence, considering." Worry flitted across Superior Sietra's face. "For Mekan to usurp the authority of another deity… He must have had assistance."

"From a Disciple of Death," Kelan guessed.

"I didn't know it was possible," Laima murmured. "A temple can only belong to one god, can't it?"

"According to our knowledge, yes," said Superior Sietra. "However, there is plenty we don't know about the god of death's abilities."

"That's why you wanted me to search the books in the library." Once again, he regretted not applying himself to the task more thoroughly.

"Correct," said Superior Sietra. "It's a tricky subject to research, certainly, but we can make some educated guesses based on Mekan's closest counterpart amongst the other deities."

"Who?" Kelan asked, uncomprehending. "Which deity?"

"I would have thought you'd guessed already." Superior Sietra closed the book that lay on the desk in front of her. "Did you know the Disciples of Life don't have temples? They make their altars in the forest."

"No." Probably he should have, but his knowledge on the other Disciples was decidedly patchy. "I didn't, but they live amongst nature, and that's ... well, everywhere."

"Precisely."

Kelan's heart gave a jolt as the implication sank in. "You mean Mekan can set up an altar anywhere, too?"

"I suspect His Disciples can, yes."

"Or steal one from another temple?" Kelan suppressed a shiver at the thought of someone trying the same in Skytower. "Why there? It seems to me that there are plenty of other perfectly serviceable places to set up their base."

"Not if they wanted to make a power play." Certainty filled her voice. "Make no mistake, picking the Temple of the Earth was an intentional choice."

Yes, and the tunnels are full of the bodies of their interred dead. The Disciples of Death planned this well.

"The question is, where are they hiding?" said Kelan. "We didn't see any Disciples of Death in Setemar."

Laima made an impatient noise. "They wouldn't advertise themselves, would they?"

"Melian did," he replied. "She was as subtle as a rampaging war drake."

"Her surviving allies must have learned from her mistakes," Laima said. "Though given the timing, it sounds like this plan has been in motion since before she attacked the capital. How long have the temple's doors been closed?"

"Four or five weeks, at a guess," said Superior Sietra. "In any case, Mekan has a foothold in Setmar. Ultimately, it'll be up to the Disciples of the Earth to oust Him from their temple."

"You think we ought to leave them to their fates?" Laima's surprise echoed Kelan's own.

"No, but it's beyond the scope of our power to interfere in another temple's business," she said. "I feared this might occur elsewhere after the infiltration of the Temple of the Flame, but I didn't realise how swiftly Mekan would act."

"He won't try the other temples, will He?" The Disciples of the Sea lived offshore, their location unknown even to the other Disciples. The Disciples of the Flame, he hoped, wouldn't be foolish enough to make the same mistake again. That left… "Like ours?"

"I refuse to allow it." Superior Sietra's voice gained a steely note. "The Temples of the Flame and Earth are more vulnerable, given their central locations, but ours is not."

"And the Disciples of Life?" He thought of Niema, whose determination to stop Corruption had urged her to leave her jungle home for the capital despite her utter unpreparedness for the chaos of the city. "They don't have temples either, though I suppose that's no guaranteed defence against Corruption."

"They're also highly attuned to Mekan's movements, considering the nature of their own gift," said Superior Sietra. "I would assume that they don't need our help, as they haven't replied to any of my attempts to reach out to their Superiors."

I hope Niema made it home. Kelan had promised to come and rescue her from the others, if they objected to her friendship with a Disciple of Death, but he hadn't counted on being drawn into another mission as soon as he'd been allowed to leave the tower again.

"What about the Disciples of the Flame?" asked Laima.

"I'll send an emissary to the capital," Superior Sietra said. "Warning them to watch for any survivors from among Melian's allies."

"You think her people are behind this?" Kelan had been sure that most of her allies hadn't survived the battle, and those who'd escaped ought to have more sense. Right?

"I would prefer that to a new and unknown entity, wouldn't you?"

There is that. "Pity the Disciples of the Flame can't use their abilities in another god's domain. Otherwise, we could ask for their help in burning Mekan's influence out of the temple."

"Exactly," said Superior Sietra. "It wouldn't surprise me if Mekan's followers were aware of that, too. Regardless, I'll send an emissary to meet with their new leader. I expect they've chosen someone by now."

"Someone better than the last, I hope," he remarked. "What should we do? Go and look for the Disciples of Death in Setemar?"

"Not yet," Superior Sietra said. "I'll send another team to join you in the morning, after I've briefed them on the situation. We don't yet know how many Disciples are present, nor how educated they are."

"Thank you," said Laima.

"It's appreciated," Kelan added. The Disciples of the Earth could last another night … or so he hoped.

By the time they landed in Setemar again, it was fully dark. Neither Kelan nor Laima had any inclination to do much except find the nearest tavern and order a decent meal and a few drinks. Laima didn't reprimand him for choosing the same tavern as the last time, though he caught her glaring at him when he exchanged a few flirtatious words with a serving girl. He'd tried to lighten the mood to the best of his abilities, but Laima remained as stubbornly silent as ever and refused to touch the admittedly foul-tasting ale he'd bought her. Unfortunately, the tavern's staff knew nothing whatsoever of the Disciples of the Earth, and no guards had shown up tonight.

"I bet they're avoiding us," he remarked to Laima as they left the tavern. "They don't want to answer more questions."

"They don't have to," she retaliated. "If our task is to find the Disciples of Death, they're not going to be known to the city guards, are they?"

"You never know." He glanced at the temple when they glided past, finding his attention lingering on the statues outside. How many of them held petrified bodies beneath? While he understood why Superior Sietra hadn't wanted to send in more Disciples of the Sky without giving them some warning first, he felt inadequately prepared for another incident.

"You don't think those statues are ... dead Disciples?" Laima followed his gaze to the temple's exterior.

"Some of them might be," he said. "I prefer our method of leaving the dead for the crows to feast on."

When a Disciple of the Sky reached the end of their life, they were laid out on the roof and given back to the sky god Himself. Rather more pleasant than burned to a cinder, in Kelan's view.

"I'm fairly sure all Disciples think their method is best." She shuddered. "I wish there was more we could do. Inside another god's temple ... why can Mekan act and not Terethik?"

"It might help if we'd had Niema with us."

Laima was silent for a moment. "Have you heard from her since she left Dalathar?"

"No, of course not," he said. "You've seen as much of her as I have."

When she didn't reply, he glanced sideways at her. "There's nothing between us. Niema and me."

"Isn't there?" said Laima. "You seemed to fall in with her and Yala as easily as with any of your other lovers."

"What?" Since their relationship had ended, he'd avoided pursuing any long-term lovers; he'd felt wretched enough at the mess he'd made of things to want to evade that responsibility for a while. "I'm capable of spending time around women without unclothing them, you know."

When she responded with a sceptical noise, he added. "Would it matter, if I had both of them at once?"

"No," she said, her tone clipped. "Not a bit."

"Right." He rounded the corner to the inn, already wishing he'd stayed at the tavern for another drink or three. With luck, by the morning, there'd be enough other Disciples in the city for him to ignore Laima's odd behaviour, and he wouldn't have to tread carefully with every word. *Not that I've ever been any good at that,* he thought wryly.

Reaching the door, he turned to her. "It wouldn't matter to you if I went back to that serving girl and ordered another drink?"

Laima stiffened. "That's your plan? Really?"

"You assume I have a plan? I'm just making this up as I go."

Her lips compressed. "Do you take anything seriously?"

"I take the possibility of our imminent deaths seriously, yes."

"You—" She broke off. "For the purposes of this mission, we have to remain on cordial terms, but that doesn't mean I forgive you."

"I didn't expect you to." Gods but he was going about this all wrong. "I made a mistake and apologised for it. If that were the end of it, you wouldn't care if I were to have one woman or twenty."

His attention travelled across her face, reading the wariness in her expression, and feeling put-out that he was responsible. She'd always been a little short-tempered, but with him, she'd shown a softer side. Until he'd screwed everything up.

Instead of replying, she swept away through the door to the inn, leaving him blinking after her. *What was that about?* Entering, he called on the nearest staff member to draw him a bath, and when he reached the top of the stairs, he heard Laima doing the same.

After the servant had left her room, he poked his head through the open door. "Seems to me that they'd save on hot water if we both used the same bath."

"Kelan."

"I ordered a bottle of Parven rice wine," he added. "It'd be a shame if I had to drink it alone."

Her lips compressed. "You're insufferable."

"You wanted an apology, didn't you?" He closed the door and made for his room, fighting a grin.

He'd scarcely closed the door when he heard her voice on the other side. "Fine. One drink—but *not* in the bath. You can bring it into my room afterwards."

"Really?" She might just want company, and to know where she stood with him. Strangely, that was scarier than the prospect of facing another group of Mekan's monsters. "I'll be there."

———

The next morning, Yala found herself in the upper city. She had little desire to pay another visit to the Disciples of the Flame, but the Superior needed to know in no uncertain terms that Yala had no intention of running around the country looking for their missing book.

Upon entering Ceremonial Square, she spied a group of robed individuals vanishing into a side street near the Disciples' Inn. *What are they doing over there?* Curiosity piqued despite her best instincts, she angled herself in that direction, and recognised one Disciple amongst their group as the high-ranked acolyte she'd run into at the inn.

Mieren slowed her pace and tilted her head, evidently having heard the tap of Yala's cane on the cobblestones. "Back already?"

"I might say the same of you." Yala indicated the inn ahead of them. "What're you doing, harassing the staff into turning away more potential guests?"

"You have too high an opinion of yourself, Disciple."

"Not a Disciple." Strange. When they'd first met, Mieren had been … not courteous, exactly, but polite. Now, by contrast, her tightened features indicated barely suppressed rage. "Is this an errand from your Superior, or...?"

Outrage rippled across Mieren's face, as if Yala had mortally insulted her entire family. "Your deity might reward traitorousness, but ours doesn't."

"Mekan isn't my deity." Wait … could she possibly be *jealous* that Superior Shralin had asked Yala to find the book rather than a high-ranked Disciple like Mieren? Yala distinctly recalled encountering the same attitude from fellow soldiers around the time she'd been promoted to captain, especially the ones who were older or more experienced. "I'm no threat to your position."

The faint flush that touched Mieren's face told Yala she'd been right in her guess. "You're too dangerous to be given such a delicate task. Superior Shralin is mistaken."

"Have you told him that?" Yala queried. "Don't worry. The book isn't in the city any longer, which makes it someone else's problem."

She knew she'd spoken carelessly, but after another restless night of nightmares featuring the island—and hearing Saren screaming from similar dreams upstairs—Yala had little patience for posturing.

Mieren took a step closer, allowing Yala to see the hint of a flame building in her eyes. "Do you think this is about a book? You might mock us, Yala Palathar, but you've been given a great honour in this task, and if you spurn our Superior's offer, you'll only implicate yourself in any further incidents."

"Honour?" Yala bit back a laugh. "If you hadn't been careless enough to lose a book that didn't belong to you in the first place—"

"Who told you that?" Sharpness entered Mieren's voice, an edge that hadn't been there before, and Yala glimpsed several of the other Disciples of the Flame watching curiously.

"Nobody." She lifted her chin. "I was under the impression that you would sooner cast yourself into your own flames than touch a book containing instructions on how to summon Mekan."

Mieren's jaw twitched. "Some sacrifices must be made to preserve order."

Sacrifices ... to preserve order? Such as murdering a monarch to prevent large-scale chaos? Preserving order had certainly been the goal of those who'd been involved in that scheme, though they'd ultimately ended up having the opposite result.

"Superior Datriem thought the same," she said, "and yet I didn't see your people claiming responsibility for Melian's rise to power."

"You know nothing of what Superior Datriem gave up for our nation," Mieren bit out. "Do you think your Disciple status earns you the right to speak to me as an equal?"

What he gave up? How closely in his inner circle had Mieren been?

"I prefer to speak plainly," Yala replied. "I'm a soldier first, Disciple second, if at all."

"You haven't been a soldier in years."

"You've never been in the army, have you?" Yala was reminded of her interactions with Melian—with someone so far removed from the reality of true sacrifice that she might as well be speaking to a child. "I never stopped being a soldier, and I never chose to be a Disciple. Besides, that isn't the reason Superior Shralin tried to hand me this absurd mission."

"Mieren?" another Disciple called. "They aren't here. According to Yielen, they flew to Setemar yesterday."

Yala's ears pricked. As he'd used the word 'flew', she could only assume he referred to the Disciples of the Sky. *They're in Setemar, are they?*

"I see." Mieren's jaw tightened. "We'll go back to the temple, then."

The other Disciples began to traipse away, but Mieren's gaze remained locked with Yala's. "I recall you were friends with the Disciples of the Sky."

"I wouldn't call us friends. Why?"

"Mere curiosity." Mieren stepped around her, not breaking eye contact. "There have been ... disturbing reports from Setemar."

"Disturbing how?" Yala's skin prickled, her mind darting back to the limp corpse she'd left in the warehouse. "Corruption?"

"The very same." Mieren's gaze lingered on Yala's scarred face. "If I were in your position, I'd consider reconsidering my decision to spurn our Superior's offer, especially if someone were to link your name to the bodies from the dockside that were handed into our temple this morning."

Fuck. Yala should have guessed that the bodies would end up at the Temple of the Flame, but she'd covered her tracks, or so she'd thought. Had Superior Shralin sent people to watch her? That or Mieren had guessed her involvement, but this was a wrench Yala hadn't anticipated.

Yala kept her expression carefully blank. "You'd be surprised. I got blamed for Melian's actions before I even knew her name."

"Indeed." Mieren gave her a last withering look before following the other Disciples of the Flame. "I'd think a little harder about your options, Yala."

12

"You're early," Saren remarked when Yala walked back into the house. "What did you do, piss off the Superior?"

"No, but I may have pissed off the person who murdered the king."

Saren fell out of his armchair. "Someone murdered the—?"

"Not *that* king, Saren."

"Oh." He scrambled upright, his hair hanging in lank curtains on either side of his narrow face. "Wait, who?"

"Mieren, a high-ranked Disciple," Yala replied. "I'm not certain, but all her talk of *sacrifices* and *preserving order* hit the same notes as Superior Datriem's own justifications. Anyway, she thinks the Disciples of the Sky are in Setemar."

"Why would they be in—?" He broke off. "Shit. You don't think they're looking for Melian's book, too?"

"I doubt they know it exists," Yala said, though the thought had crossed her mind. "The reports mentioned Corruption."

"Of course they fucking did." Saren scowled. "You're not

one of their mercenary contacts, free to run all over the country at their command. This is none of your business."

"I'm aware." If Melian's allies had indeed taken the book out of the city, Setemar was the most obvious location.

It was also the last place she'd seen Vanat alive.

"Yala." Saren pushed out of the chair, folding his arms across his chest. "It's obviously a setup. I bet the Disciples of the Flame don't even care about the book. Sending you to Setemar is the perfect excuse for them to have you stabbed on the road."

The thought had crossed Yala's mind—especially where Mieren was concerned—but she was as likely to encounter an assassin inside the capital as not. "I haven't spoken to Superior Shralin yet. He might not know, especially if his fellow Disciples are running around behind his back."

"You'd think he'd be more worried after what happened to his predecessor." Saren watched her, his sharp gaze reminiscent of the scout he'd once been. "Honestly, if this Disciple conspired to murder the *king,* you're better off pushing her into the sea and making it look like an accident."

"She tried to blackmail me," Yala said in a low voice. "She saw the bodies from the warehouse yesterday. It wouldn't take much for her to have me put away."

"She'd do worse without her Superior to keep her in line." His hands fisted at his sides. "I can guarantee that if you leave the capital, her people will be right behind you."

"And if I stay?" Yala claimed the other armchair. "I'm not walking into this without a plan. I sent word to Viam at the palace that I urgently need to see her, and I'll speak to Superior Shralin again when he's finished listening to Mieren's reports."

"Reports." Saren scoffed. "More like drakeshit. She wants you dead, and she'll make up any excuses to get you out of the city."

"There are more efficient ways to go about organising my death." Mieren had another agenda, no doubt, but Yala wasn't inclined to let a vague threat keep her penned in. "I'm inclined to think some of Melian's people did stay behind in Setemar."

"Fine," said Saren. "If you're going, I'm coming with you."

"Absolutely not."

Saren worked his jaw. "You don't need to tell me I'd be a liability if you got into a fight with the dead. I already know."

"I was going to say that if the Disciples of the Sky are already there, I wouldn't be alone," Yala replied. "Though that's assuming they aren't the same ones who left me stuck on a roof."

"Then take Viam with you."

"She'd never agree." Yala couldn't imagine her walking away from her job at the palace to come with her on this ridiculous chase. Nor should she have to. "Saren, there's a possibility that the Disciples will come after you or Viam. If they do…"

"They'll come for me first." He visibly deflated, sinking back into the armchair. "I'm fucked if you leave."

"You're fucked if I stay, too," said Yala. "I'm their priority, but they need my help, and as long as that's the case, they'll avoid doing anything too overt."

Except blackmailing me, evidently.

Saren picked up the flask he'd left beside the armchair and then put it down again. "I suppose it's for the best that this tastes like diluted raptor piss. It's probably less potent."

"Drake piss, I thought you said it was." Yala reached out with her cane and swept the flask over to her chair. "I did try to warn you that you might need to be in full possession of your senses."

"Oh, I lost those a long time ago." He gave a wry chuckle. "Look, being sober isn't going to make me any more able to fend off people who can turn me to ashes with a snap of their fingers."

"No, but it might stop you from sleeping through another intrusion." She expected him to scoff, but instead he pointed at the flask lying next to her cane.

"Get rid of that. Quickly, before I change my mind."

"Really?" Yala reached over and picked up the flask. "I'm not going to find more bottles hidden in your room?"

He covered his face with a hand. "Go on."

"Oh, no, I'm not going up those stairs. Get them yourself."

Saren gave a sigh reminiscent of his reaction whenever their squad had been assigned to cleaning duties. "You're wasted in retirement. You should be barking orders at new army recruits."

"Didn't know there were any." Yala had scarcely paid attention to the state of the army in recent years. "Go on."

"Yes, Captain."

Based on past experience, Yala would guess he'd regret the decision within a few hours, but she hadn't given him enough credit for trying. How many times had she wished she could wash away her own memories of the island? She might have turned to drink herself if it'd had any effect; she'd found that no matter how dulled her senses were, every twinge of pain in her leg brought a new reminder that she stood on solid ground and not in flight.

Viam showed up at the end of the workday, when Yala was practising knife-throwing to cover the sound of Saren vomiting into a bucket upstairs. He'd started complaining of headaches within a few hours after she'd thrown out the bottles, and she'd sent him to bed with a handful of bitterleaf that wasn't having a strong enough effect. When Yala opened the door, her former squad-mate looked as if she'd run all the way from the palace, her hair tumbling to her shoulders and her outfit unusually shabby and ill-fitting.

"I wanted to look less conspicuous, so I borrowed some clothes from a friend," she said in explanation. "The guards at the gates kept staring at me the last time I came here. I think they know my face."

"Join the club," Yala said, picking up one of her knives again. "I can only hope Setemar isn't the same."

"Setemar?" Viam's eyes widened. "Why Setemar?"

Yala told her, in brief, what she'd discovered from poking around Melian's old haunts, and her encounter with Mieren. She opted not to mention Mieren's possible involvement in King Tharen's death; it might be true, and it could cause problems for Viam if anyone else in the palace found out.

While Viam was processing Yala's revelation, Saren came staggering downstairs, holding the wall for balance.

"You look awful," Viam remarked.

"And you look like you raided a farmer's wardrobe."

"Enough," Yala said. "If I go to Setemar, I need the pair of you to keep an eye out for trouble in the capital."

"Didn't you talk her out of it?" Saren asked Viam. "This couldn't be more obvious a trap if it had a sign saying, 'drake bait' on it."

"Even if it isn't a trap, there's too much we don't know," Viam said. "Why not ask Superior Shralin if *he* thinks the book is in Setemar?"

"That's the plan," Yala replied. "Clearly, this is a developing situation, and if Corruption is involved, I have a hard time believing it isn't linked to Melian's allies. I'm just debating whether it'll be safer for the two of you if I left or if I stayed."

The three of them, reduced from seven, were all that remained of the squad she'd once flown with into battle. Their lives remained tied to hers, and her decision would influence their fates one way or another.

Viam chewed on her lower lip. "If you're going to leave, at least take one of your Disciple friends with you."

"They're already there," Yala said. "If Superior Sietra has any sense, she'll have sent Kelan, or one of the other survivors from the battle. Someone who's already seen Corruption."

Kelan would have recovered from his injuries by now, and as the Disciple who'd spent the most time around Yala, he was the obvious choice for any future missions. Perhaps that was wishful thinking on her part, as it'd be far easier if the Disciples in Setemar were on her side rather than against her.

"Say, what about the Disciples of the Earth?" Saren asked. "Don't they have an incentive not to let Mekan run amok in their city?"

Yala made a sceptical noise. "I didn't see any signs of them the last time I was in Setemar. Niema said they weren't accepting visitors."

Presumably they were hiding from the same rumours of Corruption that had brought both Niema and Kelan on Yala's tail, but it'd been weeks since then. Did they know of the events in the capital, or had they remained in ignorance?

"Pity the Disciples of the Flame can't follow their lead," said Saren. "If you leave the city, you're going to take that creepy void drake's claw with you, aren't you?"

"Of course." She turned to Viam. "I'm going to speak to Superior Shralin. Coming, Viam?'

Viam startled. "You want me to come with you?"

Yala's lips compressed. "Maybe not inside the temple. You've managed to avoid their attention, which works in your favour."

As they left the house, Yala reflected that her first mistake had been to pick up that severed leg in the first place. She'd been trying to *avoid* being taken unawares, but she'd spoken true when she'd told Mieren that she'd been blamed for Melian's actions even when she'd been living in a remote cabin far from the outside world. Somehow, trouble always found its way to her doorstep.

"What did Saren mean when he asked if you were taking the void drake's claw with you?" Viam asked, shaking her out of contemplation. "Do you expect to use it?"

"That and it terrifies Saren." Yala added, "It was acting strangely when I was at the warehouse."

"Strangely?" Viam echoed. "What do you mean?"

Yala's cane hit the ground once, twice, as she sought the words to reply. "I heard… whispering, when I was near the dead, but the voice wasn't speaking Larian. Do you think it was—"

"Him?" Viam grimaced. "It might have been. That claw is a part of His realm, a bridge between here and there."

"If it *was* Mekan, I couldn't hear Him clearly," she murmured. "That's why I wondered."

"Be careful." Viam lowered her voice when they reached the gates to the upper city. "I did look in the library at the palace, but there aren't any books on Corruption left."

"I don't expect there to be." Yala kept her head down, conscious of the way the guards' attention lingered on each of them before they let them pass through the gates. "If you hear my name connected to any new rumours, you'll let me know, won't you?"

"Of course." They reached Ceremonial Square, where Viam slowed her pace. "Ah—good luck."

I'll need it, Yala thought, veering towards the temple. *How do I always end up back here?*

Before the war, she'd never set foot inside the place, though she'd heard the stories passed around the army by former novices. Dalem, who'd left to escape Superior Datriem's cruelty, had enlightened her on the Disciples' habit of targeting children from orphanages for recruitment. While some of their acolytes came from merchant or noble families, it was rare that people of that class were willing to give up their children. They targeted the desperate instead, and when she kept that in mind, the Disciples' unquestioning devotion made far more sense.

Yala rapped on the temple door. A novice answered, to be replaced almost instantly with Superior Shralin. "I expected a visit from you today, Yala."

"Did you really." She didn't see Mieren nearby, but had little doubt that the other Disciple would have taken note of her presence. "Then you'll know I have reason to believe the book has been taken outside of the city."

"What would give you that idea?"

Was he feigning ignorance or had he somehow not realised the obvious? "The reports from Setemar. If someone's using Corruption, it stands to reason that they learned from somewhere."

"Yes," he said, "but the reports didn't mention the book."

Obviously. They wouldn't use it openly. "Given that Setemar was where Melian's mercenary allies were based for a time, I'm inclined to think one of them smuggled the book there from Dalathar."

"A logical conclusion to make." He glanced behind him, where she glimpsed the golden sheen of Dalathik's statue towering over the altar. "Some of my people volunteered to go, but I told them they're needed here."

"Did they now?" *Mieren. She wants to find the book before I do.* Part of Yala was inclined to leave her to her games, if not for her suspicions regarding the Disciples' role in the king's death, and the secrets he'd taken to the bottom of the ocean. "You trust the Disciples of the Sky to deal with the situation alone?"

"Until we have more information, I won't allow my Disciples to be diverted from rebuilding our order after the recent catastrophe." He took in a measured breath. "That said, I would be most grateful if you were to pay Setemar a visit in person."

Yala stifled a disbelieving laugh. "Gratitude? That's my payment for this?"

"You want payment?" Disbelief flickered across his face. "If you desire, I can make arrangements for a suitable payment to be delivered to you as soon as you return the book to the temple."

"I didn't say you could pay me off either," Yala retaliated. "I'm more interested in ensuring nobody will accuse me of any crimes I didn't commit, but I fear that's beyond even your power."

A sudden whiff of burning reached her nostrils; over his shoulder, Yala's gaze snagged on a figure who stood beside the altar. Facing the door, Mieren's eyes simmered with flames even from a distance. *Oh, she'll definitely find a way to get me blamed, given the chance.*

Superior Shralin gave no sign that he'd noticed his acolyte watching them. "I did say that you wouldn't be harmed within the temple, didn't I?"

"Yes, but not outside of it," she said. "Last I checked, that includes Setemar. I'd also prefer not to come back to a price on my head."

"I'll take that into consideration," said Superior Shralin. "You don't need to be that distrusting, Yala. We have the same goals."

I doubt it. "I'll go, *if* you don't send any other Disciples on my tail. Those are my conditions."

Surprise flickered across his features. "I would have thought you'd be glad of the help, but I have no intention of sending any of my Disciples outside of the city."

You might want to keep a close watch on your high-ranked associates. "Then I'll thank you for your time."

She left, before her mouth could get her into more trouble, reflecting that Mieren seemed the sort who'd go behind her new Superior's back if she so desired. For all she knew, there were others who shared the same misgivings about his decision to entrust Yala with the mission. The Disciples of the Flame might be in disarray, but the actions of their former leader had left a mark, and the stain would not easily be washed away.

Pity nobody else could destroy that damned book.

———

That night, they gave Prathen back to the forest.

Niema and the other enclave members gathered in the glade in which they'd chosen to lay Prathen to rest, a haven of vibrant trees and lush greenery that struck a jarring contrast to the grief and pain of their gathering. As was custom, they'd dug a shallow hole for Prathen's body and would pray to Yalet for three days until She had reclaimed him.

This method was supposed to allow enough time for the deceased's loved ones to say goodbye, but Niema found herself fervently wishing for a less prolonged ceremony. By the end of the first night, she was jumping at every shadow, and she was sure the others sensed her fractured nerves beneath the sorrow engulfing them.

Sorrow that Niema had no right to share in. She'd never felt so ill at ease in Yalet's presence, knowing that the goddess of light must be aware of her transgression.

When the last rays of sunlight slipped below the treetops, Niema caught the scent on the air that she'd dreaded. A rustling sounded in the trees above Prathen's grave, while the shadows seemed thicker, darker. Her sharp eyesight picked out movement amongst the branches, a clumsy, dead shape descending onto the glade. A kekin, its tail naught but bone, its fur reduced to rags over rotting flesh, and its pitted eyes devoid of life.

"Get away." She rose to her feet, her legs stiff. "Get away from here."

I can't let Mekan have Prathen.

With one eye on the dead kekin, Niema murmured a prayer to Yalet. Branches shifted, swaying at Niema's command, and a vine extended and wrapped around the kekin's fragile bones.

Get away from Prathen. The beast struggled, and Niema urged the vine to squeeze tighter. Her gorge rose as she heard bones snap.

"Niema." Hachim's voice was hushed, shocked. "Niema—what is that?"

"Hachim." She wrenched her gaze from the struggling kekin. In the dark, her enclave member's eyes were round as he stared up at her. "Help me."

Hachim recoiled when the vine released the kekin's ruined body. Even when it hit the grass, its bones kept twitching, limbs trying to reform, shadows twisting and coiling like smoke.

"The creature is infected with Mekan's power." Bile rose in her throat, but she swallowed it. "The god of life extinguishes death. I need your help."

"No." Hachim rose jerkily to his feet. "No—it can't be possible. Not here."

"Please." She whispered a prayer again, urged the greenery to unfold around the kekin's struggling form, to lay the poor creature to rest.

"Prathen!" Threl shrieked, pointing at the grave.

Niema's heart plunged downward. Shadows rose from

where Prathen lay, seeping along the grass and turning green to grey. "No. Stay away from him."

Inside the grave, Prathen's eyes opened.

Niema lunged with a strangled scream, her hands aglow with the god of life's power. "Stop!"

Green light surged from her fingertips as she prayed to the sky. The very glade itself answered, the trees rustling, the greenery stirring at her command and pushing back against the shadows creeping out of Prathen's grave.

Niema closed her eyes, every piece of her focused on one goal. *Lay him to rest. Please, Yalet. Let his suffering be over.*

She imagined, as clearly as possible, the forest itself stifling the shadows trying to raise Prathen from the grave. Greenery bloomed in her mind's eye, and she clung to that image as she repeated her prayer, again, again.

"Niema." Superior Kralia's voice jerked her out of her trance. Opening her eyes, she blinked away the green glare and exhaled a slow, shaky breath.

Prathen's grave was smooth undisturbed mass of greenery. The shadows had gone, as though extinguished, yet her Superior's presence struck like a jarring note amidst a bird's gentle song. Niema lowered her hands, seeing four pairs of stunned eyes watching her.

Then her gaze went to her Superior, who stood in the glade's opening between trees that no longer bloomed with life. Their branches had turned as grey as dust, leaves crumbling before her sight.

I did that.

"That was quick thinking, Niema." Superior Kralia's tone was neutral, but her face, half in shadow, displayed a level of grimness Niema had never before seen. Niema's stomach lurched when the moonlight shifted, illuminating more dead trees flanking Prathen's grave, which was now the only bright spot in the clearing.

"I didn't know what else to do." Niema blinked back tears. "I'm sorry."

Nobody spoke. The others continued to watch Niema as if she were a stranger, until Superior Kralia addressed them. "I would talk to Niema alone."

Niema's heartbeat thrummed, her throat constricting. One by one the others left, until she and Superior Kralia stood alone in front of Prathen's grave. "I'm sorry. I didn't mean to—"

"I asked some questions, Niema." Superior Kralia's smooth tone cut through Niema's apology. "To the other Superiors. It's rarely heard of for someone to draw on enough power to cost the life of a fellow enclave member, and there can be … consequences."

Didn't I already tell you that? "If I could have offered my own life in Prathen's place, I would have."

"Yes, I've no doubt that's true," said Superior Kralia. "However, your actions brought death to the forest."

The implication hit her. "*I* brought Mekan here?"

Her words fell like stones, precise and devastating. "Tell me the truth about Yala Palathar."

13

Kelan had expected the next morning to come with regrets, at least on Laima's part, but he didn't expect to be woken by an earthquake. Abruptly, the world lurched sideways, and he hit the floor with a thump that jerked his eyes open and left him looking up at the ceiling in dazed confusion.

He'd fallen off the bed—the bed he'd left Laima in—and she squinted at him with equal bafflement.

"Ouch." He lifted his head. "Did you feel that?"

Another tremor shook the room. *That's a yes, then.* Lurching to his feet, he steadied himself against the wall with a hand. "Was that from the Temple of the Earth?"

"I haven't the faintest idea." Laima groaned, pressing a hand to her forehead. "Gods—*why* did I let you talk me into drinking all that wine?"

"I'm a bad influence?" She hadn't needed much persuasion, from what Kelan remembered; her claims that she only wanted one drink had scarcely lasted as long as it had taken to close the door to her room. Likewise, his intention to offer her a coherent apology had vanished within minutes of him opening the wine bottle, and he'd found himself more interested in using his tongue for other matters. Laima certainly hadn't objected, though her current tone indicated that she wished she'd exercised more restraint both in wine consumption and in her willingness to let their conversation dissolve into less verbal means of communication.

A third tremor rattled the furniture. Kelan grimaced, glad he hadn't drunk enough to dim his memories of how they'd enjoyed one another's bodies, but the headache didn't help his coordination as he scrambled to gather his clothes from the floor. "I think we need to check on the Disciples of the Earth."

No other tremors followed, but from the shouts on the streets outside, the earthquake had resonated across the city.

"Do you think that was them?" he asked Laima as he finished pulling on his cloak. "If they've managed to get their powers back, it'll certainly make our mission easier."

Laima shook her head in answer. By the time they walked out of the inn, the tremors had ceased, but they headed towards the Temple of the Earth, regardless.

Kelan's first knock on the door went unanswered, but when he knocked a second time, a sweaty-faced novice poked his head out of the door. "Help us!"

A familiar decaying stench rolled out of the temple. *The dead.* Kelan reached for the blade at his waist. "We'll help."

Laima gave no argument, and they ran into the temple. This time, the lanterns on the walls of the main chamber had all been lit, illuminating the pandemonium of novices and full Disciples alike fleeing from the walking corpses emerged from the tunnels that branched off the chamber. Amongst them lay the grisly remains of the long-dead, splintering bones piled on the floor. Had they infiltrated the temple overnight?

Kelan slammed down a foot on a twitching wrist,

severing the hand, which flipped over, fingers scrabbling at his ankle. Laima brought the point of her blade into the decaying hand, and he gave her a nod of gratitude before joining the Disciples in fighting off their attackers. While the dead were in such a state of decay that they fell apart at the slightest hit, they had the advantage in sheer numbers, and kept on fighting even when taken apart.

Yet they were unarmed, Kelan noted as he tossed yet another severed limb aside. They must have come straight from their graves, and while most of the Disciples of the Earth hadn't thought to grab weapons either, he and Laima made quick work of any dead who came at them.

Finally, it was over, the dead had been reduced to nothing more than rotting bones. Some of the younger novices were crying, vomiting, or huddling in corners. More Disciples emerged from behind statues, having hidden themselves, while Superior Dovial stood amongst those who'd fought, looking as stunned as the rest.

"I gather this isn't how he intended to break the news," Kelan whispered to Laima. "So much for avoiding a panic."

Superior Dovial stepped to the front of the chamber to address the others. "Novices, go back to your rooms. Senior Disciples, go upstairs. The rest of you, gather the dead."

When he finished giving instructions, he turned to Kelan and Laima. "Thank you for your assistance. I'm sorry, but I have to deal with this. Can you come back later?"

Laima retreated towards the temple doors, but Kelan didn't move. "Why was the floor shaking earlier?" he asked. "Did one of your people manage to contact the god of the earth again?"

"No." He didn't meet Kelan's eyes. "No, I don't know where it came from, but it wasn't any of us."

Really. He was lying, but about what? "If you need our

help with anything else, let us know. More Disciples of the Sky will be arriving later this morning."

Superior Dovial nudged a pile of bones with his foot. "I fear it may already be too late."

On that less-than-auspicious note, Kelan and Laima left the temple. As the door closed behind them, Kelan studied the statues flanking the steps, wondering if the god of the earth might be more active than He appeared to be. Mekan couldn't cause earthquakes, as far as Kelan knew.

"Kelan, come on." Laima glided downstairs. "We should leave them to clean up in peace."

He joined her at the foot of the stairs. "Is it just me, or were the dead holding back?"

"What would make you say that?"

"The dead weren't trying to kill the Disciples of the Earth," he clarified. "It wasn't anything like with Melian. No casualties."

Melian had commanded the dead to grab any weapons available and to use them on any living person unfortunate enough to get too close, resulting in some of the Disciples of the Flame being brought down. Death fed on death, so it was in Mekan's favour to kill as many as possible to add to His ranks. The ones in the Temple of the Earth hadn't even been armed.

"Isn't that a *good* thing?" said Laima. "Honestly. Only you could decide an attack of the dead isn't exciting enough."

"I didn't say it was unexciting, just … inefficient." If the goal had been to cause a panic, they'd certainly succeeded; any progress that Superior Dovial had made in keeping the nature of the intrusion into their temple a secret had been thoroughly obliterated. "Pity the Disciples of the Flame aren't here to help clean up the dead. It'd save on time."

"Superior Sietra did send an envoy to meet with them earlier."

"She did," he agreed, "but I think someone needs to tell them of this new development."

Granted, enlisting the help of the Disciples of the Flame would hardly solve the major problem: namely, finding whoever had brought Mekan's presence into the temple to begin with.

Laima cut him a sideways look. "Don't tell me you want to go there yourself and leave me to greet the other Disciples alone."

"If I stay here, there's a fair chance I'll run into trouble searching for the source of that earthquake." He surveyed the temple again. "We don't both need to be here, do we? Superior Dovial clearly wanted us to leave."

She worked her jaw. "Can I trust you to handle the Disciples of the Flame's new Superior diplomatically? We don't need another incident."

Right. They have a new Superior ... and now that he thought on the subject, maybe it was worth a visit to the Temple of the Flame for that reason alone. "If their new Superior is a fraction more pleasant than Superior Datriem was, it'll be an improvement."

"If you say so." Her eyes narrowed. "Is this an excuse to drop in on your Disciple of Death friend?"

"What ... Yala?" Had Yala met the Disciples of the Flame's new leader? He'd assumed she'd be trying to *avoid* the Disciples, but he'd never met anyone else with such a penchant for attracting trouble. Aside from himself, of course. "Now you mention it, she might want to know the dead are walking around Setemar's tunnels."

"Really." Laima's tone dripped with disapproval. "You want to involve her on an official mission when she broke out of prison and defied Superior Sietra?"

"With our help, if you haven't forgotten," Kelan added.

"No, I didn't think of asking her, but she might have more information about where Mekan's allies are hiding."

Unlike him, she'd spoken directly to the god of death herself. She wouldn't thank him for getting her involved, but she had a history in Setemar already, and it was worth giving her an update.

Laima pursed her lips. "I know you. You'd better not get distracted."

"What do you take me for?" After the previous night, he'd thought they were on the same page, but Laima seemed to have drawn her own conclusions about his motives. "If I leave now, I'll be back in plenty of time to meet the other Disciples, and you know it's faster than sending a messenger."

"I suppose." She exhaled in a sigh. "Fine. But be quick about it."

"I will." He couldn't shake the feeling that he'd disappointed her somehow, but that was hardly new. *Gods, that woman is confusing.*

Now was as good a time as any to get a look at the surrounding area, so Kelan took flight and rose upward parallel to the cliffs concealing the temple. The tunnels didn't go on forever; even if they ran under the entire city, they had to come out somewhere.

Upon reaching the top of the cliffs, Kelan glided to the other side, where they circled Setemar from behind. As well as several farms scattered throughout the hills beyond, a small settlement sat in the cliffs' shadow. *Interesting place to build a village.* Yes, other towns and villages had sprung up as Setemar had expanded, but why build one on the opposite side of the cliffs to the city itself? *Oh, wait. The mines.* Setemar had been established when the Disciples of the Earth had used their abilities to extract metals from the cliffs in the days of Laria's founding. Evidently, some of those mines were still in use, centuries later.

Interesting. Kelan filed that information away and turned north, towards the capital.

———

Yala set off for Setemar at dawn. She'd wanted to leave the previous day, but it'd taken longer than she'd expected to find someone willing to give her a ride all the way to Setemar, let alone without asking intrusive questions. There weren't many travellers on the road these days, and even fewer wanting to go *away* from the capital, so she'd ended up accepting a ride from a farmer whose loud raging about the price of grain had Yala contemplating shoving him out of the wagon before they'd even left Dalathar. Since she lacked Niema's ability to soothe animals into obedience, corralling the raptors herself was likely to be more trouble than it was worth, so she resigned herself to a very long day.

At least she'd had time to give thorough instructions to Nalen to keep the undercity together while she was gone— and to make sure Saren stayed alive. The latter might be the hardest part; when she'd left, Saren had been having an involved argument with the wall about the perils of keeping the void drake's claw in the house. She'd brought the claw with her, of course, along with her other meagre possessions in her well-worn pack.

An hour into their journey, Yala was idly watching the fields of grain pass when she glimpsed an unmistakeable *human* figure in the sky. She tensed, recalling with too much clarity the first time she'd encountered a Disciple of the Sky on the road, which had ended in her discovering Vanat's corpse.

The farmer continued to rant and rave without noticing the man hovering above them, while Yala surreptitiously reached for her knife, calculating the odds of her being able to knock him out of the air.

As the figure drew closer, Yala leaned out of the cart and then recognised her pursuer's face. "Kelan, what are you *doing?*"

"Looking for you," he called back.

"Don't come any closer." Too late; he'd already dropped, and the gust of wind he'd conjured up spooked the raptors into veering off the road. The wagon swayed from side to side, the driver exclaimed and cursed, and Yala furiously gestured at Kelan to move. He did so, resulting in another breeze that knocked the wagon sideways.

The driver yelled more obscenities, while Yala clung onto the side and hissed, "Get in here."

Kelan obliged, sliding under the wood-frame roof and landing on the seat next to her. "Pleasure to see you again."

"What are you doing here?" she growled at him. "Aside from ruining my day?"

"Where are you off to in such a hurry?" he asked in turn. "Leaving the city just as I arrived?"

"Did you come from Setemar?"

His brow arched. "Staying out of trouble, I see."

"That's a 'yes', then." Somewhat vindicated, she settled into a more comfortable position as the raptors' panicking ceased. "What's going on over there?"

"Have you got all day?" He glanced at the farmer who'd been shocked into silence by Kelan's appearance that a part of Yala wished he'd arrived sooner. "Listen—I have to go, but I'll be back."

"Nice try." She leaned over and grabbed his sleeve. "You'll save me a lot of time if you tell me whether you've already seen them."

"Seen who?"

"Melian's allies," she whispered, conscious that the farmer was eying the pair of them with an expression mingling suspicion and alarm. "One of the books is missing."

"One of the books…?" He trailed off as he caught her meaning. "In Setemar? That would explain a lot."

"Why?" Her hope that Kelan would declare that his mission had nothing to do with Corruption puffed out like an extinguished flame.

"Let's just say that the Disciples of the Earth had a very good reason not to come out and talk to Niema and me during our last visit."

"Niema," she repeated. "Have you seen her?"

"Of course not. Isn't she back in the forest?"

"I imagine she's home by now, yes." She wanted to say more, but mentioning Corruption in front of their driver would likely result in them both being stranded on the roadside. "Is there anyone in Setemar with you?"

"Laima—and more Disciples are on their way," he added. "If you want me to shorten your journey, let me know when I'm on my way back."

"From where?"

"The Temple of the Flame."

"What?" She caught the side of the wagon in her hand when he lifted himself into the air. "Why are you going to *them?* They're the reason I'm on this absurd chase to begin with."

"You'll have to tell me everything later." He grinned and slipped out of the wagon, vanishing in a breeze that caused the raptors to launch into another panic.

Yala gripped the wagon's side and swore under her breath. Some things hadn't changed—including Kelan's ability to cause as much chaos as possible wherever he went

—but she'd thought he'd have more sense than to expect help from the Disciples of the Flame.

Never mind them. What's going on with the Disciples of the Earth?

———

"What do you mean, she already left?" Viam asked Saren. "When?"

"This morning," he croaked, looking even more worse for wear than he had the last time they'd seen one another. "She took a wagon south to Setemar like she said she would."

"Alone?" Viam had hoped someone would talk her out of it, but there was no deterring Yala when she got an idea into her head. She and Saren knew that better than anyone.

Saren clung to the side of his armchair like a piece of debris in a storm-tossed ocean. "She thinks it's her mission to find that book, when it seems to me that you're more familiar with it than she is."

Viam's mouth went dry, recalling the sensation of aged leather beneath her fingertips and the accompanying knowledge that she'd held in her hands the instruments that had led to the death of the king. "I thought the Disciples of the Flame might have sent someone to follow her."

"Oh, they don't want to leave their comforts behind to go hunting Disciples of Death." Saren's smile was tinged with exhaustion. "Yala said she asked for a guarantee that they wouldn't. She didn't want that Mieren to sneak up on her. You know, the king's murderer."

The king's murderer. Each word hit like a drumbeat. "Yala … met the king's murderer?"

"She didn't tell you?" Saren's smile faded. "Shit. She probably didn't want me to mention that."

Viam took a step back, then another, until she fetched up against the wall. "You didn't tell anyone, did you?"

He gave a strained laugh. "Nobody believes a word I say, trust me. Besides, she didn't know for sure."

She didn't tell me. They hadn't had a great deal of time to talk, but had Yala's omission been intentional? Or had her former squad leader yet to forgive her unintended betrayal? "Anything else you forgot to tell me?"

"I saw a war drake crawling out of the wall earlier."

"Not your hallucinations." How could Yala have left him alone in this state? "I meant concerning Corruption."

"I feel like death without inviting Mekan over for a party." He slumped. "Yala took the void drake's claw with her. That ought to stop any more incidents."

Viam's mind drifted back to her own piece of one of Mekan's beasts, which she kept at the very bottom of the chest in which she stored her clothing. "You were never tempted to learn to use it?"

"Many things tempt me. Corruption is not one of them."

That's fair, I suppose. Viam herself had only conducted the smallest experiments, when the city was already in the grip of chaos. Her knowledge had enabled her to help Yala, but she hadn't so much as touched Corruption since. *And yet she still doesn't trust me.*

"All right." She straightened her shoulders. "I'll leave you to it."

She made to leave and he called after her. "If you're that worried about Yala, follow her. Unless you're too scared to leave the palace."

"Don't be absurd." She slowed, resting a hand on the door frame. "It's a risk to stay, you know. If the king found out the truth, I'd be out of a job and potentially sentenced to death."

"For what?" he queried. "Stealing from the palace or raising the dead?"

"Both. Neither. What is *wrong* with you?" He'd always been fond of needling her—of teasing out the noble upbringing she'd tried to squash—but this cruelty was new, unwelcome. If she was to be the villain in his eyes, she might have been able to live with that, but not if it prevented them from helping Yala. "Do you intend to go to the grave believing me a traitor?"

"I don't believe you're a traitor. Traitors usually have commitment."

"How dare you?" She knew he was trying to distract from his own pain, but his words plucked at the stitches around barely healed wounds. "Besides, you're one to talk. You've not been committed to anything since the army."

"I never denied my vices, did I?"

He'd never had any shame, but he'd never had expectations piled upon him the way she had. "Try not to choke on them, then."

Saren's words rang in her ears as she made her way back to the upper city. The worst part was that he'd exposed the heart of her own misgivings. After the war, she'd been as much at a loose end as the rest of their squad. For years she'd hidden herself among the pages of books and ledgers, telling herself that she was in the best possible place to apply her skills, but when Temik had reappeared as a novice in the Disciples of the Flame, part of her had been tempted to join him. She'd initially thought his plan had been to root out the Disciples who'd killed the king, but in the end, she'd been afraid that the god of the flames would see the fear in her heart and judge her unworthy.

Viam's nails bit into her palms. Undoubtedly, the Disciples of the Flame controlled the evidence of the former king's last mission, but until now, she hadn't known the names of any of the possible conspirators outside of Superior Datriem. This Mieren might not have dealt the killing blow, might not have been involved at all, but Saren's taunts ignited a spark inside her.

I'm not committed, am I?

When Viam reached Ceremonial Square, she took a moment to collect herself, and then she walked to the Temple of the Flame.

14

Kelan left Yala's wagon and continued towards the capital, grinning to himself. *Talk about good timing.* Not that Yala would agree. Her driver hadn't been thrilled to have a Disciple of the Sky jump in and start talking to his passenger either, but there was no good way for them to have a conversation while they were on the road. He'd have to tell Yala the rest later.

Kelan glided over the houses and slums marking the boundaries of Dalathar and flew to the wall circling the upper city. The towering form of the Temple of the Flame reflected the sunlight, dazzling his eyes, and when he touched down on the doorstep, he half expected Superior Datriem to answer the door. He couldn't imagine who they'd chosen to take the place of someone who'd been a fixture in the capital since before Kelan had been born.

Instead, a novice answered his knock. "Ah—Disciple, can I help you?"

"I'm here to see the new Superior," he answered. "On orders from Superior Sietra of the Disciples of the Sky."

"Are you, indeed?" The voice came from a tall man

whose receding hair was only partially hidden by his elaborate headdress. He was half Superior Datriem's age, at a guess, and was followed by a woman who didn't wear the robes of a Disciple. She also looked vaguely familiar.

"You." He groped around in his mind for her name and came up blank. "You're one of—"

"Viam," she said a little too quickly, perhaps to stop him from saying Yala's name aloud. "I'm Viam. And you're ... Kelan?"

"Correct."

Viam was one of Yala's former squad members, which made her presence in the temple bewildering to say the least. He looked to the man he assumed must be the new Superior, who regarded him with a polite smile. "Kelan, I've heard your name. I am Superior Shralin."

"My reputation precedes me," Kelan remarked. Viam's unexpected appearance had made him quite forget what he'd intended to say. Did Yala's friend know she'd left the capital for Setemar? "Was I interrupting something?"

"No, I'll come back later," Viam stammered. "Thank you for your time."

Fear flickered in her eyes, and she darted around Kelan, vanishing down the steps. *Strange.* Maybe she didn't want Yala to find out she was talking to the Disciples of the Flame, but she probably didn't want the Disciples of the Flame to know she was one of Yala's allies either. Someone was playing a dangerous game.

The Superior, meanwhile, surveyed Kelan with an assessing stare. He was younger than Kelan had expected, without the arrogant stance of his predecessor. "Why are you here, Kelan?"

"I'm here to bring a request for your assistance on behalf of the Temple of the Earth."

"Interesting," he said. "I didn't know Superior Dovial had Disciples of the Sky running errands on his behalf."

"You might have gathered that it's a little faster for us to get around than it is for others." He indicated his feet, which hovered above the temple's doorstep. "The fact of the matter is that the god of death's acolytes seem to have taken up residence somewhere in Setemar and are proving to be quite the nuisance."

"The god of the flames does not lend aid easily," he said. "However, we did send an envoy to the city."

Yala? Does she know she's being referred to as an envoy? "You sent some Disciples?"

"Not yet," he said, "but we cannot possibly spare anyone at the moment."

"Yes, I'm sure you're all very busy." Didn't they spend all their time engaged in prayer or other joyless pursuits? He lifted his head and caught the eye of a young woman hovering behind her Superior, dressed in red robes threaded with the golden embroidery of a high-ranked Disciple.

The woman cleared her throat. "Some of us are willing to volunteer."

Superior Shralin's mouth tightened. "I have already made my wishes clear, Mieren. There is no need for any of you to risk yourselves for the sake of those who would not return the favour."

"I gather the Disciples of the Earth were dealing with this situation long before the events in the capital unfolded," Kelan supplied. "If you were to send aid to Setemar, I'm sure they would return the favour, in the event of another incident here in Dalathar.

The woman—Mieren—nodded. "Precisely."

Superior Shralin's brow twitched, while Kelan wondered if he'd walked into the middle of a rift between the high-ranked Disciples. If Superior Shralin was still trying to prove his authority to the others, it wouldn't help matters for an outsider to come and undermine his decisions, but hadn't Yala said that she was running some errand on his behalf?

"I'll give you time to consider," Kelan said. "My Superior will keep you informed."

"I will confer with my people," said Superior Shralin. "If the situation has changed by tomorrow, I may be willing to reconsider."

That was something, at least. He hadn't expected the new Superior to be any more willing to listen than Superior Datriem had been, but if Mieren's reaction was anything to go by, he'd had a shaky start.

Viam was nowhere to be seen when he left the tower. From what he recalled, she worked in the palace complex, which made her decision to visit the Disciples seem odder, but not enough for him to fly there and ask why. Whatever Laima might think, his impulsivity did have *some* limits.

He might have lingered in the city for longer, but if he left now, he'd stand more of a chance of catching up to Yala before she reached Setemar. He followed the main road southward and soon found Yala's wagon near one off the outlying villages that lay at intervals along the main road between Dalathar and Setemar. The driver must have left on an errand, because Yala sat in the wagon, and this time Kelan approached from above to avoid startling the raptors.

Yala rolled her eyes at him when he climbed into the wagon. "I thought I'd have to wait longer for you."

"You sent your driver away?"

"I gave him the money to buy supplies for the road." She rested a hand on her pack, which she'd wedged between her knees. "I take it your errand didn't go well?"

"The Disciples of the Flame, once again, refused to inconvenience themselves by coming to help us."

"I could have told you that without you needing to go to

the trouble of making the trip," she said. "Also, I'm here on the condition that they *don't* follow me."

"Why?" Would she want to know he'd seen Viam inside the temple? He decided to opt for caution for once; if he was Viam, he wouldn't want anyone telling tales to her former squad leader.

"Long story," she said. "You haven't seen any of Melian's allies yet?"

"No. I haven't." The farmer would return soon, so he plunged straight into his explanation. "However, the god of death seems to have decided that instead of building His own temple, he intends to steal someone else's."

Yala's hand gripped her pack convulsively. "He did *what?*"

"Corruption is everywhere—all over the Temple of the Earth, that is," he amended. "Their dead are crawling out of the ground, their Superior is losing control of the situation, and the perplexing part is that I haven't seen any sign of who is responsible. Not one Disciple of Death to be found."

"Nor their book, either?" Yala surmised. "One Disciple's name is Trienan, if that helps in the least. I got his name from Melian's ally."

Kelan considered this. "I'll ask around. Do you want to come with me?"

She pursed her lips, as if considering her options. "Are your fellow Disciples there?"

"Laima's there. Others will have joined her by now."

"And do all of them know what I can do?"

Well... "I wouldn't count on it, but they're not going to leave you on top of a building again, if that's what you're worried about."

From her sceptical expression, his words had not convinced her. "I'd prefer not to have to defend myself against a horde of hostile Disciples from two temples in addition to Melian's allies. Did you tell the Superior from the Temple of the Earth exactly *how* I defeated Melian?"

"No, I didn't." It was understandable that she'd be wary of the other Disciples discovering her abilities as a Disciple of Death, of course, given that even Superior Sietra had chosen to imprison her for her own safety. "Your name didn't even come up."

"Really." Yala's tone remained flat. "Is there somewhere nearby I can stay that isn't likely to be full of Disciples?"

"Yes, there's a mining village north of the cliffs," he said, recalling the settlement he'd spotted on the way out of Setemar. "I was going to look around there later."

"I'll keep it in mind." Yala swore under her breath. "My driver's back."

Kelan lifted his head and saw the farmer approaching from the path into the village. "Are you sure you don't want me to take you with me? That man might be planning to stab you in the back."

Yala gave a snort. "If anything, it's the other way around. I expect we'll make it to Setemar by nightfall."

"Safe travels." He withdrew from the wagon, reflecting that returning empty-handed might cause Laima to decry his trip to the capital as being a waste of time. At least he had the name of Melian's ally now, which gave him somewhere to start looking.

By the time Kelan glided into Setemar, he'd come up with a plan, of sorts. He traversed the city on the ground, stopping at a market to buy something to eat, and watching for any passing groups of city guards. Luck was with him, and he found the older guard he'd seen at the tavern two days prior outside the gates to the inner city.

The guard eyed him as he approached. "What?"

"I thought we were on friendlier terms," said Kelan. "I don't suppose you've seen any mercenaries recently?"

"No," he replied.

"How about ones who've been here for a while?" he asked. "I heard a rumour on the road that there's someone in the area who goes by the name Trienan… Sound familiar?"

"No."

I suppose Melian's allies had more sense than to give out their names. He tried a different tack. "Did you feel the earthquake earlier?"

"Obviously." The guard's gaze raked over him. "What are you waiting for? Go on in."

Kelan glided through the gates. "The Disciples of the Earth claimed they didn't cause the earthquake. Do you have any other people living under the city that I should be aware of?"

"If we do, they're probably hiding from your Disciples," said the guard. "Did your Superior send half the people in Skytower?"

"Oh, good, they're here." Kelan left the guard and made his way to the inn.

As he'd expected, the entire lower floor had been taken over by his fellow Disciples. He counted ten or eleven, which wasn't a large group, but the downstairs room of the inn scarcely big enough to accommodate fifteen Disciples, whose habit of hovering aboveground made them appear to take up more space than the average person.

Laima caught his eye through the lower window, and when he opened the door, she was waiting on the other side. "I thought you'd have your friend with you."

"She's coming here the normal way," he explained. "She thought arriving with me would cause too much of a stir."

Laima frowned. "You didn't even bring any Disciples of the Flame to help?"

"Their new Superior claimed they needed time to consider." He lowered his voice. "I did get the name of one of

Melian's allies who might be responsible for the situation here. According to Yala, he's called Trienan."

Laima remained unimpressed. "The name's not going to do much good on its own, is it?"

"I prefer to know who I'm dealing with." He raised a hand in greeting when he spied Lakiel behind her. "I see you've got everyone assembled."

The other Disciple responded with a scowl. "Only because you took off on some errand. Did I hear you say the Disciples of the Flame refused to help you?"

"Their Superior, not the others," Kelan corrected him. "I rather think it was the subject of some debate amongst their high-ranked acolytes."

Lakiel remained unimpressed. Had Laima told the others that he'd run away in the middle of the mission? She was acting as if the previous night had never happened, which was far from the first time he'd elicited that reaction, but not from her. *I suppose I didn't help matters by flying out of Setemar at the first opportunity.*

"Did you hear from Superior Dovial yet?" he asked Laima as they joined the others in the seating area downstairs. After flying back and forth from the capital twice in quick succession, he was glad of the chance to rest his feet while he could.

"Of course not," she said. "He's still cleaning up the mess from this morning's attack."

"And no more … earthquakes?" He tilted his head towards the window, hearing a faint sound that might have been a scream.

"What earthquake?" asked Lakiel, who'd accompanied them. The tall Disciple sometimes put Kelan in mind of a raptor, with his long beaky nose and his habit of ducking his head as though there was a low-hanging branch perpetually hanging above. "Nobody mentioned an earthquake."

"Didn't you?" He raised a brow at Laima, who shrugged.

"It didn't seem pertinent," she said. "Superior Dovial said it wasn't the Disciples."

"I'm not inclined to take his word for it," Kelan said. "In fact, if you ask me, Superior Dovial is the problem."

"I didn't," she said. "Ask you, that is. It's hardly his fault that Mekan's taken over the Temple of the Earth, is it?"

"He lied to his Disciples and forced them to hide underground for weeks," he said. "Don't you think that's not honourable Superior behaviour?"

"It's not up to us to decide that."

No ... but someone has to take charge here, and all he's done is close the doors and deny the truth. Superior Dovial had claimed to have closed off the tunnels that led into the tunnel, but the dead had come from somewhere.

Another noise from outside reached Kelan's ears. This time, he distinctly heard a scream, and as he rose to his feet, more shouts broke out from somewhere over the city wall. *What now?*

———

"I ... don't know what you mean by 'the truth,'" Niema said to Superior Kralia. "Yala saved us. She defeated Melian and prevented Corruption from spreading across Laria."

"And yet here it remains." She gestured to Prathen's grave, and the greenery that didn't quite mask the scent Mekan's presence had left in its wake. "Perhaps we were mistaken."

"Mistaken?" No. Yalet was never wrong and Yala *had* saved Laria, if not in the way that Niema had initially expected. "Maybe Corruption is too much for a single person to conquer, but Yala tried her best."

"What did she tell you?" Superior Kralia asked. "Did you ask Yala to confirm the details of the vision, to ensure that she was indeed the person you were looking for?"

What does she mean? Yala had reprimanded Niema for believing her to be their saviour without proof, but her faith was bolstered by Superior Kralia's wholehearted acceptance of Yalet's truth. Why would she now doubt what Yalet had shown them?

"I did," Niema said. "She didn't believe me at first, believing she overcame Corruption by accident, but—"

"By accident," Superior Kralia repeated. "Did she mention how, precisely, she defeated Corruption on the island?"

"The … island?" How did Superior Kralia know? The vision hadn't made Yala's location clear, or so Niema had thought, but Superior Kralia's demand sent her mind scrambling to find an adequate answer. "She said one of her squad members had been a Disciple of the Flame and knew the words of a prayer to set the island afire."

"Ah." Superior Kralia's head bowed in understanding. "It was the god of the flames who truly defeated Corruption."

"No." She spoke quickly. "The Disciples of the Flame didn't believe Yala's story. They let Mekan's followers infiltrate their ranks."

"They contacted one of the other enclaves," Superior Kralia added. "Before you returned, they sent word to us warning of a Disciple of Death by the name of Yala Palathar."

Niema's heart plunged downward as if her Superior had shoved her in the chest, straight over the edge of a cliff. "That was a rumour Melian started. She tried to get Yala blamed—"

"Because those who look into the Void have the potential to become Disciples of Death," Superior Kralia finished. "I am not entirely ignorant of the ways in which Mekan is able to access this realm, to ensnare any who are foolish enough to take up His mantle."

Niema's blood iced over. "That doesn't make her a Disciple of Death any more than it makes *me* one."

"No, but it does make you a deceiver." Superior Kralia's

mouth pinched, as if the words tasted sour. "I have no desire for you to suffer further grief, Niema, but the fact remains that you aided someone who spoke to Mekan. Who *allied with* Mekan. That is against the laws both of our enclave and of Yalet Herself."

The air tightened and the trees rustled as though in response. No… the trees *moved,* straightening upright, shedding their rotting leaves, and sprouting fresh blooms in their place.

"Come with me," said Superior Kralia. "We will see how Yalet judges your crimes."

15

As the screams rose in volume, Laima called the other Disciples of the Sky to order and they swarmed out of the inn with surprising efficiency. At the wall around the inner city, the gates lay slightly open, no longer guarded. Kelan glided upward and spied the source of the ruckus.

On the other side of the wall, a dead woman wielding a battered axe bore down on a pair of terrified guards. Her faced was caved inward as if from a heavy blow, flesh rotting from her skull, and two more dead lumbered behind her. They were also armed, and while slow moving, they took up the entire width of the narrow passage that backed onto the wall behind a row of houses, leaving the guards nowhere to flee to.

Kelan pulled out his blade and glided over the wall, landing between the axe-wielding woman and the panicking guards. One swipe of his blade and her head flew clean off, but her legs continued to move, her rotting hands raising the axe.

Kelan lifted a palm and a gust of wind swept the axe out

of the dead woman's hands. Recovering from the shock, one of the guards used his shortsword to cut the woman's legs off at the knees. She fell, hands continuing to scrabble at the ground, and the guard stared in horror. "What kind of monstrosity is this?"

"Dead." Kelan moved in with his own blade and severed one of the woman's arms. "They can't feel pain and won't stop moving until you take them apart."

The other Disciples of the Sky made quick work of the two remaining dead, but the guards remained at a distance, one of them bleeding from a cut in his hand. *I can see why Superior Dovial just sent them away without telling them what was going on.* Then again, the king's guards had hardly performed admirably during Melian's assault on the capital either.

"No more?" Kelan asked, looking up and down the alleyway that circled the outside of the wall. "Where'd they even come from?"

"They're Disciples," said Laima softly, pointing to one of the dismembered bodies. "Look."

Hells, she's right. The three dead were covered in so much dirt that it was hard to discern what they were wearing, but amid the viscera lay the tattered remains of a Disciple's robe. "Who wants to give Superior Dovial the bad news?"

"I will." Laima rose into the air, gliding back over the wall, with Lakiel close behind. Kelan, meanwhile, caught up to the retreating guards.

"Surely one of you saw where they came from," he said. "They didn't walk out of nowhere."

"No, they came through there." The younger guard who Kelan had spoken to at the tavern pointed down the alleyway from which the dead had staggered. "Out of... out of the wall."

"Out of the *wall?*" He peered at the stones, seeing no signs of a disturbance. The dead Disciples couldn't have called on Setem, could they?

Soon Laima and Lakiel returned with two Disciples of the Earth, neither of whom looked thrilled at being volunteered to help clean up the dead. Kelan abandoned his examination of the wall and went to meet them. One, a surly young man who wore a pair of thick gloves, grimaced when Kelan pointed to the remnants of their fellow Disciples.

"I don't suppose either of you know where they might have come from?" He addressed the second Disciple, a curly-haired young woman who carried a short axe at her waist. "The guards think they walked out of the wall."

The woman rolled her eyes. "The guards don't know shit."

She began scooping the pieces of the dead into a sack with rather less respect than Kelan might have expected, though the number of dead that the Disciples had to excavate from their temple that morning might have temporarily buried any reverence they had for their departed souls. The putrid stench made him gag, and to distract himself, he turned back to the wall. This time he glided down the passageway until he came to its end, where it opened into an alley that ran between two houses.

At the alleyway's end, Kelan found a bumpier section of wall, and a closer examination revealed what appeared to be a set of hinges concealed amid the stones.

Upon hearing footsteps behind him, he tilted his head and spied the female Disciple—who he'd heard the others call Pehin—approaching. "What's this? A door?"

"Old mining tunnel," said Pehin. "Nothing important."

"Isn't it?" He worked his fingers into the cracks of the door and pulled it outward, revealing a tunnel not unlike the ones that Superior Dovial had shown him inside the temple. *I think we've found the source of the dead.*

The Disciple hissed out a breath. "Close that door. Now."

"This isn't a tunnel your Superior knows about, is it?" he guessed. "Have you been leaving the temple the whole time?"

"Well, yes." A note of derision entered her voice. "Would you like being shut in a cave for weeks?"

I can imagine, as I went through something similar myself. But it wasn't the same; he'd been able to breathe clean air even when his world had been confined to the boundaries of Skytower. Yes, the Disciples of the Earth inexplicably *liked* being underground, but not being able to leave would have worn down even the most ardent follower of Setem. "Might this tunnel be how the dead infiltrated your temple, do you think?"

"No," Pehin said. "The dead were buried inside the temple itself, but these three must have found their way out."

Hmm. "Am I right in thinking you used this tunnel for purposes of the illicit sort?"

She flashed him a smile. "Our Superior is small-minded. He doesn't understand that there are certain pleasures that one cannot derive from the company of one's deity alone."

"Well, of course." The tunnel, however, was an obvious problem. "I think we should check there aren't any more dead hiding in there."

Pehin glowered at him. "We?"

"What're you two doing?" Laima glided over, looking between them suspiciously before her gaze landed on the tunnel. "Is that how the dead got out?"

"Yes, it leads into the temple." Kelan indicated Pehin. "We were going to make sure there aren't any more unpleasant surprises waiting in there."

"Good idea." Lakiel said from behind Laima. "We'll take the dead back to the temple while you two check the tunnel."

Pehin scowled, as did Laima, while Kelan fought a grin. *This is more like it.* If anywhere might contain more clues as to the source of the earthquake earlier, it was a tunnel the Disciples didn't want anyone else to know about.

Laima eyed them in disapproval before turning away. "If you want to crawl around in the dark, be my guest."

"It doesn't look dark to me." Kelan glided through the door and almost collided with a low-hanging lantern that had seemingly been wedged into the ceiling itself. Someone —presumably a Disciple—had done the same at intervals throughout the earthen passageway stretching ahead of them.

"Nice setup you have here," he commented as Pehin entered. "What if someone accidentally headbutts a lantern and knocks themselves out?"

"Don't you live in a tower from which the only exit is a steep fall to your death?" she retaliated.

"Ah, but we can fly." He reached up to retrieve the lantern, but it was solidly locked in place, as if the packed earth had somehow *grown* around it. "I assume you did this before... before the unfortunate recent incident."

"You can say it, you know," Pehin remarked, striding ahead. "Before our deity fucked off and left us to die."

Kelan's brows shot up. "I assume He can't hear you disrespecting Him?"

"If He can, he's certainly not responding." She marched on without looking back.

As he followed her around a corner, an obvious question occurred to him. "If you've been using this tunnel to sneak out of the temple, why not ask for someone to help?"

"Ask whom?" She scoffed. "The city guards can't help us. No other Disciple can do anything either."

"I guess not," he acknowledged. "When did you stop being able to access your powers? Was it all at once, or a gradual process?"

Her shoulders tensed. "Why does it matter?"

"Because if Mekan can get into one temple, he can get into others." He opted for honesty in the hopes that she'd offer the same, but she gave another sceptical noise in response.

"I'm not going to give you opportunities to figure out our weaknesses, you know," she muttered. "I have *some* pride left."

"That's not my intention," he said. "I'm trying to work out why Mekan targeted your temple. I'm here to help your Superior, remember?"

"I don't care about him," she said. "He's the one who lost all contact with our deity first. He's hardly worthy of the title."

"Nobody else in your temple can reach your deity either," Kelan pointed out. "I know the Superior is supposed to be the exception, but I doubt Mekan cares."

Whether one was a Superior or a regular Disciple, not to be able to reach one's deity must be unnerving. He'd had a hint of that experience himself whenever he'd entered another temple, but the god of the sky always returned when he left. If that connection disappeared altogether... for a start, everyone in Skytower would be in serious trouble. The tower was too far away from any towns or villages to access supplies, unless the Disciples risked falling to their deaths by climbing down to the valley, and anyone trapped there was likely to endure a miserable death by starvation.

Kelan shook off the thought. Mekan was very unlikely to reach Skytower, given the lack of hidden tunnels through which His Disciples might sneak into their home. Here, however, he had the suspicion that they'd barely scratched the surface of Setemar's network of underground passageways.

They reached a fork in the tunnel. One route was clear, the other blocked by fallen rocks that looked to have been artfully arranged to block the way through.

"Another old mining tunnel," Pehin said in explanation. "There are tons of them. That one doesn't go anywhere."

Hmm. Part of Kelan was tempted to move the rocks aside to see if she was right, but if the dead had any other ways in and out of the temple, the Disciples would find out sooner rather than later. He followed her down the other passage instead, at which point he realised the subtle presence of the god of the sky had vanished. They must be close.

Shortly after, they emerged into a wide chamber full of piles of upturned earth and with lanterns glowing in sconces on the wall.

"This is where we bury our dead," she said, retrieving one of the lanterns. "The ones that escaped and attacked us must have come from here."

"Are you sure?" The dead couldn't think for themselves. If three had separated themselves from the group that had attacked the temple, someone had told them to do so.

Either way, hundreds of Disciples had been buried here, generation after generation, all fuel for Mekan's purposes. Kelan wrenched his gaze away from the piles of earth and heard a faint thud from the tunnel through which they'd entered the chamber.

"Did you hear that?" He peered into the tunnel, hearing another thud, followed by scraping. "There's someone else in there."

"Leave it alone," Pehin hissed, cursing under her beath when he ducked into the tunnel again.

Kelan retraced his steps to the fork in the tunnel, ears pricked. A chill swept across his skin, carrying a familiar death-scent, and the scraping noise continued.

Pehin's lantern bobbed behind him. "Have you taken leave of your senses?"

"The dead are in here." His gaze picked out shifting

shadows around the rocky barrier, creeping through gaps in the piled stones.

"No." Pehin tugged on his arm, frantic. "Get away from there!"

Kelan lifted a hand to shield his face as bits of soil and debris sprayed outward, and for the second time that day, he witnessed a pile of stones collapse as a ghastly shape came crawling out from the gap.

This time, however, the creature was nothing close to human. Resembling a bird, its feathers hung off dead skin and bone, shedding viscera as its crooked wings extended.

Kelan drew his blade as its beak stabbed at them, slicing through dead skin and severing its head. As the creature's head landed at their feet, Pehin sprang back with a yelp. "What—what *is* that?"

"Not something you want nesting inside your temple." Kelan swung the sword at the beast's flailing, headless body, gagging at the smell when its innards spilled out.

A second beast came crawling through the gap the first had created, causing more rocks to fall out of the tunnel opening. Pehin screamed, throwing her lantern.

The lantern shattered upon contact with the beast, but Kelan seized on the chance to finish it off, skewering the tip of its spine until its wings stopped twitching. "Is this why you didn't want me going into that tunnel?"

"No ... no." Pehin stammered, her bravado evaporated. "Are there more of them in there?"

Kelan peered into the gap created by the fallen rocks, but no lanterns ignited the gloom in the tunnel on the other side. "I can't see. You haven't seen one of Mekan's beasts before?"

"No." Pehin shook her head, her face ashen. "They're *his?*"

"They're certainly not Setem's." He lifted one of the rocks back into place. "Your Superior needs to know about this."

For a wonder, Pehin didn't argue. While Kelan stacked

the rocks back into place—a futile effort, he was sure—she produced another sack in which to put the winged beasts' grisly remains. While no more monsters emerged, the stench lingered, and so did his apprehension. They passed through the chamber of graves without lingering to see if any more dead might be stirring, and the distant echo of Superior Dovial's voice guided them into the main chamber.

Emerging through another tunnel, they found the Superior addressing several of his Disciples as well as Laima and Lakiel.

"What is this?" Superior Dovial's eyes bulged when he saw Kelan and Pehin approaching with their grisly burden.

"Beasts from the Void." Kelan held out the sack towards the Superior. "From Mekan's realm, that is."

The colour drained from Superior Dovial's face. "The god of death stalks our tunnels?"

Didn't he already figure that out? Of course, there was a marked difference between dead Disciples rising from their graves and Mekan's own realm intruding on the Temple of the Earth.

"Apparently so." Pehin's face had regained some colour. "What should we do? Let Him invade our home?"

"You can start by disposing of those monstrosities." Superior Dovial jabbed a finger at the twitching sack. "The rest of you help to seal off the tunnels—*all* of them this time."

"That won't help," Kelan told him. "If the Void's already open here, you might as well put a small bandage over a severed limb."

Superior Dovial did not reply, but Kelan knew the truth must have occurred to him. Even if they took down every single one of Mekan's creatures, the Disciples wouldn't be safe—nobody in Setemar would be safe—until they found the people responsible.

———

During her journey back to the enclave from Dalathar, Niema had imagined facing judgment in a thousand ways. She'd dreaded the moment she'd have to stand before Superior Kralia and be judged for her crimes, and yet she'd only been able to guess at the specifics. Nobody else had ever committed the crimes she had. Colluding with Mekan. Causing the death of her fellow enclave member. Whispers followed Niema through the forest as she walked back to the hut to await her trial.

Night had fallen, and her sleepless eyes picked out shifting shadows beneath every tree she passed. The other members of the enclave had already been informed of her treachery, and she entered the hut braced for their judgement.

"She's lying!" Diaman sobbed as Niema walked in. "Superior Kralia's lying. Niema isn't a traitor. She *isn't.*"

"Don't speak of the Superior in that way," Niema told her. "She's doing what she thinks is best for the enclave."

Is she? whispered a voice in her mind. *Can the others bear to lose you, too? Another loss might break them.*

"She isn't," Threl whimpered. "I don't understand. You *saved* Prathen."

Niema slumped against the wall, her heart aching to see Ekim slumped beside the empty sleeping mat where Prathen had lain. "I didn't save him."

Ekim spoke up, her voice raspy and dull with grief. "Is it true? Did you really help a Disciple of Death?"

Niema drew her knees up to her chest, her eyes burning. "All I wanted was to save a friend. Someone without whom we would have *all* fallen to Mekan."

Her throat constricted with the truth of her crime. She hadn't confessed, not out of any desire to preserve herself, but to prevent the others from suffering further until the trial forced her to speak the words that would tear their bonds apart. If she could have taken their pain for herself, she would have.

The rest of the night passed in a blur. She slept a little, ate and drank when the others put food and water in her hands, but otherwise Niema didn't move. Scarcely breathing, she watched for the sun to reach its highest point in the sky, when Superior Kralia came to take her away.

At noon, she rose on numb feet. Grief had hollowed her, like a sunfruit's skin with its insides scooped out, leaving no emotions behind, not even fear.

Superior Kralia led her to the same clearing in which she had first set eyes on the war drake that had sealed her fate. This time she had an audience; every member of the enclave gathered around the altar, whispers rustling like branches. Superior Kralia herself did not speak, merely gesturing for Niema to kneel before the altar.

In the end, Yalet would be the one to offer a final judgement.

Niema knelt and tried to focus on her trial, but the others' distress kept plucking at her heart. Amongst the gathering enclave members, Threl sobbed into Ekim's shoulder, while Hachim whispered reassurances to a furious Diaman.

Superior Kralia stood behind the altar and addressed the gathering Disciples. "I have brought Niema here to stand trial for a betrayal of our people—and of Yalet Herself."

"She didn't do anything!" Diaman shrieked. "She didn't!"

Hachim uttered an apology, but Superior Kralia continued as if she hadn't heard either of them. "Niema, answer me this. Did you or did you not hide the existence of a Disciple of Death from your enclave?"

Truth and lies tangled on her lips, and in the end, she

spoke the words she knew Yala would have said herself. "I did not."

Superior Kralia's disapproval hit like a slap, though her tone remained neutral. "Did you or did you not use Yalet's blessing to heal that Disciple's injuries at the cost of the life of one of your own enclave members?"

"What?" This time it was Hachim who interrupted. "No, Niema tried to save Prathen. She almost gave her life."

Niema squeezed her eyes shut, tears leaking down her cheeks. She might be able to lie in defence of Yala's life, but her heart would not allow this. "I did."

Shock and pain slammed into her, fourfold, and her thoughts blanked out. *I'm sorry. I'm so sorry.*

When she came to her senses, Superior Kralia had resumed speaking. "I do not believe Niema meant for Prathen to die, but by twisting Yalet's prayers to save a Disciple of Death, she brought evil into our midst."

Niema heard nothing more. The others' pain stabbed her like blunt knives, and all she could do was curl in on herself as though by shielding her body she might shield her heart. Gradually, she became aware of Superior Kralia leaning over her, speaking into her ear.

"I never wanted this, Niema," she murmured. "If I'd known when I chose you for the mission… Yalet forgive me."

"What are you going to do?" Niema gasped through spasms of pain.

"We are not killers." Superior Kralia straightened upright, addressing the clearing once more. "We do not violate Yalet's will. However, I intend to have the Disciple of Death captured and brought before the god of life for Her to judge as She sees fit."

She's bringing Yala here. The realisation doused her pain, allowing her to crawl back onto her knees.

"As for you, Niema." Superior Kralia returned her attention to her kneeling Disciple. "Ordinarily the punishment for such a transgression would be exile from the enclave, but in the interests of sparing further suffering in the wake of Prathen's death… you will be sent to solitary confinement instead."

Confinement. In a way, that was worse than exile. She'd be out of reach of the others—and more crucially, she'd have no way to warn Yala of the danger that awaited her.

Yala. I can't let Superior Kralia bring her to the forest.

16

Yala rode in the wagon until sundown, where she stopped at a farmhouse near the village Kelan had pointed out. She paid a small fortune for a room and a warm bath that was almost pleasant enough for her to decide that it'd been worth going on this absurd journey after all.

Until she woke in the night to screaming.

Yala's eyes opened. She rolled off the narrow bed she'd been offered for the night—an improvement on her usual sleeping mat—and a thud sounded as a feathered lump crashed into her window. She might have taken it for a lost nightbird, if not for the putrid smell seeping through the glass.

I know that stench.

With an oath, Yala pulled on her trousers and belt—to which she'd attached her knives and the pouch containing the void drake's claw—and then grabbed her cane. Glad that she'd paid extra for a downstairs room, she pushed open the door and followed the strips of moonlight across the floor of the inn's common room. The front door was slightly ajar, and Yala slipped outside. Her gaze picked out three—no, four—winged monsters in the sky. *Void beasts.*

Yala shrank back into the shadows, her heart racing. She might be armed, but she didn't have a war drake as a companion this time. A spear might have managed to knock them out of the air, but her daggers hadn't the reach, and daylight would not gild the sky for hours to come.

Shifting shadows warned of the beast that had flown into her window approaching her hiding place, and a familiar fear took root inside her.

"Get out of here," she snarled, swiping with her cane. The edge hit with a solid smack, knocking the beast out of the air. Rotting guts spilled out onto the dark, damp earth, and she glimpsed a second winged shape against the moon's brightness flying in her direction, too.

How many of these fuckers are there? It was too dark to tell where they'd come from, nor if there might be worse monsters lurking out there in the night.

Someone screamed, high and loud. Yala's eyes picked out a figure cringing away from two more monsters, which ripped at their target like ravenous juvenile drakes.

"Hey!" She waved her cane in the air. "Come and get me instead."

The second monster she'd glimpsed above came diving down at her with its decaying wings beating, straight into Yala's cane. As its rotting remains scattered around her, the other two beasts continued to dive at their unfortunate human target. Yala's leg ached as she put her weight on it, her bare feet skidding through the mud, fingers scrabbling to retrieve a knife from her belt.

The young man the beasts were attacking dove aside with a yell as Yala came barrelling into him, thrusting her knife into a monster's throat. Its head flew sideways, severed, and the young man fled. His companion hadn't been so lucky; the beast's claws had ripped him open from shoulder to crotch, and his guts spilled out into the mud.

The headless beast came at her again, rotting wings continuing to beat. Yala swung the cane at her target, knocking it down into the mud, but the ones in the sky were too distant for her to aim at from the ground. Beside the farmhouse, she glimpsed the owner ducking behind a barrel, hands over his head to protect himself.

I can't fight them without a mount, Yala thought, her hand straying to the pouch where the claw's presence pulsed like a beating heart. One touch, and the god of death's attention would be on her like a beacon. All the beasts would flock to her. She'd lose any hope of finding Mekan's followers without them finding her first, but would she be able to forgive herself for leaving more of the villagers to suffer as the dead picked the flesh from their bones?

Under the moonlight, the shadows shifted like pieces of the night itself, swirling around the claw as she pulled it out of the pouch. Switching her dagger to the other hand, she ran the sharp edge of the blade over the healing cuts on her fingertips.

"Mekan," she growled. "I'm here."

The whispers—scarcely audible over the shrieks of the fleeing villagers—resolved into a single voice, one that had haunted her nightmares for weeks. *"I wondered when you would call me by name again, Yala."*

Yala's heart stuttered in her chest. *He remembers my name...* but had she expected any less?

"I'm not making a deal with you," she hissed. "I'm here to get rid of those creatures, nothing more."

"Pity," whispered the voice. *"I thought you might have changed your mind."*

"No." Despite the quiver of fear in her bones, Yala ignored the rasping voice and lifted her head to the sky, addressing the dark forms flying in pursuit of the villagers. "Come here, beasts of the Void."

Their attention was already upon her, and as she slid the claw back into the pouch, one of the beasts dove at her with its sharp beak crusted with blood.

Yala threw her dagger, which ripped through its chest to its spine and knocked it out of the air. *Fool,* she thought, as the other two beasts came wheeling towards her before she had a hope of grabbing another weapon.

With both hands, Yala raised her cane in time for the beasts' combined weight to hit her at once. She staggered, her leg scream, arms aching with the effort of pushing the sharp beaks away from her face. "Get back to the dark hole you crawled out of."

With a grunt, she gave a final heave. One of the beasts flew sideways, but the other swerved, its blood-crusted beak aiming for her eyes. Yala released the cane with one hand and swung her fist. Flesh gave way beneath her punch, and her cane followed, spearing the monster through its middle.

Her leg protested as she skidded backwards in the mud, grabbing her cane with both hands to dislodge its unwanted passenger. Sharp pain pierced her shoulders from behind, claws tugging, as a second beast tried drag her into the air.

"Get off me." She shook herself, shoulders burning, arms weighed down with the rotting carcass skewered on her cane. Gritting her teeth, she swung the cane sideways, sending one flailing beast crashing into the other, and threw herself to the ground. Even without weight on her bad leg, the impact jarred her whole body, but a glint under the moonlight showed her the way to the dagger she'd thrown lying in the dirt.

As the two beasts descended once again, she seized the

dagger and threw straight at her first attacker's exposed neck. The beast fell, directly onto her, and she gagged as she plunged her fingers into its rotting throat to retrieve her weapon.

One throw and the final beast fell, severed in two, to join its companions in the dirt.

Breathing hard, Yala used her cane for balance as she staggered to her feet. Mud and viscera caked her entire body. *It's lucky I packed more than one shirt,* she thought wryly, her mood sobering when she caught sight of the dead villager. She hadn't been able to save him, though his friend had escaped.

Would the monsters have attacked if she hadn't been here? That, she didn't know. Returning her dagger to her belt, she checked on the damage to her shoulders. The beast's claws hadn't had much power behind them, and while she'd have to be wary of infection, she'd suffered worse pain from a bloodfly bite.

As Yala limped back towards the farmhouse, the owner, who'd emerged from the barrel he'd hidden behind, shrank away from her approach. "You … how did you do that?"

"I fought in the war." No need to give specifics. "Have you seen any creatures like that before? Did you see where they came from?"

"Monsters." He shuddered. "I… I don't know. Underground."

Underground? Was that a reference to Mekan's rotting hell, or had the beasts genuinely come from somewhere under their feet? She peered at his face, but couldn't read anything in his expression but pure fear. It was too dark to see much else of their surroundings, save for a few houses, and the row of cliffs behind Setemar.

Didn't Kelan mention there were mines over there?

The man cringed away from her, reminding her of the viscera clinging to her skin. Unless he'd seen the shadows in her hands, black against the dark night ... *shit.*

Mekan had spoken to her. He'd used her name.

That was much, much worse than being known to the city guards of Dalathar.

After her role in closing the Void during the battle in the capital, part of her had suspected that if she tried to call upon Mekan again, He would strike her down. Yet He hadn't. Did He not hold grudges, or did He simply see her as beneath him, another human scarcely worth notice? In truth, she didn't know how high she was on the god of death's priority list, but she'd thought that her actions would earn her a special place in the rotting hell he called home.

I can hardly complain about my survival. Whatever the reasons, Mekan had spared her life, and given her more of an incentive to prevent whatever scheme His followers might be concocting in Setemar.

———

Kelan half expected another attack from Mekan's followers overnight, but no disturbances came. Maybe the Disciples of Death had realised they were outnumbered now that a significant group of Disciples of the Sky occupied the inn, but knowing the Void might be open right underneath his room did not make for a restful sleep. It didn't help that Laima hadn't invited him to her room this time; she'd been slightly peeved at him the previous day, to say the least, and they hadn't had a moment of privacy to talk to one another since the other Disciples' arrival.

The result was that he had to share a room with Lakiel, who snored like a raptor and talked in his sleep. After a restless night, Kelan opened his eyes at dawn to the sound of a stone clattering against the windowpane. Then another. Even *that* didn't wake Lakiel, and he rolled off the bed to see the improbable sight of Yala waiting outside the inn, one hand resting on her cane, another stone in her hand.

He raised his palm to let her know he'd spotted her, mouthing, "I'll be five minutes."

Yala would have arrived by nightfall, but he assumed she'd taken his advice to stay in the neighbouring village instead of Setemar, not that she'd be roaming the city at this hour in the morning. He gathered his clothes, dressed as quickly as possible, and glided downstairs to meet her at the door.

"You're up early."

"I had a somewhat disturbed night." Yala turned over a stone in her hand, the ends of her fingers inexpertly bandaged. "It involved lying in the guts of a dead bird."

"Charming. A new hobby of yours?"

"No, and I'd rather talk to you alone before the other Disciples wake up." Yala dropped the stone and turned away from the inn. "The village was attacked by void beasts, so I'll consider myself lucky I survived the night."

"Void beasts," he repeated. "I've seen some of those, too."

"Where?" Her grip tightened on her cane. "In the temple?"

"No, the tunnels." He studied her face, scarred and drawn. "I didn't hear anything last night either."

"The tunnels," she repeated. "I assumed it was my arrival that prompted the attack, but if not…"

"No," said Kelan. "You weren't anywhere near Setemar when the dead attacked yesterday. Twice. The second time, they came through a disused mining tunnel."

"Underground." Yala's shoulders tensed, and she winced, reaching behind her back with her bandaged hand. "I thought so … but aren't the Disciples of the Earth supposed to be able to move the earth at their will?"

"Not anymore." He eyed her shoulders, wondering if she was hurt. "They're unable to access their deity *or* their abilities, so they're reduced to piling rocks in the way of any tunnels through which Mekan might try to make an entrance. Superior Dovial refuses to entertain the possibility of hunting down the source, but I don't entirely blame him."

Yala gaped at him. "Even *he* can't reach his deity?"

"No, and they're rapidly losing control of the situation." He glided to a halt at the foot of the stairs that led to the temple.

Yala's gaze flickered over the towering statues flanking the entrance. "If those monsters came from underground, it's convenient that Mekan took the ability away from the Disciples, isn't it?"

"Exactly," Kelan said. "Superior Sietra implied that no temple is necessary for Mekan's power to work. The rules don't seem to apply to him, so the same must be true of His Disciples."

Her forehead creased. "If Mekan doesn't need a temple, why steal one?"

"To spite the other gods?" Kelan indicated the statues. "I'm told the same applies to the Disciples of Life, but they'd never do anything as crude as to steal another god's home. Also, Laima will have my head if she hears me telling you this."

"You are still at one another's throats, are you?"

"Not exactly." At this rate, he'd have to wait until they got back to Skytower to find out where he stood with Laima. "This situation is perplexing, and I'm not certain Superior Dovial is being honest with us."

"About what?" Yala narrowed her eyes. "He and the others

aren't working with someone like Melian, are they? Like the Disciples of the Flame?"

"I don't think they are." Though the more he thought on the subject, the more he was sure that some of the Disciples had surely been aware of Mekan's presence for longer than they were willing to let on. "They don't want us exploring their tunnels, though, which is going to be an issue."

"Does it matter?" she queried. "We're here to stop Mekan."

"You aren't wrong." He offered a smile. "The trouble is, every tunnel leads back to the Temple of the Earth, which runs the risk of us being arrested for trespassing."

"I'll take my chances."

"In that case, I do know of one tunnel entrance that isn't guarded." Or it hadn't been, the last he'd seen. "It's also where I ran into those beasts."

Yala's hand clenched and unclenched on her cane. "Lead the way."

Kelan glided away from the temple towards the gates out of the inner city, where he and Yala followed the outer rim of the wall to the alleyway the dead had come through. As he glided ahead, he found three sleepy guards standing in front of the door. *I should have known.*

Kelan retreated from their line of sight, holding out a hand to warn Yala. "Superior Dovial has made a sensible decision for once and appointed guards to watch for more deceased interlopers."

Yala swore. "There aren't any other entrances?"

"We can go over the cliffs and look for the mines," he suggested, "but unless someone has a map, there's a fair chance of us starving to death in a tunnel."

"The villagers who live near the mines might have a map," she said. "Or advice. They already had to bury some of those foul creatures, and it might not have been the first attack."

"If not, they're lucky not to have lost more people," he remarked. "How do you want to get to the village? Fly?"

Yala shook her head. "Wouldn't your fellow Disciples notice if they looked out the window and saw us soaring over the cliffs?"

"Yes, but it's the sort of thing they expect of me." More likely she didn't want him to carry her, which was fair. "All right, we'll take a wagon. I'll tell you everything on the way."

17

Yala found some merchant wagons on Setemar's outskirts. Kelan offered to borrow one, but Yala convinced him to pay a driver instead.

"You can't go around stealing people's transport," she muttered as the driver pocketed the coins she'd tossed him. "Or scaring their raptors."

"Yes, the raptors aren't my biggest fans," Kelan acknowledged. "I think they're jealous of my ability to fly."

"Honestly." She climbed into the wagon ahead of him, and to her relief, he followed her without startling the animals.

"I should probably have told the others I'm leaving." He glanced behind them as the wagon began to move. "I expect Laima won't complain if we show up and announce that we've caught the perpetrators."

"It's going to be that easy, is it?" She settled back against the wagon's side, stifling a grimace as the material of her shirt rubbed against the cuts the void beast had left on her back. They'd crusted over with blood, but she hadn't been able to clean the wounds properly in the darkness. Nor had she rid herself of the lingering smell of monster guts; the stench clung to her skin even after she'd disposed of her ruined clothes from the previous night.

"No, but it's nice to imagine that we'll be able to deal with this without ending up on the bad side of another Superior."

"You can't pretend you didn't want to go looking for the source of the trouble regardless of what Superior Dovial's opinions on the matter," Yala said. "Since when did you care?"

"Ah, but I'm here on behalf of my own Superior," he reminded her. "Everything I do reflects on her, which limits my capacity to make a nuisance of myself."

"I'm surprised Superior Sietra chose you for the mission, considering your role in my escape from jail," she remarked, lowering her voice so that their driver wouldn't hear the word 'jail' and assume he was carting around a pair of criminals.

"You did mitigate the situation when you saved everyone in the capital from a grim death," he said. "I gather she'd decided I'd been punished enough when she picked me for this mission."

"What was your punishment, exactly?" she asked, genuinely curious as to how the Disciples decided on such matters.

"Confinement to the tower," he replied, "and reading a truly tedious number of books."

"Reading books?" Yala gave a short laugh. "Some punishment. Better than being left on a roof."

"I have to say I disagree." He eyed her. "Are you injured?"

I thought he noticed my shoulders. "A little sore. Those monsters' claws are sharp."

"Since you haven't dropped dead, I'm going to assume its claws weren't laced with deadly poison."

Yala gave a faint snort. "No, but I'm starting to wish I'd brought a spear."

"And a war drake?"

"Not much use underground, is it?" Both of them would be thoroughly out of their element when they entered the mines.

At her request, the wagon's driver stopped near the farmhouse where Yala had spent the night. As they climbed out of the wagon, Kelan asked him for directions to the mines.

"To the *mines?*" The driver blinked at them. "Depends which one you mean. They're all over."

He pointed towards the rugged outlines of the cliffs concealing Setemar from sight. They might have hidden a thousand tunnels for all Yala knew, and even the Temple of the Earth wasn't visible from this angle.

"Thanks anyway." Kelan turned to the farmhouse as the raptors began to pull the wagon away. "I wonder…"

Yala groaned when he glided over and knocked on the farmhouse door. "Kelan, we don't need to draw any more attention."

Nobody answered the door. Kelan tried once more and then surveyed the houses clustered some distance away. "I wonder if the villagers will talk?"

"They were attacked by monsters last night. At least one of them was killed. I wouldn't want to talk to a pair of strangers either if I were in their position." They might know the beasts had come from underground, but it was highly unlikely that they'd set eyes upon the Disciples of Death. "If the Void *is* open somewhere underground, the pair of us won't be able to get rid of it."

Kelan's mouth parted. "You make a salient point. I wonder if it's worth paying another visit to Superior Shralin?"

"Was he of any use yesterday?" *Damn him.* She'd done her best to convince the new Superior not to allow any of his Disciples to follow her to Setemar, but if Melian's allies had already opened Mekan's realm, closing the Void herself was beyond her power. Kelan's, too.

I'll deal with that later. Yala cut across the rain-slick grass towards the cliffs. Daylight made it easier for her to see where she was going, but not for the first time, she envied Kelan's ability to hover above the ground; her cane kept sticking in the mud and she'd already ruined another pair of socks by the time they found the first entrance to the mines. Someone had pushed a cart in the way, blocking their path.

Kelan peered around the cart. "Looks like it was abandoned recently. Strange."

"Not really," Yala said. "If monsters started crawling out of the mines, I don't blame them for closing off every tunnel entrance they could find."

"Superior Dovial tried the same," he said. "If Mekan's already down there, He'll find a way out eventually."

"Don't I know it." Yala prodded the cart with her cane, but it didn't budge. "You can move this?"

"I could, but the villagers might not appreciate it." Kelan glided upward and pointed ahead. "There are more."

Stepping around the cart, Yala counted at least five more closed-off tunnels, and countless others were doubtless hidden among the cliffs. "It'll take all day to search all of them."

There's a quicker way, a voice whispered in the back of her mind.

Yes, there *was* a quicker way: attract Mekan's attention and follow the trail of carnage to His followers' destination.

"Yala?" Kelan turned to her; she realised her hand had idly moved to the pouch at her belt of its own accord. "You called Mekan, didn't you?"

"I didn't have a choice," she said. "Those monsters wouldn't have stopped attacking the villagers if I hadn't drawn their attention."

"You don't want to draw His attention now, do you?"

Yala lowered her hand. He was right; they were too close to human habitation for her to take the risk. "The longer we stay here, the more likely we are to be noticed by whatever might be lurking in here."

"I can scout ahead and look for clues." Kelan indicated the cliffs. "Or I can ask the villagers if they have a map."

"Unlikely, but go ahead." She found a rock to sit on and wait, resigned to seeking out Mekan's followers the less efficient way. Her throbbing shoulders reminded her she'd had a lucky escape already, but if her life had been the only one at risk, she wouldn't have hesitated to pull out the claw again.

A chill brushed the back of her neck, prickling across the claw marks the beast had left on her, and she caught a whiff of death on the air.

It might be the monsters I killed last night, she told herself, unconvincingly. The villagers must have disposed of them somewhere. All the same, she climbed to her feet and sniffed, confirming that the smell came from the mine hidden behind the upturned cart. She peered closer, but the stench vanished when Kelan reappeared in a gust of cool air.

He was also, inexplicably, carrying a lantern. "I borrowed this. Its owner thinks we're out of our minds."

"What did you say we were doing?"

"I told her I was on a mission from my Superior," he said. "To inspect the mines."

"To … inspect them? She believed that?"

"I don't think so, but she wasn't going to start an argument with a Disciple, was she?" He indicated the cart in front of them. "She told me to start here. You have good instincts."

"That and I smelled the dead." Yala took the lantern while Kelan conjured up a breeze strong enough to shift the cart out of the entrance to the mine.

"She asked me to put this back afterwards so that nobody

else can follow," he explained, taking the lantern again. "It's dark in there. Or did you want to go first?"

"No, you go on."

He tilted his head. "You aren't trying to volunteer me to be the first to walk into any monsters we might find?"

"The thought never crossed my mind." She stepped aside to let him pass. The tunnel looked scarcely tall enough for one person to stand in, let alone while hovering above the ground like Kelan did. "Whose idea was it to put the cart in the way?"

"The city guards." He shone the light ahead of them. "It seems the villagers called on them for help."

"This was their solution?" Yala ducked in behind him. "Put rocks and carts in the way of every tunnel entrance they could reach?"

It would have taken hours, and their initiative hadn't stopped the attack the previous night. Yet in their position, Yala would have struggled to think of any better ideas.

No lights existed inside the tunnel, so Yala was glad of the lantern. The scent of death remained, faint yet distinct, and after they'd walked for a short while, they came to a fork in the path.

When Kelan turned left, she whispered, "How do you know which is the right way?"

"I don't."

She ground her teeth, sniffing the air, but the lingering traces of death-scent hadn't grown any stronger since they'd entered the mine.

They found themselves in a tunnel that twisted and turned like the coils of a sea drake. Yala swore when she knocked her elbow on a wall for the fourth time. "What kind of mine is this?"

"It isn't," he replied. "It's a tunnel connecting the mine back to the Temple of the Earth. Convenient, isn't it?"

"Not for us." She came to a halt with a hiss of surprise as Kelan dropped the lantern and caught it in the same hand, causing a jangling noise to echo through the tunnel ahead.

"Ah." He lifted the lantern again. "I think we've reached the Temple of the Earth. My abilities aren't working."

"That's not where we were going." *Damn those Disciples for not drawing a map.* Though if they could move the earth around and create new tunnels at will, they probably didn't see the use in keeping track.

"We can turn back." He made to do so, but Yala caught a sudden, strong whiff of rotting flesh.

"Kelan," she whispered. "We're not alone."

A fluttering sounded, and Yala raised her cane, bracing herself. Kelan tensed and lifted the lantern, illuminating the winged shape flying out of the tunnel.

Yala swung the cane, hitting the bird-like monstrosity sideways into the path of Kelan's blade. Its wings kept beating until Kelan sliced it clean in two, and the halves hitting the ground with a wet thud.

"The Void is still open," he murmured. "I thought so."

Unease trickled between her shoulder blades. "If the Void is open *inside* the temple, do the Disciples know? Or are they about to get taken unawares again?"

Before he could reply, a faint rumble sounded below their feet, and the ground began to shake.

Niema trudged down the forest path. Two Disciples—strangers, brought from one of the other enclaves—escorted her through the trees without speaking. Both were stern-faced, clothed in reed-woven garments that were the closest to a uniform she'd seen among her fellow Disciples of Life, and while they were unarmed, Niema's experiences in the city had taught her to recognise the air of someone capable of inflicting violence upon another person.

After hours of walking, her enclave members were far enough away that their grief wasn't as overwhelming as before—or maybe it was simply that her own panic had swamped all the others' emotions. Fear for Yala, rather than herself. Superior Kralia might believe she was doing Niema a kindness in letting her live, but being led away from the enclave had the air of finality that she might have expected from a death sentence. The forest felt alien to her, as if the ground was rotting beneath her feet.

As the sun's rays had begun to slip out of sight, they reached a small hut shadowed by tall trees, with no other signs of human habitation around.

Swallowing against her dry throat, Niema addressed her captors. "This is where I'm to be imprisoned?"

"You'll be brought supplies every few days," said one of the Disciples. "If you try to leave, you'll either fall prey to wild animals or starve to death. It's your choice."

That's no choice. Niema's heart shuddered. Superior Kralia might not have intended to leave her to die, but when the sun disappeared and the dead started to emerge, nobody would come to save her.

As the two Disciples vanished into the surrounding trees, Niema sat on a tree stump outside the hut to watch the sun's last rays slip behind the treetops.

When night descended, the dead came for her.

Birds flew down, rotting wings beating, while skeletal kekins crawled along branches and dangled from their coiling tails. Heart racing, Niema picked up a long tree branch and raised it to shield herself, whispering a prayer to Yalet.

Vines unfurled, enclosing the first bird to descend upon her. The vines shrivelled and died as the dead fell to the earth, drained of Mekan's presence, but another took its place. *I can't keep doing this,* she thought, using the long branch to fend off her attacker. *I can't kill the forest to save myself.*

The sound of countless branches snapping ripped through the night, and leaves rained down upon the clearing. Dropping the branch, Niema shrank into the hut's doorway as a giant shadowy shape crashed through the canopy, sending dead birds and kekins scattering in all directions. At first, Niema couldn't discern any of the new arrival's features, until moonlight cut downward, illuminating the hollows of the war drake's massive skull.

Niema's mouth went dry. The beast was as huge as ever, though scavengers had picked most of its flesh away and nothing remained but the bones. *It can't be possible. It can't be the same one.*

"What are you doing here?" she gasped.

The beast, of course, didn't answer. Its head swung sideways, sightless eyes looking straight through her, and then gave a swipe with its ragged claws. Niema threw herself to the ground, arms over her head, and gasped in pain when the claw pierced her arm, drawing blood.

Crawling into the hut's shadow, she whispered, "Yalet— help me!"

The dead war drake moved slower than a living one would and was further impeded by the trees, but its claw swiped again, seizing her around the waist. A scream caught in her throat as it lifted her into the air and flung her sideways. Her back slammed into a tree trunk; ribs snapped like branches. A red haze smothered her vision.

"Yalet." She coughed, tasting blood on her lips, and felt the dull pressure vanish from her ribs as the god of life answered her prayers.

She's here. Yalet is still with me.

Vision clearing, Niema pushed onto her knees. The dead war drake had flung her into the bushes across from the hut, leaving her a clear route to the door—if she could avoid being impaled on those claws again.

Heart in her throat, she began to crawl. The dead war drake couldn't detect her by scent or sound, but something about her presence drew its attention all the same. Its head snapped to her, and Niema gave a panicked lunge for the door.

Bones crackled against one another as the war drake's claw stabbed a finger span from Niema's head. Wrenching the door open, she fell into a forward roll and fetched up against the wall. The beast's claw swiped at the door frame, fragile wood cracking against equally fragile bone—but the oozing shadows holding the monster's deceased body together were stronger than both. The entire hut trembled under the beast's weight, and Niema squeezed her eyes shut and offered one final prayer for her deity to spare her.

The forest answered. Life sparked below, and Niema opened her eyes to see greenery shooting upward in front of the hut, forming a shield between her and the monster. Niema lay flat, heart in her throat, as the beast's bony claws tangled in the vines while it tried in vain to reach its target.

Breathing hard, she met its pitted eyes from the other side of the shield. "I know you probably don't recognise me. Maybe you remember Yala, but she's far away from here, and she can't help us."

Gods. I'm losing my wits, talking to a dead monster. Would the beast persist at trying to reach her until her strength gave out? The dead couldn't get bored or tired, but perhaps when the sun rose, the monster would leave her in peace. She'd been vastly overestimating her capabilities when she'd imagined laying the monster to rest on her own.

A horrible realisation hit her. What if the enclave was

under attack, too? There'd been no guarantee that her departure would have led the dead to spare her fellow Disciples, none of whom had any experience fighting Mekan's creatures.

I have to get out of here.

The dead war drake continued to swipe at her, undeterred, while Niema remained prone for what seemed like hours. Eventually she must have slept, because she woke to dawn's rays poking through the hut's glassless window and the rustle of leaves. She lifted her head, seeing the dead war drake take flight, its bony wings parting the canopy. Once again, leaves and broken branches showered upon the clearing as the beast vanished into the sky.

After holding her breath for a short time in case it came back, Niema risked letting the vines withdraw enough to step out of the hut. No more dead remained, but she couldn't spend another night out here. She'd sooner risk herself out in the forest alone. The war drake's departure had cleared a gap in the canopy wide enough for the sun to pierce her vision.

It had also given her an idea. Niema found a low-hanging branch and sprang upward, climbing kekin-like into the tree. She wasn't as athletic as Threl and the younger Disciples, but she'd spent her childhood climbing trees and being higher up gave her a better view of the surrounding forest.

The enclave was too far to see from here, but when she spied a brightly feathered bird flying overhead, she whistled a command.

"Come here." She whistled again, and the bird veered towards her. Descending through the branches, Niema touched down in the clearing and urged the bird to perch on the hut's roof while she went in search of something to write on. She hadn't been allowed to bring any of her few possessions with her into isolation, and the best she could find was a large leaf fallen from a sunfruit tree. It wasn't ideal, but by jabbing a stick into the mud, she was able to scratch out a warning onto the leaf.

Yala. The Disciples of Life are hunting you. I'm their prisoner. Niema.

With a final whistle, she thrust the material into the bird's outstretched claw and prayed to Yalet to guide her hand.

"Find Yala Palathar," she whispered. "Find her … and warn her."

18

Yala scanned the tunnel floor, from which the ominous rumbling issued. "That's not the Disciples of the Earth, is it?"

"I'm guessing not." Kelan steadied himself against the wall with a hand—she guessed that he wasn't used to losing his balance—and then sprang back when the tunnel exploded in a shower of dirt.

A huge head poked its way out of the wall, resembling a raptor's. Blunted and reptilian with a long neck and sharp teeth that snapped at them. Yala backed down the tunnel, while Kelan swung the lantern into its face. The monster's teeth caught on the lantern's flame, pulling it out of Kelan's hand and plunging them into darkness.

Yala swore, scrabbling to find her weapon in the darkness. Kelan's blade had a longer reach than hers did, but without any light, it was anyone's guess as to which of them the beast would lunge for first. More dirt flew into her face, and Yala jammed the end of her cane upward into a solid target. She pushed harder, and pinpricks of light showed her that she'd wedged the cane into the beast's mouth. She tugged and the monster tugged back, pulling her off her feet.

"Yala!" Kelan's voice was laced with alarm, his hands grabbing for her.

Letting go of the cane, Yala found herself flung sideways into the hole in the wall the monster had created. The light brightened as she tumbled head over heels before she came to a dizzying halt, half-buried in dirt. Groaning, she lifted her head. She'd fallen down a narrow bumpy incline with a low ceiling, perhaps created by the reptilian monster clawing its way through the wall. At the top of the slope, the monster's shadow blocked her view of the tunnel she'd left behind.

Growling sounded, and then the unmistakeable thud of a blade reaching its mark. The monster's body sagged to the side, and Kelan appeared in its place, peering down at her. "What's in there?"

"A tunnel?" She pushed herself upright, noting that a flickering light shone from somewhere further down the slope. "Let's see where it leads."

Yala descended a few steps and came to an abrupt halt at a sheer drop. The tunnel the monster had created came out halfway up the wall of a large chamber, where several lanterns burned above a stone bench stained dark red with blood.

Kelan moved to her side, and Yala stuck out an arm. "Don't step over the edge. I think we found our Disciples."

"What?" Kelan looked down. "Oh, fuck."

"Exactly."

The altar—for it could only be that—was crude, hand-made, but the fresh bloodstains indicated its purpose. As did the jagged piece of darkness hovering above the altar, as though a set of claws had ripped a chunk out of the world itself.

"I thought I lost access to my powers because we were in the Temple of the Earth." Kelan's voice was hoarse, disbelieving. "This isn't … it can't be…"

A Temple of Death. The thought came from the depths of her mind, from the place where her memories of the island lurked, stirred by the Void's icy presence.

The slash in the world wasn't as large as the one Melian had torn open in the capital, but the patch of darkness glimmered as though a light shone on the other side. When she leaned over the edge, Kelan grabbed her arm. "Don't, Yala. Even if you survive the fall, you won't be able to get out."

"How do you know?" They couldn't see the chamber from this angle, but whoever had opened the Void had got in somehow. She dropped to her knees, gritting her teeth against the spasm of pain in her leg, and craned her neck to examine the chamber more closely. While the lanterns shone on the altar, the area in front was cast in darkness, almost hiding the figure kneeling on the floor.

As though he'd sensed them watching, the figure lifted his head and then scrambled onto his feet. "Who are you?"

"Nobody of consequence," Kelan replied. "You?"

The man—boy, really—peered up at the two of them with a mixture of suspicion and surprise. "You're not supposed to be here."

"According to whom?" Yala reached for her weapon, wondering if she could throw accurately enough to kill him from this angle. "One of your monsters dragged me through a hole in the wall. I'm not here voluntarily."

Kelan leaned over the edge. "Is there a reason you opened a portal to hell?"

"You're a *Disciple.*" The boy ran to the altar, reaching for a curved dagger that lay beside the stone. "You shouldn't be here."

Yala threw her dagger at him. The boy yelped, dropping the knife. Panic shone in his eyes, and he stumbled against the altar, clutching his bleeding hand.

Shadows stirred around the jagged slash in the world, faint whispers rising from the other side, but Yala kept her attention on the terrified boy. "Who's the leader of this cult?"

"Melian."

Yala gave a disbelieving laugh. "She's dead. I saw her with my own eyes."

"You're lying." He pushed away from the altar, his bleeding hands shaking. "She's not dead. She's coming to take command of this temple."

"Sorry to be the bearer of bad news, but it's true."

"You're lying." He crouched down reaching for the knife again. "You're lying!"

"And you're in way over your head." *Who was Melian to him?* "Where's Trienan? He's the one I'm looking for."

The boy lifted his head, his face streaked with tears. "I'm Trienan. Melian is my sister."

"Oh." Kelan swore. "Yala—"

The boy flung the knife and missed wildly, the blade clattering out of sight—but behind him, darkness stirred within the Void and the whispers resolved into a chilling growl.

A winged shape detached itself from the darkness, and Yala swore, grabbing for her second dagger. Unlike the first beast, this one resembled one of the bird-like creatures that had attacked in the night. As Yala rose to her feet, a rumbling tremor ran through the entire chamber. *That's not Mekan.*

The winged beast flew at them. Yala pushed her instincts aside and retreated up the slope, lest the next tremor cause her to lose her balance and fall straight into Mekan's embrace.

Kelan's blade swiped, missed, and the sound of more

wings beating echoed from the chamber they'd left behind. The sloping floor was uneven, impossible to run on, and as Yala backed uphill, the winged monster's claws grazed her ankles, pulling her off her feet.

"Let go," she growled, stabbing with her dagger until the dead claws released her, dead flesh parting under her blade. *I will not die here.*

Kelan's blade stabbed over her shoulder and caught the beast through the eye, giving Yala the chance to get back on her feet. The wounds in her shoulders were bleeding again, and her leg screamed with pain.

Kelan backed up with a curse. "There are at least three of those monsters in the chamber, maybe more."

"Great." It'd be a fine thing to be skewered to death in the darkness—or worse, suffocate as soil rained down upon her head. The tunnel dug by the monsters was uneven, and the way back impeded by darkness. Kelan couldn't use his abilities to get them out, and she had nothing of use at her own fingertips. Nothing but … shadow.

The sound of monstrous cries chased them uphill towards the corpse of the first beast Kelan had slain. Darkness awaited on the other side, and in a moment of wild desperation, Yala dug her hand into her pouch in search of the claw.

"Send your monsters back to where they came from," she growled under her breath.

"Yala, what are you *doing?*" Kelan hissed.

"Improvising."

"Or bargaining." He pushed his way past the monster's limp body with a grunt. "You *aren't* bargaining with Mekan, are you?"

"If I were, you'd be able to hear Him reply."

He huffed a laugh. "That doesn't mean He isn't listening, does it?"

"Please don't use up all the air in here." Reluctantly, she let him extend a hand and help her climb around the monstrous corpse. The other beasts' cries resounded from the chamber, but no claws swiped on her heels, and her feet instead stumbled over the broken remains of the lantern Kelan had dropped. *We're out.*

There was one slight issue. "The book."

"Yala?" Kelan nudged her in the shoulder. "Come on. We have to get out."

"We can't leave that temple here."

"What exactly are you proposing we do?" Kelan took a few steps forward—or back, she couldn't tell in the darkness—and cursed when he knocked into a wall. "I'd say leaving that Trienan for the beasts to feed on while we run like hell is our best option."

Damn him. As Yala reluctantly moved alongside Kelan, she muttered, "I have a hard time believing the Disciples of the Earth didn't know."

"About the temple?" Kelan swore again. "If so, we'll have to confront them."

If the dead don't get there first.

———

Kelan supported Yala on one side as they finally emerged from the tunnel. She was limping worse than usual—probably because she'd left her cane jammed in a monster's mouth—but after several lost turns in the darkness, they found the exit. Kelan exhaled in a sigh of relief when he glided out into sunlight, freed of the pressure that had descended upon him in the temple.

Yala limped past the upended cart the villagers had left behind and sat on a large rock. "Who thought setting up a

Temple of Death in an underground chamber was a good idea?"

"It *is* a good idea," he said. "If they didn't want to be found, they picked the best place to hide."

Yala swiped at him half-heartedly, and he jumped back when he saw the claw protruding from her clenched fist. "When did you pick that up?"

"Sorry." She lowered her hand. "I didn't know... I forgot I was holding that."

"You didn't know?" The curved shape made his shoulder itch with phantom pain. "*Did* you bargain with Mekan? Those beasts didn't chase us out..."

"You're as paranoid as Saren is." She pushed the claw back into the pouch at her waist.

"I'd say paranoia is a good way to react to someone carrying a piece of the god of death's realm on their person." He levitated the cart back into place, noting that it'd started to rain while they were in the tunnel. Warm droplets of muddy water dripped trickled down his face as he turned to Yala. "Do you want me to fly us back into Setemar now?"

"No." She pushed off the rock with a wince. "The Disciples of the Earth aren't oblivious, are they? Even if they aren't allowed out of their temple, some might have stumbled upon that chamber and not told their Superior."

"That or it was their blood on the altar." Either way, someone had to enlighten Superior Dovial. "I'll find someone willing to take us back to Setemar ... unless you'd rather go back to the farmhouse where you spent the night?"

Yala shook her head. "I think I've worn out my welcome there. I have somewhere I can stay in Setemar."

"All right." He glided downhill to the village, found a farmer getting ready for the market, and spun a story about the pair of them being abandoned on the roadside by an unscrupulous wagon driver. They were both covered in dirt, which added credence to his story and convinced the farmer to take them all the way around the cliffs to Setemar's outskirts.

"One of these days, your stories are going to come back to bite you," Yala told him as they climbed out of the wagon.

"Would you rather have walked?" He reached to help her and she reluctantly took his hand.

"Too many people know my face in the capital." Her feet touched the ground, and she released him. "I don't need to deal with the same nonsense here."

"I'm more conspicuous than you are." His sky-blue robes were striking even when covered in mud. "Want to come back to the inn to clean yourself up?"

"No, I'll stay at Vanat's old house. Nobody else has moved in there, and it's a better place to lie low."

"Good thinking." It'd slipped his mind that one of Yala's former squad-mates had lived in Setemar for a time. "Ah—do you want me to tell the other Disciples what we found?"

"Which Disciples?" She raised a brow. "Start with the Disciples of the Sky and see if you can get their support. Then we'll find out how much Superior Dovial knew."

That won't get rid of the Temple of Death ... but I know who can. "And ... the Disciples of the Flame?"

"No." Yala gave a firm headshake. "Absolutely not."

"Who else can get rid of the Void?" He let the uneasy silence hang between them as the wagon departed, the sound of wheels bouncing on the uneven road uncomfortably reminiscent of the tremors under their feet. How far *did* the tunnels stretch? Did the entire city sit upon a Temple of Death?

Yala's mouth pulled into a frown. "You're right, but I don't trust them."

"They sent you here."

She gave a short laugh. "If they could have sent anyone else, they would have."

"I can avoid mentioning your name in my report, if it helps."

"No, they'll already know I'm involved." Her manner gained a resigned air. "Listen, if you see anyone called Mieren, avoid talking to her. She's bad news."

"Mieren?" His mind jumped back to the woman who'd challenged her Superior. *Ah. Her.* "I'll keep that in mind."

"Also, while you're in Dalathar, you won't mind paying a visit to Saren, will you? Ask him for my spare cane."

"I will." It wouldn't take him much longer to visit Yala's friend, and who knew, maybe he'd find out why Viam had been visiting the Temple of the Flame the previous day too. "I should probably tell the others before I leave."

———

Laima waited for Kelan in the inn's doorway, a hand on her hip. "Why are you covered in mud?"

"Bathing in mud is said to have health benefits." He moved closer, dropping his voice. "I went for another look around the mines."

"Alone?"

"No, a certain friend from the capital showed up this morning."

She took a step back. "You went with *Yala?*"

"I assumed you were sleeping."

Not strictly true—and from her tight expression, she knew it, too. "What did you do, dig your way out with your bare hands?"

"Surprisingly close to the truth." He summed up what they'd found, and by the time he'd finished, Lakiel had joined

Laima at the door. He, unlike Kelan, looked well-rested—and annoyed.

"Why didn't you wake me up first?" he asked.

"You were sleeping." *And snoring like a slumbering raptor.*

"You went into the mines?" he said. "And you found—?"

"A Temple of Death, yes," Kelan finished. "Or some approximation of one, complete with a bloodied altar and an opening straight into Mekan's domain."

"And the Disciples of the Earth…?" Laima trailed off.

"I don't know how aware they are of the illicit activities taking place beneath their feet," said Kelan. "You might want to pick someone more diplomatically minded than me to ask their Superior."

"They haven't invited us back into their temple yet," Lakiel said. "Not since yesterday."

"The villagers were attacked last night," Kelan told him. "It's not just the Disciples who are in danger from the monsters in Mekan's realm."

Laima grimaced. "You have a plan, don't you? You and Yala?"

"*Yala* is here?" Lakiel asked.

"Yes, and I'd appreciate it if you didn't tell Superior Dovial yet," Kelan said. "She's here on behalf of the Disciples of the Flame."

Laima stared at him. "She works for *them*?"

"They're trying to manipulate her." If the book she'd been sent to find had been inside the Temple of Death, he hadn't seen it, but he'd been preoccupied with the winged monstrosities the Void had spat at them. "They want her to find Melian's surviving allies. I intend to tell them that we did."

"Now you're going to visit the Disciples of the Flame?" Lakiel asked. "That wasn't one of Superior Sietra's orders, was it?"

"No," he admitted, "but I imagine they'll be more likely to listen to me now that I've seen the Temple of Death with my own eyes, and it'll be quicker than Yala going back to the capital. I won't be long, and Superior Dovial might have decided to speak to you again by the time I get back."

Laima gave another sigh. "If you *did* find a Temple of Death, we'll certainly need the Disciples of the Flames' help. Don't screw this up, Kelan."

I was just thinking the same thing.

After the bird had departed, Niema began her escape. There was one slight hitch: another living person approaching. *Oh, no.* It'd slipped her mind that someone would have to come to deliver her meals, and she climbed down her tree to await her visitor.

She'd expected the hostile Disciples who'd escorted her to the clearing and was startled to see Superior Kralia of all people approaching instead. Words tangled in her throat, and in the end, she simply pointed to the canopy—battered from the war drake's collision—and to the shredded thorns she'd shielded herself within.

"I had to protect the enclave," said Superior Kralia, her voice tinged with weariness. "The dead attacked us, too."

No. "I could have helped."

"Your motives cannot be trusted," Superior Kralia said. "Truly, I am sorry. It was a mistake to ask you to leave for the city, and I take full responsibility for what became of you."

An unexpected rush of recklessness seized Niema, born from sleeplessness and desperation. "What would you have done in my place? I could have helped a Disciple of Death or see all of you destroyed. You can't say I made the wrong choice."

"Enough." Superior Kralia took in a breath. "I hoped that being away from the enclave would have enabled you to reflect on your decisions."

"I'm not saying I don't regret my silence." Niema turned her gaze downward. "If I'd told you the truth when I returned, Prathen would have still died, and the others would have suffered all the more."

"I'm surprised that you would so readily give up on your fellow enclave members, Niema," said Superior Kralia. "Given how close you stood to Mekan, it seems inevitable that He and His followers would have corrupted you, too."

Niema's eyes stung. "Yalet protects me. She wouldn't have helped me survive last night if I was on Mekan's side."

Superior Kralia's mouth pinched. "Regardless… I've been speaking to the other enclaves to arrange for you to be sent somewhere further away, where the Corruption that follows you cannot reach the rest of us."

The implication chilled her. "And if it's not me? What if the dead keep attacking you even when I'm gone?"

"We will eradicate it." Eyes flinty, Superior Kralia gave Niema one last cutting look. "Farewell, Niema."

Then she was gone, vanishing into the surrounding forest. Niema held her breath, then exhaled. *I should have asked about Yala.* Yes, that might have tipped off her Superior that she intended to escape, but how long did she have until the other Disciples arrived to escort her to her new prison? She'd sent Yala a message, but there were no guarantees that her warning would reach her before the Disciples of Life did.

Calm down, she told herself. Superior Kralia might have forsaken her, but Yalet had not. If she could find her way to shelter while the sun was up, before the dead returned at night, she might stand a chance of survival.

Niema stretched out her senses to be sure that nobody was around, and then she walked until the rustling trees swallowed the clearing behind her. Every hour, she picked a tree to climb and check for landmarks, but it wasn't until noon that she spied a long thin depression between the trees that stretched in either direction. *Is that a river?* Most rivers, she knew, led north, towards Laria's major cities.

Niema began to move through the treetops. Her senses remained alert, attuned to every living creature that might be nearby, human or otherwise. Kekins, climbing through the branches, watched her curiously. Bright birds flitted across the sky. Bloodflies swirled in thick clouds. No signs remained of the enclave, and the others' heartbeats were already growing fainter.

I'm sorry. I'm so sorry.

Niema continued north, towards the river.

———

Kelan left for the capital at once. He might have stopped to wash some of the dirt off his face so the Superior wouldn't refuse him entry, but the rain took care of that, and his cloak was soaked through by the time he reached Dalathar's upper city.

He glided over the wall, over Ceremonial Square, and touched down on the Temple of the Flame's doorstep. A novice answered his knock, looking aghast when he dripped water all over the entryway.

"I'd like to speak to your Superior," Kelan said. "He's expecting me."

The novice dipped his head and ran inside while Kelan held out his sleeves so that the heat emanating from the temple would dry off some of the rainwater. Countless candles burned beneath the statue of Dalathik's likeness, depicting the god of the flames as a serpentine form, haloed in fire.

Superior Shralin approached Kelan. "Is there a reason you look like a half-drowned skirrit?"

Has a sense of humour, does he? "You recall my mentioning that the Disciples of the Earth were dealing with incursions from the dead? It turns out there's a Temple of Death underneath Setemar, and I decided it was prudent to inform you."

Superior Shralin's eyes grew wide. "Explain."

Kelan wouldn't normally have tolerated such a command from anyone other than his own Superior, but he decided on balance that arguing wouldn't be worth the fuss. "There was an altar. An opening into the Void. Monsters. Oh, and a would-be novice who claimed Melian was still alive. Those things put together make a temple, I believe."

The Superior's mouth dropped open. "You met a Disciple of Death?"

"Yes," he said. "Trienan, he called himself. Unfortunately, we were attacked by monsters and had to flee, which prevented us from finding out more."

"We," he repeated. "You met with Yala Palathar?"

"I gather you're the one who sent her to find Melian's surviving allies?"

"She told you that?" Superior Shralin drew in a breath. "How many Disciples were there?"

"We only saw one, but I assume it was a group effort to open the Void," he said. "It'll take a group effort to get rid of them, too."

Superior Shralin ignored his pointed tone. "Have you informed the Disciples of the Earth of this?"

"I expect my fellow Disciples of the Sky are telling Superior Dovial as we speak." *If he lets them in.* "However, they have no access to their abilities, and inside a Temple of Death, neither do I."

"The same, I assume, would hold true of *my* Disciples."

Right. Kelan had overlooked that small detail. Without their abilities, closing the Void was out of the question, and most of his arguments were rendered irrelevant. Most, but not all. "Not if the beasts got *out* of the tunnels, which they did, on several occasions. They've been attacking the villagers."

"I am sorry to hear that," he said, "but without access to Dalathik's fire, it's impossible for us to get rid of Mekan's beasts permanently."

"Why not try?" The woman who'd argued with the Superior during his last visit stepped into view, golden-threaded robes reflecting the sunlight streaming through the windows.

Mieren. The very person Yala had told him *not* to talk to.

"I told you," said Superior Shralin with barely restrained impatience, "I do not give you permission to leave the city."

"It sounds like the Disciples of the Earth would appreciate the help," Mieren said. "So would the people who live in and around Setemar. Why shouldn't some of us go? It'll take a few days to reach Setemar, and the situation might get worse the longer we wait."

No doubt they'd take offence if Kelan offered to carry them, but he could imagine Yala's irritation if he showed up with the very Disciple whom she'd warned was untrustworthy.

"Should I leave you to discuss amongst yourselves again?" Kelan asked, conscious that Yala had also told him to visit her friend, and that if the two Disciples came to blows, he did not want to stand in the path of Dalathik's rage.

"Yes..." Superior Shralin's glare smoothed out into a neutral expression. "I quite agree."

Taking the hint, Kelan left the temple and followed the directions Yala had given him to her new home. The unassuming row of tenement buildings was a considerable step up from the cabin in the jungle she'd lived in beforehand, though doubtless lacking some of the comforts of the Disciples' inns.

A short time passed before the door opened. A dishevelled man whose long hair curled past his shoulders squinted at him with bloodshot eyes. "You're… Kelan, is it? If you're looking for Yala, she's gone."

"I know. She and I just escaped an unpleasant death in the mines."

Saren groaned. "Please don't tell me she asked for *my* help."

"No, she wanted me to fetch her spare cane."

"What did she do with the other one?" He led Kelan into a room that was as spartan as Yala's cabin had been, containing little except a couple of battered armchairs and some wooden boards which appeared to have been used for target practise.

"You probably don't want to know." Kelan located the spare cane leaning against a wall in the corner.

"Glad there's someone in Setemar on her side." Saren leaned an elbow against the wall and studied Kelan's dripping wet cloak. "She refused to take me with her, and Viam … well, she wouldn't go."

"Speaking of whom." Kelan had quite forgotten Yala's friend's odd behaviour the previous day. "Did you know your friend Viam was visiting the Temple of the Flame yesterday?"

"What?" Saren pushed away from the wall. "Shit. I provoked her, but I must have pissed her off beyond measure if she went to *them*."

"Isn't she the one who taught Yala how to raise the dead?" He thought back to Viam's startled reaction when she'd seen him inside the temple. "She must have assumed the Disciples wouldn't recognise her."

"They might not have." Saren gave a faint smile. "You know, our squad members were targeted by Melian's lot because we were the only people in the nation that had seen the Void and had the potential to become Death's Disciples. But half the city witnessed Melian rip open the Void in Ceremonial Square. If the Disciples of the Flame wanted to take out all the possible risks, they'd have to set the whole of Dalathar on fire."

"They still think of Yala as a bigger risk than anyone else, don't they?"

"Well, she defied the god of death to His face, so they're more likely to remember her than the rest of us." Saren chuckled to himself. "I know, I know, Yala would want me to talk some sense into Viam. I don't have much going spare, but I'll try."

"Yala will appreciate it." He hefted the cane. "This, too. I'll let her know."

As Kelan left the house, a brightly coloured bird crashed headlong into his face. Blinking in confusion, he held out a hand to catch his avian assailant, which carried what appeared to be a large leaf in its beak. A closer look showed several words had been daubed onto the leaf with mud.

"You're a conspicuous-looking messenger," he remarked. "Looking for someone in particular?"

The bird tilted its head as if to consider him, then opened its beak and allowed him to extract the leaf. He could make no sense of the rain-smudged writing except for the first word—*Yala*—and the last—*Niema.*

Kelan knocked on Saren's door again.

"What?" came the voice from within. "Don't tell me you ran into trouble already."

"No, a messenger bird." When Saren opened the door, Kelan held out the leaf. "I don't suppose you can make sense of this? I think it's for Yala."

"Weird." Saren held out a hand to take the message, his brow furrowing. "Who wrote this?"

"Niema," he said. "Disciples of Life can command animals, and she wouldn't have known that Yala isn't in the capital."

"Fucking hells." Saren fumbled the leaf in his hand. "The Disciples of Life are coming to arrest her."

"You're joking, aren't you?" He tried to read over Saren's shoulder, but he didn't have the patience to disentangle the words when it was easier to accept Saren's reaction as genuine. "They must have somehow found out she's a Disciple of Death."

Saren swore. "It sounds like this Niema's in trouble. She's a prisoner."

"By her own people?" *Shit.* He'd told her, half-jokingly, that he'd be more than happy to come to her rescue if her fellow Disciples objected to her friendship with Yala. He hadn't counted on immediately being confined to Skytower and then sent on another mission straight after achieving his freedom.

"Yes, and she's being attacked by the dead."

"Oh, is that all?" He and Yala could hardly go to Niema's rescue when they already had her hands full in Setemar, but if the Disciples were coming for Yala, their paths would collide sooner or later. "I'll give her the bad news."

———

Vanat's apartment hadn't changed since Yala's last visit. Aside from a light coating of dust upon the sparse furniture, he might as well have gone out to the market, not to his death. A lump rose in her throat, which she swallowed, and she set about changing out of her muddied clothes and re-bandaging her wounds. It would have been easier if she'd had someone else to help, but she didn't need to draw more attention from people who recognised her face.

What a fucking mess we're in. A Temple of Death. The Void. Melian's *brother.* Worse, that damned book must be down there in the chamber they'd been forced to flee, and even if she found another way in, the monsters from the Void were far too much for a single person to deal with. Like it or not, she needed the other Disciples' help. Including the Disciples of the Earth… if they hadn't taken Mekan's side.

When she'd finished binding her cut hands and shoulders, Yala left the house and walked the short distance to the Disciples' inn. The Disciples of the Sky had congregated outside, while a female Disciple—Laima—gave them instructions. Without her cane, Yala's steps were uneven, her pace slower, but she held her head high as she approached their group.

"It's you," said Laima. "The Disciple of Death."

Whispers rose among the others, while Yala's hand crept towards her remaining dagger. "Yes. Did Kelan tell you what we found in the tunnels?"

"A Temple of Death." Laima's tone was disbelieving, but a worried murmur travelled among the other Disciples. "Or a place that resembled one."

"With an opening to the Void," Yala added. "Have you spoken to the Disciples of the Earth yet?"

"No," said Laima. "I intended to wait for Kelan's return, since he's a witness. Is that where you're going?"

Yala's shoulders tensed. "I don't believe I have an invitation into the Temple of the Earth."

"Yet?" echoed one of the Disciples. "You shouldn't be here, Disciple of Death."

Yala met the eyes of the Disciple who'd challenged her, a heavyset man whose shoulders strained at his cloak. "Superior Shralin of the Disciples of the Flame asked me to come here. If you'd rather fight the dead alone, be my guest."

"We're going to speak to Superior Dovial," Laima decided. "Yala can come with us or not, it's your choice."

The others didn't like the idea, given the way they muttered among themselves, but they'd come to help the people of Setemar. That put them on the same side.

Now she needed to convince the leader of the Disciples of the Earth of the same.

20

Viam didn't dare leave the palace complex again until the morning after her failed attempt to enter the Temple of the Flame. She'd barely had the chance to introduce herself before Kelan's arrival had stopped her from getting any further. *I would make an absolutely terrible spy,* she thought as she steeled herself to make a second attempt.

The palace was a difficult place in which to keep secrets. She and the other staff shared dormitories, which were an improvement on the army barracks, but which meant she had to carefully invent excuses every time she left the palace complex or else rumours would sprout up among the other staff members like weeds. The gods only knew what they thought of her behaviour yesterday, after she'd run back from the Temple of the Flame as if they'd sent a wild drake to chase her down.

Her face burned with humiliation at the memory. *Not this time.*

Viam walked out of the palace gates and came to a startled halt when she recognised someone waiting next to King

Larial's statue. Saren had put on some kind of absurd floppy hat to shield his face from the bright daylight, which also had the bonus of keeping the rain off his face. Viam had scarcely been outside a minute and already rainwater plastered her hair to her forehead.

"Saren." She crossed the square to meet him. "What are you doing here?"

"Warning you."

"*Warning* me?" Yala had warned Viam that he'd be in a delicate state while he fought off the effects of alcohol withdrawal—and that was assuming he didn't lapse back into old habits while she was gone—and she'd assumed he'd stay at home until Yala's return. Not that he'd walk all the way here to see her.

"You visited the *Disciples of the Flame?*" He whispered. "You're lucky you didn't end up on a pyre."

"What gives you the right to give me advice?" Gods. Kelan must have told him, which meant there was a good chance Yala knew, too. "You're the one who implied I wasn't doing enough."

"I didn't tell you to walk into the war drakes' den with a slab of meat strapped to your face." He made a rude gesture in the general direction of the temple which made Viam instinctively reach for his arm and drag him out of sight. "Our Disciple of the Sky friend paid me a visit."

"I thought so." She released his arm. "He told you I was at the temple, didn't he?"

"It's lucky he did." Saren peered at her. "Have you lost your wits?"

Viam stiffened at the accusatory note to his voice. "You don't need to tell me I'm betraying Dalem's memory by even considering joining them."

"Dalem wouldn't care, not now Superior Datriem's gone."

He shook his head, his hat sliding down his forehead. "It's your life to throw away."

"I'm not throwing my life away. I'm trying to help Yala." She pushed a handful of damp hair off her forehead.

"Seems more like a good way to piss off two gods at once."

"What—Dalathik and Mekan?" Viam frowned. "Because I already used Corruption? Would Dalathik care?"

"You're asking the wrong person." He grinned. "You know, it's funny how the only two members of Yala's squad who ended up surviving are the most useless of the lot. Maybe that's *why* we survived."

His words stung despite Viam's best efforts to insulate herself. "Yala survived too."

"Yala would walk out of the hells themselves if she could." Saren pushed his hat up, regarding her with shadowed eyes. "She wouldn't want you doing this. You know that."

"The Disciples killed the king, Saren," Viam said quietly. "Don't you want to know what else they're hiding?"

"No," he said. "I *don't* want to know."

"Yala does," Viam said. "It's less dangerous for me."

Saren gave a laugh. "They won't *tell* you anything. You'd be a novice for the first few years, spending all your time cleaning latrines and polishing the Superior's shoes. Is that what you want to do with the rest of your life?"

"All right, all right." She turned back to the palace gates. "It was just an idea. I'm flattered that you came all this way to warn me, but—"

"It's not just about you." His tone gained a newly urgent edge. "According to our Disciple of the Sky friend, the Disciples of Life are coming to arrest Yala."

Viam whipped around. "Have you been hallucinating again?"

"No—well, yes, but this one was real." He shuddered. "Niema sent a note warning her to run."

That can't be possible. "Why would they arrest another Disciple?"

"Don't ask me," Saren said. "Luckily, Yala isn't here."

"Luckily?" Yala might be in Setemar, but only as long as it took her to find the missing book and stop Melian's surviving allies. "That's not—"

From the other side of the palace gates came a series of thuds that sounded like several pairs of heavy boots striking the ground, and then the cry of a wild animal made both Viam and Saren jump.

"Fuck me," Saren said. "Was that a war drake?"

"Sounded like it." *What's going on in there?* "I'll look."

Viam ran to the gates, where the guards moved aside to let her back in. Both flinched when another screech rang through the air. Definitely a war drake.

Heart in her throat, Viam ran through the palace grounds towards the noise. She veered around the back of the administrative building and skidded to a halt. Two guards led a fully-grown war drake by a chain looped around its neck, while none other than King Daliel followed.

"What are you doing with that?" Shock pushed past her usual sense of decorum. The war drake was barely restrained; they hadn't covered its mouth with a muzzle, and it was making its disapproval as clear as possible.

"You there," said one of the guards, spotting her. "Stay back. This thing has a nasty bite."

"I know that." What were they thinking, bringing it so close to the monarch? "Didn't you hire a trainer?"

"We can handle it." The guard gave a sharp yank of the chain, and the war drake screeched in protest. She'd forgotten how huge they were up close, each tooth as long as one of her fingers and sharp as a whetted blade. Its wings were folded against its back, bound with ropes.

"Ah, you're one of the scribes, aren't you?" King Daliel approached and the impulse to drop to her knees warred with the desire to back away in case the beast broke free of its chains.

"Yes." She settled for a short bow. "Ah—is there a reason your guards brought a war drake into the palace grounds?"

"Yes, on my orders," he said. "As a test."

A test? "Your Majesty, I used to be in the flight division, and—I don't think that beast is properly restrained."

"Did you?" He hastily stepped aside when the war drake's clawed foot shot out, forcing the guard to throw his weight against the chain to prevent it from breaking free. "I didn't realise anyone here had experience with these beasts. They're quite … ornery, aren't they?"

At that moment, the beast gave a lunge forward. The guard lost his grip on the chain and stumbled. Claws flashed, and the man bellowed in pain, blood pouring from his leg.

Viam backed away. "I'll get help."

Screams followed her as she ran around the corner, narrowly avoiding a collision with Brenat. "What's going on?"

"A war drake." Viam winced at another scream. "They need a healer. Is anyone available?"

"Shit, I don't know." Brenat gestured to the administrative building. "Might be someone upstairs."

Viam hurried towards the door. "Why would they bring a war drake into the palace grounds without proper equipment?

Brenat raised an eyebrow. "There's proper equipment?"

"Well, yes." Had the king's guards forgotten everything about the wild beasts they'd once tamed? Yes, he'd eliminated the entire flight division, including the beasts' trainers, but one would think someone in the palace would remember. *Oh, right. Someone does. Me.* "Mostly to keep them biting your fingers off before you even get into the air."

Brenat nodded in understanding. "His Majesty must intend to bring the war drakes back. He's already expanding the barracks."

Viam's spine stiffened. "Why?"

"Why else?" Brenat said. "He's rebuilding Laria's army."

———

Kelan reached Setemar by midmorning and made for Vanat's old house first. Yala didn't answer the door, which didn't surprise him. He hadn't expected to find her lying idle, and when the inn yielded no answers either, he glided towards the Temple of the Earth.

A novice answered the door, and inside the main chamber, Yala stood surrounded by Disciples. Her arms were folded and her stare defiant. "There you are, Kelan."

Hadn't she wanted to avoid drawing attention? Granted, she might have grown impatient and decided to explain the situation to Superior Dovial in person. In the awkward silence that ensued, Kelan held out her spare cane. "This is yours."

"Thanks." Yala took the sturdy wooden cane from him. "Can you confirm what we found in the mines? I already told Superior Dovial, but I think he wants to hear it from you, too."

Superior Dovial's eyes narrowed a fraction. "Yes, I would like to hear your account, Disciple."

Sensing a trap, Kelan nevertheless spoke. "I assume Yala told you we found a Temple of Death in the mines, complete with an opening into the Void. If you don't believe us, we can show you."

"This is absurd." Superior Dovial glared between them. "We have inhabited this temple since before Laria's first monarch wore a crown. There can't possibly be another temple here."

"I couldn't reach my deity in there," Kelan added. "Which is usually a sign that I've entered a temple belonging to another god."

The colour drained from Superior Dovial's face. "I do not believe this."

"You saw the monsters for yourself, didn't you?" Kelan attempted to sound sympathetic, but his patience was beginning to wear thin. "We found the temple by accident through a hole in the wall, but there's likely to be another entrance that's easier to access. Do you have a map of the area near the mines?"

From the expression on the Superior's face, Kelan might as well have asked if he had three heads. "No, we don't."

He's determined to be difficult, isn't he? "Your Disciples know the area, don't they? If anyone wants to volunteer to help us search, we'll do our best to make sure they don't come to any harm."

Within limits. It was unwise to make any guarantees where Mekan was involved.

"Preposterous," Superior Dovial said. "There is no Temple of Death, and I refuse to tell such dangerous lies to my Disciples."

"Please have some sense," Yala said. "The last Superior I met who called me a liar ended up being stabbed in the back by one of his own Disciples."

The fury that sparked in Superior Dovial's eyes sent his fellow Disciples retreating and caused even Yala to take a step away from him.

"Leave," he said. "All of you."

Nobody argued. Nor did anyone speak until they were

outside the temple. While his fellow Disciples glided ahead of him, Kelan kept pace with Yala as she descended the stairs.

"I realise that I'm not the best person to make judgements on proper behaviour," he said, "but I think you're the only person I know who would dare speak to a Superior in such a manner."

"He doesn't outrank me." Yala's cane hit each step with a solid thud. "I don't fit into your hierarchy. Besides, he was never going to listen to us."

"You make a valid point, but I'm afraid I have some more bad news."

"What?" Yala reached the foot of the stairs. "Let me guess, the Disciples of the Flame are sending the very person I told you to avoid?"

"Worse." He glanced ahead at his fellow Disciples to make sure none of them had lingered behind to eavesdrop. "Niema sent a warning that the Disciples of Life are coming to arrest you for colluding with the god of death. Or so I assume. Her note didn't give specifics about your supposed crimes."

"You've got to be fucking joking." Yala's free hand curled into a fist. "They're coming here?"

"No, they think you're in the capital," he said. "They're also likely travelling on foot, which gives you ample time to prepare."

"Is that supposed to be *good* news?" Yala resumed walking. "Is Niema coming with them?"

"They arrested her, too."

"Shit." Her mouth hung open. "That would explain why we didn't hear from her sooner."

"I know." Niema herself had taken a major risk in returning home, given that her people viewed anyone who associated with Disciples of Death as an affront to their very existence. "If I knew where they imprisoned her, I'd get her out."

"Might be better than staying here to save Superior Dovial's ungrateful hide." Yala twisted to glare at the temple. "I'm inclined to leave him to his fate, but I won't let the villagers become collateral damage."

"Wouldn't it be easier to get rid of a Temple of Death if we had a Disciple of Life with us?"

Yala's jaw twitched. "Yes, if she can reach her deity in there, which is no guarantee."

"She might be able to," Kelan said. "Superior Sietra implied that Yalet and Mekan are similar in that they don't need temples."

"Why did Melian's allies build one, then?" She walked on, her cane striking the cobbles. "They might not need temples, but Niema's people live deep in the jungle. I doubt they bother with maps that would help outsiders find them."

"If she managed to send us a warning, she might be trying to escape." That didn't mean Kelan would be able to find her location, of course. "Our other option is to find unambiguous proof to present to Superior Dovial."

"What proof?" Yala scowled. "The corpses of those monsters?"

"He's already seen some of those." Kelan's thoughts went back to the previous day's venture into the tunnel where he'd first encountered Mekan's beasts. "I think I might know where to start looking for the other route into the Temple of Death."

"That hidden tunnel?" she guessed. "Isn't it guarded?"

"They might be open to persuasion." When Yala raised an eyebrow at him, he added, "If we want to get inside, we'll have to figure something out. A diversion."

"Might be worth a look," Yala acknowledged. "It's better than waiting for Superior Dovial to see sense. I've met his sort before. You know, the ones promoted based on nepotism rather than merit."

"Superior Dovial was appointed by Setem Himself," Kelan said. "No Disciple would cast doubt on their own deity's choice."

"Nobody wanted to challenge the king's decisions either." Yala angled towards the gates out of the inner city. "The problem with people is like him is that their mistakes have a tendency to get other people killed as well."

"True enough." He lifted his gaze to the wall. "Do you want me to meet you on the other side? I can distract the guards myself. That way you won't be blamed."

"Distract them with what?"

"Still thinking of ideas," he admitted. "If we had a well-timed attack from the dead…"

"I'm not raising the dead in the middle of Setemar, Kelan."

"Pity Niema isn't here to conjure up a swarm of rodents or birds." He glided higher, until he hovered on a level with the wall. Unlike in the capital, the guards solely patrolled on the ground, so standing on the wall was less likely to be met with a spear in his back. Still…

"Kelan," Yala hissed at him. "Please don't do anything outrageous."

"Wouldn't dream of it." Kelan gave her a wave. "I'll meet you on the other side. Try to keep the guards at the gate talking, if you can."

He glided over the wall to a nearby rooftop, where a precarious-looking stack of barrels outside a tavern caught his attention. *Sorry for this.*

He conjured up a breeze and took aim. A crash resounded as the barrels toppled over, rolling in all directions. At a little more prompting from him, one of them began to tumble down the street that ran alongside the wall. Kelan glided to the alleyway where the guards had moved away from the tunnel entrance in search of the noise.

"Runaway ale barrels," he told them, pointing over his

shoulder. "I think the tavern's owner would appreciate your help."

One of the guards took a step forward, but the others didn't budge.

"I can watch the door," Kelan offered. "I won't let anyone get out, dead or alive."

With a grunt of thanks, the guards moved in the direction of the noise. Kelan waited until they'd vanished out of the alleyway, and then he found the hidden hinges and pulled the door open. As he exposed the tunnel's entrance, he heard the unmistakeable thud of Yala's cane striking the ground.

"You," she said to him as she appeared in the alleyway, "are nothing but trouble."

"I agree." He turned back to the tunnel's opening. "Let's see what they're hiding in here, shall we?"

21

Once they entered the tunnel, Kelan closed the door behind them. A lantern shone directly above their heads, and more lined the tunnel ahead.

"The Disciples were sneaking outside all along, were they?" Yala remarked.

"Their Superior couldn't expect them to stay underground indefinitely. It's no wonder they grew frustrated." Kelan took the lead, ducking under a low-hanging lantern. "This tunnel ends in the chamber where the Disciples bury their dead, so you'd think the Superior would have been a little more vigilant."

"He's as deep in denial as Superior Datriem was," Yala said. "Ah—speaking of whom, how was your visit to the Disciples of Flame?"

"Unproductive, as expected." He glided around a corner. "The monsters came out of an old mining tunnel, and the Disciple who was with me seemed entirely too keen to change the subject."

Yala might have found his own evasion of her question suspicious if not for the admittedly unsuitableness of the tunnels for conversation. Her gaze roved over the smooth stone walls as they walked, her hand resting on her remaining dagger and her ears pricked for any noises.

Their footsteps echoed in the gloom, but she didn't hear anything else until they came to a fork in the path. One route was blocked by a wall formed of rocks that looked to have been placed by hand.

"This is where the monsters come from," Kelan murmured, "but using my abilities to move these is likely to make a great deal of noise."

Yala gave the rocks a poke with her cane, but they'd been wedged in such a way that there were no gaps large enough for her to pry them apart. "Do it anyway."

"You might want to duck."

Yala shielded her face, remembering the time he'd blasted the roof of her cabin clean off. A breeze lifted her hair, becoming a force that hit the wall of rocks like a battering ram. Dirt flew outward, splattering Yala's face, and her ears protested at the noise of the rocks thumping into the tunnel on the other side.

Kelan lifted his head. "I believe our transgression has been discovered."

Yala swore. As her hearing returned, she picked up the unmistakeable clamour of shouts from the direction they'd come from. "It's probably not in our favour to collapse the tunnel on their heads."

"Definitely not, but I can slow our pursuers." He lifted his hands and made a motion as if he was pulling on a rope. Some of the rocks he'd knocked aside came flying out of the tunnel and landed behind them, forming a considerably more precarious wall than the one Kelan had knocked over.

Yala, meanwhile, stepped into the tunnel they'd unearthed, and a familiar death-scent caught in her nostrils. "Shit. The dead are in here."

"Are they?" He glided into the tunnel, which had no lanterns to guide their way. "I'm glad I didn't commit vandalism without cause."

"Wish I'd brought a lantern." Some light shone from behind, but the route ahead was smothered in shadow. Yala tested the ground with her cane as they walked, and death-scent grew stronger with each step.

At the tunnel's end, blood splattered the wall, thick and viscous. Some of it had dried, but it couldn't be more than a day old, and the smell of the dead hung in the air like miasma.

"What happened here?" she murmured. "There aren't any bodies..."

"Three attacked yesterday." Kelay surveyed the blood pooling on the floor. "They were Disciples of the Earth."

What had they been doing in here to begin with, if the tunnel had been out of bounds? A thought took root in Yala's mind, digging deep. "You know... the Disciples of the Earth might have been desperate enough to make an appeal directly to Mekan to leave them alone."

Kelan's mouth twisted with distaste. "No. A Disciple would never sacrifice their own, and Mekan doesn't under-stand any other language, does He?"

"If they were desperate..." Yala trailed off, hearing the thump of rocks hitting the ground. "Shit. They'll blame us for this."

"No, they won't," Kelan replied. "There aren't any bodies."

"Sometimes you're entirely too optimistic."

A moment later, several Disciples of the Earth ran into the tunnel behind them. They did not look pleased.

That could have gone better, Kelan thought.

The Disciples of the Earth flanked him and Yala, escorting them through the tunnels to their Superior. From what Kelan gathered, they hadn't known what else to do, and he thoroughly regretted bringing Yala with him. As a Disciple, Kelan was likely to be let off easier than Yala was, especially given her outburst earlier.

A few Disciples of the Earth watched curiously as Yala and Kelan were escorted into the main chamber. Superior Dovial strode to meet them, a muscle ticking in his jaw; from his demeanour, Kelan had the impression that if he'd had access to any of his usual abilities, he might well have brought the ceiling down on their heads.

"We found them in the old mining tunnel," one of the Disciples told their Superior. "They distracted the city guards watching the other entrance."

"How dare you make a mockery of my hospitality." Superior Dovial spat out the words and then took in a breath. "You should return to your Superior in disgrace, Disciple. As for *you*, Yala Palathar—"

Yala tensed when he spoke her name.

"I should have paid more attention to the stories about you," he went on. "Yes, I've heard of Yala Palathar, Disciple of Death. Saviour of the nation, according to some—and according to others, a dangerous killer."

Kelan spared a brief glance for the other Disciples, wondering what they thought of their Superior's raving, but they regarded Yala with open horror.

"It was my idea," he ventured. "I thought the dead that attacked us yesterday in the mining tunnel might have come from the temple Yala and I found, and I wanted to check there weren't others in there."

"The temple you *claim* to have found," said Superior Dovial. "I refuse to believe it."

"How do you explain the dead rising inside your own

temple?" Yala interjected. "I have no intention of making an enemy of you, but someone conducted a blood sacrifice in that mining tunnel. You can look for yourself if you don't believe me."

"There was blood all over the wall and not a single body to be found," Kelan added. "I don't know who was responsible for putting it there, but you might want to have a closer look at the three bodies that escaped and attacked the city guards yesterday."

"That's enough," Superior Dovial said through gritted teeth. "It's beyond my authority to punish another Disciple, but if you ever set foot in this temple again, I will treat you as I would any other trespasser. Now, leave."

At a gesture from his Superior, a Disciple of the Earth moved to escort Kelan to the door. Laima waited on the steps outside, her arms folded across her chest and her mouth taut with anger.

"Kelan, what were you thinking?" She didn't wait for him to speak before launching into her tirade. "I *know* it was your idea, not Yala's, but she's the one who's going to take the fall for your mistake."

A thread of guilt twisted inside him. "It wasn't my best idea, but someone was trying to contact Mekan in those mines. They performed a blood sacrifice."

Laima's eyes widened. "Are you accusing the Disciples of the Earth of allying with Corruption now?"

"No." Given her cagey behaviour, Pehin had known something was amiss in there, but her genuine fear at the dead monsters' attack made Kelan doubt that she'd been responsible for killing those Disciples. "I'm only telling you what I saw."

"Your problem is that you *don't* think, Kelan." She glided down the steps, and he followed. "After all the work we did to make a good impression. Superior Dovial is never going to accept our help now."

"He doesn't even believe the Temple of Death exists." When Laima sighed, he frowned. "You *do* believe me, don't you?"

"I believe you *think* you saw a temple."

"And Yala?"

"She's a Disciple of Death."

"Doesn't that mean she's *more* likely to recognise a Temple of Death for what it is?" Kelan glanced over his shoulder and saw the temple's doors had closed. *Shit.* "The same goes for a blood sacrifice, come to that."

Laima tugged on her sleeve without making eye contact with him. "There's never been a Temple of Death in Laria before. There's no comparison to make."

"Yala's seen one," he said. "Look, I'm not trying to argue with you—"

"As far as lies go, that's not one of your best, Kelan."

Stung, he followed her away from the temple. "Laima, I thought we were here to stop Mekan from infiltrating the Temple of the Earth. We can't do that by disagreeing about whether He is here at all."

"That's not the issue." She angled towards the inn. "Also, I *thought* you were going to bring the Disciples of the Flame to help."

"They can't use their abilities inside another temple," he reminded her. "Also—what if some of the Disciples of the Earth *did* make a sacrifice to Mekan?"

"Then that's their problem, not ours." Laima reached the inn's door and pulled it open. "I don't want you to get into even more trouble, Kelan."

He followed her inside. "What do you think they're going to do to Yala?"

"Since she's not a member of another temple, I imagine they'll handle her as they would a regular trespasser."

Sorry, Yala, he thought. *I'll have to get you out of there later.*

———

Niema continued to make her way through the forest, keeping a steady pace. She stopped to pick fruit that was safe to eat and to relieve herself in the bushes, but otherwise, she walked throughout the day. The trees kept the sun off her face and prevented her from being showered in the mid-afternoon storm, but they also hindered her pace and made it difficult to tell if she'd lost track of the route to the river.

In the end, all she could do was keep going, and pray to Yalet to safely deliver her to her destination.

Sunset arrived too soon. This time Niema had no shelter between her and the oncoming darkness, and as the sun slipped below the treetops, a familiar dread took hold. The light fled, and shadows came to life around her, expelling dark shapes that exuded the foul stench that had become all too familiar to Niema.

"Yalet protect me," she murmured.

As she prayed, the forest answered, rising to push the dead away from Niema. Skeletal birds tangled in vines, kekins swung into thick branches—and yet they kept on coming, as if Niema exuded death and not life.

As if they knew she'd killed Prathen.

Above the trees, a vast shadow fell overhead. *The war drake.*

She ran, panic seizing her, as the dead continued to assail her from above. Kekins with claw-like hands, birds with their bright feathers rotted away, humans—

Two living humans, standing in her path.

No.

Niema put on a burst of speed, her mouth forming prayers to keep the dead at bay. Then she saw the sight she'd hoped for, the gleam of water under moonlight, glistening between the trees.

The war drake's shadow descended, and she gave a final desperate sprint. The ground ran out as Niema skidded to a halt, too late to stop herself from tumbling over the edge into the river.

Hands caught her shoulders before she fell, pulling her back. Niema twisted around, the moonlight illuminating her rescuers: the pair of Disciples of Life who'd escorted her to her place of confinement.

Gasping for breath, she doubled over. "The—dead—"

"Niema," said the Disciple on the left—male, serious-faced, and holding her tightly enough for her arm to bruise. "You escaped."

"Wait. Please." Her words tumbled out, desperate. "The dead are following me. It's not safe."

She straightened and her gaze picked out a campsite near a canoe sitting on the river's edge. *Are they the Disciples that Superior Kralia sent after Yala?*

Rustling sounded, and a dead kekin jumped out of the trees. The Disciples released her shoulders, exclaiming, and Niema ran for freedom.

Niema hadn't moved more than a few handspans before the very undergrowth below her feet came to life, wrapping around her ankles. As she squirmed to free herself, another dead kekin came scampering out of the bushes, its bony tail lashing, its teeth bared.

"I told you." She twisted around, addressing the two Disciples behind her. "The dead—they're everywhere."

An idea hit her. Niema whispered a prayer to Yalet, and

the kekin keeled over, stripped of the unnatural force that had returned it to life. At the same time, the life drained from the tendrils holding her feet. She kicked them away, repeating her prayer.

"Hey!" The second Disciple—female, with her hair styled into a thick knot—came after her, only to come to a halt when the dead war drake descended, its bones gleaming under the moonlight.

"Watch out!" Niema threw herself flat on the ground, uttering an urgent prayer. "Yalet—help us."

The female Disciple spoke a prayer of her own. The war drake's bony claws raked at the air, tangling in vines that moved at the Disciples' command. The trees rustled, the forest itself coming alive to form a barrier between them and the war drake, and despite herself, Niema found herself praying in synchrony with the others. The war drake kept struggling, bony wings beating, claws straining to reach its target.

"This unnatural beast." The male Disciple addressed Niema. "You've seen it before, haven't you?"

"It's a dead war drake," she rasped. "I don't know where it came from."

Branches creaked, the trees pushing against the unnatural force that kept the war drake moving, long after its life had expired.

"You must know where it came from," said the female Disciple. "It's following you, isn't it?"

"I don't know why." Both truth and lie, as she didn't know for certain. "It wants to kill, nothing more. That's how Mekan's magic works. The dead only know how to make more dead. They can't think for themselves."

The female Disciple exchanged glances with her companion. "In that case, you'll come with us."

A thrill of dread raced through Niema's nerves. "Where? Where are you going?"

"We're hunting the Disciple of Death," said the male Disciple. "And since you're here, you can take us to her."

22

The Temple of the Earth wasn't the worst place Yala had been held captive in, but it won a prize for the most irritating. The room the Disciples had put her in was more of a guest room than a prison, with a proper bed and other wooden furnishings, though the lack of windows gave everything a cave-like feel. More comfortable than being stranded on a roof, certainly, and they'd even let her keep her cane—but her patience thinned with every hour that passed.

Novices brought her meals, but kept a wary distance, pushing the food tray through the door and quickly closing it before she had any chance to run. Evidently, word had spread about her abilities—rumour or accurate, she didn't know—but even if she'd managed to get out of the room, she wasn't familiar enough with the temple's layout to run to the exit before she was inevitably caught.

Around early evening, Superior Dovial finally returned. Hearing footsteps, Yala rose to her feet, resting her hand on her cane.

The Superior entered the room and closed the door

firmly behind him. "No fewer than ten of my fellow Disciples are outside the door," he told her. "In case you were considering running."

Yala raised an eyebrow. "I'd take it as a compliment, but one lone person against an entire temple of Disciples is hardly a fair match, even Disciples who find themselves without their gifts."

A muscle ticked in his jaw. "Were you never taught to respect your Superiors? If you want to survive as a Disciple, I suggest you start learning."

"I'm no Disciple." *And you haven't earned my respect,* she added. "Being a Disciple requires one to pledge oneself to a deity, not form a temporary alliance with a god to prevent a city from being annihilated."

Superior Dovial studied her face. "I heard the rumours, but I find it hard to believe that the capital was in such dire straits that the king had to call upon *you* to help instead of the Disciples of the Flame."

"The king was hiding in his palace," she replied. "The Disciples of the Flame were swindled by one of their own. I don't know what rumours you heard, but I *did* prevent Mekan from destroying their temple, and I'd be happy to help you do the same if you give me a chance."

Superior Dovial shifted on his feet as if uncomfortable. "It gives me no joy to keep you here. I will ask the guards to take you to the city jail in the morning, once we've fixed the damage you did in the tunnels."

"What?" Yala's grip tightened on her cane. "Did you see all the blood in that tunnel? Don't you want to know how it got there?"

He drew in a breath. "I don't know what you and the Disciple of the Sky were doing in there, but I can assure you that my people weren't responsible."

"Was I carrying a bloodied weapon at the time?" she questioned. "Was Kelan? Nobody in their right mind would believe we were responsible for all that blood, especially as there were no bodies."

"Nevertheless, I won't allow you to cause any more trouble inside our temple."

"Out of interest," she said, "what exactly does creating a temple entail? I assume it's not as simple as taking a building and filling it with statues and altars."

His response was terse. "That is also a matter for Disciples."

Worth a try. "If the Disciples of the Flame were to send an envoy, would you let *them* look around your tunnels, or would you order them to leave, too?"

"If they refrain from trespassing where they aren't allowed, they won't have anything to worry about." He withdrew from the room. "I shall speak to the guards in the morning."

He wanted to move her to the city jail, did he? She stood a higher chance of being able to get out of there than out of a temple of solid stone, though it'd be a fine thing to end up a wanted fugitive on top of her other supposed crimes.

Maybe when the dead attacked again, the Superior would change his mind, but as night approached, she found her hopes retreating. Had Mekan's followers changed tactics after she and Kelan had found their temple? She'd half expected retaliation, but none had come, and if Trienen was anything like his sister, he'd be scheming, not sleeping.

Yala's thoughts circled with no answers forthcoming. Eventually she slept, waking twice when tremors shook the room and filled the temple with the sound of stone scraping against stone. No screams followed, though, and she fell back asleep without any more visitors.

At dawn, Yala's eyes cracked open to a nervous novice pushing a tray of food and a waterskin into her cell. He squeaked in fright when he saw her watching him and scrambled to his feet, leaving the tray on the floor.

"Relax, I'm not going to attack you," she said, her voice scratchy from sleep. "Is the Superior awake?"

The boy withdrew, closing the door behind him. Yala sighed and went to pick up the tray and waterskin.

As she took a drink, the Superior opened the door and walked in. His shadowed eyes indicated he hadn't slept any better than she had. "You'll be staying here for another day. The city guards, regrettably, have other issues to attend to today."

"What issues?" Suspicion unspooled inside her. "Was there another attack from the dead?"

"No," he answered. "Some disappearances in the local village, as I understand it. The guards have requested our help."

"Disappearances." Her memories flickered back to the mines, and to the farmhouse and village. "The Disciples of Death might be retaliating against us for our discovering their temple. Were the missing villagers by any chance taken underground?"

Superior Dovial shook his head. "The mines are all closed. No tunnels are open."

That doesn't prove anything. "If you let me out of here, I can show you the way to the place where we found the altar."

"You must know that isn't possible," he said. "I will update you when we're ready to move you to the city jail."

"Wherever they were taken, the villagers might not have long to wait for help," she warned. "Generally, obtaining the favour of the god of death involves sacrificing others' lives."

His mouth tightened. "You have personal experience with this?"

"I've never sacrificed anyone," Yala said, "but I've seen Melian do it. She tried to sacrifice me, in fact."

"I see." From his tone, she couldn't tell whether he believed her or not. "I believe it'll be easier if you stay out of this, Yala."

Damn him, she thought. *The Disciples of Death have made another move. And if I don't get out of here, those people will die.*

———

Kelan had no opportunity to help Yala escape the Temple of the Earth until the following morning. The Disciples of the Sky had little sympathy for Yala's situation, even when he pointed out that they'd be glad of her help if the dead attacked again, but no such attacks took place in the night.

The atmosphere at breakfast the next day remained tense.

"Did any of you feel those earthquakes last night?" he asked the other Disciples as they gathered in the inn's common room. "Something's going on underground."

"Something's going on in the village, too," Lakiel remarked. "I heard the servants talking... someone mentioned disappearances."

"Disappearances." Kelan stiffened. "From the village near the mines?"

Near the Temple of Death?

"It's all the guards are talking about, apparently," said Lakiel. "I'm going to ask them if we can help."

Kelan doubted the guards outside the tunnel would be fooled by a diversion twice in a row, but these disappearances might be a reason to look past Yala's supposed crimes in favour of the bigger picture. Did Superior Dovial know of these disappearances? Kelan certainly wasn't welcome at the Temple of the Earth, but when Lakiel and several others left the inn to talk to the guards, Kelan went with them. So did Laima, who stuck close behind Kelan as if she expected him to start trouble again.

The older guard he'd spoken to the other day plainly hadn't had being accosted by a group of Disciples of the Sky on his plan for the morning.

"Yes, there were disappearances," he growled, in response to Lakiel's question. "We've already sent some people to the village. You don't have to get involved."

"Are they going into the mines?" Kelan queried. "Is that where the villagers were taken?"

"We have reason to think they're underground," he said, with obvious reluctance. "That's why we requested the help of the Disciples of the Earth."

"And they said yes?" Kelan raised an eyebrow. "I thought they weren't leaving their temple."

"Didn't you get kicked out yesterday?"

Well... yes. "We had a disagreement, but we have the same goals. So does my friend, but she's been unfortunately detained."

"She's the one who got arrested by the Disciples of the Earth," Lakiel added in disapproving tones. "Kelan, I suggest you stay behind."

"I've been in the mines before, remember? I can show you the way."

"There's no need, if the Disciples of the Earth are going there." The older guard narrowed his eyes at Kelan. "You're lucky not to have been arrested, too, Disciple."

"I wasn't the one who performed a human sacrifice inside one of the mining tunnels." Kelan lowered his voice. "I can guarantee the Disciples have no intention of helping. What if they never show up?"

He grunted. "The Superior gives them orders, not me. There's nothing I can do."

Typical. The guards' hands were tied, he knew, but the villagers' lives would be lost due to the Superior's inaction.

"What's going on over here?" asked a light, feminine

voice. Pehin stepped into view, alongside the sour-faced Disciple of the Earth who'd helped them dispose of the dead the previous day. "Are you volunteering to go looking for the missing villagers?"

"Are you?" Kelan glided to meet her. "I'm surprised Superior Dovial let you leave."

"He didn't," she replied. "We slipped out of the temple while he was talking to the city guards."

"Did you now?" An idea occurred to him. "Did you know a friend of mine is incarcerated inside your temple? Would it be possible for her to slip past the guards too?"

"Depends on what she did." Amusement flickered across her face. "Nice job getting kicked out, by the way."

"She did the same as I did—told the truth." He lowered his voice a little. "Yes, there was trespassing involved, too, but we found evidence of human sacrifice inside the mining tunnel you showed me."

The colour seeped out of Pehin's face. "You found... what?"

Kelan had wondered if she'd been involved, but her obvious terror dispelled that notion. "We found a large amount of blood, which I would guess belonged to the bodies that attacked us by the wall. In response, Superior Dovial expelled me from your temple and arrested Yala."

Pehin gaped at him, her face ashen. "That not right."

"I'm glad someone thinks so." He glimpsed Laima watching them with disapproval, but he pushed on. "Is there anything that might convince your Superior to change his mind?"

"Is Yala really a Disciple of Death?"

"Best ask her that yourself."

"Nice evasion." A hint of a smile returned to her mouth. "All right, I'll help. If I get caught near her cell, I'll come up with a cover story."

"Tell him the guards have offered to take Yala off his hands," he said. "Say that you've promised to escort her to the city jail. I doubt he'll follow you and check."

"You're going to break Yala out of prison?" Laima spoke from behind him, sounding disgusted. "You're unbelievable."

"What's the alternative?" His gaze travelled over the towering cliffs. "Yala will almost certainly be able to find those missing villagers, if they're where I think they are."

Pehin shot him a grin. "On it."

As she hurried off, Laima's glare deepened. "Can you honestly say that you wouldn't have done the same if the villagers hadn't gone missing overnight? You and Yala have been scheming since she arrived."

"Not everyone agrees with Superior Dovial's approach to the situation," he said. "Like Pehin. I can guarantee some of her fellow Disciples will have misgivings, too. Will keeping a Disciple of Death inside their temple do anything to help them get rid of Mekan?"

"You're asking the wrong person," she said. "I'll leave you and your fellow miscreants to dig your own graves."

Laima approached the other Disciples of the Sky. Some of them had returned to the inn, but the others appeared to be having a heated argument over whether to take the guards' suggestion to stay away from the village. With Laima's current mood, he opted not to get involved, and instead found a side street from which to watch the temple.

After a short time, Pehin reappeared at the top of the stairs. She and another Disciple flanked Yala, who was dressed in what appeared to be a novice's cloak. Kelan fought the urge to wave at her, instead gliding up to the rooftops to wait for them to be out of sight of both the temple and the city guards.

"I should have known it was your idea," Yala said when he

dropped down into an alleyway to meet them. "You've been corrupting Disciples, have you?"

"We're capable of corrupting ourselves," Pehin said with a grin. "Except *your* kind of Corruption. You're a Disciple of Death, right?"

"No." Yala shrugged out of the borrowed cloak and tossed it at the startled boy who'd accompanied Pehin. "How long before the Superior realises I'm gone?"

"Whenever he next goes to the jail. It'll be a while, given the missing villagers."

"Missing villagers." Yala's grip tensed on her cane. "Is anyone looking for them?"

"Yes," said Pehin. "Us."

"Are you?" Scepticism filled Yala's voice. "I don't see your Superior falling over himself to offer volunteers."

Pehin chewed on her lower lip. "Most people in the temple don't know anything about what's going on the outside. Superior Dovial is keeping us in the dark, and I've had enough. Right, Hashet?"

Her companion grimaced. "You know how much trouble we might get into? Going out to the tavern through the hidden tunnel is a minor infraction, but this…"

"There's a world of difference between sneaking out to go drinking and searching for captives inside a Temple of Death," added Kelan.

Pehin flinched. "Is that where they are?"

"Almost certainly," Yala answered. "I wouldn't be so keen to throw my life away, if I were you."

"You don't have to come inside the temple," Kelan interjected, feeling sorry for the young Disciples. "We just want to find the villagers, but we don't know the tunnels as well as you. What was the plan?"

"The plan?" Pehin exchanged glances with her fellow Disciple. "Use one of the hidden passages to get to the mines. What's yours? Are you going to fly to the village?"

"If my fellow Disciples want to join me." He gestured in the general direction of the street where he'd left them arguing. "Either of you need me to carry you?"

"I don't like heights." Hashet looked as if she might pass out with her feet planted on the ground, and his companion shook her head, too.

"You can meet us on the ground," said Kelan. "If you're certain. Remember the villagers aren't Disciples. They're completely powerless."

"I know." Pehin sucked in a breath. "If Superior Dovial doesn't catch us on the way, we'll meet you there."

"And if you change your mind, I won't blame you," Yala added.

As they left, Kelan frowned at her. "Were you trying to get rid of them?"

"Maybe." Defensiveness laced her tone. "I know they did me a favour by getting me out, but I don't trust *anyone* in that temple, whether they're on Superior Dovial's side or not."

"Fair." He spied several Disciples of the Sky rising into the air, above the rooftops. "We'll draw less attention if we go with them."

"Unless your people hand me back to Superior Dovial."

"I'll make sure they don't." He extended a hand. "How do you want to do this?"

"The same way as last time." She moved in front of him, folding her arms over her chest with her cane gripped firmly in one hand. "Let's get this over with."

Kelan grasped her arms from behind and took flight in a leap that would have startled anyone who wasn't used to flight. Yala didn't make a sound, and as they rose into the air, Laima spotted them at once.

"Where'd those two Disciples go?" she asked Kelan.

"To meet us on the other side," Kelan answered. "They know all the shortcuts through the mines, but I gave them a fair warning of what they're in for. Are you coming, too?"

"I'm going with the others to help the villagers," she replied. "I'm not going to waste my time looking for imaginary temples."

"Just asking." He scanned her companions and counted four, five, other Disciples. "You know we're on the same side. All of us."

"Agreed," said Yala. "Even Superior Dovial, though I'd appreciate it if you could refrain from turning me in."

Laima pursed her lips. "I told Kelan he's welcome to dig his own grave, and you can do the same."

"I'm sure Trienan's already taken care of that," Kelan remarked, though with little humour. "I wonder… do Disciples of Death bother laying their dead to rest at all?"

"You'll have to ask one," Yala said. "Or consult that accursed book, if I ever find it."

Right. The book. Her mission had slipped his mind, considering how much of a ruckus her arrival in Setemar had caused. For now, they needed to focus on finding the villagers and stopping the Disciples of Death, wherever they might be hiding.

23

"How does one go about creating a temple?" Yala asked Kelan, as they flew over the cliffs. It felt less secure than flying on a war drake, though she'd freely admit her own bias; most people wouldn't be comfortable sitting on the back of a giant winged reptile who would happily eat them. "A regular temple, that is. Not Mekan's."

"Well…" Kelan began after a short pause, evidently not having expected the question. "It depends on the Disciples. They have to find a location that's going to work for all their followers, while fulfilling whatever requirements the deity needs. And then they need to find someone to build it."

"I'm not talking in a practical sense, Kelan," she said. "There's no need for elaborate buildings, as long as the deity listens to you."

"Obviously," he said. "That's what distinguishes Disciples from non-Disciples."

"Yes, but even Disciples can't just point at a random house and declare 'this is a temple now'. Can they?"

"There are other rites involved," Kelan acknowledged. "I

can't say I'm an expert on my *own* temple, though, let alone the others."

"And the Disciples of Death?" She jabbed a finger down at the cliffs. "How'd they figure out how to make their own temple?"

"I assume they used that elusive book of ours."

Right. The book. The centre of all their trouble. If she could rescue the villagers *and* retrieve the book, her own part in this ought to come to an end.

And yet.

When they reached the other side of the cliffs, Kelan touched down next to the mines. Yala tested the muddy ground with her cane and approached the other Disciples of the Sky.

"How many villagers are missing?" When nobody answered, she sighed inwardly. "Like I said, I'm on your side. There are lives at risk here."

One Disciple spoke, haltingly. "Seven. The guards said the tunnels haven't been disturbed recently. They're looking around the village instead."

"Are they sure about that?" Kelan followed Yala's gaze to the upturned cart blocking the mine entrance through which the pair of them had discovered the Temple of Death. "Where else can they possibly have gone?"

"Might've been taken by mercenaries," said a younger Disciple. "Isn't that more likely?"

"The city guards are still collecting reports," added one of the others. "We didn't want to crowd them, but we'll talk to them afterwards."

"Agreed," Laima said. "We'll split up to search the area first."

As the Disciples organised themselves into groups, Kelan moved to talk to Laima. From their body language, they appeared to be arguing. Not wanting to get involved, Yala moved to the mine entrance. The cart didn't look to have been touched since the previous day, but there was bound to be another entrance to the temple somewhere. Didn't all the tunnels form part of the same network?

And just where are the Disciples of the Earth?

Yala watched the Disciples of the Sky organise themselves into groups and split up, and her gaze snagged on the farmhouse she'd spent the night at. Was anyone inside? When she drew nearer, she saw curtains had been pulled over the windows, which struck her as an odd choice during daylight hours. Maybe its owners had been amongst the villagers who'd been take, or they were trying to protect themselves.

A familiar death-scent arose, and Yala's ears pricked at a fluttering sound like small wings beating. Her gaze landed on a bird that had landed on the grass near the farmhouse, its neck bent at an unnatural angle. Shadows coalesced around its wings, which continued to beat.

"Yala…" Kelan glided to a halt beside her. "Where'd that come from?"

"I didn't see." She watched the bird flutter upward in a lopsided dance, her skin prickling. "This is where Mekan's beasts attacked us the other night."

Yala veered towards the farmhouse door, her cane sliding in the rain-slick mud, and spied movement through the gap at the curtain's edge.

A buzzing arose in her ear, like a bloodfly, and resolved into a familiar whisper.

"Yes…"

The voice didn't address her, but she recoiled all the same. *Mekan.*

Kelan sucked in a sharp breath. "You heard that, too, didn't you?"

"Yes." She hadn't even touched the claw. What in the gods'

names was going on in that room? Reaching the farmhouse's door, she gave it a firm shove. "Locked."

Kelan glided forward, extending a hand. "Want me to open it?"

Yala inclined her head. Air rushed from his palm, knocking the farmhouse door inward.

Death greeted them on the other side. Crimson stains smeared the entryway as if someone had been dragged over the floorboards, and a partly opened door on the right revealed a cloaked figure whose face she recognised at once. "Trienan."

The boy's eyes widened when he saw Yala and Kelan. "You... what are you doing here?"

"I should be asking you the same." She advanced on him. "What did you do to the villagers?"

He backed away, tripping over the end of his cloak. On the other side of the door, a number of robed figures gathered around a heap of blood-soaked bodies. Trienan's allies were dressed in clothing that appeared to have been stolen from the Temple of the Earth's laundry room, which might have been laughable if not for the villagers' bodies lying with their throats sliced open, nor the pulsing darkness that oozed around their corpses.

"What the fuck is this?" Yala demanded.

The Disciples of Death—all of whom looked scarcely older than twenty—turned to stare at Yala and Kelan, evidently not expecting the interruption. At their feet, the blood soaking the floorboards mingled with shadows, thick as oil.

"*Yes...*" whispered the god of death. "*More.*"

"You have no idea what you've done, have you?" Shit. So many dead... and worse, they'd made the sacrifices out in the open, not underground.

The nearest Disciple, who was clutching a bloody knife,

came at Yala. She swung her cane at his elbow, breaking his grip on the knife. Kelan seized the weapon and propelled it straight at another would-be Disciple, who fell with a choked cry, her blood mingling with the unfortunate villagers'. Yala's cane cracked into the man's skull, and he slumped downward into the mass of shadows on the floor.

The darkness expanded, and a Disciple vanished with a shriek when a claw-like hand emerged from the shadows and pulled him inward. *Fuck.* Mekan's realm tore open, and Yala glimpsed horror dawn upon the Disciples of Death as they realised that they'd unwittingly trapped themselves in the same room as the Void.

The darkness expanded, creeping towards the door as Yala backed away. She and Kelan made for the exit, while the Disciples panicked and tripped over one another in an effort to escape.

Yala emerged from the farmhouse, gripping her cane. Kelan was close behind her, and as Trienan came sprinting past, Yala snagged his arm. "Don't even think about running. Those people's blood is on your hands."

"Let go of me." He tugged at the sleeve of his robe, his eyes wide and terrified. "This is your fault. If you hadn't interrupted us, Mekan would have spared our lives."

"He doesn't spare anyone, fool." Disgusted, she gave him a shove through the farmhouse's open door, where darkness fed upon the Disciples unfortunate enough to fall into its path.

Behind her, Kelan waved to a pair of Disciples of the Sky, who'd come to see what was going on. "We have a situation."

"What's going on?" asked one of the Disciples.

"The villagers are dead," Yala told them. "Tell your people to stop the search and come here at once."

The Disciple's reply was swallowed by a loud cry, a sound that had haunted her nightmares for years. Her gaze snapped back to the farmhouse, whose walls trembled, muffled screams resonating from within.

Kelan swore. "Is that what I think it is?"

"Yes." Dread coiled around the base of Yala's spine. "A void drake."

The two Disciples of the Sky had stopped, their jaws agape. If they'd been present at the battle in Dalathar, they'd know the last void drake she'd encountered had killed several of Kelan's fellow Disciples and nearly taken Kelan's own life.

"Go on." Kelan lifted a shaking hand. "Fetch the others. We're going to need them."

Everyone in the area would have heard the noise. Some Disciples of the Sky were already gliding over to join them, though they sensibly kept their distance from the farmhouse. Its walls continued to tremble, darkness licking at the underside of the door like the tongue of some great beast.

Kelan faced the other Disciples. "How many of you are armed?"

"All of us," Laima replied. "But that's not enough, is it?"

No. It isn't. Yala closed her eyes and reached for the claw, tracing its edges through the fabric of the pouch.

"Yala… what are you doing?" Kelan asked.

"Negotiating." Her fingers slid across the claw's sharp edge and the shadows answered the call of her blood.

———

When the sun rose, the Disciples of Life did, too. They bound Niema's hands with ropes made of vines and pushed her into the canoe. Then they rowed north, following the river.

The water's current carried them swiftly, covering distance far quicker than Niema had when she'd first left in search of Yala. At the time, she hadn't known how far from home her journey would take her.

Nor how soon she might have to leave again after she returned.

The other Disciples hadn't told her anything except for their names, Kelik and Shetrem, and answered all Niema's questions with monosyllables. They were hunting Yala, she knew, but it'd take days to reach the capital even at their current pace. What was their plan when they arrived? Unanswered queries battered at the inside of Niema's skull, along with a pervasive urgent desire to escape before night fell again.

They rowed upriver for several hours before Niema set eyes on the first non-Disciples she'd seen in days. A man and woman sat inside a small cart pulled by two raptors, following a narrow dirt track.

Niema took in a steadying breath and then whistled between her teeth. The raptors' heads cocked, the cart swaying on its wheels, and the people inside grabbed the edges to keep from losing their balance. Niema ceased her whistling. She didn't want to harm anyone, and the wood-frame cart looked fragile enough to break at the slightest provocation. Realising her intentions, her two captors ceased their rowing.

Yalet forgive me. Niema leapt out of the canoe, staggering when her feet hit the bank. She gave another whistling command, and the raptors pitched forward. The two people inside the cart, thankfully, had the sense to leap clear before their transport tipped over sideways. Another whistle, and one raptor ripped its way free of the wooden frame.

The second ran lopsidedly at the Disciples' canoe, towing the remnants of the broken cart. Hoping it kept her captors occupied for a while, Niema ran up to the freed raptor and whistled. The beast bowed its head, allowing her to climb onto its back. Climbing with her wrists bound was awkward, but she had no time to stop and remove them.

The beast was a head taller than her and well-built, but unlike war drakes, they weren't bred to carry humans. As soon as it lurched into motion, she had to grip its sides with her legs and press her chest against its neck to keep from being flung aside. The rocking motion of the raptor's gait made it impossible for her to concentrate on where she was going, and before long she heard the warning sound of the other Disciples in pursuit.

"Yalet preserve me." Niema whistled, barely keeping her balance as the raptor picked up the pace.

A challenging whistle rang from behind her. The raptor tipped sideways, dislodging her into a bush. Niema tumbled, a sharp sting in her neck warning that she'd landed near a bloodfly nest.

Their humming ignited an idea in her mind. Niema whistled, not at the raptor but at the insects forming a thick, viscous cloud above the bushes.

Triumph rushed over her when the bloodflies surged upward out of the nest and straight at her pursuers. The bulbous creatures were small but numerous, and cries of pain came from the other Disciples. Freeing herself from the bushes, Niema hurried to catch up to the raptor.

She gave a whistled command and then turned her back, exposing her bound wrists. At her instruction, the raptor's blunt teeth sank into the vines tying her hands together and ripped them free.

Shaking off the vines, Niema climbed back onto her steed's back. With her hands free, she could better keep her balance as her mount picked up speed. She kept the river within sight to ensure she was going in the right direction, but her ears picked up the sound of her pursuers before long.

A sharp whistle sounded, and then loud humming that

raised the hairs on her arms. *The bloodflies.* Niema gave a quick command to her raptor to veer sideways off the path, but its feet weren't built for the jungle terrain, and the jolting motion soon had Niema clinging grimly to its neck. A bloodfly's bite stung the back of her hand, followed by another.

Niema whistled, but she couldn't command both her steed and her attackers at the same time. As the humming mass of insects encased her, the raptor ran in a panicked circle, and she lost her balance, rolling into the bushes once again.

Niema lay on her back, breathless. Forcing a whistle between her teeth, she urged the swarming insects to cease their attack.

"You can't escape, Niema," called the male Disciple, Kelik. "Surrender yourself and you won't be in any danger."

Niema lurched to her feet, whistling a command to the raptor, but Shetrem, the other Disciple, let out her own high-pitched whistle.

The raptor veered into Niema's path and knocked her off her feet. Once again, her back slammed into the bushes, and the two Disciples closed in.

"Danger?" she wheezed. "You can't do me any harm. It's against our vows."

"Those are your vows," said Kelik. "Not ours."

What does that mean? Disciples of Life aren't allowed to harm other living creatures. Isn't that a basic tenet?

Niema sat up. Shetren seized her arms from behind, binding her wrists with vines and then applying a second rope vine to her upper arms, too. Kelik seized her and shoved her back into the canoe.

The Disciples climbed in and began to row. Niema sat, head bowed, shoulders hunched. *They're allowed to harm others. Yala is in more danger than I thought.*

As time passed, Niema fell into a stupor, looking up only

when the sound of large wings beating cut through the air. She lifted her head, spying a dark splotch against the sky that she thought at first was a swarm of birds until she made out its vast wingspan.

No. It can't be.

Kelik swore. "What's that beast doing out here?"

Was it really the same one? Niema squinted, her gaze filling in the blanks. Most people would take the war drake for a living one, mistaking shadows for scales, but the dread in her heart told her she looked upon the same beast that had driven her from her home.

Shetrem slowed her rowing, tilting her head back. "Is it following us?"

Niema's heart gave a quiver to see the dead war drake in daylight, although she knew rationally that the god of death's power wasn't dependent upon the sun cycle. The dead didn't need to sleep, though she hadn't seen them during the day since the battle in the capital.

The war drake continued to fly northward, following the course of the river. Even if it wasn't tailing them, they were certainly heading in the same direction … but where?

"It's going somewhere," Kelik said, echoing Niema's thoughts. "Perhaps its master called it back."

"It doesn't have a master." Yala had brought it back, true, but Yala was nowhere near the southern jungles. She was in the capital. Wasn't she?

Shetrem ignored her. "It's bound to Mekan, the same as all His creatures."

"Mekan doesn't have a voice here." Niema's own voice was small. Undoubtedly, she'd brought the god of death into the forest from the mere act of saving Yala's life, but the war drake's behaviour was perplexing to say the least.

What do you want? she thought.

"If it's bound to Mekan, that beast can lead us to the

source of His monsters." Kelik indicated the shadow of the war drake. "It seems you did us a favour by trying to run away, Niema."

"Why?" Niema shivered at the stark satisfaction in his expression.

"We'll follow that beast," Shetrem said. "And it'll take us to its master."

24

Kelan didn't hear the god of death's answer to Yala's request. A wrenching sound echoed from inside the farmhouse, punctuated by screams that drowned out all other noise.

The void drake's sharp teeth ripped through wood and stone alike, its huge head protruding through the roof and into the light. One wing emerged first—thick, leathery, and covered in black-grey scales not unlike a war drake. Also like a war drake's were its claws, curved and sharp enough to flay a human from head to toe. Kelan's shoulder twinged, remembering the pain of his last encounter with those claws.

"Not this time," he murmured, drawing his blade. His fellow Disciples did the same, and by mutual assent, they rose aboveground and formed a semicircle in the air.

"Aim for the eyes," he told the others. "Also, try not to get hit."

Laima made a frustrated noise. "That's not helpful, Kelan."

"Well, it's all I've got." Fear constricted his chest as the beast released a chilling cry, one that conjured up images of oblivion, of a dark pit leading into eternity.

It's not natural fear, thought the part of himself not immobilised by terror. *It's some construction of the god of death's... as if He needs any more advantages than he already has.*

As the beast continued to rip its way through the farmhouse roof, Kelan tried to look for weaknesses instead. The trouble was, the void drake's body was thick with natural armour which left few vulnerable spots to target, and fighting from a distance wasn't an option either. *We should have borrowed spears from the guards. Why didn't we do that?*

The guards themselves were notably absent, and aside from his fellow Disciples, the only other fighter present was Yala. She stood with her feet planted on the ground, one hand on her cane, and the other extended. Shadows curled around her palm, matching the darkness swirling out of the ruined farmhouse.

I hope she has a plan, because I certainly don't.

The beast finally freed its other wing and took flight, opening its maw to reveal rows of sharp teeth. Its oil-black scales gleamed under the daylight, claws raking at the air. Kelan hefted his blade, cold sweat rising on the back of his neck at the mere thought of going close to that creature again.

"Hold and fight," Laima called to the others, her voice uneven. "We have orders. Terethik is on our side."

Right. The god of the sky was on their side ... but was Mekan present within this monster?

Their group scattered as the void drake flew at them. Kelan swung his blade, the metal glancing off the beast's claws. His heart plummeted when a spear-sharp claw swiped perilously close to Laima's shoulder.

"Up there!" she called to the others, rising in flight.

They regrouped, forming a semicircle of sharp blades. The other Disciples had learned a few tactics since the last battle—perhaps on Superior Sietra's instructions—but due to his injury, he hadn't fought in the sky since that disastrous day.

"Where are the guards?" he asked out of the corner of his mouth. "If we get it on the ground, their spears might be able to reach it, but not if they're hiding alongside the villagers."

"What about your friend Yala?" Lakiel held his blade in a shaking hand. "Can't she control that monster?"

Kelan's mouth parted in disbelief—*now* the others were eying Yala hopefully, as if they expected her to come to their rescue.

"The Disciples of Death are the ones who summoned that monster," he told them. "Yala didn't, and I don't think they can control what it does."

The beasts from the Void were something altogether different than the dead that existed in *this* realm, he was sure, but this was not the time to ponder the limits of Mekan's power. The void drake surged upward in a beat of wings, and their group scattered once again. Kelan dodged its claws, but its tail swung around and caught him square in the chest, knocking the air from his lungs. He fell, his vision swimming as he fought to keep his balance in midair.

"Kelan." Laima flew in front of him, her blade flashing, the edge bounced off the beast's scaly foot.

By some miracle, Kelan had kept hold of his weapon, which he gripped hard as he flew at its wing. His strike pierced the sinew from behind—a lucky stab—but its spear-sharp spine came perilously close to his eye and forced him to wrench his blade free, leaving only a shallow wound.

A second Disciple followed Kelan's lead, but void drake's claws flashed, skewering its target in mid-air. Kelan's stomach dropped to see the robed figure impaled on the monster's claws.

Panic washed over him. This wasn't a fair fight. They

weren't warriors, and the beast was no ordinary creature. *Where are the fucking guards?*

His gaze landed on Yala. She *still* hadn't budged, her eyes closed even as the unfortunate Disciple's body hit the ground. What was she doing?

Laima's scream made his head snap up again. The beast's claw had sliced open her arm and blood gushed outward in a crimson trail.

"Hey!" he shouted.

The beast's head turned towards him. It flew, hardly slowed by its torn wing, and he hastened to drop in flight. Extending his arm, he held the blade out as far as it would go. If the beast took his bait and flew lower, he could reach its vulnerable spots without—

The void drake's claws flashed out, tearing the blade loose from his hand, and sending it tumbling into the mud below.

Fuck.

Kelan plunged into a dive, the beast's claws raking at his heels. Picking up speed, he scanned the ground for the blade he'd dropped but instead glimpsed two of his fellow Disciples hiding beneath the cart that blocked the mine entrance. Kelan couldn't say he blamed them in the least, and part of him wanted to join them—if not for Yala standing alone on the path, and for the mental image of her disdain and disappointment if she saw him fleeing. That was enough to convince him to lunge for his dropped sword.

Claws snagged at his cloak, flinging him aside, and Kelan slammed onto his back in the mud. Tasting blood at the back of his mouth, he watched the beast descend for the kill.

Then its head turned to the lone figure standing upright without a trace of fear.

———

Shadows rose from the claw, tugging at Yala's hand, as if trying to drag her into the Void from which it had emerged. Through her half-closed eyes, she saw blackness consume the farmhouse and screeches and cries rang out above as the beast flew in circles around the Disciples, its claws slashing and striking.

"God of death," she whispered, closing her bleeding fingers around the claw's edge. "Take my blood and help me stop this."

A thud resounded as a body fell out of the air, limbs askew, body skewered. Gritting her teeth, she tightened her grip on the claw until its edge sliced deep into her fingers. *Answer me!*

Someone crashed into her. Her eyes flew open, her cane skidding as she lost her balance. Trienan's hands scrabbled to take the claw from her grip, his expression half-crazed.

"Get off me." She punched him in the face with the hand that held the claw, its sharp edge raking across his cheek.

He released a shrill scream, blood pouring from the wound, and the shadows around the claw thickened, drawn to the spilled blood. Yala's fingertips tingled. The claw grew *heavier*, the shadows stretching towards Melian's brother.

A cry from above signalled the fall of another Disciple, whose body hit the ground with a grisly thud. *I have to stop this.*

Yala swung her cane at the boy, knocking him off his feet. He moaned, pressing a hand to the bloody gouge in his cheek. "Don't … please…"

"You opened the Void." Another body fell out of the air. Kelan. *Shit. He'd better not be dead.* "I'll consider sparing you if you tell me how to stop that monster. Can it be controlled, like the dead?"

The boy's mouth gaped. "No. The creature is Mekan's alone."

Damn. She'd killed a void drake with a regular weapon, but she'd been on the back of a war drake at the time. On the ground, she had no reach.

The image of her last flight entered her mind, unbidden. *Don't be absurd,* she told herself. The dead war drake would be long gone by now, decayed to nothing if not destroyed by the Disciples' flames.

Or would it? Mekan's shadows could keep a creature moving far beyond its body's expiration, and while its dead wings might have carried it far away from Laria, a part of her knew instinctively that the beast endured. Maybe the fight and blood loss had addled her brain—or Mekan's madness had wormed His way in there—but she was certain that His creatures wouldn't fly too far from their master.

A tortured cry from above told her the void drake had skewered another Disciple. The cloaked body fell, and Yala dragged her gaze away when Melian's brother jerked upright, a knife in his hand.

Yala seized his knife hand with scarcely an effort, wrenched the blade free, and slashed his throat.

The god of death's attention was like a sharp breeze on the back of her neck, an unseen pair of eyes fixating on hers, and a rasping whisper in her ear. *"You."*

"Bring my steed." She held up the claw, which trailed shadows and blood, and spoke in a clear voice. "Now."

"Blood."

"Yes, blood." Yala's fingertips numbed as she lowered the claw so the shadows could lap greedily at the crimson slash in Trienan's neck. "I've given you blood enough for this. Bring me my war drake."

"Yala." Kelan gasped her name. He'd pushed himself upright, unsteadily. Mud caked the back of his cloak, and his hair was plastered to his face, but he didn't look to be mortally wounded. "Take shelter. There aren't enough of us."

"Not yet." She shook her numb hands and spied odd greyish stains on her fingers, creeping from beneath the bloody cuts. "There's no running. If we flee, the monster will kill the villagers instead."

"Do you want to get ripped to shreds?" His tone rang with defeat. "The others are hiding in the mines."

She opened her mouth and closed it, knowing the scepticism her words would entice. *I called the dead war drake.* And her request had reached its target; her fingers remained numb, her steps unsteady, as if something vital had been sucked out of her. She leaned on her cane for balance as she straightened upright, and Kelan glided to her side.

"Come on." He took her arm and gestured towards the upturned cart in front of the mines, which had moved to create a gap large enough for a person to walk through.

Inside the tunnel crouched several other Disciples, including the two Disciples of the Earth who'd offered to help find the villagers. Yala let Kelan steer her past the cart, where she caught the eye of one of the Disciples.

Pehin's mouth gaped open. "What … what is that?"

"A void drake," Yala said. "That's what'll end up in your temple if your Superior doesn't come back to his senses."

A chilling cry sounded. Kelan released Yala's arm and turned back to the descending beast, which had noticed its victims fleeing.

As he took flight with his blade in hand, Yala gripped the shadow-soaked claw and growled at the deity on the other side. *Why can't I control that thing? Is it alive, or dead?*

Kelan swerved, dodging the void drake's claws. Her heart plunged as he dropped in flight, but he caught his balance. He landed on his feet next to the mine, blood soaking one side of his face, and called to the Disciples inside. "We're outnumbered. Can one of you go and ask your Superior for help?"

"He'll never agree," Pehin said. "If that monster follows us, we're dead."

"You're dead if you stay here, too," Yala snapped. "You volunteered, didn't you? Do you want to watch everyone get slaughtered?"

The void drake landed outside the mine, the impact sending clods of mud flying into the air. Yala darted behind the cart to avoid being impaled, but one swipe of its claw sent their shelter flying. The cart shattered into wooden shards, and the beast's claws snagged the second Disciple of the Earth, yanking him off his feet.

Pehin screamed, "Hashet!"

"Pehin!" Hashet twisted and screamed, hands scrabbling at the ground as the beast dragged him by the leg. "Setem, help me!"

The ground gave a sudden tremor. Yala staggered back into the mine, and the beast took flight with a beat of its wings.

Hashet screamed. An odd blue glow suffused his face and hands, dazzling Yala's eyes.

"Setem!" He cried out the name of his god, his gaze rapturous. "I felt Him! He's back!"

He was still grinning when the void drake descended once again. Sharp claws pierced through the crown of his skull, ripping his head in two. Red misted the air, and the glow faded like an extinguished candle flame.

"Hashet!" Pehin screamed, her voice raw. "Hashet!"

"Be *quiet*," Yala hissed at her companion, trying to see where Kelan had gone. He'd flown out of the mine's entrance, dodging the void drake's gore-drenched claws—but it was the second winged shape in the sky that caught her attention.

When Kelan landed beside her, Yala whispered, "Can you distract that monster for a minute? I've got this."

"You've got what?" Understanding dawned when she jabbed her bloody hand at the approaching shadow, which had taken on a distinctly winged shape. "All right."

Kelan flew out into the open, circling the beast, and Yala watched with her heart in her mouth. The void drake slashed, catching his arm, yet the dark shape in the sky grew closer and closer.

It's really here. Relief swamped her, enough to make her forget the pain in her leg and the odd numbness in her hands. She felt as light as air as she ran out of the mine to her steed.

The dead war drake's body had decayed, leaving nothing but scale and bone. Shadows had replaced sinew and muscle, oozing out of gaps in its scales, but its sheer size still rivalled the void drake, and by a miracle only the god of death could provide, the beast had endured.

When its claws touched down in the mud, she was ready. Using her cane to gain leverage, Yala clambered to sit between its shoulders. Shadows swirled upward like smoke, both from the beast and from her own hands. Her heart gave a momentary lurch—an acknowledgement of the precariousness of her perch upon a creature that ought by rights no longer be able to fly—but Kelan's descent warned that the void drake had spotted the new arrival.

Yala gave a silent command to her steed. In a wingbeat, the war drake flew at the void drake. Their collision rattled every bone in the war drake's fragile form, but the shadows held firm, its body impossibly sturdy beneath Yala's legs. She reached for her dagger and then flattened herself against the war drake's back as the two beasts clashed, claw scraping against claw, bone against bone, scale against scale.

Yala clung to her steed, gasping, "Up! Fly up!"

The war drake released the void drake and surged upward, the second beast flying in pursuit. With another command, she urged her steed to change direction, its claws raking across the void drake's face. One eye burst in a shower of crimson.

Kelan's blade skewered the beast's wing from behind, ripping through the sinew and eliciting a screech of agony and fury. He caught her eye with a grim nod and pulled the blade free, trailing dark blood.

Bolstered, Yala urged the dead war drake to press its advantage. Its claws scraped against the void drake's scaly hide; the beast's retaliatory strike caused her dead steed's bones to rattle again. Shadows oozed out, and Yala was forced to flatten her body and grip the war drake's bony neck with both hands.

The war drake flew wide, tilting on one side, and the rush of flight ensnared her. Once again, she reached for her dagger, and as the war drake flew towards its adversary, she flung her weapon.

Her knife missed the beast's eye by a mere finger span. Its retaliatory swipe jarred her steed's bones, her injured leg giving an aggrieved twinge. An unpleasant thought hit her— if the war drake took too much damage, would it simply fall apart? Yes, the shadows might hold it together, but that didn't mean she'd survive if her steed collapsed underneath her.

"Yala!" Kelan held up her dagger. She flew towards him with a nod of thanks, leaning over the war drake's side to retrieve her weapon.

Wheeling around, she took aim, and this time she didn't miss. Her blade plunged into the beast's other eye, and her steed's claws followed, plunging straight through its skull.

The void drake fell, a heavy weight of bone and scale striking the ground with a crash that was surely felt throughout the entire village.

Yala clung to her steed, her vision swimming. For a dazed

moment, she imagined that she might blink and see her squad running towards her. Waiting for her to land.

Her eyes cleared, but her squad made no appearance. She was alone, clinging to a dead beast in a mockery of flight. Darkness encroached on her vision as she brought the war drake to land, breathing hard, her body spent.

When she next looked up, the other Disciples of the Sky had come out into the open. Warily they approached, keeping their distance from both Yala and the fallen monster. *Right. They think my steed might attack them.*

With reluctance, Yala swung her good leg over the war drake's side and slid down to the muddy ground. The impact brought a jolt of pain and unsteadiness that caused her to stagger, grabbing for the nearest solid surface, which turned out to be the war drake's bony leg.

Kelan landed beside her. "Yala—are you all right?"

"I'm fine." She let go of the war drake and willed herself not to pass out. "The Void…"

"Never mind the Void." He eyed the war drake. "Is that monster under your control?"

"Yes." She spied several other Disciples flying downward, but only Kelan had dared to get near the war drake. "You can go."

"That's nice," said Kelan.

"Not you." She pointed at the war drake with a shaky finger. "Better keep your distance."

Kelan peered at the monster's empty eyes. "Has it been flying around Laria since the battle in the capital?"

"Must have been," she murmured. "I didn't expect it to come back."

"Yes, you did." Kelan gave a slight smile. "You know, we're going to have a harder time proving you aren't a Disciple of Death after this."

2 5

After the incident with the war drake, Viam didn't know what to expect from the king. Nobody in the palace administrative building knew any more than she did about his supposed plans to rebuild the army. After Saren's warning, she knew another visit to the Temple of the Flame was out of the question, and besides, *they* wouldn't know the king's plans.

Had Rafragoria made another move against Laria, or was this more of a preparatory decision in case of another incident in the capital? The latter seemed more likely, but between that and the Disciples of Life's apparent pursuit of Yala, Viam found herself unable to rest.

She woke at dawn with the burning desire for action, which to her, meant the library. This time she had a clear aim in mind: the Disciples of Life. While Yala had befriended one, Niema had left the city long ago and had likely been as cagey with her secrets as most other Disciples Viam had met. There was no dedicated section of the library on the Disciples, but they'd been entwined with Laria's history from the start, and surely the Disciples of Life were no different.

Viam selected a stack of books from the history section and settled down to read. She was swiftly drawn in, yet no mentions of the Disciples of Life occurred in any accounts of Laria's founding. The first time, she thought the omission unintentional. The second, too. By the third, she was sure there was something amiss.

Weren't they here from the start? She took note of every mention of the other Disciples, growing more and more baffled. The Disciples of the Flame hadn't been a cohesive order in those days, but they were extensively documented for their role in establishing King Larial's government. Even the Disciples of the Sea, who were no longer present in Laria, had calmed the oceans to make it possible for subsequent waves of settlers to cross the turbulent seas between their nation and Rafragoria. The Disciples of the Earth were responsible for building the first cities, the Disciples of the Sky for their help clearing the land for farming—but not a single mention of the Disciples of Life. What was she supposed to make of that?

Viam jumped out of her seat when she saw Brenat standing in front of a shelf, watching her curiously. "Brenat. I'm not late for work, am I?"

"No. Sorry I startled you." Brenat stepped forwards to pick up one of the discarded books. "What are you reading?"

All excuses fled Viam's mind. "I was reading up on…"

"The role of the Disciples in the founding of Laria?" Brenat read the back of the title she'd picked up. "Rather dense for this early hour, isn't it?"

Viam shrugged. Not to be deterred, Brenat picked up another book she'd discarded. "Want me to put these back? Were you looking for anything in particular?"

Another shrug. "I'll put them back. I was just… curious."

"About the Disciples?" Brenat began stacking books, ignoring Viam's protests. "I'm sure you'll find what you need somewhere. There are more books here than anywhere else in Laria combined, including the Temple of the Flame."

Noting her reaction to the last part, Brenat tilted her head. "Is this to do with why you were visiting their temple?"

Viam found herself offering part of the truth. "I considered joining the Disciples of the Flame."

"*Joining* them?" Brenat fumbled and almost dropped the stack of books in her arms. "Why would you do that? They're as dull as paint."

Viam picked up two books without looking at Brenat. "Some would say the same of me."

"Who?" Brenat snorted. "Someone who didn't see you wrangle a war drake, I'm guessing."

Viam slid the books back into place on the shelves, heat rushing to her face. "I've never liked how the Disciples hoard information. If I want to study the Disciples' history, why should I have to become a member of their order?"

"Oh, now you're making sense." Amusement laced Brenat's voice. "You want to pledge yourself to a deity to get access to His library?"

"It's the Disciples' library, technically, not Dalathik's." Viam picked up two more books and returned them to their shelves.

"I thought that was the same thing," said Brenat. "The Disciples are compelled do what Dalathik tells them, aren't they?"

"Yes, but He doesn't talk to them directly."

Brenat gave her an odd look. "Isn't that normal? I don't know much about the Disciples, but I think we'd have a wildly different relationship with their gods if Dalathik lived in their temple."

True enough. The gods didn't communicate directly with humans—except, of course, for Mekan.

"Maybe." Viam returned the last book to its place on the

shelf. "Though I've heard the Disciples of Life receive actual visions from their deity."

Did they hear Yalet's voice? Might there be any similarities with the way Mekan communicated with His followers? Strange, for two deities so diametrically opposed to share any traits at all. Including a lack of information, which she might have found more curious than frustrating if not for the Disciples of Life's supposed pursuit of Yala.

"They also live in the jungle, far from human contact, don't they?" Brenat said. "Don't tell me that's your next idea."

"No." What could she say? That they were trying to arrest a friend of hers? They shouldn't even have the authority to do so, but the Disciples had always operated outside of the regular laws. "Have they ever come to the city before?"

"I think some of them visited once, but that was before old King Tharen died…" Brenat trailed off, peering out of the nearest window. "Your clawed friend is back."

A familiar muffled screech caught Viam's ears. "Oh, no."

She moved to the window, where two guards led the war drake by a chain looped around its neck. At least they'd put a muzzle on its mouth this time, but its growl emanated displeasure. What were they doing, giving it a tour of the palace grounds?

"I'm going to see what's going on."

Leaving Brenat staring out the window, Viam ran for the door, hoping she'd be able to stop the king's guards from losing any more limbs.

———

Despite Yala's victory over the void drake, the atmosphere among the surviving Disciples of the Sky remained as tense as the air before a storm. The farmhouse's ruin scarcely covered the lingering traces of Mekan's presence, and while the Void hadn't grown any bigger since she'd slain the monster, Yala knew it was only a matter of time before another beast came out.

Nobody wanted to go near the farmhouse and check. The Disciples of the Sky had lost half their number and half the rest were injured, and she could hardly blame them for wanting to tend to their dead instead of watching for more horrors. Kelan, who was as shaken as the rest, offered to carry her back into Setemar to tend to her wounds.

"I'm not injured." Her bleeding fingers no longer hurt, in fact. "You are."

"They're just scratches." Blood continued to seep from a cut on his forehead, while his sleeves were sliced to ribbons. Likely his cloak had fended off some of the damage, though it wasn't as tough as drakeskin. "Ah—there are the city guards."

Yala's gaze went past the Disciples, who'd begun to gather their dead, and spied a group of guards congregating. They made no effort to approach the Disciples, as if they expected to be reprimanded for hiding among the villagers and letting others die in their place. "Cowardly fuckers."

"What should we do with him?" Kelan indicated the body of Melian's brother near the open door to the farmhouse.

"Good question." Yala dragged her gaze from the guards and poked Trienan's body with her cane, nudging him onto his back. His stolen cloak was sopping wet with mud and water, but she made out a distinctly square shape in one pocket.

"Is that what I think it is?" Kelan watched as Yala fished out a small book with a rain-damp, weathered cover. "The book you were sent here to find?"

The cover bore no title nor any markings. Though damp, the surface held the tough, scaly texture of drakeskin. "It just might be."

Yala slid the small book into the pouch at her waist, shivering when her numb fingers brushed against the void drake's claw. *What is happening to me?*

Melian's book might contain answers, but she'd have to wait to assuage her curiosity. If this was indeed the book the Disciples of the Flame had sent her to retrieve, her quest here was over, yet leaving Setemar seemed a selfish endeavour. Mekan's realm remained open, and the monstrous corpse of the void drake was a beacon for anyone else who might want to summon the dead. If any of Trienan's allies had survived.

"Do you want me to take you back to Setemar?" Kelan asked her. "We're asking for volunteers to take our dead back to Skytower, but some of us will have to stay. I'll be with the latter."

"I'll go to Setemar," she decided. "I'd like to find out why this book caused the Disciples of the Flame to entrust *me* of all people to find it."

Their flight was short, tense, and neither of them spoke until they landed outside the inn and Kelan released her. "You really should get someone to look at your wounds."

Yala stepped away from him, fingers clumsy on her cane. "I'd rather be certain that your fellow Disciples aren't intending to hand me straight back to Superior Dovial."

"Yala, you slew a Void drake with your own hands," he said to her. "Nobody will dare touch you."

"We'll see." She tried not to think too hard about how natural it had felt to call directly to Mekan, to summon the dead war drake to her side. "What are you going to do?"

"I'll help move the bodies," he said. "I imagine Superior Sietra would prefer them not to be manipulated by Mekan."

Yala's pragmatism told her that handling corpses with Mekan's shadows still at her fingertips would end badly, but more worrying was that her hands kept twitching whenever she looked at the blood streaking Kelan's face. She clenched her fist pointedly and said, "You should put a bandage on, too."

"Yes, Captain."

She grunted but let his use of her old title slide. "Come on."

Nobody in the downstairs room of the inn raised an objection to Yala's entrance, but most were too busy binding broken limbs and stemming the bleeding from lacerations inflicted by the monster's claws. She retrieved some bandages from the first-aid kit someone had brought into the room and passed one to Kelan.

From what Yala could see, the Disciples had a basic idea of how to tend to wounds, but the real problem was the shock. Some of them wouldn't have been in a real battle before, and while the inn's staff did their best to help, she counted at least two Disciples sitting in chairs, their gazes fixed at a point somewhere the distance.

This is going to be a problem. The Disciples of the Sky weren't soldiers, although Laria's militaristic ways would have seeped into their education as novices. The way they'd fought the void drake had been proof enough that they'd been trained in the use of weapons, but they didn't work together, not like her squad had. If another void drake attacked—or, gods forbid, more than one of them—they'd find themselves in serious trouble.

Yala waited for Kelan to go and help with the injured before she had a closer look at the wounds on her fingers. The shallow cuts would heal quickly, but even after washing her hands, her fingertips retained a grey tinge. If this was an effect of her use of Mekan's power to call the dead war drake to her side, she fervently hoped it was temporary. After she'd wrapped bandages around her fingers, she went to leave.

The door opened first, and more Disciples entered,

carrying large sacks that Yala inferred must contain the dead Disciples who'd fallen in the battle.

"You're still here?" Laima spotted Yala near the door. "I thought you left."

To her alarm, a familiar tingling sensation sprang to her fingertips. *Not the time, Mekan.* "Yes, I'm here. I was told this was the place for Disciples to seek medical attention."

"You don't look injured."

Yala held up her hands to reveal the bandages she'd used to cover her greying fingers. "Be glad it's not worse, for your own sakes."

"She's not wrong," Kelan said from behind her. "Someone needs to send an update to Superior Dovial. Laima, do you want to come with me?"

Laima's mouth thinned. "He won't want to hear the news from you, Kelan."

"Do the others look in any state to offer a report?" Kelan looked beseechingly at Yala. "Right?"

"I'm not going to give him the chance to lock me up again," Yala informed him. "I'll stay here."

"I thought so." His eyes lingered on the pouch at her waist. "Let me know if you find any… new insights."

Right. The book. She had no intention of reading Melian's tome in the same room as a group of hostile Disciples, so she nodded. "Good luck with the Superior."

While Kelan and Laima departed for the Temple of the Earth, Yala left the inn and headed back to Vanat's old house. Reading a book didn't strike her as the best use of her time, but she was none the wiser as to how to close the Void without the help of a Disciple of the Flame or Life.

Perhaps the book would shed some light on the solution, but even if not, part of Yala was curious to know how this innocuous tome had led a man to betray his nation—and had led the Disciples of the Flame to betray him in turn.

After closing the door to Vanat's house, she sat in the battered old armchair and cracked open the aged drakeskin spine. Her immediate impression was that the book was a translation, written in an older Larian script that was made harder to read by the fading ink and occasional splash of rain on the pages. Yala surmised from the introduction that the text's author was a scholar from the early Parvan Empire, and that he'd been writing before Laria had even existed as a nation.

"This is the fifth volume of the travels of … Mavilangran." She stumbled over the unfamiliar name. "What is this, a travel journal?"

The answer was yes, and Yala had scarcely read two pages before she'd developed a headache. Mavilangran's style was tediously verbose, focusing mostly on the minutiae of his day-to-day routine while aboard a ship instead of the more interesting aspects of his voyage to find and explore distant nations.

Reading is Viam's pastime, not mine, Yala thought. There had to be something relevant in here, but somehow Mavilangran made an encounter with an angry sea drake sound as dry as a rain-starved field.

Impatient, Yala began skimming through the pages, and then stopped when she laid eyes upon a hand-drawn map. The familiar lines formed the continent of Laria and the surrounding islands all the way up to the Rafragorian peninsula, but neither was labelled as such. *Is this one of the first maps of Laria ever drawn?*

She turned the page. *In a storm, we were cast upon an unfamiliar shore,* she read. *There, we found an unexpected settlement, inhabited by individuals who claim to be dedicants of the Hierarch of Bone, the One of Shadows, the Creeping Void. I have never seen the like in all my travels...*

Recognition thrummed within Yala. Her fingers slipped

on the pages as she fumbled to the next page, to reveal the hand-drawn sketch of an island.

Yala lifted her head, her heart beating erratically as unwelcome images flashed behind her eyes. A temple, nestled within the jungle, upon an island wreathed in fog.

Except with one major difference. The island described in the journal had been inhabited by a thriving people, and despite the Temple of Death's dominance, the jungles had brimmed with life, not death and destruction. These people had lived full lives in the shadow of death—before Mekan had turned on them.

Yala continued to read Mavilangran's accounts of his interactions with the island's people, and his observances on their relationship with the god of death. He didn't refer to Mekan by name, merely titles like The One of Shadows or the Hierarch of Bone. Their leader, too, referred to as the Hierarch, and his accounts of the man made him seem surprisingly open to sharing his temple's secrets with a strange foreign scholar who didn't understand the language.

The Shadowed One takes payment in blood, in the sacrifice of the self and others, Mavilangran wrote. *As strange as it might seem, these people have learned to give what they can without succumbing to death themselves. It is quite remarkable.*

Yala lifted her hands, driven to lift the bandages to expose the grey beneath. Something had *changed* during the battle, and yet she still lived and breathed. Who was to say it was impossible to live in a place that seemed designed for the dead alone?

A sudden tremor shook the room. Yala sprang to her feet, the book sliding from her lap. *What was that? Not Mekan again?*

She listened out but didn't hear any screams. Rattled, she picked up the book again, finding she'd jumped several entries ahead to the point where Mavilangran had left the island behind. He and the inhabitants had parted on pleasant terms, or so Yala gathered.

The next entry, however, brought the scholar to another unfamiliar shore. This one was even more familiar.

"He did come to Laria." The descriptions of its long beaches and wild forests didn't quite fit with Yala's impressions of the northern shore, but she knew enough to be aware the continent had been wild and untamed before King Larial had arrived with the first settlers.

Except…

We met with some friendly but wary locals, she read. *They make their homes within the forest and claim to have a deep reverence for all life.*

Yala sat, the book falling open in her lap, her mind reeling.

The man had met with the Disciples of Life. Niema's people, it seemed, had been present on the continent before Laria had even existed.

26

While Kelan's instincts told him to avoid the Temple of the Earth after his prior banishment, he suspected that the other Disciples would downplay Yala's role in vanquishing the void drake when they reported the incident to the Superior if he wasn't present to remind them that she'd saved all their lives. That fact alone might prevent her from being imprisoned again, so he brushed off the others' furious stares as he entered the temple and launched straight into his explanation of the attack.

"A Disciple of Death saved us?" Superior Dovial's voice was brittle, his eyes haunted. "No, she simply wanted to distract us from her escape from custody."

"Trust me, everyone at the battle saw her kill that void drake," Kelan told him. "If not for her, we'd all be dead."

"He's right." Laima spoke grudgingly. "We didn't have a chance. And the Void is still open. None of us can close it, including Yala."

An uneasy silence ensued before Superior Dovial spoke

haltingly. "The Disciples of the Flame—I'm told you paid them a visit."

"They aren't coming." Kelan knew he should be trying to regain Superior Dovial's trust by allowing him to take control, but he was conscious that every moment the Void remained unwatched, it might spit out another horrifying monster. With Yala exhausted from the last battle, they stood little chance of surviving another. "We need to watch the Void and strike instantly against anything that emerges."

Superior Dovial lowered his gaze. "If I order my Disciples to leave the temple, I'm condemning them to death."

"Would you sacrifice the lives of the villagers instead?" Kelan tried and failed to keep the impatience out of his tone. "They're the first people who'll be targeted, and too many of them have already died."

"We'll have them evacuated and brought to Setemar," said Superior Dovial. "If we had access to our deity, we would be able to offer more help, but this is all we can do."

"You can fight, can't you?" He indicated the blade at his waist, stained to the hilt with the creature's blood. "Our own powers can't physically injure anyone, but we manage."

"Nevertheless." The Superior's jaw tightened. "I am sorry for those who were lost, but we have no other options."

Coward. He bit back the word, aware that most people would have made the same decision. The Disciples of the Earth weren't trained in combat, let alone to fight monsters like the void drake. Behind their Superior, some of the other Disciples exchanged urgent whispers. Kelan scanned the chamber and spied Pehin lurking near the back. She'd seen her friend Hashet killed right in front of her, which was bound to put her off any more excursions into daylight, but... come to think of it, hadn't Hashet claimed that he could sense his deity moments before he'd died?

Of course, there was a chance he'd imagined the whole

thing as a result of his terror, but how to explain the tremors that had shaken the earth when Hashet had faced the monster, or the bluish glow around his hands that resembled the Superior's dying altar?

"I think you should ask for volunteers," Kelan said to Superior Dovial. "You might be surprised. Not all your people want to hide underground."

A flush darkened Superior Dovial's skin. "They obey my orders."

"They trust you to keep them safe," he corrected. "What if the next opening to the Void shows up inside the temple? There's already at least one inside the mines."

"You've crossed too many lines already, Disciple," said Superior Dovial. "If your people want to give their lives in tribute, I respect their decision, but it's not for me or mine. Nor will we ally with Disciples of Death. That's my final word."

Damn him, Kelan thought. *He* is *a coward, and he's going to get more people killed.*

As Kelan opened the temple's doors, a violent tremor ran underfoot. Teeth rattling in his skull, Kelan glided above the steps, hearing the tremor continue to reverberate in the temple's walls. Even the statues of Setem on either side of the door trembled, and he had a hard time believing Superior Dovial hadn't noticed. He knew a losing battle when he saw one, however.

Kelan suspected he wouldn't find Yala at the inn and glided straight to her friend's old apartment. He knocked on the door and heard the answering thud of her cane hitting the floorboards.

Yala appeared in the doorway. "Oh, it's you."

"Found anything useful yet?"

She held up the book in a bandaged hand. "Turns out it's a historical journal, not an instruction manual for Corruption."

"Is it?" He followed her into the house, which consisted of a single room not unlike the one she'd left behind in the capital. "Written by whom?"

"An eccentric scholar from the old Parvan Empire." She took a seat in a battered armchair and flipped open the book. "It did shed some light on how King Tharen found out about the island. Look at this."

"He visited the Temple of Death when it was inhabited?" Kelan peered at the pages Yala showed him, which were covered in hand-drawn illustrations of what appeared to be tunnels or chambers fanning out from a tower-like construction in the centre. "Is that the island? The layout looks like the Temple of the Earth."

"Does it?" She held up the pages with bandaged fingers, her brow scrunching. "I don't see the resemblance, but I never saw the island when it was anything more than a ruin."

"The people this scholar met were all acolytes of the god of death?"

"Apparently so," Yala answered. "That's not all. He visited *Laria*, afterwards, and met the forerunners of the Disciples of Life."

Kelan blinked. "People lived here before King Larial?"

"Looks that way." Yala flipped the page to show another hand-drawn map. "I've never been a keen historian, but the stories they tell us about Laria's founding certainly don't mention anyone was already here."

"Interesting." He had to concede that the drawings did indeed resemble Laria's coastline. "If the book's not an instruction manual for Corruption, why are the Disciples of the Flame so desperate to retrieve it?"

"I imagine they don't want all their hard work keeping the island hidden from public knowledge to go to waste."

Hard work. Like murdering the king. Kelan glanced

down at the floorboards. "I assume you felt the earthquake, too?"

"Yes." Her lips pursed. "Is Superior Dovial still refusing to let his people leave?"

"Regrettably so," said Kelan. "He claims that the only way to save the villagers is to evacuate them from their homes, and he's otherwise content to wait until the temple collapses."

"Might be the quickest way to be rid of him." Yala's tone sobered. "I'm starting to think I shouldn't have made such an effort to dissuade the Disciples of the Flame from sending assistance."

They can get rid of the Void. Then again, so could the Disciples of Life. "Do you intend to give them the book?"

"When I've finished reading it." Rapping on the front door caused her to rise upright. "Who's that?"

"No idea." Kelan moved to answer the door and was greeted with Laima's scowling face on the other side. "Oh, hello."

"I followed you," she said before he could ask the obvious question. "Since you're supposed to be at the inn."

"Where else could I talk to Yala about sensitive matters?" he asked. "I meant Corruption."

Laima sighed. "The others are completely demoralised, Kelan. As you managed to get yourself kicked out of the Temple of the Earth, I think you should be the one to go back to Skytower to ask Superior Sietra for advice. Don't you agree?"

"This time I left of my own volition." When she glared at him, he added, "I'll go, but if you want someone to give instructions…"

Yala tensed. "Don't look at me."

"Why not?" he queried. "Haven't you been in this kind of situation in the army?"

"We suffered defeats, but nothing this hopeless," she responded. "Also, the other Disciples just saw me command a dead war drake. Why in hell would they want to take orders from me?"

"She has more sense than you do," Laima told Kelan. "What are you thinking?"

He shrugged. "I just thought they might want to hear a motivating speech from the person who brought down that monster."

"Motivation?" Yala echoed. "If anything else comes out of the Void, we're all fucked. Sorry to be the bearer of bad news."

"Best not tell them *that*." He lifted a hand in farewell. "I'll be back."

He left the house on Laima's heels, and she gave him a weary glare. "I wish you'd *think* for once. You had the chance to regain Superior Dovial's favour and you insisted on needling him again."

"Would that have worked?" He doubted so. "His only plan involves staying in the temple indefinitely. I can't see that strategy ending in anything other than his own demise and that of his fellow Disciples."

"What else is he meant to do?" she asked. "We tried fending that beast off and half of us ended up dead."

I know. There had to be another option, but he was woefully short on ideas. "One of the Disciples of the Earth claimed to have been able to reach Setem when we were fighting the void drake."

"Which Disciple?"

"The one who was killed. Not Pehin, her friend, Hashet." He thought back to the battle. "I'm sure the ground trembled when he called Setem's name."

"It just trembled five minutes ago, Kelan," she said. "If that has anything to do with the god of the earth, only His Disciples will know."

True. "All right. I just thought it was worth mentioning."

"Maybe not to Superior Dovial," said Laima. "It's hardly going to help convince him to volunteer any assistance if we remind him that one of the two Disciples who did come to help in the battle ended up slaughtered."

No... but if he was right, how did Hashet manage to reach Setem when nobody else can?

———

Niema's captors continued to row upriver. The war drake had disappeared into the distance, but the river only flowed in one direction. They didn't need to be able to see their target to know they were heading the right way.

Towards Yala.

"What are you going to do her?" Niema asked the other Disciples after a long stretch of silence. "Why do you want to hunt down someone who's done nothing to you?"

"She is an agent of Corruption," said Kelik. "We cannot let Mekan gain access to this realm. If you do not agree, you are Mekan's agent, too."

"She saved my life." Talking to her captors was like conversing with a bird taught to repeat only a small handful of phrases, but Niema found herself compelled to persist. "There might be other Disciples of Death out there who are far more dangerous. Like Melian."

"Yala Palathar is the only Disciple of Death known to us," said Shetrem. "She will be judged by Yalet Herself. Should she resist, we will enact Yalet's judgement upon her with our hands."

"You can't mean you'll kill her." Cords of dread tightened

around Niema's heart. "Whatever happened to the vows you swore to the god of life?"

Even if they'd sworn different vows to the ones she knew, Niema didn't understand how hunting an innocent woman could possibly be Yalet's desire.

"We swore to serve the god of life's command," said Kelik, "and we will do whatever is necessary to scourge Corruption from this world. Including, if necessary, taking the lives of those who seek to destroy Her."

Gods. Was this not the first time they'd killed in Yalet's name? "This isn't what Yalet wants. It can't be."

Neither Disciple replied. Their brief conversation was over, and they lapsed into silence once more.

The war drake didn't reappear until dusk. The Disciples slowed their relentless rowing and picked out a spot on the bank to stop for the night. They did not undo Niema's bonds, although they did offer her water and some dried fruit to chew on. Niema was lightheaded with hunger and exhaustion, yet her mind refused to rest. The night would be her best chance to escape.

The Disciples prayed to Yalet, urging the nearby trees to form a shield around them to protect against the dead. *Or to keep me caged,* Niema thought, watching the sky for the inevitable moment the dead war drake made a reappearance.

Soon the beast circled overhead, the moonlight reflecting off its smooth bones. *Why is it following me?* Did the beast somehow remember her after all? So much information concerning the god of death remained shrouded in mystery, and while it was certainly possible that the beast was leading them to Yala, Niema trusted that Yala wouldn't have called upon Mekan again unless she felt she had no choice in the matter. Moreover, if she'd been pushed to use Corruption to challenge another Disciple of Death, Niema's captors would have far more to worry about than Yala's supposed transgressions.

Had Yala received Niema's warning? Even if she had, was it possible to outrun a pair of Disciples of Life who were determined to enact their deity's will at any cost? Niema didn't know, and her growing doubts encompassed her own fate. Would her captors go as far as to kill one of their fellow Disciples if they believed it would rid the realm of Mekan's influence?

The war drake slipped out of sight beyond the vines that formed a tent around their camp. Niema glanced at her captors, who lay on their sleeping mats, unmoving. Then she sat up, the movement awkward with her hands bound. She whispered a prayer, urging the vines to part to let her climb out. They did so, and she held her breath at the rustle of leaves, but the other two Disciples didn't stir.

Niema climbed out of the makeshift camp and scanned the surrounding forest for any signs of a living creature. Spying a nightwing bird, she whistled a command and the bird flitted over to her. She led the way, skidding down the bank towards the canoe, and then gave another faint whistle. The bird's sharp beak pecked at the rope-like vines binding her hands until they loosened enough for her to shake herself free.

Niema climbed into the canoe and grabbed an oar. Then she began to row, holding her breath at every splash and thud as the oars scraped against stones on the riverbed. She kept up a faint whistle that urged the bird to follow her, yet doubts whispered in the back of her mind. Yalet would keep her safe from any predator, but Her abilities only extended to the living, not the dead.

With each passing moment, Niema found her hands clenching tighter on the oars, her throat constricting. She rowed harder, as though to outrace her own panic, but darkness encroached on the edges of her vision and her breath rasped in her throat. Even her prayers to Yalet tasted sour on her tongue. Only the motion of the oars—left, then right— kept her from giving in to the impulse to curl in on herself like a wounded animal.

Niema's heart gave another quiver of dread when she glimpsed the war drake's shadowy outline against the light of the moon.

"What do you want with me?" she whispered.

The war drake gave no reply, of course. Neither did the god of death, though Yala knew His power alone kept those wings beating.

Mekan… and Yalet. Two deities eternally opposed, except Kelik and Shetrem believed Yalet wanted them to kill in Her name.

Could it be true? Did they somehow not experience the pain and sickness that every other Disciple of Life felt whenever another living creature was harmed?

Was a Disciple of Life ordered to kill any more unlikely than a Disciple of Death turning out to be the saviour of Laria?

She had no answers, and Niema's hands trembled with exhaustion as she rowed, shoulders hunched, one eye on the shadow in the sky. Yet the beast didn't descend. Maybe she was too far out of reach, though the dead war drake didn't appear to be heading north any longer. Its path was listless, meandering, and when it vanished into the dark sky, some of the tension seeped out of Niema's weary bones.

At the first opportunity, Niema grabbed a fallen leaf from the bank and daubed a sharp stick into the mud, scratching out a brief note to Yala. *They're coming. Following the river.*

Niema gave the note to the nightwing to hold in its beak, whistled her command, and then settled into the canoe for a long night of rowing.

27

Yala might have spent the rest of the day reading, but Kelan's departure brought a rush of frustrated energy that refused to dissipate. That fact remained that more people would die if someone didn't find a way to cut off Mekan's realm, and if she didn't try to convince Superior Dovial to change his mind, the blood of innocents would be on her hands. In a literal sense. Glad she'd had the forethought to bring her drakeskin gloves, Yala fished them out of her pack and slid them onto her hands. Her army-issued gloves fit well enough that they wouldn't impede her ability to hold a weapon, but they hid the inexplicable grey markings that stained her fingertips.

With the gloves on, Yala picked up her cane and left the house. The streets were quiet and the few people she passed hurried along with their heads down. She did spot a group of city guards near the wall, and while part of her wanted to reprimand them for not being of any help whatsoever in the clash with the void drake, who was she to judge people simply for wanting to stay alive?

Her attention landed on the Temple of the Earth. Oddly,

the doors lay open, and as she moved closer, two robed figures appeared in the doorway.

Yala ducked into a side street. *Those aren't Disciples of the Earth.* Nor did they wear the blue robes of the Disciples of the Sky, but pure white with gold embroidery. Yala's heart gave an unpleasant jolt when she recognised Mieren, the female Disciple of the Flame who'd challenged her back in the capital, alongside a second Disciple she didn't know.

Had Superior Shralin changed his mind? Or had Mieren decided to act alone? They'd gained access to the Temple of the Earth, which suggested they intended to help. Yes, Mieren was as trustworthy as a Rafragorian general and her friend was likely no better, but her arrival might be the reprieve Yala and the others needed. Nobody else in Setemar had a chance of sealing Mekan's realm.

Yala watched the newcomers descend the stairs outside the temple. The brief temptation seized her to hand the book over and return to the capital, washing her hands of the matter, but she squashed the desire down. The book was no less dangerous in Mieren's hands as it had been in Trienan's, and if the Disciples of the Flame had indeed come here to get rid of all traces of Mekan, Superior Dovial wouldn't have told them about the Temple of Death. Not when he still didn't believe it existed.

Damn them.

While the Disciples of the Flame headed towards the gates out of the inner city, Yala made straight for the inn. She opened the door and walked in on a room full of startled Disciples of the Sky, several of whom jumped to their feet as though they expected her to pull a knife on them. *Or raise the dead, maybe.*

"You might be interested to know that there are two Disciples of the Flame in the city," she told the gathered Disciples. "I just saw them leave the Temple of the Earth."

"They came to help us." Visibly relieved, Laima crossed the room and beckoned to another pair of Disciples to join her. "We can show them the way to the village."

One of them might be at cross-purposes with her own Superior. She didn't voice her suspicion aloud; the Disciples needed a morale boost, and besides, the quicker they were rid of Mekan's realm, the better. Yet even if the Disciples closed the opening to the Void in the farmhouse, there was no guarantee they'd think to look elsewhere.

Granted, Mieren might not return to the capital immediately, either. Not when she didn't have the book.

Yala's instincts urged her to keep her distance, but when Laima and the others left the inn, she followed.

"They must have already left," Laima observed as they reached the gates. "They'll have a wagon, I expect. We'll meet them there."

"Isn't it more convenient for you to carry them?" When the Disciples eyed her, Yala added, "Just an observation. I don't know what instructions Superior Dovial gave them."

"We'll find out," Laima said tersely. "Lakiel, Dakam—go and talk to them. I'll wait here."

Her two companions took flight, gliding over the wall, but Laima returned her attention to the inn.

"You aren't going with them?" Yala asked.

"Someone has to keep an eye on the others." Her expression shadowed. "Most of them are injured. I hope the Disciples of the Flame can handle the Void by themselves."

"It won't be enough if they don't destroy the underground temple, too." Yala lifted her head as the Disciples rose into the air on the other side of the wall. This time they each carried one robed figure, and they glided towards the cliffs. *Interesting.* Yala would have assumed being carried around would be beneath Mieren's dignity, though it was undeniably more convenient to shortcut over the cliffs instead of following the road.

Laima watched, too, though she didn't reply.

"The underground temple," Yala repeated. "I know you don't believe it exists, but even if it's not an actual temple, Mekan's followers were hiding there. If any have survived, that's where they'll be."

Laima's mouth thinned. "If you're right, those tunnels are a maze. Only the Disciples know the way around."

"Exactly," Yala said. "I don't think Superior Dovial is willing to confront the extent of the trouble they're in."

"Superior Dovial isn't a war general," she said. "Maybe if he was, you'd show him more respect, but you can't expect him to mobilise his people to face an enemy they can't see."

"I don't expect him to. I expect him to display a minimum of common sense." Yala's gloved hands curled into fists. "Superior Shralin sent me here to find Melian's allies. I'm not here because I want to be, and the quickest way to be rid of me is to take me to the mines so I can help those Disciples get rid of all traces of Mekan's realm."

"Really." Laima looked her over. "I saw you control the dead. I'm not placing my life in your hands."

"I rather think it's the other way around." A smile twisted Yala's lips. "Trust me, I'm not the one who holds the advantage. If you decide to 'accidentally' let go of me while we're in the air, there's nothing to stop me hitting the ground like a dropped groundfruit and making a mess."

Laima muttered a curse under her breath and then strode behind Yala. Unlike Kelan, she made no effort to ease the shock of being yanked upward into the air, and Yala's dangling leg ached at the jolting motion as they rose higher over the cliffs.

On the other side, Laima descended just as rapidly and

released her on the grass—directly in front of the two Disciples of the Flame.

"You." Mieren's expression barely registered surprise. "I wondered if you were here, Yala Palathar."

"Believe it or not, I did keep my word." Yala rested her cane on the muddy grass and gestured to the farmhouse. "If there are any Disciples of Death surviving—"

The farmhouse burst into flames without so much as a blink from the Disciples. White fire flared, brighter than any natural flame, and extinguished itself with equal suddenness. Nothing remained behind save for a smoking ruin.

Yala jabbed her cane at the thin trail of smoke seeping out of the farmhouse's remains. "You do realise that any Disciples of Death might have been in that house, don't you?"

"Good," said the male Disciple who'd accompanied Mieren.

"Their *book* might have been in there," Yala went on. "The book your Superior sent me to retrieve."

Mieren eyed her. "I doubt it was. If there was anyone alive in there, they'd have shown themselves."

"Not necessarily," Yala said. "Melian's allies are a bunch of cowards who mostly died as a result of their foolishness when they opened the Void."

A breeze against her back prompted her to glance behind, seeing that Laima had left, and so had the other two Disciples of the Sky.

"Was that your friend?" Mieren's mouth twitched imperceptibly into a smile. "We told the others to leave, but I suppose someone of your particular status has trouble making friends amongst the other Disciples."

Yala ignored the taunt. "Why'd you send them away? Did you have something else you wanted to do here?"

"Obviously." Mieren's friend indicated the mines. "There's trouble down there, and we're going to stop it."

So they do know. "I thought Superior Dovial didn't believe the Temple of Death existed."

"A temple?" Mieren repeated. "A Temple of Death? There's no such thing."

"That's what it looked like to me." Yala gestured towards the visible outline of the upturned cart near the mines. "I'm not sure where the main entrance is, as I found it by accident when Mekan's monsters attacked."

"Really."

"Yes," Yala replied. "There was an altar, and another opening into the Void."

Mieren watched her through narrowed eyes. She and Yala had a score to settle, no doubt, and her actions now depended on whether she prioritised helping the Disciples of the Earth over her grudge. Finally, she spoke. "Fine. Lead the way, Disciple."

Not a Disciple. Her reply went unvoiced, though her instincts urged her not to step into a dark tunnel alongside the two Disciples who had no reason to show her any more mercy than they did Melian's surviving allies. Yes, Superior Shralin had promised that Yala wouldn't be harmed inside the Temple of the Flame, but that promise meant next to nothing out here in the mines.

Did Superior Shralin give them orders to come here? The question lingered on her tongue, but it wouldn't do to provoke a fight. If Mieren and her friend discovered she'd overcome Mekan's beasts with the aid of a dead war drake of her own, there was little doubt of her fate.

Heat seared her face when the Disciples raised their hands, and she took a sharp step to the side. Flames shot past, engulfing the cart blocking the mine's entrance. The smell of burning filled the air, thick and cloying, and Yala fought her very instinct as she approached the mines first.

"Do either of you have a lantern?" she asked.

"There's no need." The male Disciple held up a flame in his palm; of course, they didn't need to light a candle when their hands could serve as the same, but she'd had no intention of relying upon the two Disciples as a light source.

"You know the way, don't you?" Mieren indicated the tunnel ahead. "Go on."

Shoulders tensed, Yala plunged ahead into the darkness. As the familiar scent of death surrounded her, her fingertips tingled underneath her gloves. Yet none of Mekan's creatures appeared, not until they reached the spot where the beast had ripped open the tunnel wall. The decaying corpse of the raptor-like creature stank even worse than the last time she'd been in here, and even Mieren wrinkled her nose.

Yala gestured behind the creature to the sloping tunnel its claws had created. "This is the only way through. It's a steep slope and there's a drop at the end, so be careful."

She'd spoken using her captain's voice without thinking; when the Disciples blinked at her and didn't move, she added, "I'm not trying to trick you. I'll go first."

Nudging the monster's body aside with her cane, she stepped gingerly around it. She'd expected to run into one of Mekan's creatures before she'd had to crawl down the slope that led to the chamber, and the lack of any enemies unsettled her. Had the Disciples' mere presence scared off the dead?

Wait. I forgot to mention they'll lose their powers in there.

She turned back, but they hadn't followed her into the tunnel. Perhaps they thought she was trying to lure them into a trap. "Come on. It's this way."

Bending her head to avoid the low ceiling, she walked down the slope with careful steps. As she heard the Disciples enter the tunnel behind her, she pointed ahead with her cane. "It's here..."

She reached the tunnel's edge and stopped, disbelief

flooding her. The chamber was empty, the slab of stone had gone, and not so much of a sliver of the Void remained.

"That can't be right." Yala lifted her head. A glance behind her told her that the Disciples had neglected to follow her downhill, and so she climbed back up as carefully as she'd descended.

The Disciples weren't in the tunnel opening. They'd retreated, taking the source of light with them. Foreboding shivered in Yala's bones. She'd needed the Disciples' help to destroy the temple, but if it no longer existed, there was nothing to stop them from doing the same to her.

Yala drew her dagger and held it in a loose grip as she climbed around the creature's body. "You know, if you weren't going to follow me, you might have told me *before* I went to the trouble of crawling the way through that tunnel."

The two Disciples waited for her outside the hole in the wall, standing between her and the way back. The white flames they carried in their palms appeared larger than before, reflected in their eyes, and her sense of foreboding intensified.

"What's the problem?" she asked. "Changed your mind about wanting my help?"

Had they known they wouldn't find anything down here? It seemed impossible that a temple could just vanish, but in the end, the altar had been its main feature and so had the Void. The former would have been easy to carry off, but the latter... *The Void. Where did it go?*

"Well?" she pressed when the Disciples didn't answer. "Are you just going to stare at me instead?"

"We saw your beast on the way here," said Mieren. "That dead war drake."

Ah. Understanding, she released the last shreds of hope that she'd get out of this tunnel without drawing blood.

"It's Mekan's creature, not mine," Yala corrected. "I didn't know it was still around until I came here."

"And yet the beast spared your life." Mieren lifted her flaming hand. "You claimed not to be a Disciple of Death, but your actions say otherwise."

"This isn't about me. It's about protecting the people of Setemar." Yala held her weapon at the ready. "Your Superior asked for my help. I imagine he'll be quite pissed off if you kill me."

Or not. The king had been the most powerful man in the nation, and that hadn't mattered in the end.

"Superior Shralin is, I believe, ineffective as a replacement."

Yala's brows shot up. "Isn't that sacrilege? Aren't you worried Dalathik will strike you down for disapproving of His choice?"

"Not when I remain loyal to Superior Datriem." Mieren exchanged glances with her companion—enough for Yala to gather that he agreed with her. "Many would disagree with his choices, but he is the reason Laria has lasted this long without being embroiled in conflict with Mekan."

I was right. She does know he killed King Tharen.

The male Disciple swung a flaming fist at her and Yala smashed her cane into his knees. He fell with a cry of pain, but his companion struck before Yala could dodge. Scorching pain shot up her arm; her vision blurred, and the cane fell from her grip. A second blast narrowly missed her shoulder, striking the corpse of the dead monster instead. The monster vanished in a white flash, dead skin and bone becoming ashes and leaving her nowhere to hide from their next assault.

She gripped her dagger in one hand, staring them down. Her adversaries might have fire at their fingertips, but like the other Disciples, they hadn't been formally trained in combat. That was her only advantage.

That, and her knowledge that even the Disciples of the Flame weren't immune to Dalathik's fire.

The male Disciple scrambled to his feet, but Yala grabbed his cloak with her knife hand and pulled into the path of Mieren's next attack. A horrible scream ripped from his throat. Yala's stomach turned over as the stench of burning flesh filled her nostrils. The Disciple cried out again when Yala's blade raked across his forearm, and then she shoved him at his companion.

Mieren spat out a curse and performed a series of gestures with her hands. Abruptly Yala's knife grew too hot to hold; though her gloves blunted some of the impact, she was unable to stop herself from dropping the weapon. *Shit.*

Swiftly Yala dropped to the tunnel floor. The impact jarred her injured leg, but the flames grazed her side instead of incinerating her. Teeth gritted against the pain, she threw herself into the gap in the wall and rolled over.

"You can't hide, Yala," Mieren called after her. "No temple can protect you."

This might not be a temple anymore, but I can make it your tomb.

Yala rolled to the side, letting the slope carry her downward until she neared the edge of the sheer drop. She came upright, breathless, arm and leg burning, hoping that the element of surprise would be enough. She'd lost all her weapons, save for one.

The sound of Mieren and her companion entering the tunnel prompted her to reach for her pouch. Mekan's shadows would have no impact on their fire, but when her gloved fingers brushed the claw, familiar whispering reached her ears.

Was the Void still open somewhere in the tunnels, or had

the temple been moved elsewhere? She might be able to do more if she was able to remove her gloves and touch the shadows with her bare hands, but the two Disciples were already descending the slope. There was no time.

Yala half-sat up, angling her body so that the Disciples wouldn't be able to see the chamber on the other side...nor the claw she gripped in her gloved hand.

"Yes, you've got me." She wheezed out a breath. "Very brave of you, cornering an injured civilian."

"You called yourself a soldier," Mieren said.

Her companion didn't speak. A red-raw patch of skin marred the entire left side of his face; patches of his hair were singed clean off. Fury reverberated in his eyes as he raised a clenched fist.

Yala struck. The claw's sharp edge pierced his ankle and he tripped, tumbling over the sheer drop into the chamber. His shrill scream rang out before the unmistakeable thud of his body hitting the ground.

"You..." Mieren pointed at the claw with a shaking hand. "You *traitor.*"

"Me?" A laugh rose in Yala's throat. "Your Superior murdered the king, yet you have the nerve to call *me* a traitor?"

"Like him, your death will serve a greater purpose." She lunged and Yala seized the end of her robe. Pulling down the Disciple to her level, Yala buried the claw in Mieren's chest.

While she was still choking on her last breath, Yala shoved Mieren over the edge, to join her companion in the Temple of Death.

———

Superior Sietra seemed to be expecting bad news. She took Kelan's report of the deaths of her Disciples in grim silence, one hand clenching and unclenching at the side of her high-backed chair as he spoke.

"I should have sent more people," she murmured, her head bowed. "I am truly sorry."

"It wouldn't have made a difference." Kelan was aware that his words weren't particularly reassuring, but he knew she wanted the truth. "If not for Yala, we'd *all* be dead."

She lifted her head, grief clouding her expression. "Yala Palathar has earned a pardon several times over. Are there any surviving Disciples of Death?"

"If there are, they're hiding," he said. "Yala killed Melian's brother. He had in his possession a book that the Disciples of the Flame wanted her to find."

"Oh?" Her gaze sharpened. "Which book?"

"I don't know, exactly." He thought back to his brief conversation with Yala before he'd left. "There was no title, but Yala said it was a historical journal of some sort, written by a scholar from the old Parvan Empire."

"I see," said Superior Sietra. "Tell Yala that I'd very much like to see the book for myself, after she's finished with it."

Kelan raised a brow. "Do you think it's better than any of the books I found in the library?"

"It might be," she said. "Depending on its contents."

"Yala said it wasn't a handbook with instructions as to how to use Corruption." Why the Superior would be interested in a *book* at a time like this was beyond him. "This scholar was writing an account of his travels which included the island where Yala encountered the abandoned Temple of Death. He also visited Laria, before … well, before it existed. It's fascinating, but not necessarily relevant to our current dilemma."

"Tell me more," she said. "Anything is potentially relevant."

"Well…" He raked through his thoughts for anything that

might be of note. "The people he met in Laria—or whatever it used to be called—sounded like the Disciples of Life, and they predated King Larial by several centuries at least."

"Indeed?" She nodded. "Yes… I always wondered why the Disciples of Life aren't mentioned in accounts of Laria's history."

"What does that have to do with Corruption?" He gave up on humouring her interest. "I thought you wanted me to research Mekan, not Yalet. Though the Disciples of Life are also trying to arrest Yala, as if she doesn't have enough problems."

"*Arrest* her?" Superior Sietra's eyes widened in genuine shock. "On what grounds?"

"Being a Disciple of Death, I think," he said. "We received a warning from a friend of hers, whom they also arrested. I can only assume the Disciples of Life have no idea that Mekan's trying to take over the Temple of the Earth and that should probably be their priority instead."

"Nevertheless." Her tone regained its grave undercurrent. "The Disciples of Life are the only people outside of the Disciples of the Flame who are known to be able to overcome Corruption in any capacity. If they declared Yala an enemy…"

"Not just her. Remember Niema, who visited Skytower?" Guilt twinged in his chest. For all his promises to help her, he hadn't even tried. "They imprisoned her, too, for defending Yala."

"I see." Superior Sietra's jaw tightened. "Their reaction is understandable when you consider the risk Corruption poses to their home, but it's certainly inconvenient to those of us who know the truth."

"Especially when Mekan can only be countered by the Disciples of Life and Flame," he added. "Do any of your books explain why that is?"

"No, but it's one of the reasons I wanted to research the subject. The gods of flame and life were responsible for banishing Mekan, according to some stories, which might why their magic alone can counter the Void."

"And ours can't," he said. "Nor the Disciples of the Earth. Are we doomed to be ousted, too?"

"Not at all," she said. "A temple is only as strong as its Superior."

True. He'd seen evidence of that with his own eyes, and he had to trust that Superior Sietra was stronger than Superior Datriem, than Superior Dovial. "I hope someone better takes over the Disciples of the Earth before they all get killed."

"So do I," she said. "I'll send another team to join you in Setemar. You can decide if you want to go with them. I know it can't have been easy watching your fellow Disciples die."

"I'm fine." Was he? He hadn't personally known any of the Disciples who'd died, but the effects of being surrounded by death and destruction were bound to take a toll. Yala would know more about that sort of thing than he did, he was sure. "I'll go back. I don't mind flying in the dark."

"If you're certain." She gave him a once-over. "Get someone to check that cut first. We can't have you dropping dead of an infection."

Kelan grinned despite himself. "Yes, Superior."

He took her advice to fly to the infirmary to ask a healer to check on the places where the beast's claw had slashed his face and arms, and then he dropped in at the cafeteria to grab something to eat. He had no appetite, but he'd need the energy for the long journey back to Setemar. The other Disciples sat in huddles in the mess hall, exchanging whispered rumours. No doubt they'd heard about the deaths of the others and perhaps knew Superior Sietra would be asking for more volunteers; Kelan finished his meal quickly and left before they could start asking him questions.

Once outside of Skytower, he took the quickest route across the countryside to avoid wasting any light. Even then, dusk came quickly, swallowing the sun's last rays. Kelan navigated more by instinct than by any landmark. When he passed over a stretch of dark forest, he picked out a winged silhouette in the sky.

Is that the dead war drake? He adjusted his flight path to avoid a collision and then came to a confused halt in midair. The war drake appeared to be bigger than the other one, though he was too far off to make out its features. It wasn't anywhere near Setemar either, but Kelan kept one eye on the dark shape as he glided onward. Strangely, he could have sworn there was a human-shaped shadow above the beast, but the dark shape melted into the sky before he could be certain whether it had a rider.

Strange, but for once, Kelan's exhaustion outweighed his curiosity. It was fully dark by the time he glided over the city wall, and he had to amass a great deal of willpower to enter the inn through the front door rather than slipping in through an upstairs window and collapsing into bed.

Laima and the other survivors had gathered in the downstairs room, and when he entered, expectant faces greeted him.

"Another team is coming to join us in the morning," he told them. "Or earlier, if they fly through the night."

"Good," Laima said around a yawn. "I hope we won't need them now the Void's closed, but it's better to be sure."

"The Void's *closed?*"

"Yes, the Disciples of the Flame were able to stop Mekan's forces," said Lakiel. "We're very grateful for them."

Kelan hadn't expected them to keep their word. "The Disciples of the Earth have their temple back?"

"They never lost it," Laima said. "We'll visit them in the

morning and ask if they've regained access to their abilities. We decided to give them time to mourn the dead."

What dead... oh, right. He recalled the unfortunate Disciple who'd been killed by the void drake. "Are the Disciples of the Flame staying at the inn?"

"No." Laima frowned. "I haven't seen them since we left them at the mines. I assumed they returned to the capital after they finished dealing with the Void."

"Does Yala know?" He expected the question would be answered with a scowl, but Laima dropped her gaze instead.

"She was with them, too."

"They took Yala?" Disbelief bled into his voice. "Really?"

"She went with them voluntarily," Laima retaliated. "Don't look at me like that. I didn't tell them she was here."

Had they gone back to the capital? No, it'd take days for them to travel by foot when they didn't have the ability to fly. What had Yala been thinking?

He was halfway out the door before his thoughts caught up with him; while Laima called his name, he didn't turn back. Perhaps he was being paranoid, but none of the others would have had any inclination to check up on Yala. Nor had they believed his warning that Mekan's allies had created a Temple of Death, and if the Disciples of the Earth hadn't regained access to their abilities, Mekan's influence remained.

Kelan glided to Yala's friend's house and rapped on the door. When it swung open, a dagger brushed against his throat. "Oh, hello, Yala."

Yala lowered her knife. "Don't startle me like that, Kelan."

"What's wrong?" His gaze dropped to her arm, which was heavily bandaged. "Where are the Disciples of the Flame?"

She worked her jaw, and then spoke with an air of resigned acceptance. "I killed them."

"You … killed them." Whatever he'd expected to hear, it wasn't that. "I assume you had good reason?"

"What do you think?" She beckoned with a bandaged hand. Behind her, more bandages littered the floor, along with a bottle of some kind of ointment that he assumed she'd brought with her. "The fuckers tried to burn me alive."

Walking into the same room as a killer was not his most intelligent decision of the day, but Yala had never hidden her nature, and if it came to it, he'd rather meet his end by her knife than at the hands of the dead. "Did they destroy Mekan's temple first?"

"Not exactly." She sat in her armchair, wincing. "They saw the war drake and drew their own conclusions."

"At least they closed the Void beforehand." Another possibility hit him. "Do you think their bodies will, ah, rise from the dead?"

"I hope not." She ground her teeth. "I had to leave them in the Temple of Death, which is bound to cause problems, but I'm not sure it *is* a temple any longer. Someone moved the altar, and the Void wasn't there."

"Who moved the altar?" Perhaps Yala and Kelan's discovery had prompted the Disciples of Death to move their temple elsewhere, but he hadn't thought any had survived the incident at the farmhouse.

Yala grunted. "There's something dodgy going on in those tunnels, but if I start poking around, the Disciples of the Earth will find out what I did to the people who came to help them. Never mind that they acted against the orders of their own Superior when they came here."

"They didn't come for the book?"

"They never knew I had it," she replied. "That doesn't mean Superior Shralin won't have my skin seared off my bones for killing two of his Disciples." Her hands clenched at her sides, and darkness leaked between gaps in the bandages like blood.

Kelan peered at her hands. "Is that supposed to happen?"

"I haven't a fucking clue." She peeled back the bandage on one hand, revealing greying fingertips. "They've been like this since I brought back the war drake."

That doesn't seem good. "Does the book explain anything?"

He scanned the room and spied the drakeskin-bound tome on the floor next to the first-aid kit.

"No," she said. "There are no instructions on how to use Corruption, let alone why Mekan was able to usurp Setem's temple."

"My Superior expressed an interest in the book." When she cut him a glare, he hastily added, "I didn't make any promises. She's already been researching Corruption, like I told you."

"Better to know her enemy, I suppose," Yala said. "And to think I entertained the idea of handing Mieren the book and walking away."

"*Are* you going to leave?" he asked. "I wouldn't blame you if you did."

"Not if there's a horde of angry Disciples waiting for me in Dalathar," she retaliated. "If I return the book to the Temple of the Flame, I'll have to give the Superior the bad news."

"Not necessarily," Kelan said. "They walked into a Temple of Death. Let the Superior draw his own conclusions."

Yala's hands clenched, leaking more shadows. "They deserved it. Mieren conspired to murder the king, even if she didn't commit the deed with her own hands."

"Did she now?" Kelan tilted his head. "Then taking her life in turn ought to earn you a commendation."

"Don't start," she growled. "You know that this hasn't solved anything. Mekan is still squatting in the Temple of the

Earth, and I can't think of any way to oust Him that doesn't involve inviting more Disciples to Setemar who'd happily see me dead."

She might have a point. He was too tired to think of any alternatives, and despite the crazed glint in her eyes, Yala looked much the same. "Ah, you should know I thought I saw a war drake on the way here. A living one, that is."

She blinked. "Where?"

"South of here … much further south," he amended. "It was dark, but I could have sworn someone was riding it."

"A soldier?" Her brow furrowed. "I thought most of them were in the capital. The soldiers, not the war drakes. They left."

"I thought the same," he said.

"Right." She gave a snort. "Why not add a live war drake to our list of problems."

"I think I prefer the dead one, too." He glided back to the door. "See you tomorrow?"

"If someone doesn't stab me in my sleep."

"I pity the person who tries."

She killed the Disciples of the Flame. Was he surprised? Not entirely. He had blood on his hands, the blood of his fellow Disciples even … but he'd prefer not to imagine the potential consequences of her killing two other Disciples inside a Temple of Death.

28

I *fucked that up,* Yala thought, idly watching the shadows leak from her fingertips. She'd been lying low in Vanat's house since her return from the mines and had expected her next visitor to have come to take her to account for her crimes. An irrational belief, she knew; nobody was likely to find the bodies except the Disciples of Death, if any survived.

Nevertheless, she couldn't face the other Disciples of the Sky yet. Her burned arm throbbed despite the ointment she'd daubed on the wound, and her fingers remained grey-stained beneath the bandages. She thumbed through the journal again to distract herself, squinting at the pages in the dim light of the candle she'd set on the low table next to her armchair.

She'd already skimmed all the way to the end and confirmed that the journal contained no instructions to speak of, although the text had answered questions that had plagued her for years, such as how the island had become known to King Tharen. Mavilangran's words created images of a temple bustling with life and Disciples gathering outside to greet the locals, which stood at a stark contrast to her memories of the overgrown ruins she'd encountered.

Yala's gaze snagged on one passage. *"They also have a number of dwellings beneath the flagstones of the central square. I do not know who lives underground—the higher ranked of the Hierarch of Bone, perhaps—but my brief glimpses showed an extensive network of caves running below the temple.*

Her blood chilled at the memory of the island itself wrenching apart as though torn open from within. At the time, she'd been too focused on running for her life to examine the island's exposed innards from which Mekan's beasts had emerged, but the scholar's descriptions evoked an uncomfortable similarity to the chamber in which she'd left the dead Disciples of the Flame.

Get a grip, Yala. There are only so many ways you can design an underground chamber. It doesn't mean anything.

If there'd been an opening to the Void deep within the island all those years ago, too, Mavilangran's journals didn't say, but it was strange to think that the temple on that island had existed for years, maybe decades. What had changed after the Parvan scholar's visit that had turned the island into a ruin? To build a thriving civilisation in the shadow of death seemed a paradox, but the temple's mere existence indicated that Mekan didn't always kill His Disciples.

What was different about them? She dismissed the question, irritated with herself for pondering the merits of remaining Death's Disciple when two Disciples of the Flame had tried to burn her out of existence a few hours earlier.

As for the Disciples of Life … even if they wanted to arrest her, Niema couldn't hurt a plant without flinching, so Yala had a hard time summoning up any fear of *them.*

Strange that they'd lived on the Larian continent for longer than anyone had been aware. With the hundreds of years that had elapsed since then, it was anyone's guess as to whether the other Disciples were aware of their history. *I suppose that depends on how many of them have read this book.*

Regardless, the scholar had been more interested in this world than in the one where the god of death was supposedly chained. The journal wouldn't tell her why her fingers kept leaking shadows like blood, nor how to remove Mekan's touch from her skin.

"Is this it?" she murmured. "Am I doomed to be under the god of death's influence for the rest of my existence?"

For all she knew, her own demise was no guarantee He would leave her in peace. Mekan had not spoken directly to her since she'd called the dead war drake, nor she Him, but He certainly wouldn't tell her why her fingers had turned corpse grey. Nor could she ask Him why He'd decided to usurp someone else's temple instead of building His own.

Or could she? Yala put the book aside and delved into her discarded pouch. Her bandaged fingers fumbled the claw, its edges gleaming under the candle's light. The fresh blood of the Disciples of the Flame mingled with the older dark stains, and shadows flickered at its edges.

Faint whispering resolved into a single word. *"Blood."*

"Yes, and...?" Yala's pulse stuttered. "Haven't I given you enough blood?"

"Your flesh is mine."

"No, it isn't. Do you *always* kill your Disciples, in the end?"

No response came this time. Was He even listening to her? He could certainly communicate with humans when He wanted to, but the voice didn't sound as though she was the intended addressee.

"Why did you mark me?" The question was useless; she already knew the answer. Mekan had marked her because she'd made a request of Him and asked for more than she had been able to give in return.

Otherwise, His vocabulary seemed limited to references to death, blood, and sacrifices. Did Mekan have no other thoughts to occupy His immortal mind? He knew her name, of course, but even then, He hadn't struck her down in fury for closing the Void back in the capital and thwarting His plans.

A daring thought nudged into her mind. Mekan might be the god of death, but His ability to interfere with the world was dependent upon access to dead bodies. Otherwise, fear was His main weapon, and after her clash with the Disciples of the Flame, she had a hard time fearing the power she'd used to save her own skin.

Moreover, from what she'd seen, only *living* people could open the void, and with the limited number of Disciples of Death in existence, Mekan couldn't afford to be picky. Maybe that was why He'd spared her life.

Is it really that simple? Surely not, but if the people on that island had lived in relative harmony with the god of death, there must be a way to survive her own choices.

You aren't my master, Mekan, she thought, *but I might master you.*

Kelan's night was restless, punctuated by nightmares, and he woke with his shoulder aching as though it'd been stabbed with a thousand knives. The sound of Lakiel's snoring from the other bed prompted him to give up on the idea of getting more sleep, so he dressed quietly and glided out through the open window rather than risk meeting one of the others on the way downstairs. He'd managed to avoid too many questions the previous night, but he was sure Laima had figured out that Yala was still in the city. She'd never have guessed the fate of the two Disciples in the mines, of course, but if

Mekan's beasts made another appearance, he'd have to come up with a convincing reason not to send another plea for help from the Disciples of the Flame.

Not that anyone is likely to listen, Kelan thought as he glided upward, above the Temple of the Earth and the curving cliffs beyond. His conversation with Yala the previous night, while unsettling, had been a reminder that but she had more sense than Superior Dovial did even when she was half-unconscious from exhaustion and with shadows oozing out of her fingers. Really, it would save a lot of time if someone were to lock Superior Dovial in his altar room and then ask the other Disciples to offer their opinions in place of their fool of a leader.

Kelan's thoughts were shaken back to the present when he caught sight of a dark blot in the sky. The war drake? He was sure he hadn't imagined the *living* war drake he'd seen on yesterday's flight, but this one was surely Yala's steed. She'd sent it away, but the beast had come back. To help her?

It can't have a sense of purpose, he reminded himself. *It's dead.*

Kelan glided over the cliffs towards the winged shape in the sky, confirming it matched Yala's steed, and that it carried nobody upon its back. Except… was it holding something in its mouth? Kelan flew closer, and the dead war drake's mouth opened. The object—which turned out to be a dead bird—plummeted past Kelan, a large leaf fluttering in its wake. A leaf covered in smudged writing. With a rush of guilt at how easily he'd forgotten Niema's plea for help, Kelan extended a hand to catch the leaf.

He glided away from the dead war drake in case it became aware of his presence and then studied the leaf. The note was unsigned, but the scratchy handwriting certainly belonged to Niema. Shorter than her previous note, it consisted of a few letters that rearranged themselves in Kelan's mind several times before he made out the word 'river'. *River ... like that one?* Even from this height, it was easy to spot the winding blue line known simply as 'the River' to most people in the capital. If Niema's fellow Disciples intended to reach Dalathar quickly, using a boat was much faster than walking on foot, or attempting to navigate poorly maintained roads and dense jungles in a wagon pulled by raptors.

He couldn't tell if Niema's note was a plea for help, but if it was, he'd be better off approaching alone. Yala would be irked at him for leaving without her, but it would not help Niema's cause if Yala decided to bring her army-issued knife —or worse, raised the dead and pissed off the god of life in the process.

Kelan followed the river south. Minutes trickled by, in which he saw little except for a few small villages and settlements, including one that might have been Yala's former home. Destroying her house hadn't been his best idea, he'd freely admit, and that it had been far from his worse decision in recent months only underlined how swiftly his life had unravelled.

Air buffeted him from behind, a warning that the dead war drake was heading the same direction.

"What do you want?" He veered to the side, watching the beast out of the corner of his eye. It wasn't following him, he didn't think, but its flight path matched the flow of the river.

Unnerved, he continued flying, keeping a steady distance until the war drake doubled back and began to fly in the opposite direction. Strange behaviour, even for a dead monster.

The river cut right through swathes of forest, into Laria's beating heart, and for some reason he found himself thinking of Yala's revelation that the Disciples of Life had been present before anyone else had ever arrived on the continent. Here in the southern jungles, wild and untamed despite a few hundred years of human interference, it was easy to believe that the god of life alone held sway.

Kelan passed a larger settlement on the water and flew higher to avoid being spotted by any people who might be awake at this hour. When he descended again, he picked out a disturbance on the river, a blot moving upstream that swiftly resolved into a human figure. *Is that...?*

Niema. She sat in a canoe, gripping an oar with such intensity that if she'd had any strength in her twig-thin arms, she might have snapped it in two. She'd obviously been travelling for hours, and despite her death grip on the oar, she looked ready to pass out from exhaustion.

Kelan flew closer, calling her name. "Niema."

She looked up. "No. I can't fall asleep. This is too important."

"You aren't asleep." He held up the leaf she'd written her warning on. "Your handwriting is awful."

"That note was for Yala," she mumbled.

"You don't want me to get you out of here?" He caught up to her canoe and doubled back, gliding alongside her. "You *could* stay on the river, but it'll still take you a few days to reach Setemar at this pace."

"Setemar?" She lifted her head, her expression clearing as she realised she was talking to an actual person and not an exhaustion-induced hallucination. "That's where Yala is? She did get my warning, didn't she?"

"Yes, but I was under the impression you were a prisoner." He peered down the river behind her, but he didn't see any other canoes. "On the run, are you?"

"Two others are following me." Her shoulders hunched. "There might be more—what are you doing?"

Kelan swept past her, his cloak fluttering behind him. "Going to take care of that problem."

"Don't hurt them!" She stopped rowing and twisted around in her seat, her eyes widening.

Kelan laughed. He couldn't help it. "You haven't changed a bit. Are you asking me to spare people who are trying to kill you?"

"They're not trying to kill me!" she protested.

"They're after Yala," he said. "Aren't they? Are you sure they won't do her any harm?"

"Of—of course not. They're going to put her on trial before the god of life."

Kelan stopped mid-glide. "Have they ever trialled a Disciple of Death before? What does that entail?"

"Superior Kralia didn't tell me," she mumbled. "She doesn't trust me. Because of Yala."

Of course she doesn't. He could only imagine how badly the experience had shaken Niema, yet she'd chosen to focus her efforts on warning Yala rather than saving herself.

"I can take you directly to Yala, you know," he told her. "Are you sure you'd rather stay down here?"

Niema's head bowed. "I don't want to lead them to her."

"That won't be an issue." He grinned. "It's much quicker to travel by air. Remember?"

"Stop right there!" The shout was followed by the thunder of footsteps. Not humans. Raptors.

Niema's eyes widened. "It's them."

Ah, he thought, *there are our Disciples of Life.*

29

Yala read the journal until she couldn't keep her eyes open an instant longer. Between one blink and the next, she drifted off to sleep.

And dreamed of the island.

She flew above the forest on the back of a war drake, looking down at the jungle and the ruins within. The wide stone area in front of the temple had split open, revealing not the Void, but a series of underground chambers, staircases and passages spiralling downward into the island's depths.

She woke with the image imprinted on the inside of her eyelids. *Damned book.*

Yala dressed for the day and weighed her options. She'd walked away from the fight with the Disciples of the Flame with countless new bruises, but her burned arm was less painful than the previous day and she'd retained the use of both hands. If she was to ensure nobody found their bodies, now was the time to act.

Assuming Mekan's power hadn't already raised them from death.

There was also the question of who'd moved the altar, but whoever was down there in the tunnels, Yala intended to confront them alone. She chose her route carefully to avoid walking past the inn, and once she was out of the inner city, Yala confirmed the back entrance to the Temple of the Earth was still guarded. The Superior had likely taken more precautions after her and Kelan had broken in. *The village it is, then.*

Yala picked up a meat pie from the market as well as a lantern to take with her, and then set about trying to find a merchant with more thirst for coin than sense. As she'd expected, the locals refused to travel too close to the ruined farmhouse, too spooked by the stories of the events the previous day, but she dug deeper into her coin purse with each person she approached until a merchant finally agreed to take her to the village.

"Aren't you're the one who was flying on the big … thing yesterday?" He flapped his arms in demonstration as she climbed into the wagon. "They said she was a woman with a scar on her face and a cane."

Yala's heart sank. "No. That's not me."

"I won't tell anyone," he said in a booming voice that caused several locals to glance in their direction. "I heard the stories. Did you really fly in the army?"

"That part is true." She'd hoped to shut him up, but he kept peppering her with questions as the raptors pulled the wagon out of the city.

"They were saying you performed some kind of arcane magic on the beastie," he remarked. "Is that true?"

"Of course not." Gods, she ought to have walked instead.

"Ridiculous, right?" he went on. "You're not one of those Disciples. You aren't wearing a cloak."

"Well observed." He seemed harmless enough, but his

rambling would guarantee that anyone he ran into would know he'd taken her out of the city by the morning's end.

Twenty minutes later, they reached the burned-out mess that had once been a farmhouse. Yala hopped out of the wagon while the merchant was in the middle of asking yet another question and ducked behind the gutted ruin of the farmhouse until she heard the rattle of wheels receding into the distance.

Removing her gloves, Yala adjusted her grip on the lantern and approached the mine entrance. She'd been too exhausted and injured to move the cart back into position the previous day, and a sizeable gap lingered between the cart and the mine entrance.

She climbed inside and followed the tunnel, using the lantern to guide her way to the hole in the wall. Not a sound disturbed the silence, and if not for her vivid memories of the dead monster erupting in flames, she might never have known she'd been engaged in a vicious fight to the death on this very spot.

Yala hesitated for a moment and then climbed through the hole, descending slowly this time with her cane braced for balance. Upon reaching the rim of the hole in the wall, she peered down into the chamber. No altar ... and no bodies.

Shit. Who removed them? Or did they walk away of their own accord? She held the lantern over the edge, trying to see into the chamber, but any other entrances or exits remained hidden in shadow, and it was abundantly clear that the two dead Disciples of the Flame had gone.

Or had they? An idea pricked at her mind like a bloodfly's bite. Putting down the lantern, Yala reached into the pouch at her waist and ran her fingertips over the claw. Shadows seeped out of its edges, coiling around her greying fingers like smoke.

"I killed those Disciples, Mekan," she murmured. "Bring them to me."

If she could call a dead war drake from the gods-knew-where, surely the dead Disciples would be reachable, too. If any dead were nearby, the claw would draw them like prey-birds to carrion. Her fingertips tingled, and a faint whispering thrummed in her ears. She turned her head to the left, and the whispering grew louder, the shadows thickening around her hand.

"That way?" she guessed. "I can't walk through walls, Mekan. You're going to have to offer more than that."

Yala let go of the claw and picked up her lantern, retracing her steps up the slope and into the tunnel through which she'd entered. Then she put down the lantern a second time and pulled out the claw, repeating her request.

The shadows coiling around the claw surged westward, as if prompting her to walk in that direction. Picking up the lantern once more, Yala continued along the path she and Kelan had been following before the monster had ripped open the tunnel wall. Her ears picked up indistinct thumping sounds from somewhere ahead of her. *Is that the dead?*

Reaching a fork in the tunnel, Yala rounded a corner and ran into three Disciples of Death.

For an instant they stared at one another. The three wore the same bloody, dusty robes as the ones she'd found in the farmhouse and were armed with daggers. They must have survived the carnage and escaped.

The first Disciple lunged at her. Putting down the lantern, Yala brought her cane across the young man's skull. He toppled without a word, and the second Disciple, female and around a decade younger than Yala, raised her knife. Yala parried easily, her cane smacking into the woman's wrist and sending her weapon clattering away into the darkness. Bringing out her own dagger, she slashed at the Disciple. Her burned arm was stiffer than usual, but the blade cleaved open her assailant's arm, and the young woman fell into a sobbing, bloody heap.

Upon seeing the Disciple whom Yala had struck on the head, she screamed. "He's dead!"

The third Disciple tried to flee. Striding forward, Yala grabbed him by the scruff of his neck with her knife hand. The movement jarred her throbbing arm, but the man went limp, recoiling from the shadows trailing from her fingertips.

"Tell me where your temple is," she growled.

"No." He yelped when Yala's dagger scraped the side of his neck. "No, no…"

"You started this when you ambushed me." She adjusted the dagger's angle so that it pushed against his throat. "Where's your altar? Are there any more of you down here?"

Yala's dagger bit into the skin of his throat and he whimpered but didn't speak a word. She tried another question. "Where'd those monsters disappear to?"

That, she didn't understand. Yes, the beasts might have retreated into Mekan's realm, but it seemed unlikely that they'd flee the tunnels when there were so many vulnerable human targets nearby.

The young man moaned. "I'll tell you everything. Let me go."

"All right." Yala removed her dagger and gave him a shove, causing him to trip over the young woman sprawled on the ground. "Go on. Talk."

When neither of them answered, Yala moved closer. "Let's start with an easy question. How did your people drive the god of the earth's influence out of His own temple?"

She had her suspicions, of course, but only someone who'd been directly involved would be able to give a clear answer.

"We didn't," whispered the female Disciple. "We didn't know… when we came here."

"Was this all Trienan's idea?"

"Trienan's dead," said the young man, holding a trembling hand to his bleeding neck. "You killed him."

"Yes, I did." Trienan hadn't seemed that sure of himself either; at a guess, he'd been waiting for Melian to come and give him further instructions. "He's the one who asked you to build the temple, but there was another god here too. Setem."

"His people… doubted." The male Disciple gasped out the words. "They chose our way instead."

"Some Disciples of the Earth helped you." She'd guessed as much, but how deep did their treachery go? Whoever had been involved, she doubted these fools could tell her whether the Disciples of the Earth turned to Mekan out of desperation after losing contact with Setem—or if they'd been partly responsible for their deity's departure in the first place. "Tell me … where did Setem go?"

"There are no gods here but me."

The response was a whisper directly into her ear, as though the speaker stood behind her. She jerked her head sharply to the side, but the lantern she'd put down showed no more intruders, dead or otherwise.

"Mekan." The shifting of shadows drew her gaze to the three fallen Disciples. The one she'd struck on the skull began to stir, soundless, shadows nudging his limbs upright. The two survivors both screamed, crawling from their rising companion.

"Call yourselves Disciples of Death?" Yala stuck out her cane to trip them, but a tremor rocked the earth underfoot and caused the two surviving Disciples to fall into a heap again. Yala braced her cane against the ground to keep from losing her balance, too. "What *was* that? Are you the ones who've been causing the earthquakes?"

"No." The male Disciple clung to his companion, moaning. "No. It's Him… He's here."

"Mekan." Not Setem. The god's power resided in the earth, but if Mekan's influence stretched beyond the temple—or rather, below—"Where?"

"Down." He gulped. "Far, far down."

The image from Yala's dream burst into her mind once more. The ground wrenching open, monstrous beasts tearing their way free.

We were looking in the wrong place, she thought. *What Mekan did to the Temple of the Earth was a distraction.*

The Void had been beneath their feet the whole time.

———

The Disciples who'd come in pursuit of Niema did indeed ride raptors, and to Kelan, the sight of humans precariously balancing on the flat-headed reptilian creatures' backs was more amusing than threatening. Both were thin and wiry, like Niema, but wore fierce expressions that were more soldier-like than he'd have expected from the Disciples of Life. The female Disciple had her hair tied up in a knot that was somewhat windswept from riding, while the male's face was splotched with what appeared to be bloodfly bites.

Niema's face blanched with fear. "They're dangerous, Kelan. If they see you helping me…"

"Dangerous? You mean they're allowed to kill?" Wasn't that against Yalet's tenets? "Interesting."

"It's not *interesting,* it's *wrong.*" Niema hunched over in the canoe. "Don't—"

"Sorry." Kelan called on the god of the sky, sending a fierce gust of wind to knock both raptors backwards. The Disciples both tumbled off their steeds but recovered surprisingly fast, rolling to their feet.

The male Disciple faced Kelan with a hard stare. "You're here to help the traitor?"

"Traitor?" He glanced between them, observing that both Disciples did indeed have the leaf-shaped birthmarks on their necks that marked them as Disciples of Life. They also had numerous bite marks on their necks and arms, in addition to the ones on the male Disciple's face. *Was that Niema's doing?*

"Let me talk to them first." Niema rose upright and made to step out of the canoe.

"They don't look like they want to talk." Kelan tensed when the two Disciples whistled sharply. The raptors changed course, charging at Niema's canoe.

Kelan glided forward and grabbed Niema around the middle, yanking her out of the canoe. She made a noise of protest but let him lift her into the air, while the raptors halted on the riverbank at another whistled command from their riders.

"Out of interest, where were you going?" he called down to them.

"Are all Disciples of the Sky friends of traitors?" asked the male Disciple, ignoring the question. "Are you a friend of the Disciple of Death, too?"

He means Yala. "I can't say I'm friends with any Disciples of Death, no. The last few I met tried to kill me."

"Corruption must be eradicated from the world," said the female Disciple. "No exceptions."

"Cheery, aren't they?" he remarked to Niema, who didn't answer. He could feel her trembling with exhaustion and a surge of anger at her companions arose within him. Raising his voice, he said, "If the best way to fight Corruption is with the aid of a Disciple of Life, you won't mind if I borrow this one, will you?"

"Kelan!" Niema hissed.

"Niema is a traitor who is marked by the god of death Himself," insisted the female Disciple. "She befriended a Disciple of Death and committed a terrible crime against our own, and she will face justice at the hands of the god of life."

"Really? I don't see Mekan's mark." He adjusted his grip and pretended to examine Niema's face, mostly because he was a little concerned that she might faint and slide out of his grip if he didn't pay close attention. "You should know, the god of death has usurped the Temple of the Earth. If you're set against Mekan's dominion, you might want to focus your efforts there instead of against one harmless Disciple."

"Mekan is our sworn enemy, and it is our imperative to rid the world of all His followers," the male Disciple retaliated. "Return Niema to us."

"She's not Death's Disciple," Kelan told them. "And if she was, it's illegal for you to capture and judge a Disciple who doesn't belong to your own order."

"We do not adhere to the common law."

"That doesn't mean those laws don't apply to you." Not that most people would stand in the path of a pair of militant Disciples of Life. *I think it's time to leave.* "If you have no intention of helping the Disciples of the Earth to rid their temple of Mekan's influence, Niema and I will deal with it ourselves."

Both Disciples whistled, sharp enough to hurt his eardrums. A black smear rose from the bushes, resolving into a cloud of bloodflies.

Kelan launched into flight, and Niema yelped as they climbed higher into the air. Sharp stings erupted along his neck and hands, but Niema released a whistle of her own, causing the bloodflies to change direction. Not for long. An instant later, the buzzing returned, and a sharp pain in his wrist prompted him to release Niema with one hand to dislodge the insect from his arm.

She gave another yelp, her legs dangling. "Watch out!"

"Now, it'd be a tragedy if my face got covered in bites like your unfortunate friend over there."

While Niema once again directed the insects to change direction, Kelan picked up speed until the cloud of insects vanished in the breeze left in their wake. Niema stopped whistling and sagged in his grip with a quiet groan.

"That was fun." He glanced down at her. "Are you all right?"

"No." She trembled again. "They'll come after you, too."

"I thought they already were." Kelan adjusted his flight path to make sure they were still following the river. "What does your Superior want with Yala?"

"To put her on trial before Yalet Herself," Niema mumbled. "But they implied that murdering Mekan's followers doesn't count against their vows, which includes Yala *and* me."

"You aren't Mekan's follower." Kelan cut above a swathe of forest to further avoid the Disciples and their swarm of angry insects. "What would give them that idea?"

She was silent for a moment, and then spoke quietly. "They found out I saved Yala's life and healed her from near death."

"Oh." He considered this. "Yes, I can't imagine saving the life of a Disciple of Death would be in line with your deity's tenets."

"It's worse." Her voice was a ragged whisper. "I borrowed the life of my enclave members to heal her, without knowing, and—and one of them died."

Ah. Kelan racked his mind for something comforting to say. "You didn't know. They can't possibly blame you for something you had no control over."

Niema began shaking with silent sobs, and for the lack of any other adequate words, Kelan simply held her until they reached the outskirts of Setemar.

Upon seeing the cliffs shadowing the city walls, Niema stirred. "Wait, is it true? That... that the Disciples of the Earth need my help?"

"You don't have to do anything, but I thought you'd want to know Yala's here, too."

"Yala's *here?*" She twisted in his arms. "Then ... she doesn't know."

"Fortunately, I was visiting her friends in the capital when your note arrived and was able to pass on the warning," Kelan said. "Your handwriting is terrible, by the way."

"I was running for my life!" Her indignant tone almost sounded like her old self. "They'll catch up soon. Setemar is closer than Dalathar is."

"It'll still take a few days."

"Or less." Her shoulders stiffened. "They're following that beast over there."

He followed her gaze and spied a familiar bony winged shape ahead of them. "You've seen the dead war drake, too?"

"I thought it was following me," Niema mumbled. "Is ... is it following Yala, too?"

"In a manner of speaking." He didn't have time to explain Yala's risky bargain with Mekan before they reached Setemar, and he was probably better off letting Yala explain to Niema herself. "I think it's drawn to the dead, and this city is infested with them."

Niema shuddered. "Put me down over there."

"There?" She'd pointed at a patch of trees near the city, so he obliged and flew downward. "Any reason?"

"I need to replenish my strength." They touched the ground, and Niema dropped to a crouch and whispered a prayer. Eyes closed, she murmured Yalet's name. Her palms glowed green, and the surrounding plants began to wilt; when she opened her eyes, some of the exhaustion had faded from her face.

"You know, most people would just take a nap if they were tired," Kelan observed.

"I don't have *time* for a nap," Niema insisted. "If Mekan's infested the city, I have to help."

"We'll find Yala first." He lifted her into the air again and they glided over the city's outskirts. Once they'd crossed the city wall, Kelan flew to Yala's house first.

When he released Niema, she examined the row of narrow apartments in front of them. "I know this place."

"This is where Yala's staying," he said, knocking on the door. "If she's in. She was acting strange the last time I saw her."

She killed the Disciples of the Flame. Again, it was up to Yala to decide how much to share with Niema, but when nobody answered the door, a flicker of worry stirred. He hadn't expected her to sit idle all day, but he'd hoped she'd exercise a little caution. There was no telling whether Superior Dovial still intended to have her arrested—nor whether anyone had discovered the bodies of the Disciples she'd left behind in Mekan's chamber.

"Are there other Disciples of the Sky here in the city?" Niema peered over the rooftops. "I don't see any."

He inclined his head. "They're at the inn. Superior Sietra sent a second group after we lost several of our people fighting one of those void drakes, so if they're here, Laima and the others will be giving them instruction."

Niema flinched. "I should have been here. I never should have gone home. If I hadn't—they wouldn't have come after Yala."

"They would have," he said, with certainty. "She was at the

centre of their vision, wasn't she? Sooner or later the truth would have reached them."

Niema's gaze turned downward. "They thought she was our saviour. Can you blame them for turning against her when she didn't turn out to be what they expected?"

"They might feel betrayed, but their priorities are out of order." He indicated the cliffs which housed the Temple of the Earth. "So are theirs. They tried to arrest Yala, too, and I sincerely hope they haven't repeated their mistake."

Kelan veered in that direction, moving slower than usual so that Niema could keep up. She wasn't wearing any shoes, and she'd replaced her clothing with the reed-woven garment she'd worn during their first meeting before she'd learned the hard way that the city required hardier attire.

When they neared the front of the temple, Niema lifted her gaze to the forbidding statues on either side of the doors. "I would introduce myself to the Disciples of the Earth, but … are they truly serving Mekan now?"

"Not directly," Kelan said. "They locked Yala in a cell as a Disciple of Death, but they're also too scared to leave the temple to help fight off Mekan's monsters."

"That's not much of an endorsement." She lifted her chin. "Take me to your people first."

"Are you sure?" He had to admit she'd be far safer there than the alternatives, and Niema was in dire need of a reprieve from being chased or attacked. "All right, but I don't think Yala will be there."

The inn's downstairs room was even more crowded than the last time. In addition to the injured Disciples from the previous day were a number of new faces. *I thought so. The second team showed up.*

"This is Niema," he announced as they walked in. "She's here representing the Disciples of Life."

"Bit late for that," someone muttered.

A flush crept over Niema's face, but she held her head high as they crossed the room to a free corner. He let her take the only spare seat, reasoning that she needed it more than he did, and addressed the nearby Disciples. "Has anyone heard from Superior Dovial today?"

"No," Laima answered. "The Disciples have locked their doors again and aren't taking visitors."

"That's inconvenient." Had there been a new development overnight, or was the Superior's paranoia spinning out of control again? "I assume they haven't regained access to their deity?"

"Not to my knowledge." Laima eyed Niema with suspicion. "Is that why you brought a Disciple of Life here?"

"Partly," he evaded. "Ah, have you seen Yala today?"

"Didn't she leave with the Disciples of the Flame?" asked Lakiel. "I thought they went back to the capital."

"They did, but Yala stayed," he replied. "I gather she thought Mekan might try another route to attack the Temple of the Earth."

Was that where she'd gone? Surely not, if Superior Dovial had closed the door to visitors… but there were other routes into the temple. Through the mines.

As if in response to his thoughts, the ground trembled, rattling the furniture and causing the Disciples' conversation to cease.

Niema jumped in her seat. "What was that?"

"No idea. It's been happening since we got here." Kelan surveyed her hunched frame. "You need more suitable clothing. I can go to the market, but it might be easier if you borrow a spare cloak from the laundry room."

"I'm not dressing like a Disciple of the Sky." She sounded scandalised at the very idea.

"I'm insulted," Kelan said. "You can skip the cloak, but you can't walk around the city without shoes."

Another tremor shook the room, this one more intense. Several chairs fell over, their occupants leaping to their feet, and thumps sounded from upstairs, too. The whole inn quaked, and a rumbling sound emanated from below that sounded like a great beast stirring below the earth.

Niema, clinging to a chair, stared wide-eyed at him. "That not the god of the earth."

"No, it isn't." If his hunch was right, and Yala had gone back to the mines… "I think Yala might need our help."

30

Viam extended a hand and dropped the strip of meat on the ground in front of the war drake. The beast's nostrils contracted; jaws opening, it snapped up the meat in a quick bite. While its head was bowed, Viam used the stirrup to climb onto the war drake's back.

The watching guards gawped at her as she settled in the saddle and took hold of the reins. With a whispered command, she urged the beast take several steps forward, its wings bunching against its back.

"Can you fly?" one of the guards called to her. "Go on, show us."

"I'm not going to fly," she informed them. "This beast isn't trained to tolerate human riders yet. It'd probably drop me in the ocean."

What am I doing? she'd found herself thinking more than once. *They're wild animals. They have to be retrained from scratch, and that's not my job.*

Yet here she was. Part of it was because if Yala had been in the capital, Viam was certain that she'd have somehow found a way to get in on training the wild drakes, and another reason was the king's unpredictable habit of leaving the palace on excursions. Viam had no desire to see the monarch disembowelled by a war drake's claws.

"That was impressive." A young guard moved closer, and the war drake's head shot out. Its teeth snapped a finger span from the man's petrified face.

"Don't make sudden movements," Viam warned. "I'll put the muzzle back on."

She slid off the beast's side and reached into the bag at her waist for another piece of meat, which she tossed at the war drake as a distraction. While it was occupied chewing, she readied herself to put the muzzle back on, moving with practised ease forged from doing the same countless times under much tenser circumstances.

How things change, and yet all too often we end up back where we started.

By the time she'd hurried back to her quarters to change into clean clothes, she had scarcely half an hour before work started for the day, which left no time to go to the library. Not that she'd had much more luck teasing out information on the Disciples of Life during her brief visits over the past couple of days. She'd made a little more progress when she'd switched her focus to reading mythological accounts of how the other gods had banished Mekan to the Void, despite their lack of consistency. Some versions of the story had Dalathar taking on Mekan single-handedly, some involved Yalet too, and others claimed Mekan had voluntarily exiled Himself from the other deities without needing to be banished at all.

None, however, gave meaningful instructions as to how to handle Mekan without any aid from the other deities.

As Viam was leaving the staff dormitory, she heard a familiar voice calling her name. "Hello, Brenat."

"You look troubled." Brenat fell into step with Viam, and they crossed the palace grounds. "Is it those war drakes?"

"The guards are going to get themselves killed if they aren't careful," she admitted. "They need to rehire some proper trainers, assuming any will come back."

"Must be a well-paid job," Brenat remarked.

"Not enough to justify the risk," Viam replied. "Novices were the ones who did grunt work like mucking out the war drakes' pens. *That* was a thankless job, I can tell you."

Brenat laughed. "I'll have to make sure they assign me elsewhere."

"They're not going to make you sign up to the army again." The mere idea made Viam's heart sink. "You went through conscription already, right? Which unit?"

"Foot soldier," she replied. "Didn't see much combat. You?"

"I was in the flight division."

"Right, you used to fly on one of those war drakes … oh, is that why you've been helping the guards?"

"How else would I have learned how to handle those beasts?"

Brenat shrugged. "I just thought it was one of the things you've read every book on."

"You think I figured out how to handle a war drake from a book?" Viam laughed. "Definitely not."

With her mood somewhat improved, she and Brenat reached the administrative building, where they found none other than King Daliel talking to one of the staff members. Just in time, Viam managed to stop herself from kneeling; she didn't want him to get annoyed at her for making unnecessarily overt gestures of respect.

"Viam." The king smiled at her. "Just the person I was looking for. You were helping the guards, weren't you?"

Viam blinked, her mind taking a moment to catch up. "Ah —sorry I didn't ask your permission first, Your Majesty."

"That's not necessary," said the king. "I'm glad we have one person among the staff who knows how to handle those creatures. You've worked with them before?"

Viam nodded. "I was in the flight division in the army."

"Good," he said. "I was starting to think nobody here had ever seen one before."

"Do you think they'll be necessary?" she asked. "The war drakes?"

"I hope not." King Daliel's expression turned sombre. "However, at one time, the war drakes were one of our strongest assets."

"They were also dangerous to everyone, not just the enemy." Granted, they faced a far more cunning adversary today than they had when Rafragorian soldiers and their sea drakes had been the worst they'd expect to face on the battlefield.

Should she be the one to tell him the truth? Not all of it, of course, but the king was good-hearted, trying to do what was right to keep the people of Laria safe. How could he do that when he didn't truly know what he was up against?

"True," he acknowledged, "but it's worth being prepared, I think. You don't mind giving the guards some instruction, do you? I assume not, because you've already been spending your free time doing exactly that."

"Ah… no." A sense of resolution came over her. "I don't mind, but I also had something else I wanted to talk to you about, Your Majesty."

"Oh?" He regarded her with a curious smile. "What is it?"

"I—have some information for you," she said. "May I speak to you alone?"

Surprise flickered through his features. "Yes, I can arrange that."

————

Yala watched the dead man rise to his feet as tremors shook the ground, each stronger than the one before. The female Disciple screamed when her dead companion's knife ploughed into her chest, blood blossoming over the front of her borrowed robe.

Her body had scarcely hit the ground when shadows surged, yanking her upward like a puppeteer's strings.

"Fuck." Yala shoved the third Disciple at his companions and backed away as the two dead Disciples fell on the living one. Her stomach turned over at the sound of his fading screams, but she kept moving, bracing her cane against the wall to keep from being knocked over by the tremors.

The wall gave way beneath her hand. Yala stumbled as the ground lurched, tripping over the lantern she'd unthinkingly placed on the ground. In the same instant, two figures burst out of the wall in a shower of soil and debris.

A foul stench rolled out, brought by the new arrivals, and the tingling in her fingertips left no doubt as to their identities. The Disciples of the Flame's bodies were already far more decayed than two people who'd been dead less than a day ought to be, but their now dirt-smeared white robes were intact enough for her to know which was Mieren.

"Back to annoy me again, are you?" The unfortunate Disciple of Death's screams had faded, leaving Yala as the sole living target in the tunnel, and the odds of her being able to hack five dead people to pieces with a single dagger were not spectacularly high.

"Haven't I given you enough blood?" Yala spoke to the god of death, lifting her knife hand to expose the shadows seeping through her fingertips. "You can let me have one of them, surely."

The dead did not cease their attack. Yala brought her cane

up defensively, knocking down the first dead man to reach her. The second, Mieren, she stabbed with her dagger. When the ground gave another heaving shudder, Yala yanked out her blade before she was dragged down with Mieren's corpse.

Dead hands grabbed her from behind. Yala rammed her elbow backwards and spun her cane, smashing it into the man's knee. Bone cracked, but the man didn't release her. His grip was surprisingly strong, and painful against her burned arm.

"Get *off* me." With a heave of her shoulders, Yala freed herself, eyes watering with pain. Her fingers fumbled her dagger; her arm burned as if it had been set ablaze once again.

A sword swung, cleaving the dead man's body in two. Yala took a step back, clutching her injured arm, squinting at her rescuer. "Kelan."

He wasn't alone. Niema stood beside him, staring at the dead Disciples with wide, haunted eyes. "Yala."

"You have a good sense of timing." Yala gave Melian's body a shove, sending her into the path of Kelan's sword, too. "Nice to see you again, Niema."

Mieren's body fell before Kelan's blade and Niema hurried forward, green light flaring to life in her palms as she called upon the god of life.

"Don't overextend yourself." Yala knocked one of the remaining dead aside with her cane. "I don't know who's controlling these bastards. I can't get Mekan to listen to me."

Niema ignored her warning and raised her palms, green light flowing over the dead's shadowed forms. Their limbs stopped twitching, the shadows receding, and the five dead were reduced to corpses once again.

As the light washed over her, Yala's fingers spasmed with sudden pain, like invisible needles had been driven underneath her fingernails. The shadows that had been seeping out of her hands receded, vanishing under the bandages wrapped around her greying fingers.

The colour drained from Niema's face, and Kelan caught her shoulder as she stumbled against him. "You aren't going to faint, are you?"

"Might," Niema slurred. "Those … are Disciples…"

"Of the Flame, I know." Yala clenched her hands, hoping that Niema hadn't sensed the painful reaction her deity's magic had elicited. "Nothing stays dead in here."

Kelan reached back and picked up a lantern, which he must have brought with him. "Looks like we got here just in time."

"How did you know where to find me?" Yala re-sheathed her dagger and found her own lantern; by some miracle the flame had stayed lit after she'd kicked it over.

"Guesswork," Kelan replied. "You were making a lot of noise, too."

"I heard you've been having even more fun than I have, Niema." Yala fished her gloves out of her pockets and pulled them back on, covering her bandaged fingers. "What's this about the Disciples of Life coming to arrest me?"

"They're coming to take you to Yalet for judgement." Niema pitched forward; she'd have fallen flat on her face if Kelan hadn't caught her by the shoulders.

"Come on, you're exhausted," he said. "We'd better get out of here."

Yala sensed that now was not the moment to inform the others that the entire network of tunnels might lead to Mekan's domain. She was in no fit state to fight with her aching leg and throbbing arm, coupled with the intermittent spasms in her fingertips, and Niema was far worse off. What had the Disciples of Life done to her?

When they exited the tunnel, Niema sank onto the

nearest rock, her face ashen. She had no visible injuries and wore clean clothes that she must have purchased or borrowed them since arriving in Setemar, but her drawn expression reminded Yala of a prisoner of war.

"Niema?" She leaned on her cane to study her companion's face. "Did your Superior torture you?"

Niema's shoulders hunched. "No. She didn't want to do me any harm. None of them did. They only wanted to protect the enclave."

"They blamed her for things she wasn't responsible for," Kelan supplied. "They put her on trial and exiled her into the forest, leaving her to get attack by the dead. Then sent assassins to capture her when she escaped to save her own skin."

Yala frowned. "Assassins? From the Disciples of Life?"

"No," Niema mumbled. "Not assassins…"

"They might as well have been." Kelan levitated the cart back into place over the mine's entrance. "She said they had a convenient exemption from the vows against harming another living creature."

"Of course they did." Yala sank onto another rock, her leg aching and her burned arm throbbing. "I bet the Superior always had a secret group of assassins ready to call upon when she needed them. It's amazing how quickly they can drop their own principles as soon as there's a challenge to their established order."

Kelan leaned against a large rock across from Niema and Yala. "If it's any consolation, Superior Sietra has granted you permission to safely visit Skytower, Yala. I'm sure she'll extend the same invitation to Niema."

"I'll take that under consideration." Yala scowled. "The Disciples of Life will have to wait their turn. We have a situation here. If I'm not mistaken, the Temple of Death was never restricted to the chamber. It's much deeper underground."

"What?" Kelan lifted his head. "How'd you know?"

"The last surviving Disciples of Death told me," she said. "They implied the entire network of tunnels has been compromised by Mekan."

"How?" Kelan asked. "We can't destroy all the tunnels. I'm pretty sure the people living above wouldn't much like that."

"The whole city is a Temple of Death," Niema whispered. "We're doomed. If Mekan has got His claws into everyone in Setemar…"

"He hasn't," Yala said. "He *has* managed to ensnare some of the Disciples of the Earth, which might account for how easily He was able to get into their temple."

Kelan's brows lifted in surprise. "They betrayed their own god?"

Niema gasped and slid off the rock. "No. That's impossible."

Yala grunted. "The Disciples didn't share the details, but after what I've seen in the past few days, I'm not going to make judgements on what the god of death is capable of."

"The Disciples of the Earth have closed the doors to outsiders again," Kelan added. "Possibly for related reasons."

"Typical." Yala tapped her foot against the rock. "They're dooming themselves if they stay in that temple for much longer, whether they're loyal to Mekan or not."

Niema clambered back onto her rock. "They might not be. Superior Kralia implied that Mekan can get into *any* temple, whether it belongs to Him or otherwise."

"Superior Sietra said the same." Kelan nodded to Niema. "But she said the same is true of your god. Yalet."

Niema's shoulders slumped. "That doesn't matter. We're too late to stop Him."

"No, we aren't." Yala spoke loudly to dispel her own doubts as well as Niema's. "There's no reason to believe Setem is gone."

"No." Kelan pushed away from the rock he'd leaned

against. "Yes—I saw that Disciple use his abilities before he died. Hashet. Did you see, too, Yala?"

"I was a little preoccupied." She frowned, recalling the flash of blue light that had briefly ignited before Hashet's demise.

Niema looked between them. "He reached Setem? Are you sure?"

"It certainly looked as though he did." Kelan glided forward, his expression brightening. "He was... around there."

Yala's exhaustion wouldn't let her stand and examine the area he indicated, but there were no physical signs of Setem's presence. Only a fuzzy memory of a tremor, a light, and then Hashet's gruesome end.

"He wasn't near the mines," Yala observed. "Has anyone gone more than a handspan from the temple in weeks?"

"Except for the Disciples' illicit night-time excursions?" Kelan said. "I doubt they thought of trying to call their deity while drinking and fucking. Not if they didn't want to bring the roof down on their heads."

Yala rolled her eyes at him. "If you're right, I wonder what would happen if we helped some of the Disciples leave the temple?"

"Worth a try," Kelan agreed. "Superior Dovial has his people trapped by fear more than anything else, and if you ask me, some of the Disciples would be glad to get away from him."

"I thought you said some of them were working with Mekan." Niema pushed to her feet. "The Disciples."

"Yes," said Yala. "I don't think it's all of them, and they might have been trying to get back to the gods ... any god."

If they'd left their temple and set up another base elsewhere, they might have been able to strike back against

Mekan. Intentionally or not, Superior Dovial had been as much of an adversary as Trienan and his allies had.

"How do you propose we convince them to leave?" Kelan queried. "I'm not averse to the idea of corrupting a few Disciples, but I've been kicked out of the temple twice and you nearly got arrested."

"There's that." Yala gingerly lowered herself off the rock. "What we need is to talk to some of them without their Superior hovering over our shoulders."

"Pity they aren't using the back tunnel to sneak into the local taverns any longer," Kelan remarked. "Then we might have had a chance."

Niema stood, too, and took a few steps away from the mine. "What about me? I shouldn't even be here. I'm marked by Mekan, Superior Kralia said."

"Drakeshit." A surge of anger restored some of Yala's energy. "Your people were on this continent before the other Disciples showed up, did you know?"

"What?" Niema dropped to a crouch, and the grass around her began to shrivel and die. A glow ignited around her hands, and Yala once again braced herself as pain prickled her fingers under her gloves. She held her breath until the glow faded and Niema stood, her stance no longer as unsteady as before.

"I was reading an old journal written by a scholar," Yala said, "and it sounds like your people lived here at the same time as the people who initially inhabited that island. We both know who's still around today, and it's not them."

Niema's eyes rounded. "How can that be?"

"Your Superior isn't the most forthcoming individual, is she?" Kelan glided away from the mine entrance, too.

Niema ducked her head. "She's doing her best. And if it's true… we survived because Mekan didn't. We can't exist in the same space."

"According to whom?" Yala clenched her fists, trying to ignore slightest wisp of shadow escaping from her gloved hands. "She wasn't alive in those days. None of us were, and the Superiors have good reason to ensure the past stays buried where they think it belongs."

"I think *my* Superior is trying to uncover the truth," said Kelan, "but her success depends on whether we survive the present. Any ideas?"

Yala thought. There was only one option, really. "I'm going to corrupt some Disciples."

31

Late afternoon the same day, Viam found herself seated in an armchair in a luxurious suite that served as the king's main receiving room. King Daliel sat in a high-backed chair edged with gold serpentine carvings that were uncomfortably reminiscent of the statues in the Temple of the Flame. She'd never been in this room before; in the army, most ceremonies had taken place outside in the courtyards, and it had always been Yala who had commanded attention when her squad had received commendations from the king. The rest of them were little more than part of the scenery.

Now? She'd carried too many terrible secrets for too long, yet with the one man who might be able to help giving her his undivided attention, the words refused to come.

King Daliel spoke in kind tones. "You did want a private audience, didn't you?"

She nodded, trying to ignore the two guards standing next to the doors who were apparently included in that private audience. Given his father's fate, she could hardly blame him for taking precautions. "I'm sorry, your Majesty.

I… I was a soldier, and my squad leader was always the one who spoke for me."

"A soldier." Understanding flickered across his face. "I can only apologise for what you endured in defence of our nation."

Why would he say that? Isn't he the one who's thinking of bringing back the army? Of course, there was a marked difference between waging a decades-long campaign against a neighbouring nation and defending one's country against an unnatural threat from within its own borders.

"What did you wish to tell me?" he asked. "Speak. There's no need to be afraid."

"I was on the last mission ordered by your father." She forced out the secrets that rose in her throat like bile. "My squad—in the flight division—were probably the last people to take orders from him."

His polite smile froze. "Is that so?"

"Yes." She pushed onward. "I don't know how much he told you, but our last mission was to claim an uninhabited island before Rafragoria, and he sent my squad there ahead of the rest of the army."

"Yes … that makes sense," King Daliel said. "I read the reports, but they were sparsely detailed, given the unthinkable tragedy that followed the mission."

Viam nodded. "We were never asked for a full report either. I understand why, but—I thought you should know that what we saw on the island was not so dissimilar to the events that occurred in the capital a few weeks ago."

King Daliel was silent for a moment, his body still enough for her to know she'd shocked him. She didn't dare look at the guards to see if they mirrored his reaction. "What did you see?"

"A—a temple, devoted to Mekan." She swallowed. "Monsters. They'd already killed the Rafragorian contingent. I believe their team unthinkingly awakened the Void when they set foot on the island, and we flew straight into the same trap."

"Yet you escaped."

"Barely." Viam squeezed her eyes shut, tears intruding on her vision. "One of my team died to save us. When we returned to Laria, everyone had bigger concerns than the island, understandably, and…"

"Then I disbanded the flight division," murmured King Daliel. "I see now that I made an error in doing so."

"My squad leader went straight to the Disciples of the Flame," Viam went on. "You can imagine that the tale would sound outrageous to anyone who hadn't seen the island with their own eyes, and—and they dismissed her story."

"It's understandable that Superior Datriem would have wanted to avoid causing further strife and panic," said King Daliel. "I confess that I banished the Disciples from the palace for a time, after my father's death. I was angry, irrationally perhaps, that they didn't protect him."

Viam's heart jolted in her chest. *They didn't … they killed him.* King Daliel might have unknowingly saved his own life by sending the Disciples away. "I heard… I heard the Superior was close to your father."

"Yes, Superior Datriem was one of his closest advisors," he said. "I wish I'd trusted him sooner. He would certainly have known the dangers that awaited us, given the Temple of the Flame's extensive collection of texts on Corruption."

His words rang in Viam's skull, and the memory of a book bound in drakeskin crept to the forefront of her mind. "They have books on—Corruption?"

"Of course," he said. "There is nowhere safer in all of Laria, is there?"

It's not possible. Is it?

If he was right, the original owner of the books from

which King Tharen had learned of the island and which Melian had used to learn Corruption … had been Superior Datriem.

———

Yala and the others returned to Setemar on foot. They walked slowly, for Niema's sake, though Yala was glad of the reprieve. Niema had insisted on applying Yalet's healing gift to Yala's burned arm to lessen her pain, but her expression remained grim and haunted despite Kelan's best efforts to raise her spirits. As they walked, they discussed and dismissed plan after plan for talking to the other Disciples without being challenged by Superior Dovial.

"If we could get a message in there, it would help." Yala racked her mind for ideas. "Like one of Melian's recruitment posters."

"That's how she found her followers?" Kelan tilted his head. "Niema, you can help, can't you? You sent a message to Yala. Two, in fact."

"Kelan, I think a bird would stand out more in a tunnel than in the sky," Yala said. "Besides, there are no windows. The only way in and out is through the front door or through one of the tunnels."

"We could try another diversion near the back tunnel." Kelan indicated a pair of raptors pulling a wagon along the road. "A runaway raptor is less likely to be blamed on me than another incident involving ale barrels."

"I'm not going to cause a scene," Niema protested.

"You might not need to." Yala lifted her head, spying the shadowy outline of the dead war drake in the sky above the cliffs. "Not if that monster gets any closer."

Niema flinched. "You aren't controlling it, are you?"

"No…" Yala dropped her gaze to her gloved hands. "Not that I'm aware of."

"How would you be unaware?"

Not wanting to tread further down that road, Yala back-tracked. "If you want to send a note to the Disciples, you'll need something to write with."

"Something that isn't mud this time," Kelan added. "It's a miracle anyone was able to read your last message."

"Go on, then." Niema gestured to a row of shops ahead of them. "I don't have any money. You can get hold of some writing materials, can't you?"

"I have to admit I've missed how refreshingly straightforward you are." Kelan departed with a grin, while Niema and Yala waited for him on a bench.

"This isn't going to work," Yala muttered. "The guards won't leave the back door unattended again… unless you approached them in person, I suppose."

Niema flinched. "You want me to expose myself?"

"They don't know your face," Yala said. "If you explain that your Superior sent you to help, they won't turn you away."

"They might." Niema fidgeted in her seat. "Or they might refuse to deliver a message to anyone other than the Superior."

"Wouldn't you prefer that to setting a group of raptors loose?" Kelan glided downward and handed Niema a quill and some paper. "Write a note and ask for it to be delivered to the Superior, and then send another message to the regular Disciples while the guards are distracted."

"Saying what?" Niema took the quill in one hand and placed the paper on the bench to write on. "If I write a message asking them to betray their Superior, and it gets intercepted by someone loyal to him…"

"Say you're here to help vanquish Mekan and bring back

their deity," Kelan suggested. "Ask anyone who's interested to meet outside the mines. They're bound to have several ways out. Even if some of them get caught on the way, others might make it there without being hauled back into the temple. I don't see their Superior trekking all the way over to the mines in person."

"No… definitely not." It wasn't a perfect plan, by far, but Yala had to admit he'd covered most bases. "Maybe send a skirrit instead of a bird. Less conspicuous."

"True." When she'd written out the notes, Niema summoned a small rodent with a whistle and urged it to follow her towards the inner city's wall.

Yala kept her distance, but Kelan kept gliding over to check on Niema's progress with the city guards.

"Will you keep still?" Yala hissed at him. "They're going to figure out we're involved if you keep bouncing around like a wild kekin."

"She's a good liar," Kelan said. "The guards are listening to her."

"Then let her do her job." Yala lifted her head as the shadow of the war drake passed over the rooftops again. *Damn, that's close.* Wait…

"There are two of them," Kelan observed, head titled back. "That's not a dead war drake either."

"No." The war drake was undoubtedly *alive,* its dark scales gleaming in the sunlight, and a rider sat upon its back. Not a soldier. The figure didn't wear armour, nor did they carry a weapon. "Who…?"

"I'll check." Kelan took flight, and Yala seized a handful of his cloak and yanked him back down. "What?"

"Don't give them an excuse to attack us." Suspicion prickled at the edge of her mind, and a flash of green light in the sky above confirmed her guess. "They're Disciples of Life."

"Niema." Alarm flitted across Kelan's face. "We were wrong about them taking days to catch up with her."

Yala groaned under her breath when he overtook her, gliding towards the temple's back entrance. When shouts of anger followed from the guards, she inferred that he'd obliterated any chance they had of making a stealthy approach. Reaching the adjacent street, she peered around the corner and spied the guards running out of the alleyway, while Niema stood awkwardly nearby.

Yala waited for the guards to vanish before she darted around the corner to join the others. "Kelan, *what* did you do this time?"

"I told them we were under attack from hostile war drakes," he said. "They could hardly call me a liar when the evidence is right above their heads."

"My people are here!" Niema's body shuddered. "They're coming for me, and for you."

"Calm down," Yala said. "We won't get anywhere by panicking. Did you give your message to the guards?"

"Yes, but they never had time to take it to the Superior, thanks to him." Niema jerked her head at Kelan, who was in the process of pulling open the tunnel door.

"Your little rodent messenger did make it inside the temple." He gestured through the door. "Come on. What better place to hide than under the Superior's nose?"

"You want to go *into* the temple?" Yala asked.

"Why not?" he queried. "I can guarantee the last place those Disciples will expect to find Niema is in a temple compromised by the god of death, and you'll be able to pass on your message to more of the Disciples of the Earth, too."

Niema opened her mouth in protest and then closed it. "I don't know the way…"

"I do." Resigned, Yala climbed through the door and beckoned Niema to follow her. "Kelan, the guards will have expected *you* to go into the tunnel. We need someone to stay out here and keep their attention off us."

This wasn't ideal—Niema had never been in the temple before, and Yala hadn't seen as much of it as Kelan had—but they might be able to ensure Niema's message reached some of the other Disciples. Moreover, if Niema was able to prevent Mekan's forces from advancing any further into Setemar, she'd be best positioned to do so from inside the temple itself.

"I'll lead the way," Yala murmured to Niema. "This tunnel leads into the room where they bury their dead Disciples. We aren't likely to be ambushed in there... not by the living, anyway."

Niema gave a quiet whimper. "They're here. They already found me."

"I know." Yala sympathised with her, but there was no time to panic. "Superior Dovial won't let them into the temple, not if he's barred his doors against outsiders. Kelan will do his best to keep them distracted, too."

They advanced through the tunnel, using the light of the lanterns wedged into the ceiling to guide their way. When they neared the fork in the tunnel, Yala's fingers began to tingle again; she clenched her fists and willed Mekan to leave her be.

Niema slowed her pace. "I can sense people ahead of us."

"Who?" Yala listened, not hearing anyone, but Niema's ability to detect any nearby living creatures was much sharper than her regular senses. "Can you identify them?"

"No," Niema whispered back. "I can recognise my enclave members, but only because I've known them for so long. Not strangers."

"How close are they?" Yala gripped her cane and walked around the corner, where someone had replaced the rocks that covered the other branch in the tunnel.

"Not that near." Niema trod behind her on quiet feet. "I'll know if they're close enough to hear us."

"Handy," she said. "Can you use your abilities inside the actual temple? Kelan said you might be able to."

"I don't know," Niema said. "Before the Temple of the Flame, I'd never visited the home of another deity."

"And you had other things on your mind there," Yala recalled. "In Skytower, too."

Niema's gaze dropped. "I don't know that we can rely on my abilities to help us, if I'm infected by Corruption."

"You aren't infected." *I am,* she thought, a prickling sensation rising in her fingertips as they drew nearer to the room containing the Disciples' graves. "Don't be ridiculous."

"The dead *are* following me, though," Niema said. "What if I can't get rid of Mekan's influence and I make things worse instead?"

"Let's assume that isn't an option." Yala emerged into the chamber where the Disciples' dead had been laid to rest. Fresh earth covered their tombs, but shadows stirred in the corners. *Not now, Mekan.* She listened for human voices instead and caught an indistinct murmur from one of the tunnels branching off, but she couldn't tell which direction it led.

Niema came to a stop. "It's *them.* My people are in here."

Yala swore under her breath. "That tunnel must lead to the main chamber."

It also meant Superior Dovial had let them into the temple, which dispelled her argument that he'd refuse them entry—but also confirmed that Niema's abilities did work inside another deity's home.

"This one is empty." Niema indicated one of the narrow passages with a trembling hand. "But there are a *lot* of people in that direction."

Yala peered through the tunnel she'd indicated. "Might it lead to the rooms where all the Disciples are confined?"

If the Disciples of Life were in the main chamber, Superior Dovial would be there, not watching the other Disciples. This might be their only chance to get their message directly to the others.

"I think so," Niema said faintly. "But—*all* the passages end up back in the same place."

"The main chamber." Yala knew that, but they'd come too far into the temple to risk retreating. "We know which way to avoid. I doubt there are many people wandering around unsupervised."

She took the lead into the tunnel, glad of the lanterns placed at intervals to show the way ahead. After a short time, they came to a row of identical wooden doors from which whispers and muttering issued. *Here they are.*

Picking a door at random, Yala walked into a chamber full of robed figures who couldn't be older than sixteen. Most sat on cushions or sleeping mats, playing cards or dice, and some jumped to their feet at their sudden appearance.

A young man addressed them. "Who are you?"

"We're here to help," Yala said to the Disciples. "Did your Superior forbid you from leaving your rooms?"

"Yes," said the novice. "Nobody is allowed in or out. No exceptions. That includes you."

"I'm no Disciple," Yala told him. "Is everyone in the temple shut in their dormitories? Including the full-ranked Disciples?"

"Except the highest ranked ones," the novice answered. "Why are you here?"

"To help them." Yala surveyed the room. "Did you by any chance see a skirrit carrying a note a while ago?"

"I did." A young woman held up a scrap of paper. "It dropped this."

Good. "Read that note. Decide what you think. Oh, and can you do me a favour and not mention you saw us?"

She didn't wait for a reply, instead she backed out of the room and moved to the next door. As soon as someone heard the disturbance, they'd call for the Superior, and she couldn't reasonably expect everyone to obey her request for silence.

The next room contained a group of full-fledged Disciples who'd gathered around a table, upon which sat the skirrit that Niema had sent into the temple to deliver the messages. As Yala closed the door behind her, all eyes turned in her direction.

"Who are you?" asked several voices, some addressing Yala, others directed at Niema.

"Nobody important," Yala answered. "I'm here to help you."

"You sent this." A burly male Disciple waved Niema's note in the air. "You're with Pehin, aren't you?"

"Depends what Pehin's intentions are," Yala said. "Ours are to stop Superior Dovial from holding you all hostage and help you regain access to your deity."

"Pehin thinks we should betray our Superior and walk out," said the Disciple. "That won't help us regain Setem's favour."

"What if the alternative is to stay in here until the god of death kills you all?" Yala asked. "Staying in here is what's stopping your connection to your deity from coming back. I'm not going to give you orders, but I think you should be offered the choice. This isn't a Temple of the Earth anymore. It's a Temple of Death."

Objections broke out, which Yala shushed with a glare. "Where is Pehin? I want to talk to her."

"Nobody knows," another Disciple said. "She does whatever she wants."

"Sounds like your Superior doesn't have complete control

over you." Yala's gaze slid between them, while Niema whistled for the rodent's attention. "Remember you're bound to Setem, not to Superior Dovial. Your deity won't fault you for trying to find Him."

"Yala." Niema whispered in her ear. "Someone else is coming this way."

"Shit." Yala faced the Disciples. "We'll be waiting near the mines at the village for anyone who wants to join us."

If we don't get caught. While the Disciples passed the note amongst themselves, conversing in low voices, Yala pushed the door open. The sound of footsteps prompted her to walk as swiftly as her leg would allow, knocking on each door they passed. She heard Niema whistling to the skirrit to deliver more notes into the various dormitories, but the corridor ran in a straight line, and at the end stood a single figure.

Superior Dovial.

"You." He jabbed a finger at Yala. "I thought I heard a rodent in the tunnels."

How pleasant. Covering Niema with her back, Yala drew herself upright and attempted a mimicry of Kelan's nonchalance. "Sorry for bursting in like this, but you barricaded the doors. I have an urgent message for you."

"You *dare* to come back in here after you escaped custody?" he snarled. "You should be in jail."

Brushing past Yala, Niema dropped to her knees before him. "Superior Dovial, I am honoured to meet you."

Yala's surprise and alarm melted into a rush of satisfaction at his slack-jawed expression. Recovering himself, Superior Dovial addressed Niema. "Who are you?"

"I am a Disciple of Life." Niema stood tall. "I apologise for entering your home in such a manner, but it's my belief that your entire temple has been infected by Mekan. I was sent here by my Superior to help you."

"You aren't the first person to make that claim." His eyes

narrowed. "Moreover, you arrived here in the company of a criminal."

"I was not aware that Yala broke any laws." Niema straightened upright, meeting his eyes. "She saved the capital from the dead, and I believe she can do the same here."

"Superior Dovial!" a voice called from behind him. "Superior Dovial—we have visitors."

"Who now?" he demanded. "I thought I told you not to let anyone in."

"They're from the Disciples of Life," said the robed figure. "And they claimed they're looking for an escaped convict."

———

No, Niema thought. *Not this. Not now.*

She'd assumed Superior Dovial himself had answered the door, that he'd sent the Disciples of Life away—but deep in her heart, she'd known that they wouldn't give up that easily. Not when they believed themselves to be arbiters of justice sent to scourge every trace of Mekan's presence from this realm.

Including her … and including Yala.

Disciples of the Earth flanked them both as their Superior led the way into the main chamber. A commotion had broken out on the doorstep, where the two Disciples of Life who'd been pursuing Niema argued with someone on the steps outside the temple. Niema could make a shrewd guess as to the source of the disturbance, and her hunch was confirmed when she caught sight of Kelan's blue cloak outside the door.

"What is going on?" Superior Dovial asked the newcomers. "Are you really from the Disciples of Life?"

"Yes, and I'm afraid we're here with bad news," said Kelik. "One of our own has allied with the Disciples of

Death and may have come here to trick you. *He* was with her, too."

"I was?" Kelan sounded surprised. "I seem to be in several places at once lately."

Yala caught Niema's arm. "Come on. Let's go, while they're distracted—"

"Where?" Niema backed up a step, straight into a cloaked Disciple.

"Don't worry," whispered a feminine voice in her ear. "I'm going to help you get out."

"Pehin," Yala muttered. "I wondered where you were hiding."

"Sounds like you've been busy, too," Pehin remarked. "Come with me."

Niema had little choice but to let Pehin guide her and Yala into the same tunnel through which they'd entered the main chamber. The Disciple of the Earth planted herself in the way. "I'll keep them occupied. My friends will show you to the way out."

Two more Disciples beckoned Yala and Niema to follow them through an open wooden door. Shouts rang out from the main chamber, so they hurried across the dormitory past groups of curious Disciples to another door at the far end. They left the room and Niema was alarmed to find Pehin waiting for them on the other side.

"This place might seem like a maze, but it's easy enough to navigate when you've been here long enough," Pehin said in response to Niema's confusion. "Out of interest, why are your own people coming to arrest you?"

"They think I betrayed them by befriending Yala." Niema took in a quick breath. "Where...?"

"That way." Pehin pointed down a tunnel that plunged into darkness. "I thought your friend wasn't a Disciple of Death."

"I'm not," said Yala. "The Disciples of Life tend to view anyone who's had any contact with the god of death as tainted, and those two are particularly militant. Right, Niema?"

There was more to it than that, but Niema nodded. "They think we're traitors, and they'll think the same of you."

Pehin laughed. "Oh, I'm used to that by now. I'll see how many people I can bring to the mines. Does that sound good?"

Yala inclined her head. "I'll see you there."

32

Kelan watched Yala and Niema's escape out of the corner of his eye, doing his best to keep the Superior's attention on himself instead. The Disciples of Life had left their war drakes outside of the city's limits, mercifully, but they'd arrived far sooner than he or Niema had expected.

"He's a liar," said the male Disciple of Life. "An agent of Mekan."

"I'm not an agent of Mekan," Kelan corrected him. "I'm here on behalf of my own Superior to *stop* Mekan. It seems to me that we're at cross-purposes as a result of our Superiors' commands, not our deities'. That doesn't mean everyone who disagrees with you is allied to Corruption."

"That remains to be seen," said Superior Dovial. "You cannot be trusted any more than your friend Yala can."

"And these people?" He indicated the Disciples of Life. "They're effectively assassins acting on their Superior's orders. You want to let them run around your temple unchecked?"

"We are no assassins," said the Disciple. "We are here to

purge the nation of Laria of any traces of Mekan and His allies."

"Which includes committing murder," Kelan added. "I'm not going to tell Superior Dovial how to run his temple, but I assume he doesn't want *more* dead bodies in there."

Shouts rang out from deeper in the chamber, suggesting that Yala and Niema's escape had been discovered. When Superior Dovial turned his back on the door, the two Disciples of Life attempted to enter.

Kelan barred the way. "Now, I happen to know you captured and tortured a friend of mine, so I wouldn't let you into *my* temple. You don't have any authority here either."

"Neither do you,' said the female Disciple. "If you stand in our way, I will call upon Yalet to aid me."

Two can play at that game. Kelan lifted a hand and conjured a breeze. "Yours isn't the only deity present, and there are rather more of my people than there are of yours."

The Disciples of the Sky had come out of the inn to see what was going on, though none were close enough to hear their conversation.

In response, one of the Disciples of Life whistled, and the sound of beating wings carried over the rooftops.

"Oh, come on." Kelan watched the huge form of a war drake rise above the rooftops. "That's hardly fair."

"Enough!" Superior Dovial reappeared in the doorway. "Kelik, Shetrem, I apologise, but I'm going to have to ask you to leave. We have two criminals on the run inside our temple."

"We can find them," said one of the Disciples of Life. "Provided this Disciple is not allowed to interfere. He's already aided in the escape of one of those criminals."

Superior Dovial gestured to Kelan without looking him in the eyes. "He will never set foot in here again."

"Let's hope I don't have to." He also hoped that Yala and

Niema would manage to find their way out before the Disciples of Life caught up to them, but if he took another step closer to the temple, he'd be at their mercy as well. Especially if his theory that the Disciples of Life were able to use their abilities inside any other deity's temple was accurate.

He glided down the steps and found a group of Disciples of the Sky gathering outside the inn, including Laima, who greeted him with a scowl. "Don't tell me you were causing trouble for Superior Dovial *again.*"

"Did you see those two war drakes?" He gestured to the reptilian form vanishing behind the city wall. "They brought Disciple of Life assassins to hunt down Yala."

"Disciple of Life... assassins?" she repeated. "I thought Yala left the city."

"No, she didn't," he said. "We're in deeper trouble than I thought. The tunnels underneath Setemar *are* the Temple of Death, but those Disciples are more interested in arresting Yala than evicting Mekan from the city."

Laima's mouth fell open. "If you're right, what are we supposed to do? Evacuate the whole city?"

"I don't know," he said, "but we're pretty sure that the only way for the Disciples of the Earth to regain their connection to their deity is to leave the temple. Superior Dovial, as you might imagine, isn't a fan of that idea, and he's flat-out refusing to tell them the truth."

Laima groaned. "Kelan, you can't turn the Disciples against their Superior. I know Yala thinks she can do whatever she likes, but our Superior gave us orders."

"To stop Mekan," Kelan retaliated. "Didn't you feel the earthquakes earlier? They're getting worse, and the Disciples of the Earth are powerless to join the fight against the deity occupying their temple as long as Superior Dovial keeps them imprisoned."

"What's your and Yala's big plan, then?"

"The Disciples of the Earth who want to help us fight are going to escape through the mines near the village," he said, addressing the rest of the Disciples, too. "Do any of you want to come with me to meet them?"

Nobody offered a word of support, including Laima. *It's going to be like that, is it?*

Yala and Niema followed a winding route through the tunnels deep below the cliffs. Pehin had given them a lantern with which to see the way ahead, but these tunnels were little used and often hard to traverse. Niema frequently had to use her abilities to make vines shoot up from the earth and push aside large rocks blocking their path, and soon Yala's leg burned with the exertion.

Seeing her discomfort, Niema moved in to help. Her hands glowed faintly, and the pain lightened a little, though her fingertips stung in the same instant.

"Thanks." Yala rubbed her shin. "I understand why the Disciples didn't want to make it easy for outsiders to get into their temple, but it seems futile for them to bother when they're opening their doors to assassins now."

"I didn't expect them to catch up to us so quickly," Niema said quietly "They didn't have war drakes the last time I saw them."

"Do you think the Superior helped?"

"I hope not," she said. "If they did, she'll be close behind them."

And she'll come to arrest both of us or worse. As if they needed another enemy.

Footsteps came fast on their heels. Yala tensed, and Niema spun around. "Sorry. I forgot to check if anyone was following. It's not the Disciples of Life..."

The footsteps grew louder, and Pehin came sprinting up to them, breathless and holding a lantern. "Sorry."

"You're early," Yala observed. "What is it?"

"Someone told the Superior." She bent double, gasping as though she'd run all the way from the temple. "Or he guessed our plan. He's been asking the Disciples of Life to help close off all the non-essential tunnels."

"Instead of dealing with Mekan?" Yala swore. "How many people did you convince to join us?"

"A few," Pehin answered. "Not enough."

"I guess we'll have to see if they make it out." They continued to walk, and as silence filled the tunnel, an unasked question arose in Yala's mind. "Did you ever find out what happened in that mining tunnel?"

"No." Pehin turned her gaze away. "I haven't had many opportunities to get out of the temple in the last few days."

"You knew, though, didn't you?" Yala pressed. "Those bodies that attacked us. Who killed them?"

"I don't know." She slowed her pace, the lantern dangling from her hand so that her face was cast in shadow. "I heard stories, but I wasn't involved."

"Stories about some of your fellow Disciples trying to contact Mekan?" Yala's words elicited a sharp intake of breath from Niema, but she continued. "I know they did. I heard directly from a Disciple of Death before I killed him."

"You did what?" Pehin tripped over a rock, almost dropping the lantern. "When?"

"It doesn't matter," Yala replied, sensing Niema watching her, too. "They're no longer a threat, but I want to make sure you aren't, either. Have you ever spoken to Mekan?"

"No." Pehin gulped. "No, but some of the others… I heard them talking, saying they might be able to reach Setem if they bargained with Mekan."

"By killing their fellow Disciples?" She assumed that was

how the three bodies had ended up wandering around the city, similarly to the fate that had befallen the Rafragorian soldiers on the island.

"I think it was an accident," Pehin mumbled. "I didn't know them well, but when they started scheming to meet in that tunnel, I decided I wasn't going to take the risk."

"Good call." She glanced at Niema, who'd stopped in her tracks. "What is it?"

"Someone's behind us." She fiddled with the hem of her borrowed shirt. "I don't think it's the Disciples of Life, but there are quite a few people."

"Ah—it's the first group of Disciples." Pehin backed up several steps. "I told them to take different routes in order to avoid attention."

"I hope they weren't followed."

"They weren't. Don't worry, I'd know if there were unfamiliar voices among them."

Yala would have to take her word for it; the murmur of voices was scarcely audible to her ears, but it made sense that people who'd spent their lives underground were sensitive enough to sound to distinguish one Disciple's voice from another at the other end of an echoing tunnel.

Yala watched Pehin vanish around a corner, and she returned within a minute with several other Disciples in tow. The group was smaller than Yala would have liked, maybe fifteen in total, but they made too much noise for Yala's liking.

As the group of newcomers overtook them, Niema let out a sudden gasp. "I can sense my people."

"The Disciples of Life?" Yala caught Pehin's eye. "How close are the others?"

"I don't know," she said. "They all took different routes, like I said."

"I'll go," Niema offered. "I'll find the Disciples of Life. If I hand myself over to them, it'll win you time to escape."

"You can't do that, Niema," Yala insisted. "They'll kill you."

"No." Niema turned on her heel and faced the tunnel behind them. "You have to help the Disciples of the Earth."

"That doesn't mean you have to make a martyr of yourself." Damn. They could ill afford to waste time arguing, but Pehin had stopped walking as well.

"They aren't alone," Pehin whispered. "They must have intercepted the other group on the way out of the temple."

The murmur of voices reached Yala's ears, resolving into shouts. Before Yala could stop her, Niema broke into a sprint, and Pehin followed fast on her heels.

Dammit. Yala saw the Disciples of the Earth who'd been ahead of her had made to turn around, too. "Don't stop," she snapped at them. "Get out while you can."

The Disciples bolted, while Yala followed the discordant shouts until she came to a blockade. Pehin was involved in a heated argument with the Disciples of Life, who'd barred the other Disciples of the Earth from getting through the tunnel, while Niema stood nearby with her fists clenched at her sides.

"Let them go," she said to the Disciples of Life. "Take me instead. I'm the one you wanted, aren't I?"

"And me." Yala projected her voice so that it echoed off the tunnel walls.

As soon as the Disciples of Life turned their attention onto Yala, Niema darted forward, weaving between the Disciples of the Earth until Yala had lost sight of her. The other Disciples of Life pursued her, and a flash of green light blossomed. Roots sprouted from the earth, becoming twisting vines that spanned the tunnel from floor to ceiling.

"Don't stand there," Yala hissed at the gaping Disciples of the Earth. "Come on."

The Disciples of the Earth came to their senses and ran away from the vines surging from the spot where the Disciples of Life struggled against one another. Yala stared at the solid wall of green Niema had conjured; when the wall began to crack, she hastened to catch up to Pehin.

Fervently hoping that Niema had been right about the Disciples of Life not harming one of their own, Yala followed Pehin's lead through the tunnel until they reached daylight.

When they emerged, some of the Disciples of the Earth shielded their eyes as if they'd never seen the sun before. Understandable, given how long they'd been trapped inside in the dimly lit tunnels, but Yala found herself wondering how a group of people who flinched from sunlight would ever stand a chance of facing up to a god. The second group of Disciples were huddled together near the mines, equally apprehensive.

"Can any of you sense your deity?" Yala asked them. "If not, you'll need to move further away."

"No." One of the Disciples pointed shakily at the sky. "Not with those things flying around."

Yala spied three winged shapes above, two living and one dead; the latter was close enough for her to make out the shadows seeping between its bony wings. "It won't hurt you."

"You're really a Disciple of Death," said another Disciple. "How are we to trust you won't betray us?"

"It's a bit late for second thoughts," Yala told them. "I'm here to stop Mekan, and preferably to avoid getting killed in the process."

"Agreed." Kelan came gliding down, further startling the Disciples. "Apologies for being late. I had some difficultly convincing the other Disciples of the Sky to come and help."

Pehin tilted her head back to the sky. "I don't see any."

"Exactly."

"The Disciples of Life took Niema," Yala told him. "She

used her abilities to block the tunnel and buy us time to escape, but they won't give up that easily."

"Shit." Kelan scanned the Disciples of the Earth who'd opted to leave. "We need to find their deity…"

"Yes, we need to go somewhere that isn't on top of Mekan's temple." Yala strode away from the mine entrance towards the area where they'd fought the void drake.

Pehin indicated the rain-slick mud in front of the mines. "That's where Hashet…"

"He managed to call Setem." Kelan glided to that spot and beckoned to the other Disciples. "Over here."

Most of the Disciples of the Earth wore sceptical expressions, but some followed Pehin's lead. A few moments passed, and then a Disciple let out a cry of surprise. There came a crack, and a flash of blue light, and he held up a small rock, which had cracked clean in two. "Setem… He answered me."

The other Disciples rushed towards him with shouts of surprise and relief; some fell to their knees, uttering prayers.

"It worked." Kelan glided back to Yala's side. "We might just be able to oust Mekan after all."

"Don't speak too soon." Most Disciples of the Earth remained ensconced inside their temple, and now Niema had been forced to block one of the few remaining routes out. "We need to get Niema away from those fanatics, preferably without their war drakes tearing off our limbs."

The living war drakes were nowhere to be seen, but the dead one continued to circle the cliffs, as if it was waiting for Yala to call upon its aid. She might well need its help to make a swift exit when the Disciples of Life inevitably came for her, but she allowed herself a minute to share in the relief of the Disciples of the Earth. Some had fallen to their knees, foreheads pressed to the earth, sobbing in gratitude.

Yala met Pehin's eyes and saw her face was wet with tears,

too. She'd seen her friend die for the discovery that might just have saved them all.

"We have to get to the others." Pehin raised her voice, wiping her eyes with the back of her hand. "They need to know it's possible to reach Setem."

"No." Yala positioned herself between them and the mines. "If you go back in there, you'll lose access to your deity and you'll be at Mekan's mercy."

"I'll go alone," Pehin offered. "I don't mind taking the risk to get word to the others."

"Would Superior Dovial believe you?" He certainly wouldn't take Yala or Kelan's word for it, and she could imagine the lies the Disciples of Life might have told him, too.

They have Niema.

"I'll take some of the others." Pehin faced the group, some of whom had raised their hands to volunteer.

As Yala watched them, a familiar tingling sensation arose beneath her gloves, and the war drake's shadow fell from overhead. "Stop that."

"Can it hear you?" Kelan lifted his gaze to the sky. "Or see you? It doesn't have eyes anymore."

"No." Yala shook her hands as though to dislodge Mekan's influence by sheer force of will. "I don't know what it's doing."

A rumble travelled beneath her feet, and Yala's attention went to the Disciples of the Earth. "Damn. If Mekan does anything underground, we won't be able to tell if it's Him or them."

"Better than them having no access to their deity at all." Kelan watched Pehin beckon two other Disciples to follow her. "I should go with them."

"It'll take too long." Uneasy, she clenched and unclenched

her tingling hands and willed the war drake to fly higher before the Disciples took its presence as a threat.

The ground heaved, more violently than before. The cliffs shuddered, and the thud of falling rocks formed a cacophony that almost drowned out the whispers arising from the claw Yala carried at her waist. The tingling in her hands intensified to sharp pain.

Then Mekan's voice spoke, uttering words like rock scraping against bone: *"Thank you for the sacrifice."*

33

Viam walked out of the palace after her meeting with the king and made straight for the gates instead of heading back to the staff dormitories. She knew Brenat would be waiting to bombard her with questions, and her instincts told her to consult Yala before deciding how much to share of her conversation with King Daliel with anyone outside of their squad.

With Yala absent, that left only Saren as a potential confidant, and while thinking of their last encounter still brought the sting of humiliation, she'd been meaning to ask if he'd received another update, both on the situation in Setemar, and on the Disciples allegedly pursuing Yala.

Viam knocked on the door of the apartment and Saren opened the door with one hand raised to shield his face from the sunlight. "Oh, it's you."

"Nice to see you, too," said Viam. "I have news."

"Don't tell me you went and joined the Disciples of the Flame after all."

"No, but it turns out those books that King Tharen used to find the island used to belong to Superior Datriem." She closed the door behind her. "There was never a collection of books on Corruption in the palace. They were in the Temple of the Flame all along."

"Him?" Saren burst out laughing. "That's priceless. The old hypocrite was secretly collecting tomes of Corruption?"

"Yes, but if King Daliel hadn't barred the Disciples of the Flame from the palace for not protecting his father, Melian would have found the books a lot sooner."

Some of the mirth faded from Saren's face. "Barred them from the palace? Didn't think the king had it in him."

"He did, and it might have saved us all." When Saren frowned, she added, "If he'd discovered his father's research, Superior Datriem would have had to choose whether to assassinate another monarch and risk Laria falling into chaos —or do nothing and risk the information reaching the public."

"If you think that makes me feel sorry for him, you're mistaken."

"That's not what I meant." Viam rubbed her forehead, already regretting this excursion. "I wanted to tell Yala, but she's not here… unless you've heard from her?"

"No, I haven't." He absently studied one of the wooden targets that Yala had propped against the wall. "I thought that being sober would make the world make more sense, but at least then I could blame the drink for everyone around me being out of their minds."

Viam cleared her throat. "It probably won't help if I told you that I'm training war drakes again."

"You're doing what?"

"War drakes," Viam repeated. "The palace guards are clueless. They have no idea how to handle those creatures without getting ripped to shreds."

"Obviously." Saren snorted. "So King Daliel's lost his wits, too."

"He thinks we might need the flight division in case of another incident in the capital," she said. "He told me so himself."

"You *spoke* to him?"

"Where else would I have found out he banned the Disciples of the Flame from the palace?"

Saren groaned. "And there I thought you were the only one of our team who had their head screwed on the right way. I also thought you were glad to have put those days long behind you."

"Have I ever said that?" Viam's tone was more defensive than she'd intended; she hardly blamed Saren for coming to that conclusion. "If the king asks for volunteers to join the flight division, will you sign up?"

"Fuck, no."

"Then what do you want from me?"

"What do I want?" he echoed. "I want that island to get the fuck out of my dreams."

The honest response surprised her. "That's beyond my power. If I could stop your nightmares, I'd be able to handle my own."

His bloodshot eyes locked with hers. "You too?"

"I lived through it, too, Saren." Had he forgotten, or had he thought she'd cast the memories aside along with her uniform? "I miss the flight division. I know you don't think I do, but… training those war drakes is the closest I'm ever going to get to what we had."

A wry smile formed on his face. "I know. Hells, maybe I'll volunteer after all. Getting myself killed in the saddle might be all I have to offer in the end."

"Don't say that."

"We can't all be Yala." He lowered his gaze to the floor. "You know, I think what I never got over was that our last mission showed Yala was only human, like the rest of us. She always seemed untouchable, until she met a force that even she couldn't hold back."

"Death." Viam's eyes stung with unexpected tears, thinking of Dalem, of Machit, of those who would never again fly as part of their squad.

"Doesn't mean she won't *try*, I know," Saren added. "If she was still our squad leader, I might have followed her into the abyss, but she doesn't need us."

Doesn't she? Viam had assumed otherwise, but her conversation with the king had reminded Viam that her position in the palace gave advantages as well as risks—and so did her unexpected new occupation with the war drakes. "She might."

"Viam, she's a *Disciple of Death*," he said. "Besides, she's in Setemar. What can we do from here?"

An idea formed in Viam's mind. "I can think of one thing she might appreciate."

———

"Thank you for the sacrifice."

The cold voice hit Niema like a slap, causing her to stumble down the temple stairs. The Disciples of Life on either side of her seized her arms to prevent her from falling, hard enough to bruise.

"What... what was that?" She twisted to see over her shoulder and gasped in pain when the Disciples yanked on her arms, hauling her the rest of the way down the stairs. "Didn't you hear that?"

Mekan. The voice couldn't have belonged to anyone else, and it'd come from inside the Temple of the Earth.

Niema hadn't seen anything out of place when the two Disciples of Life had led her out of the maze of tunnels, except that nobody had been inside the main chamber. The echo of voices from the tunnels had made her assume the Superior was dealing with more escapees, but Niema's captors showed no curiosity, nor did they slow their relentless pace.

And they hadn't heard the voice, either.

"Don't run." Shetrem loosened her hold on Niema's arm as they followed the curve of the wall to the city gates. "It's pointless."

"I heard *Him*." Dread coiled inside her heart. "The god of death. He was thanking someone."

A brief, futile hope assailed Niema when she caught the eye of one of the guards outside the gates, but they moved aside to let the three of them pass without seeming to care that she was a prisoner. *Nobody else heard the voice except for me. Who was the god of death thanking?*

As they reached the other side, the sound of beating wings came from above. A third war drake cut across their path, and Niema's heart gave a jolt when she saw the figure sitting on its back.

Superior Kralia.

A sense of unreality washed over her. Niema blinked, shaking her head to dispel the vision, but the Disciples showed no surprise at the sight of their leader riding on a winged steed, leading them to a deserted street.

"Superior Kralia." Shetrem knelt before the descending war drake, and after a moment, Kelik did likewise.

The war drake's claws touched the ground. Atop its back, Superior Kralia regarded her with an expression of pity mingling with regret. "I was saddened that you ran, Niema. I thought your isolation would lead you to repent for your choices, and yet you came straight here to aid the enemy."

"Yala Palathar is here, in this city." Kelik climbed to his feet. "She's been coaxing the Disciples of the Earth to turn against their Superior. It's my belief that Niema has been helping her do it."

"Yala isn't the one you want," Niema whispered. "She's trying to *help* the Disciples of the Earth. They're being held hostage inside their own temple while Mekan tries to recruit or murder them."

"That's quite enough." Superior Kralia took in a breath. "Kelik, Shetrem, you will go back to the Temple of the Earth and continue to aid the Superior with banishing this evil from their midst."

"Mekan is underground—" Niema's mouth closed when Superior Kralia let out a sharp whistle. The war drake lifted a claw until the sharp edge touched the skin of Niema's neck. Watery terror seized her entire body, and she hardly dared breathe until the claw lowered to the ground again.

The other two Disciples had departed, leaving her alone with Superior Kralia.

"Why did you bring those creatures here?" she whispered. "They're steeds for soldiers. They used to belong to the army. I thought…"

I thought you were better, she might have said. *I thought you were more devoted to Yalet than any of the rest of us. I thought you were set against harming others.*

But she'd been wrong, sickeningly wrong, and the truth set her world ablaze.

The Superior whispered a prayer, quietly enough that Niema didn't catch any words until the end: "I am sorry for what I must do, but this is necessary."

Niema spoke through numb lips. "Why are you doing this?"

"It is my duty to rid this city of Mekan's influence," said Superior Kralia. "All of those who ally with Him, must be scoured from this realm, and Yalet will provide the strength we need to do this terrible task."

"Terrible," Niema repeated. "You're going to kill the … the Disciples of Death."

"Yes," she said, "and if you have any love for Yalet left in your heart, Niema, you will take Yala Palathar's life with your hand. Or else you will be a Disciple of Life no longer."

Her words struck Niema like a hammer to the chest, cracking her ribs and leaving her heart laid bare. "No."

"I'm giving you a chance to earn Yalet's forgiveness," said Superior Kralia. "It might seem cruel, but Mekan's followers are no longer part of the living world and are therefore not subject to your vow against taking lives. If you do this, She will forgive you. No, She will embrace you."

"I can't." This couldn't be Yalet's will. "I can't. I won't."

"You're a child." Superior Kralia's pitying expression returned. "You cannot fathom the evil that was unleashed when you saved Yala Palathar's life. You must correct this wrong with your own hands."

Objections rose to Niema's tongue, only to be stifled when Superior Kralia whistled again. She tensed, expecting the war drake to strike, but the beast didn't move. Instead, a strange pressure filled her skull and her vision flickered, as though a watery curtain had descended over her eyes. The whistling echoed in her head, wrapping around her thoughts, and when her vision returned, the world was altered. Not her surroundings—the cobbled street of Setemar hadn't changed a bit—but her mind was oddly at peace.

"There," said Superior Kralia, her voice sad, pensive. "I will return to our allies and bring them here to aid in the fight. When I return, Yala Palathar will be dead."

Niema nodded. "I understand."

No treacherous thoughts remained; her mind consisted of one objective.

She was Yalet's soldier, and she had a job to do.

When Kelan heard the god of death's voice, he and Yala both halted in their tracks. "You heard that, too?"

"What sacrifice?" Yala stared up at the cliffs and then dropped her gaze to the mine opening they'd left behind. "Shit. Who was Mekan talking to?"

"Your guess is as good as mine." He glided to the tunnel entrance, and Yala ran behind him, her cane smacking the earth. Upon reaching the mines, he glanced over his shoulder at the Disciples of the Earth. None of them had reacted to the voice, suggesting they hadn't heard anything, but the dead war drake's shadow dipped lower than ever.

"I'm going in," Yala told him.

Kelan started to object and stopped himself when she lifted a hand, revealing the shadows coiling outward from where her glove met her wrist. "If you're sure."

The winged shadow passed overhead again, and when Kelan lifted his head to the sky, he counted three reptilian forms circling Setemar from above in addition to the dead war drake hovering over the cliffs. Whatever had possessed the Disciples of Life to take up flying on war steeds? They must believe Yala was dangerous enough to warrant sending their deadliest Disciples, yet they were oblivious to the real threat. Unless they'd heard Mekan's voice, too, but even that was no guarantee they'd cease their campaign against Yala.

"Kelan." Pehin came running up to him. "Where'd Yala go?"

"To find the god of death," Kelan answered. "At least, I think she has. I wouldn't go back into those tunnels."

"But what about the people still inside the temple?" The colour had drained from her face. "We can't leave them to die."

Another tremor shook the cliffs, and the thud of rocks striking the ground warned of another landslide.

"The front doors are easier to access," he told Pehin. "If you want to help, gather your people and approach Setemar from the outside. I'll try to send some of my people to help you, but I can't guarantee they won't have their hands full."

As for the Disciples of Life? Kelan intended to remind them that their imperative to banish Mekan ought to supersede their desire to recapture Niema and set their winged monsters loose against Yala.

Kelan rose into the sky, careful to avoid flying into the path of the dead war drake and flew over the trembling clifftops. There were indeed three living war drakes circling Setemar's rooftops, but before he could check if any of them were carrying riders, Laima waylaid him in midair. "Kelan, what in *hells* did your friend Yala do?"

"What—the earthquake? That's not her." Air buffeted them from one of the passing war drakes, and Kelan dropped in flight. "Did another Disciple of Life show up?"

"The Disciples of Life must have sent their best warriors to help us fight Mekan."

"That's not why they're here." Unfortunately. "Have you seen Niema?"

Another gust of air knocked into him, and Kelan turned to look at the newcomer. The third war drake was considerably larger than the first two. Its rider was clad in odd armour that appeared to be made of thousands of overlapping leaves, and she surveyed the pair of them with an imperious expression.

"I am Superior Kralia," she said. "I believe you are part of the delegation sent by Superior Sietra of Skytower, correct?"

"Yes," Laima replied. "Ah—the others are at the inn. Would you like to join us?"

This is Niema's Superior? Kelan kept an eye on the war

drake's sharp claws as he and Laima flew over the rooftops and touched down in front of the inn. The war drake landed in the street with scarcely an impact; surely only a Superior could exert that level of control. The beast was a wild animal at the core and bringing it into a crowded city carried enough of a risk that she must be confident of its absolute obedience.

The beast sat still, deceptively placid, while Laima dropped to her knees in a gesture of respect and so did the other Disciples who were outside the inn. With reluctance, Kelan did the same. From the ground, the beast appeared even larger, its rider more formidable.

"We were sent to help the Disciples of the Earth." Kelan rose upright. "Mekan has infiltrated their temple and ousted their own deity, with the aid of a few rogue Disciples of Death. We've dealt with most of them, but there's some, ah, disagreement on how to proceed."

He didn't see the other two Disciples, nor Niema either. *Where is she?*

"That is our purpose here," said Superior Kralia. "We have come to rid the city of all traces of Mekan's presence."

"You'll have to ask Superior Dovial first," Kelan said. "He's refusing to let anyone leave the temple—"

The earth gave another violent shudder. Kelan jerked into flight, as did several of the other Disciples, but the sound of stone scraping against stone made his teeth rattle even while in the air. Dust showered down from the shaking cliffs in a curtain of greyish brown.

The war drake growled, but Superior Kralia silenced it with a whistle. "I'm told there's a troublemaking Disciple of the Sky attempting to aid the Disciples of Death. That's you, I believe."

"Wrong." Laima glared at him, but he pressed on. "I'm pretty sure Mekan caused that earthquake. He's hiding beneath the city itself, and if any of his allies survive, they're down there, too."

And what of the voice? Had anyone else heard Mekan speak, aside from Yala and himself? Someone had offered a sacrifice…

"Then I will eradicate them all." Superior Kralia's steed took flight, blasting dust into their faces, and the sound of wingbeats mingled with the continued rumbling from the cliffs.

"Kelan," said Laima. "Are you trying to get us alienated by every other Superior in the country?"

"That woman tried to kill one of her own Disciples," Kelan told her. "She also put a death sentence on Yala's head. I wouldn't trust her to help us."

His gaze turned towards the Temple of the Earth, where he saw Niema standing on the stairs. Startled, he flew closer, braced for her captors to appear from within the temple, but the doors remained closed.

"There you are." He caught up to her on the stairs. "Wait—are you going back into the temple? Why?"

"I need to get to Yala,"

"That wasn't an answer." Her voice was much too calm for someone who was supposed to be on the run from her own Superior, and her expression was as blank as one of the carved statues next to the door. "Did you talk to your Superior, or did you manage to avoid catching her attention?"

Niema's lips compressed. "I need to get to Yala."

"I heard you the first time." *Something's wrong.* "Yala went into the mines. Did you hear the voice?"

Niema ignored him and knocked on the temple's door. Hard. The sound resonated, almost as loud as the tremors, and to his utter astonishment, the door gave way before Niema's touch.

Carnage awaited on the other side.

34

Yala moved through the tunnel, using her borrowed lantern to guide the way. She'd removed her gloves, but she didn't need to be able to see the shadows coiling above her palms to know which way to walk.

Her steps halted when she came to the barrier that Niema had created, formed of vines stretching from floor to ceiling. *Ah, shit.* The vines formed a thick wall that looked as solid as rock, but she put down the lantern and pulled out her knife anyway.

She'd scarcely touched the vines before the shadows leaking from her hand coiled outward, and the vines began to rot away before her eyes. Green turned to grey and crumbled until no traces of the wall remained. Her presence certainly wouldn't help keep Mekan out of the tunnels, but He was already here and the shadows urged her onward like a compass.

Yala knew she was near to the temple again when she saw the bloodstains. Red darkened the soil, streaking the tunnel floor, and leading her to the bodies of two Disciples of the Earth. They lay positioned as if they'd cut one another's throats in simultaneous strikes. Her fingers tingled, and she clenched her fists to keep Mekan's power from leaking out.

Around a corner lay a cave containing a bloodstained altar. Robed bodies littered the floor, including one that lay across the altar itself, blood fountaining from the gaping hole in his throat. Superior Dovial.

That's what they did with the altar. It was the Disciples of the Earth who took it from the Temple of Death.

Yala broke out of her reverie when one of the bodies stirred, and her hand tingled. "Don't even think about it."

A second tunnel branched off the cave, and Yala moved past the altar and the unfortunate Disciples to follow the path back to the main chamber. Screams rang out, and Disciples ran in all directions in chaos that made it quite impossible for her to tell which were agents of Mekan and which weren't. More blood splattered the floor, and lanterns lay where they'd been knocked free of their sconces by the relentless tremors racking the temple.

The front doors burst open. Yala did a double-take when she caught sight of Kelan standing on the steps, next to— *Niema.* She'd got away from her captors, but where had the other Disciples of Life disappeared to? Weren't they supposed to be preventing this very disaster?

"Yala." Kelan peered over her shoulder. "What's going on in there?"

"Mekan's made His move." She met Niema's eyes and was unprepared for the intense hate staring back at her. Disarmed, she placed the lantern on the floor. "It's bad. Really bad."

A winged shape dropped from the sky. Kelan grabbed Niema, pulling her out of the path of the skeletal war drake's descent. The beast landed on the steps in front of Yala, its head bowed.

"Did I call you?" Yala addressed the war drake. "You're more reliable than the living ones."

Yala mounted her steed, mostly so that the Disciples of the Earth would have a clear path through which to exit the temple. As the war drake took flight, she called to Kelan. "The Superior is dead. Everyone in that temple needs to get out."

She didn't hear his reply; as the beast rose in flight, a spear flew past her head. Yala looked for the source and spied two guards approaching the stairs. As the second spear left the guard's hand, Yala flew downward and caught the weapon in her free hand.

"I'm going to pretend you didn't throw that at me." She spun the spear, pointing it back at its owner. "Help the Disciples of the Earth get out. There's been a massacre."

Yala flew towards the inn, where most of the Disciples of the Sky scattered in alarm when they saw her skeletal war drake mount.

"Oh, pull yourselves together," she snapped. "The beast is under my control, which is more than I can say for the dead attacking the Temple of the Earth. I'm sure one or two of you can help, can't you?"

The ground gave a visible heave, and cracks sprang up on the street leading up to the temple's doors. A thrill of dread rushed through Yala's blood.

Turning to the other Disciples of the Sky, she said, "If you weren't already aware, this entire city is a Temple of Death. We need to order an evacuation."

Nobody moved for a heartbeat. Cracks continued to spread through the street, growing into fissures, and as the Disciples of the Sky finally began to rise into the air, Yala urged the war drake to veer towards the city wall. Leaning over the side, she shouted at the guards in front of the gate.

"Everyone needs to leave the inner city! If you don't, you'll get buried alive!"

She flew around the inside of the wall, repeating her warning to every group of guards she passed. Tremors interspersed her shouts, and she was relieved to see groups of locals running from their homes and making their way to the city gates.

On the other side of the wall, she spied a group of skeletal bodies staggering through the street. *Shit.* Mekan's power was spreading throughout Setemar, and upon seeing the oncoming dead, some of the locals turned and began fleeing back into the inner city instead.

"Don't go back there!" she shouted to them. "Keep running!"

She flew the war drake to the street where the dead roamed, spilling out of a local cemetery. Many were armed with swords and spears, ready to kill at Mekan's command.

Yala flew downward, extending a hand, and addressed Mekan. "You owe me. They're mine."

Darkness surged from her hand, mingling with the shadows fuelling the walking corpses. They stopped in their advance, but she didn't have time to ensure every dead body had ceased to move when the dead Disciples inside the temple had likely begun attacking, too. The others didn't deserve to die for their fellow Disciples' treachery.

Some of the Disciples of the Sky had come to their senses and hovered above the city, shouting warnings to the locals and urging them to leave at once. If that didn't get their attention, the tremors continuing to shake the ground certainly would. The cracks splitting the street in front of the temple had spread further, spiderwebbing beneath houses and roads alike, but the person standing on the temple stairs didn't seem to have noticed. Niema, watching Yala's approach with an expression of strange indifference.

"There you are. Is Kelan in there?" Yala flew nearer, extending a hand.

Niema's lips moved, forming a prayer. Green light flared, and with a sudden jolt, the dead war drake tilted sideways. Yala scarcely had time to brace herself before the shadows holding the war drake together vanished, tipping her over onto the temple's steps. She rolled over, shielding her face, and the war drake's body fell upon the temple steps in a shower of bone.

Pain racked her shoulder from the impact, her leg protesting beneath her, but Yala had managed to keep hold of the spear, which she used to push herself upright. "Niema, what are you doing?"

Niema gave no reply. She wore the same empty expression, her hands and face aglow with eerie green light. She'd used that power before, but Yala had never seen her act like this. What had she done, offered some dangerous bargain to her deity and put herself into a trance? Or had her fellow Disciples of Life been responsible?

"Yala," Kelan's voice shouted from inside the temple. "Watch out. She's not herself."

"I must eradicate all traces of Mekan from this world." Niema raised her glowing hand, pointing a finger at Yala.

Light streamed from her finger, and Yala rolled to the side again, the spear slipping from her hand. Her fingers twitched and spasmed in pain, as though she'd plunged them into a bloodfly nest, and burning agony shot up her leg as she was forced to put her weight on it to stand upright.

A blast of air hit Niema from behind, sending her pitching forward down the temple's stairs. She landed on her feet, scarcely seeming to notice the impact, and Kelan came gliding forward to block her from reaching Yala. "Niema, what's going on with you? Did you forget Yala was on your side?"

Gritting her teeth against the pain, Yala reached for the spear again. "Niema, I don't want to hurt you, but you need to come to your senses."

"I don't think she's in her right mind." Kelan glided down the stairs towards her. "Niema—"

A crack ripped through the ground, perilously close to the where Niema stood, but she didn't seem to notice. She stood still, like a tree whose roots went deep enough to withstand a storm, her face as blank and calm as one of the dead Yala had left on the other side of the wall.

A possibility tickled at the back of Yala's mind. Like Mekan, Yalet couldn't exert direct influence over people. What about Her followers? She couldn't imagine such practises were widespread, but when she considered how fragile her fellow Disciples' vows against harming any other living creature had turned out to be—*that's it.*

"It's your Superior, isn't it?" She tried to catch Niema's eye. "She can influence humans as well as animals and she has some kind of hold over you."

"What?" Kelan landed in front of Niema, his face ashen. "Your Superior commanded you to kill Yala?"

Yala recalled the vow that Niema had sworn to keep the true nature of her mission a secret from Yala when they'd first met. The vow had caused Niema physical pain when she'd tried to drop hints, and if this vow was equally binding, she'd die before she broke her word.

"I am Yalet's hand." Niema raised a glowing palm. "I have a job to do. Get out of the way."

Yala reached for her dagger with a spasming hand and found herself gripping the claw instead. Mekan's cold voice whispered in her ear. *"I can destroy this one with ease."*

"Please don't."

"If you will destroy Yalet's servant, you will be greatly rewarded."

"I won't." No. If Niema was truly under a spell that only her Superior could break, Yala would simply have to force Superior Kralia's hand.

She pulled out the claw and lifted it high into the air, a silent demand rising from within her heart. *Give me everything you owe me, Mekan, for the lives of those Disciples of the Flame.*

Shadows pulsed from her hands, the tingle of Mekan's power supplanting the pain Niema's attack had caused. Screams drifted out of the temple, and then a dead man emerged, blood pouring from his gaping throat. Superior Dovial.

"Shit," said Kelan. "He's really dead."

"He is," Yala said, "and if they don't want to join him, the other Disciples need to get the fuck out of there."

"I tried. They're lost without their leader, and they wouldn't listen to me." He glanced at Niema, who watched the dead Superior with the same strange detachment in her expression, before returning her attention to Yala.

"I can handle her," Yala said. "Go and put your fellow Disciples to work."

Kelan took flight, while Yala grabbed her discarded spear and faced Niema.

"I don't want to hurt you," she repeated. "You don't want to hurt me, either. You swore a vow against doing harm to any other living creature, in fact."

Niema lifted her hands in answer, the god of life's energy pulsing outward in a green haze. Superior Dovial's body fell, crumpling, and Yala's hands began to spasm again.

———

Niema faced Yala, her hands bathed in the light of Yalet's presence. Part of her was aware of the cracks in the ground fanning out from the temple to the city walls and beyond. In the background came the sound of fleeing civilians, weapons clashing, cries of the dying. Yet one simple command kept her fixated on her target.

Eradicate Corruption. Destroy Yala Palathar.

Yala stood amid the crumbling bones that had once been her steed, gripping a spear, her face smudged with dirt. She spoke, but her words meant nothing to Niema, who raised a hand to call upon the god of life once more. The ground gave another heave, this one strong enough to send them both staggering, and a wider crack ripped the street wide open. From within, shadows surged upward, coiling in the air like smoke. Mekan's realm, close enough for her to taste the rot on her tongue. Her stomach curdled, but her Superior's command rang in her skull yet again. *Eradicate Corruption. Kill Yala Palathar.*

Yalat herself had climbed the stairs to the temple, climbing over Superior Dovial's corpse. "Everyone out! Now!"

Niema raised a hand, but air blasted into her from behind and knocked her head over heels. Each thump of her fall jolted in her skull, along with her Superior's command. *Eradicate Corruption. Kill Yala Palathar.* Her chin smacked into a stone stair; she bit her tongue, tasting blood.

Kelan glided past her, an apologetic expression on his face. "Sorry, Niema."

Niema clambered to her feet, only to be knocked over again by the other Disciples of the Sky following Kelan's lead. As they vanished through the temple's open doors, they left behind them the growing crack in the earth, from which darkness stirred.

For an instant, the command in her head was smothered by Mekan's laughter.

"Come a little closer, Disciple, so that I might claim you too."

———

Kelan ran through the main chamber of the temple, calling a warning to any living person he passed. Not being able to fly meant he'd swiftly lost track of his fellow Disciples of the Sky among the crowd of living and dead Disciples, but he did run into Yala near the door.

"Might be safer for them to escape through the tunnel," he observed, catching sight of the widening crack at the foot of the stairs. "Where's Niema?"

"Distracted by the dead, I hope." She moved through the chamber; in addition to the shaking floor, she'd dropped her cane somewhere, and carried a spear instead. Shadows wrapped its length, flowing from her fingertips. "Where are those Disciples of Life?"

"That's a good question." He hadn't seen if they'd remounted their war drakes or if they'd returned to the temple prior to handing Niema over to their Superior. "I think we underestimated how many Disciples of the Earth Mekan managed to get on his side."

Many had died, but that didn't make them any less dangerous, especially with Niema no longer fighting with them. He'd thought she was acting strangely, but to know her Superior had been responsible—her actions had defied the very essence of what it meant to be a Disciple of Life. He'd wondered, in the past, whether the immense powers the Disciples of Life possessed might have been wielded against their fellow humans if they hadn't been restricted by strict vows against causing harm, but he never could have expected their Superior to violate their vows such a manner.

Under the general clamour inside the main chamber, he picked up on the sound of frantic shouts from one of the tunnels branching off the entrance chamber. Hearing, Yala veered in that direction. "That's where the Disciples' dormitories are. There might be people hiding in there."

"Novices," he guessed, running down the tunnel ahead of Yala. "Which door?"

"All of them." Yala opened the first door they came to, revealing a room full of small and frightened novices huddling together on sleeping mats.

Kelan beckoned to the novices. "Your temple isn't safe. The *city* isn't safe. You have to get out or you'll die here."

"Our Superior told us to stay," one of them said.

"He's dead," Yala said from behind him, in her usual blunt manner. "If you don't want to join him, get out."

"Really, Yala." A couple of the novices had begun to cry, but Kelan couldn't summon up any words of reassurance. "Run. You'll be safe if you get outside."

I hope, he added silently, as they ran to the next room. They repeated their message to the few Disciples they found within. Unlike the novices, most of the full-fledged Disciples had taken the initiative and left their rooms of their own accord, but some had gone deeper into the tunnels to avoid the dead rather than fleeing the temple.

"Go towards the back exit—it's quicker," Kelan said to a group of Disciples they passed on the way towards the chamber where they interred their dead.

Yala limped behind him, swearing; her bad leg must be bothering her again. He too was conscious of the small cracks appearing in the tunnel walls and floor with each new tremor, and the steady stream of dust pluming in the air.

The chamber of the dead lay ahead, but that was where their progress ended. The entire room was full of vines, a writhing mass of greenery that swamped the Disciples' graves and blocked most of the other tunnel entrances, too.

Yala halted behind him. "The Disciples of Life have been busy."

"Did Superior Dovial give them permission to do this?" He attempted to edge around the mass of green, hearing a loud commotion from one of the other tunnel entrances. "This isn't helping anyone."

"No, it isn't." Yala extended a hand. Shadows coiled outward, and when they made contact with the vines, the plants shrank, their green leaves becoming grey. Yala yanked back her hand, trailing shadows. "Didn't want to kill all of them…"

She'd cleared enough of a path for Kelan to reach the tunnel that led to the exit, but another blockage awaited. Disciples jostled against one another, their path obstructed by someone who stood at the fork in the tunnel. *The Disciples of Life.*

"This is where they've been hiding?" He attempted to see past the crowd, but Yala caught his arm.

"I have to go," she said. "If I get near them, I can't promise Mekan won't use my hand to kill them."

"I thought He couldn't control what you did."

"He can't. Just my hands." Yala cursed under her breath. "I don't understand, but He can't control the living. He *can* control the dead, and I'm not going to give Him another corpse."

Green light flared from the tunnel in front of the disjointed gathering of Disciples of the Earth. With reluctance, Kelan nodded to Yala. "All right. I'll try to deal with this."

He peered amid the Disciples of the Earth and spied another wall of vines obstructing the tunnel. The two Disciples of Life stood like a pair of sturdy ancient trees, preventing anyone from passing.

"What are you doing?" Kelan called. "We need to get out of here before the dead catch up to you."

"This temple is infected by Mekan," insisted the female

Disciple of Life. "Including its inhabitants."

"You're joking, aren't you?" The woman didn't look as if she'd cracked a joke in her life, but surely not every single Disciple present was an agent of Mekan. "You're welcome to fight the god of death to the end of existence *after* we get out of this cave, but we're wasting time."

"Corruption must be eradicated." The male Disciple of Life raised a hand, and more vines shot outward from the walls and floor.

The resulting tremor further destabilised the tunnel, and soil rained down upon their heads. *Damn. If they aren't careful, they'll do Mekan's job for Him.*

Someone screamed. The coppery scent of blood filled the air, and a Disciple fell, impaled on a blade-like vine. A second collapsed, too, choking and gasping.

"You—" He gaped at the Disciples of Life. "You're doing what Mekan wants."

"*Exactly,*" whispered a bone-chilling voice, and Kelan saw the colour drain from the Disciples' faces.

"We do as Yalet wishes," said the female Disciple. "We serve no other."

A booming crash sounded above, like a huge chunk of rock falling from a great height. Then another.

"Everyone out!" he shouted. "If that was the city wall—" *It's right on top of us,* he finished silently, drawing his blade.

The tunnel collapsed on one side, dirt showering them. Kelan drove forward, slicing the vines that blocked the way, deafened by the crashing thuds from above. At every crash, he flinched, expecting the ceiling to cave in on their heads, but despite the soil and bits of stone raining down on them, the tunnel held firm.

Until the door came within sight. There came a final deafening crash, and with his last breath, Kelan gasped a prayer to Terethik.

A shower of dirt pressed upon Kelan's shoulders, only to be pushed back by the breeze he conjured to his hand. His deity was back, but a breeze couldn't hold back a storm. He held up his arms like a shield as he glided through a haze of rock and dust, hoping that he'd stopped some of the other Disciples from being crushed.

Coughing dust, he flew upward, his blurred vision showing him dazed Disciples of the Earth emerging from the ruins of the tunnel. The wall had collapsed on one side, and the inner city beyond had vanished beneath a sickly white smoke rising from somewhere in front of the temple.

Kelan flew higher, above the ruins of the wall. The ground had split in front of the temple, widely enough to swallow up most of the buildings on each side. If anyone inside the temple had survived, they'd lost their only means of escape, and the people in the inner city, too.

Kelan dropped in flight, stomach sinking. The gates had collapsed along with the wall, crushing guards and civilians alike beneath its iron weight. Bodies lay sprawled amid the ruins, and a blue cloak caught his eye like the glare of the sun.

Laima lay beneath the fallen gate, blood streaking her face beneath the haze of grey dust.

"Laima." Kelan landed beside her, speaking through numb lips. "Laima. Please…"

"She is mine, Disciple." The cold voice shook the very ground on which he stood. *"They are all mine."*

35

———

Kelan reached for Laima's hand, his head ringing with each piece of stone that hit the ground on either side of the twisted ruin of the gates. He'd heard the god of death's voice, yet he refused to believe Laima was dead. His fingers slid into hers and her hand twitched, shadows creeping below her wrist.

"Stop that." He let go, choking on bile. "Let her go, Mekan."

"She is mine... the city is mine."

Repulsed, he looked for the source of the voice, but it came from nowhere and everywhere at once. The city was Mekan's, and the god of death couldn't bring back the departed, only a twisted imitation. As for Yalet—if She was capable of such a feat, the cost would be too high, he was sure. He'd ask Niema—

Niema. Was she still under Superior Kralia's command to kill Yala? He wrenched his gaze away from Laima and flew towards the inner city, squinting into the haze. Somehow the temple had remained intact despite its steps having been cleaved in two, and he spied a figure clinging to the side of one of the statues in the entryway. Even through the whitish film over his vision, he recognised Yala, next to the great statues of the god of the earth Himself which trembled along with the rest of their temple. His gaze picked out more Disciples of the Earth hiding amongst the ruined buildings on either side of the street.

An ear-splitting screech sounded, deep from within the cracks in the earth. Kelan's body shuddered, a primal fear arising from the depths of his very soul. A second screech, and a winged beast ripped its way out of the ground, its claws tearing at the edges of the chasm and sending the panicking Disciples of the Earth fleeing further into the ruins.

"Niema, get down!" Yala's voice was a hoarse shout. "Get down!"

That was when Kelan caught sight of Niema. She perched on the edge of the chasm splitting the street, so close to the edge that it was a wonder she hadn't tripped during one of the many quakes that had shaken the ground. She didn't seem worried about falling in, nor did she show any fear as she faced the oncoming beast. She lifted her hands, aglow with Yalet's power, and the impulse rose in Kelan to fly to her side—but there was no telling if she'd turn that power against him as well as Yala.

Skirting the gaping fissure in the earth, Kelan glided over to the temple and landed next to Yala. She clung to the statue, her face ashen, her attention riveted on the beast that had risen from the chasm in the earth.

"It's the same as the island." She gave a fierce shake of her head, her gaze clearing. "Why did she have to destroy my steed?"

"She did?" A closer look revealed the broken bones of the dead war drake littering the steps where they'd fallen. "Niema..."

The other woman remained in the same spot, heedless of her proximity to the void drake. Raising her head to the sky, she let out a shrill whistle. An answering cry resounded, and Kelan saw Yala's eyes widen as the same realisation hit both of them in the same instant. Yala shrank into the temple's shadow, but Kelan remained outside to watch the living war drake answer Niema's call.

"Those Disciples of Life won't be pleased." Yala wore an expression of grim satisfaction as the two reptilian beasts crashed into one another, claws ripping and tearing.

"They're dead," Kelan said. "I'm pretty sure they are, anyway. The wall collapsed on them."

Dull pain thumped inside his chest, a reminder of the other lives that had been lost, but if someone didn't find a way to stop Mekan's beasts, more would soon join them.

"More's the pity." Yala held onto the doorway with one hand, her face drawn with pain, her fingers streaming shadows. "Mekan wants me to join Him."

"Please don't." He didn't know if he had it in him to survive another loss. "We can't stay here. It's only a matter of time before the whole temple collapses."

"I know, but I'm sure the solution *is* here," Yala replied. "The temple is where this all started."

A dead Disciple appeared, raising a knife in his hand. Shadows leapt from Yala's hands, halting the dead man mid-motion.

"Impressive," he said. "Can you do that to Mekan's void drakes?"

"No. Don't ask me why." She gestured through the open doors. "If there's anyone alive in here, I'll send them out. I can trust you to get them to safety?"

Her words pierced the pain and grief. *I can trust you...* Too many had already died, but he was among the few people able to leave the inner city without walking straight across the gaping hole of the Void or climbing through the ruin of the collapsed gate. He had to see if anyone else needed his help.

The reptilian beasts continued to clash, a blur of scales and claws within the white smoke seeping out of the crack in the ground. He flew higher, alarmed at how much bigger the chasm had grown in the past few minutes alone. Would it eventually swallow the whole city, sucking the living and dead alike into Mekan's domain?

Kelan skirted around the street towards the inn, which had miraculously remained upright. Several Disciples of the Sky cowered in the downstairs room. *Shit. The injured must have stayed behind.*

"You can't stay in there!" he called to them. "You're safer in the sky than on the ground."

"Even with those monsters?" Lakiel emerged, limping, one hand wrapped around a bandaged arm. Blood streaked his face from a cut across the bridge of his nose. "They'll kill us."

"They're too busy taking one another to pieces to worry about us." Kelan indicated the chasm. "Anyone who isn't too injured—there are people hiding in the inner city who need our help. We're their last hope."

A couple of others emerged, warily, as Kelan rose into the sky. He scanned the inner city for survivors amid the dust and debris. Most of the civilians had fled, but he found a few Disciples of the Earth hiding amid the ruins.

"How many survivors?" he asked them. "Where?"

"A—around." The Disciple coughed, spraying dust. "Where's Pehin? She said she was going to save us."

Pehin. He'd quite understandably forgotten the Disciples who'd been left behind on the other side of the cliffs, the ones who'd regained their connection to Setem. "She's with the others. We have to go."

Evacuating each Disciple one at a time was a slow process, and with each new tremor that shook the ground, Kelan braced himself for a new horror to emerge. Dark shapes stirred within the whitish haze above the chasm, and gruesome cries split the air as Kelan pulled a groaning novice out of a pile of rubble.

"Where… is the Superior?" the novice asked him.

"Dead." Kelan carried the boy over the wall and left him in the first street he came to that was free of rubble and carnage. He returned to the inner city, where the haze had spread further, encompassing the temple and the cliffs. *Like the island*, Yala had said. The island, dominated by a Temple of Death, where the ground had ruptured to reveal the Void at its heart…

Having run out of Disciples to rescue, Kelan went looking for Pehin. He flew high above the haze masking the cliffs, relieved to find the smoke hadn't spread to the other side yet.

The group of Disciples of the Earth was easy to spot from their robes. They'd moved some distance from the mines, following the dirt track that eventually ended up in Setemar. When he descended, Pehin came to accost him. "What in the hells is going on over there?"

"Trouble," he said grimly. "Your temple is falling apart from the inside and the city itself is under attack. Oh, and your Superior is dead."

"No." Pehin stopped. "*No.*"

He'd thought she'd *wanted* him gone. "I helped some of your people get out, but the inner city is buried in rubble."

"We're too late," Pehin murmured. "If the god of death has claimed the whole *city*, we're all doomed."

"He hasn't, and you aren't." The other Disciples closed in behind her, firing questions at him about their friends they'd left behind, but Kelan raised his voice over theirs. "I have to go back and help people in Setemar, but I had a quick question. Was there a temple already here in Setemar when the Temple of the Earth was built? Were the tunnels already underneath the city?"

The Disciples' answer was a uniform look of blank confusion.

"Does it matter?" Pehin kicked a rock, her eyes haunted. "The Superior's dead. We're finished."

"It matters," he replied. "Mekan's influence runs deep. If the tunnels were already here and weren't always used by your people, it'd explain how He ensnared some of your fellow Disciples from inside your own temple."

"There are… stories," one of the Disciples said. "They say the god of the earth guided the first Disciples to Setemar, where they found tunnels already inside the cliffs, as if they were waiting for us."

"Don't tell another Disciple that," one of the others snapped. "Superior Dovial would never—"

"Superior Dovial is dead," said Kelan, "but your god is still with you, and your fellow Disciples are waiting in Setemar for you to bring Him back to them. Unless you'd rather let Mekan have Setemar for Himself?"

"No." Pehin lifted her head, eyes glittering. "Setem never deserted us, and the city is *ours,* not Mekan's."

"It is," agreed another Disciple, and a general murmur of assent passed among their group.

"What do you want to do?" Kelan asked them. "I'll help if I can, but there's only one of me. I can't carry you all at once."

"We'll get there," Pehin said. "And we'll pray for a miracle."

I think we all need one of those, Kelan thought.

———

Niema stood on the edge of the Void. Her head swam with confusion; while her Superior's commands urged her to follow Yala into the temple, the glow in her hands seemed insignificant compared to the yawning chasm in front of her. The reptilian cries of the beasts clashing above awakened the instincts that Superior Kralia's orders had blotted out; pain tugged at her heart as she sensed the agony of those trapped in the ruins, the sharp sting of lives snuffed out. A growing whisper in the back of her head told her she was supposed to *save* lives, not take them.

Niema recoiled. Tears burned her eyes and seared her cheeks, mingling with dust, and her hands wavered in front of her face. Hands that had almost taken Yala's life.

Yala. Niema's gaze snapped away from the Void and to the temple's steps, littered by the bones of the dead war drake. Yala must have gone inside; by destroying her steed, Niema had cut off her only route of escape that wasn't through the temple itself.

"What have I done?" she murmured.

The cries of the reptilian monsters' clash continued to erupt from within the crack in the earth. A third pair of wingbeats joined them, and Niema shrank away, recognising Superior Kralia atop the war drake's back.

I can't let her know the spell has broken. Niema clambered up the ruined stairs to the temple's doors, which hung open, the statues on either side miraculously intact. On swift feet, she darted into the main chamber. Most lanterns had been extinguished, leaving the tunnels cast into darkness. Squinting, she made out a figure she thought must be Yala.

"Yala." She coughed, inhaling dust. "Yala—I'm sorry. I'm here to help."

Niema stiffened as the figure moved towards her, revealing muddied robes and a sharp knife clutched in one hand. As she stepped away, the dead Disciple collapsed into a puddle of shadows.

Behind him, Yala faced Niema, holding a bloodied spear

in one hand and the curved claw of a long-dead void drake in the other. Shadows flowed from her fingertips like trails of smoke. "Please don't try to kill me again."

"I'm not." A shudder racked Niema. "I broke her spell, but if Superior Kralia finds me, she'll give the order again."

"All the more reason to avoid going outside." Yala gestured around the darkened chamber. "I'm sure the solution is somewhere inside the temple. The Disciples of the Earth … they didn't build this place. I'm almost certain the tunnels beneath Setemar already existed when they moved in and reshaped the cliffs to form their temple."

Niema's heart gave a jolt. "You think this temple once belonged to *Mekan?*"

"The chasm looks the same as the one on the island," Yala said. "There were tunnels, there, too, extending deep underground. I think the Disciples of Death were long gone by the time the Disciples of the Earth arrived, but it was more convenient for them to adopt their subterranean network of tunnels and chambers as their own."

"But … that means Mekan was right." The truth clamped over her heart like a vice. "If this was always His temple, we can't force Him out. Can we?"

"He isn't here." Yala held up the claw, trailing shadows. "Neither are His followers, which is why He keeps trying to poach other Disciples. I imagine He was overjoyed when Superior Dovial closed the temple's doors and trapped everyone in here with their terror and paranoia."

"How do you know?"

"I don't, but He tried to claim me, too." Her fingers clenched around the claw. "He can't open the Void alone. If not for humans pledging themselves to Him, He'd be less than nothing."

A screeching cry from outside warned that the reptilian fight had reached the doorstep. Three sets of claws tore at each other; Superior Kralia's mount had joined in the fight, too. The void drake had an obvious advantage in its indestructible nature, but the war drakes were bred for combat and were under the control of someone with the god of life's power at her fingertips.

On the war drake's back, Superior Kralia looked nothing like herself. Her face was set in an expression of intense concentration as her beast's claws ripped into her target, and part of Niema wondered what would happen if she stood back and didn't interfere even if the beasts dragged each other down into the abyss together.

What kind of Disciple of Life would think that? she thought. *She's your Superior... even if she did force you to kill.*

"I don't know what to do," Niema whispered.

"Now is not the time to have a crisis." Yala staggered into Niema when the ground gave another tremor. "Shit. This place is going to fall apart."

The cracks spreading up the stairs had reached the temple's doorway and the main chamber, and a rumble through the ceiling brought dust showering upon their heads.

"We can't stay here." Niema braced a hand against the city wall, staring out at the carnage of the inner city. She couldn't see a single living creature except for the beasts in the sky; the dead and living alike had scattered amid falling debris.

Was it too late to stop Mekan's wrath from spreading until Setemar became a city of corpses?

"I know." Yala joined her, limping heavily and watched the winged beasts continue their bitter clash.

One had fallen—the war drake that had had no rider— leaving two combatants to tear and rip at one another above the crack in the ground. A spasm of fear shook Niema's heart. *No. I don't want her to die. If she does ... Mekan will win.*

Stumbling down the steps, she glimpsed the Void, a mass

of grey and black seething with darkness, entirely blocking their path. "We're trapped."

"Guess I'll have to improvise." Yala lifted a hand—the fingertips were black as pitch—and the fallen bones of the dead war drake began to rise into the air from the steps where they'd scattered.

"What are you doing?" Niema stared in fascinated horror as shadows poured from Yala's hands, binding the bones back together until they formed a semblance of a living war drake.

"I don't know about you, but I don't want to be on the ground when this place falls down." Yala held her hands up, and billowing shadows surged from her fingertips. The beast's wings beat, more shadow than flesh, and when it lowered its head into the temple's doorway, Yala clambered onto its back. "And I want to find the missing Disciples of the Earth. We need them."

Niema cringed back when Yala extended a hand to her. "You want me to fly on that monster?"

"You didn't think I'd leave you on the ground, did I?"

"I tried to kill you."

"Your Superior tried to kill me," Yala corrected. "Come on. At least this war drake won't try to eat you."

Hesitantly Niema took Yala's hand, and shadows rushed to coil around Niema's arm. She yelped and yanked her hand back, a familiar whisper grating against her ear. *Join me, Disciple.*

"Ignore Him!" Yala reached for her hand again. "He can't claim you as long as you're breathing."

The steps trembled, the crack widening. Niema lost her balance, but Yala caught her arm and pulled her onto the dead war drake's back. Niema's leg swung over the mass of bone and shadow, and a scream caught in her throat as they soared upward into the sky.

If she didn't look down, she could almost convince herself they rode on a living creature, but a monstrous scream from below prompted her to drop her gaze. From the jagged slash in the ground, horrors crawled to the surface. She glimpsed a ghastly winged creature that resembled a giant bird, feathers peeling from rotting flesh, its cruel beak crusted with blood. More beasts crawled out into the light or flew upward on wings of darkness to surround the pair of them and their steed.

Niema drew her arms around her chest in a futile effort to keep the darkness from touching her. The shadows merged with the fog, all-encompassing, and she could no longer feel her deity's comforting presence.

Yala shouted a warning, too late. A claw reached out, snagged Niema's foot, and pulled her downward into the darkness.

———

From the dead war drake's back, Yala saw Niema vanish into the void. *Fuck.* If anyone could survive that fall, it was Niema, but there were no guarantees.

The dead war drake flew higher, wheeling above the cliffs, its bony mass once again held together by Yala's command. Sickly white smoke covered the entire inner city, seeping out of the Void. Within, she picked out a couple of hovering figures who didn't ride on steeds. *Disciples of the Sky.*

Yala flew in their direction, over the ruins of the collapsed wall. When the dust and smoke cleared from her vision, she counted more Disciples of the Sky than she'd expected. They'd spread out above the street, leading a group of robed figures. The Disciples she'd helped evacuate through the mines. Why had they come back to Setemar, where their deity no longer resided?

Yala flew closer, spying Kelan hovering near the front of their group. "Kelan, what are they doing here?"

"Good timing," he called to her. "I was starting to worry the temple had fallen on you."

"You didn't answer my question."

"Ask her, not me." He indicated Pehin, who appeared to be organising the Disciples of the Earth into a formation. "They're testing the limits of Setem's power."

"Didn't I help them escape this very trap?" Yala flew lower, conscious of the panicking civilians in the streets who fled from her descending steed. "What can they do, pray for the entire inner city to fall into the ground and take Mekan along with it?"

"It looks like the temple's already collapsing." Kelan's face was smudged with dirt, and there was a grim sense of resignation to his tone. "I think they're praying for a miracle."

Will they get one, though? The god of the earth might have lived in the very ground beneath their feet, but Mekan's realm had grown to encompass their entire home. What hope did they have of ousting Him?

"This is the place." Pehin caught sight of Yala's steed. "Whose side are you on?"

"Mine." She surveyed the gathering Disciples. "Did you know your temple was likely built on top of the god of death's?"

"I told them," Kelan put in. "They said they wanted to try anyway."

"That's right." Pehin looked as frightened as the rest, but they'd assembled in rows across a wide street near the city wall, their stances firm. "Mekan wasn't here when our ancestors moved in. He hasn't been here for years."

I know. "True, but His realm is now open. Even if His followers are dead, I wouldn't count on Him giving up."

"I don't expect him to," said Pehin, "but Setem is on our side. I believe that now."

A murmur of agreement followed. At Pehin's command, the Disciples fell to their knees and pressed their palms to the ground. A faint blue glow arose from each figure, and as they began to pray, their voices melded into one single hum that permeated the air.

Will that be enough? Yala glanced behind her at the ruins of the inner city, from which monsters rose above the city wall. There were too many, and the Disciples of the Earth had positioned themselves out in the open.

Yala alone couldn't stop the monsters, but she readied her spear all the same, facing the first beast to rise over the wall.

A cry sounded at her back and she glanced over her shoulder. *War drakes.* Four, five beasts bearing Disciple of Life riders, approaching the city at speed.

A winged bird lunged over the wall, and Yala retaliated with her spear, plunging it into the beast's rotting skull and ripping through its eye socket. As its body tumbled onto the buildings below, the war drakes drew closer, their riders' hands aglow with green light. Instinct told her to join them, but she also knew from experience when it was better to stand back and let others fight instead. If she stayed within their line of sight, they'd take her for an enemy as well, so Yala urged the war drake to fly over the city wall.

Whitish smoke mingled with shadow above the gaping slash in the street. Yala flew higher, keeping one eye on the Void, and the other on the war drakes soaring towards Setemar.

Until, with a quake that shook the world, the cliffs split in two.

Cracks split the Temple of the Earth wide open as if a

pair of giant hands had reached down from above and ripped the cliffs apart like the skin of a sunfruit. The booming shudder resonated in the air, sounding oddly like the sound of the Disciples of the Earth's humming prayer.

Yala lay flat against her mount, soaring higher, certain that when she looked down at the temple, she'd see the Void in its place. There was a strange symmetry to the way the cliffs had split, peeling open the roof of the temple and revealing the main chamber in its entirety. Without the cave-like feel of its enclosed walls, the chamber would have been almost unrecognisable, if not for the statues of past Superiors against its back wall.

The statues had survived the quake, but not for long. The large, robed figures shuddered, dust raining down and creating plumes of smoke around their feet. The one at the end of the row caught Yala's gaze; it had almost shuddered off its pedestal, yet its body somehow remained upright. With a sharp crack, it hit the ground, first one foot, then the other.

Walking. The statue was *walking*.

With a tremendous grating noise, the other statues of past Superiors came to life, too.

———

Niema fell into nothingness, a familiar voice whispering in her ear. *"I can help you, too, Disciple. I can take away your pain."*

"You don't know anything about me." Maybe she'd become corrupted and twisted from within after what she'd done to save Yala, but there was no turning back the clock, no undoing her choices. If she died today, Yalet would have to judge her as she was.

"Your god will not save you."

"You're wrong." Niema whispered a prayer to Yalet—a

simpler one, not a command, but a plea for her god to take what was left of her and use her life to rid the world of this terrible wrong.

Her body jerked to a stop. Her eyes flew open, legs dangling over oblivion, a hand grasping the scruff of her neck. She twisted her head to see her rescuer. Superior Kralia, perched on her war drake's back, had grabbed Niema's shirt as she fell past, but she might let go, sending Niema into the Void.

Niema took in a shaky breath, closed her eyes, and continued her prayer to Yalet. "Take my flesh, take my bones if you will, but please rid the world of this evil."

A growl sounded. Her eyes opened again as one of the winged monstrosities rose before her and her Superior, carrying the stench of rotting flesh. *This is it. This is the end.*

Her body jerked but didn't fall; Superior Kralia lifted her upward. "Command, Niema. Remember the command."

"What—kill Yala?" She choked on the word, then cringed as a blast of rotting stench wafted into her face. The beast shot out a clawed foot, and in desperation, Niema whistled, shrill and loud.

The beast's claw halted a finger span from Niema's face. Heart in her mouth, she whistled again, the same command she might give to a living animal, and the dead beast's claw dropped to its side. Despite being Mekan's creature, it was *listening* to her.

"Go away," she whispered. "Leave us alone."

Another whistle, and the beast launched into flight, vanishing into the smoky darkness emanating from the Void.

Niema's vision swam. She'd have given into unconsciousness, if not for her precarious position, and the array of strange noises arising from above. Thumps sounded, too uniform to belong to falling ruins, and a humming noise that surely didn't belong to Mekan's creatures filled the background. Then came the cry of a war drake, followed by another.

"They're here," Superior Kralia said softly. "We can end this fight."

"How?" The Void was endless, a gaping ruin, yet the Disciples of Life shone like beacons in a dark night as they flew into the smoke to join their Superior.

They prayed to Yalet, a resonant song that Niema couldn't help but join; as did Superior Kralia, her voice louder than the rest.

The sides of the sheer cliff began to shake. Superior Kralia's war drake leapt into flight to avoid being dislodged in a shower of dirt. Niema swung precariously from her Superior's grip, and the smoke cleared, showing Mekan's beasts retreating into the chasm. The Void had shrunk, noticeably, its jagged edges creeping away from the temple.

The temple, which had split open, and from which large humanoid figures had emerged. Niema blinked, certain her mind was playing tricks on her—the figures were far too large to be human, but they certainly weren't Mekan's beasts either.

"Setem has returned," Superior Kralia proclaimed. "He has answered His Disciples."

"That can't be—?" Niema broke off with a gasp when the war drake lurched upward, and the receding smoke revealed the nearest humanoid figure was a *statue*, walking as though it possessed a mind of its own.

As Niema watched open-mouthed, the figure swung a massive fist at one of Mekan's creatures. The beast plunged into the shrinking chasm, and more stone warriors came thumping down the ruin of the temple's stairs to join their ally. Murmuring prayers came from the Disciples of Life circling above, but the louder prayer came from the other side of the wall, from the Disciples who'd delivered a miracle.

Superior Kralia's voice rose once again, chiming in with the other Disciples of Life. Green light suffused their group, washing over Niema, too. The darkness retreated, shadowy smoke evaporating, as their collective faith pushed against Mekan. Niema felt no pain, yet her heart contracted with regret and sadness to know that this would be the last time she prayed in unison with her Superior, that their harmony had forever been broken.

They prayed until the patch of darkness shrank into a glare that hurt to look at, and no longer did she hear the voice of the god of death. Mekan was silent.

ods, Yala thought, watching the Void shrink beneath the collective power of the Disciples of Life. Yet the real miracle was the giant statues that had come to life at the Disciples of the Earth's command, each step of their stone feet an earthquake, their huge fists rising to crush Mekan's beasts with ease.

"Astonishing." Kelan hovered in the air beside her. "Pehin told me that all her people are taught this prayer, but I don't think the Superior knew what its effects would be. It's supposed to be for emergencies only."

"Every time I think the gods are out of surprises." The gaping hole in the ground remained, but the smoke had seeped away, the Void receding out of sight. Her hands, too, had faded from black to grey as Mekan's power left this world. "Mekan made a mistake when He tried to recruit Niema. She'd never have joined Him."

"Nor would you."

"Obviously." There'd been times at which Yala had worried that the claw would seize control and draw her into Mekan's waiting embrace, but that was what Mekan *wanted* her to believe. He thrived on the knowledge that people came to Him in their darkest moments, when He seemed like their only option.

As the last trace of the Void vanished, the war drakes slowed their flight; Yala belatedly realised the smoke was no longer hiding her from their sight. *Shit.* She'd lost her cane a while ago and every part of her felt bruised, but there was nothing to stop the Disciples of Life from directing their collective prayer at her steed and causing her to fall to a painful demise.

Yala found the Disciples of the Earth gathered near the ruins of the gate. Some Disciples of the Sky were there, too, levitating blocks of stone out of the way to clear a path to the inner city. Kelan beside one of the dead bodies crushed beneath the gates; when Yala flew lower, she recognised Laima's face.

"Kelan." Words failed her. "I'm sorry."

He inclined his head without looking up. *Gods.* There were never adequate words to sum up the suddenness of death or the sheer randomness of lives taken by the unthinking beast of war.

Air buffeted Yala, and a war drake passed overhead. Superior Kralia caught her eye—a challenge—and Yala urged her own steed to follow. The Superior controlled her beast with as much finesse as an expert rider, but the glazed expression in the war drake's eyes and its placid obedience were as alien to Yala as a void drake. Holding her breath, she guided her own steed to land in the deserted street where Superior Kralia waited for her.

"You're Superior Kralia," Yala said. "I suppose you've wanted to talk to me for a while."

"If you are Yala Palathar, Disciple of Death, then yes. I have."

"That's not what I am."

"What are you, then?"

Yala gave her a considering look. "A soldier."

"A soldier." Distaste filled the Superior's words. "A killer."

"I saved lives today. I didn't take them."

"Yet you ride an abomination." She indicated the dead war drake. "You carry a piece of the Void upon your person and wield shadows from your fingertips."

"A weapon is a weapon," Yala said. "I won't apologise for using any means to save others from Mekan."

"You're lucky you didn't become His instrument."

"It wasn't me who built a temple on top of a network of tunnels that once belonged to the god of death." Yala searched the Superior's expression. "Did you know of that part of Laria's history? If your people have been here as long as I think they have, I'm guessing so."

Surprise flitted across her face. "What manner of accusation are you directing at me?"

"The same I have for the Disciples of the Flame." Yala reached for her pouch and pulled out the battered book of Mavilangran's travels. "I owe this to their Superior, but it's certainly been enlightening to find out how many Superiors are fond of hoarding knowledge."

"You know nothing of us," said Superior Kralia.

"I think I do." A bitter smile twisted Yala's mouth. "What do you do, pass on the truth from one Superior to another and expect the rest of your people to live in happy ignorance?"

"It is a terrible burden I take upon myself," she said. "Only one who has no doubt in their faith in Yalet can know the truth of Mekan without being corrupted."

"You aren't so different," said Yala, before she could help herself. "Mekan controls His followers using fear. Your deity is supposed to be incorruptible, yet you took away the will of one of your own Disciples because you had no faith in her."

She trailed off, braced for a blow, but the Superior didn't move. "Someday you may understand the choice I made, if you live that long."

Superior Kralia took off in a beat of wings, leaving Yala and her dead steed behind.

———

Niema woke in the ruins. At first, she wondered if she'd fallen unconscious during the battle and had dreamed of Mekan's defeat—but the jagged crack in the road was empty, with no traces of the Void. While the Temple of the Earth was in a sorry state, several fearsome statues stood amid the ruins. At their feet knelt the Disciples of the Earth, and Niema hastily fell to her knees, too. It seemed the polite thing to do.

She jumped when a shadow fell over her, and the dead war drake put down a bony claw at her side. Upon its back sat Yala, who extended a hand. "Can you try not to fall off this time?"

Niema tensed, but no shadows reached to grab her. "Where is my Superior?"

"Not here. She sensibly left the Disciples of the Earth to rebuild their temple."

Shakily, Niema let Yala pull her onto the war drake's back. "They're going to rebuild their temple in the same place as before?"

"I don't think it's the best idea either," Yala said, "but they were here for hundreds of years, and their dead were laid to rest inside the temple. Some are part of the walls themselves."

True. Already the split in the cliffs had sealed, the temple made whole again. Around the ruins of the wall gathered the shaken residents of the city, and beyond the city's limits, the Disciples of Life had landed in a field.

"I wouldn't advise you to go over there," Yala told Niema. "I'm surprised Superior Kralia didn't take my head off."

"I need to talk to her."

"You're not trying to martyr yourself again, are you?"

"No." Niema didn't fear death; all her fears had burned away when she'd faced the void, but her desire for answers had not. "Take me to her."

Yala flew the dead war drake across the rooftops to the spot where Superior Kralia sat atop her own steed in front of her gathered Disciples. When she spotted Niema, her eyes narrowed a fraction. The other war drakes pulled away from Yala's dead steed as they came to land.

Niema climbed shakily down and faced her Superior, her hands clenched at her sides. "Did you hope I'd die? Is that why you left me behind?"

"No," said Superior Kralia.

"Then what?" Her voice cracked. "Are you going to send more assassins after me? Or take me back to the enclave only to exile me once again?"

"I have done you wrong," said Superior Kralia.

"Yes," Niema said quietly. "You have."

"Will you forgive me?"

"No." She squared her shoulders. "And if that means exile, so be it. I'll keep my faith with Yalet elsewhere."

"I understand." The Superior's face showed deep tiredness, as if more than the battle had exhausted her. "You did as your faith directed you. No ordinary Disciple of Life could have done what you did."

"No ordinary...?" Niema's mouth went dry as she recalled the way the monster from the Void had ceased its attack at her command. "How? I'm not—a Disciple of Death."

"You are not that either, but something else."

The words stung, but Niema was too weary to feel the full impact. "Then... what?"

"I'd very much like to find out," said Superior Kralia. "And I would like to invite you to return to the enclave, if you so desire."

"I can't."

"You would rather walk alone?"

"I would." A lie, but what choice did she have? "I just have one request. I would ask that you leave Yala alone. You saw for yourself that she's not Mekan's creature."

"She's a force unto herself." Superior Kralia's gaze travelled to the war drake upon which Yala sat. "She's dangerous, and if she isn't careful, she will cost all of us dearly."

Her words held the hint of certainty that made Niema wonder if Yalet shown her another vision that Niema hadn't been privy to. If She had, though, Niema knew better than to ask for the details.

"However," the Superior went on, "I will honour your request."

"I will visit my enclave one last time," Niema added. "I owe them that. And then…"

And then… who knew. She'd changed too much, too deeply, to return to the life she'd once known.

"Then do as you will," said Superior Kralia. "May Yalet's blessing be upon you."

———

Skytower felt different when Kelan returned late that evening. Darkness had fallen a while ago, but he and some of the others had decided to return as soon as they'd gathered their fallen fellow Disciples from within the ruins of Setemar. The city had suffered too much damage for them to be able to return to the inn for the night, and terrified civilians crowded every building in the outer city. Only the Disciples of the Earth had dared return to the area behind the ruins of the city wall, and in the end, he and the others had left them to rebuild their temple.

Once he'd determined that the Disciples of Life didn't intend to turn on Yala or Niema again, of course. He was glad when they didn't; his people were in no shape to fight another battle.

Kelan adjusted his flight path to land directly outside the Superior's office, avoiding the crowded platform where he'd be bombarded with questions. Explaining to the Superior would be hard enough, and the knowledge that Laima was gone seemed twice as final when he voiced the words aloud. When his voice wavered, she didn't interrupt, but waited for him to continue until he'd finished his tale with the revival of the Temple of the Earth.

"It seems unwise to rebuild on top of the ruins," he added. "But they have history there, too."

"That is true," said Superior Sietra. "I do wish Superior Dovial had survived. I have an inkling that very few of his fellow Disciples knew of the history of their temple, but he almost certainly knew a little."

"So does Superior Kralia," Kelan added. "The Disciples of Life are entangled in this, too. Have been for hundreds of years."

"Yes, we'll have to look into that," she said. "It's lucky their faith in their deity is unwavering."

"Lucky?" he echoed. "They tried to turn one of their own people into an assassin against her will."

"Their behaviour was reprehensible," she said, "but if Mekan tries to infiltrate our temple, we need to find ways to resist Him."

"I think He prefers cities," Kelan said. "Densely inhabited places. Though He does like trying to steal other deities' followers, too."

Including me, he thought. That, he was sure, was why he'd heard Mekan's voice and others had not.

"Yes." Her mouth turned down at the corners. "I am sorry, Kelan. For Laima, and for the others who were lost, too."

He blinked, unprepared for the riot of emotion that her words stirred within his chest. Was this what Yala and the others had felt after returning from the war having lost their squad-mate, and knowing that the world they'd left behind would never return? Perhaps. He hadn't asked, hadn't wanted to lay his burdens on her, when she was already shouldering the weight of the world.

Eyes stinging, he groped in his mind for a change of subject. "The book. I left it with Yala … is that a problem?"

"No," she said. "However, I have a job for you. It might be a worthy distraction."

"Oh?" Kelan had his doubts, but he was willing to listen to anything that took his thoughts away from Laima, off the chasm of grief that awaited.

"I want you to pay a visit to the Disciples of the Flame."

———

Yala arrived back in the capital the day after the battle to the sound of applause. Cheers and shouts echoed from somewhere ahead of the wagon, and Yala peered over the side, trying to work out where the noise was coming from. Ceremonial Square, she thought. Strange.

Yala waited for the wagon to slow and then climbed out, catching her balance against the side of the vehicle. She'd recovered her cane from the temple's ruins—largely thanks to Kelan—but while the Disciples of the Sky had returned home the previous night, she'd been left to travel the slower route. Her bruised and battered body had objected to riding through the night, so she'd stayed at an inn on the way back from Setemar.

This time, she'd made sure there weren't any mines or tunnels anywhere within reach.

Yala opened the door to the house and called upstairs to Saren. "It's me."

"Is it?" He appeared in the stairway, more alert than she'd expected. "I dreamed you showed up with a parade earlier. What is that racket outside?"

"I haven't a clue," she answered, putting down her pack. "I just got back."

"I can see that." He crossed the room and peered out the window. "Hey ... it's Viam."

"Good timing." Yala went to open the door, finding Viam pacing outside. Her usually styled hair was in disarray, her clothes dishevelled and stained with what appeared to be mud. "I thought you were at work."

"I had the morning off." Viam entered the house, looking a tad sheepish. "Ah, and I thought you might come back today."

"Did you?" Where—oh, right. "Did the Disciples of the Sky already arrive?"

She dipped her head. "Since I wasn't at work, I decided to wait for you."

Yala hadn't seen her from the wagon, though she'd been a little distracted by the volume of noise from the upper city. "What in the world is going on out there?"

"It's ... ah, a military parade."

"A *military parade?*" Yala sank into an armchair, her mind refusing to process any more surprises. "What are those people cheering for? Not the king's execution, I hope."

"No. The king wanted to see if he has support among the public, and I think he does."

"A few years too late." Saren gave a laugh. "Does he want to join his father in the ground?"

"He's trying," Viam protested. "Listen, Yala, I had something I wanted to show you."

"Now?" Saren frowned, then shrugged. "All right."

"What?" Yala had the distinct impression she was missing an inside joke. Hadn't the two of them barely been on speaking terms when she'd left? "What are you two scheming?"

"We have something to show you," Viam said. "If you aren't too tired."

I am. Any scheme that involved Saren was worth exerting herself to investigate, though, in case he brought more trouble to her doorstep. "Please tell me you didn't help him steal his liquor back."

"I'll have you know I haven't touched a drop." Saren huffed. "I'm wounded, Yala."

"It's not far from here," Viam said. "You don't have to come…"

"Yes, I do." Whatever had mended the years-long rift between the two of them had done what Yala herself had never been able to achieve, and her curiosity overcame her desire to lie down and sleep. "Let's go."

As they walked Yala gave the others the abbreviated version of her experiences in Setemar, including a needed reassurance that the Disciples of Life were no longer hunting her down.

"Shit, and I thought I was having a bad week," Saren remarked as they crossed a bridge over the river. "Where is Niema now?"

"She went back to the jungle," said Yala. "To see her enclave and say goodbye. I don't know what her plan is afterwards."

"I can't believe the Disciples of Life are that ruthless."

Viam had been so fixated on Yala's story that she'd almost walked into a streetlamp a couple of times. "I've been trying to research them, and there's barely anything in the palace. Not even in the records of Laria's founding."

"I can tell you why that is," Yala said, "but it'll take another hour or more, and I want to know what you've been doing."

"Save the academic debate for later," said Saren. "We're here."

Yala came to a confused halt in front of what appeared to be an old stable. Viam darted inside and exchanged a few words with a man who was dressed in clothing similar to her old uniform, who beckoned Yala with a gloved hand. She followed him to a paddock where a young war drake paced in circles, and her heart gave an uneven jolt.

"Where did you get that?" Yala watched the reptilian beast continue to pace, indifferent to her presence.

"The king has been training them," Viam explained. "So… I asked if I could take one for my own. Well, for you."

"For *me?*"

"You always missed flying," Viam said. "I forgot how much *I* missed it until recently."

"Hey." Yala gave a whistle, and the war drake ceased its pacing and snapped its teeth at her. "Nice to meet you, too."

"I knew you'd get along," Saren said. "I heard the king was hiring trainers, you know."

"Now?"

"Yes," said Viam. "I didn't mention your name, but if you wanted to…"

"Not yet," said Yala, though her traitorous heart gave a leap. "I have other matters to deal with first, like the Disciples of the Flame. I have the book they asked for."

"You're not going to give it to them, are you?" Saren asked. "They sent assassins after you."

"Yes. They're dead." She'd left out her own role in their

fates, the same as she hadn't given the details of Mekan's attempts to ensnare her. "They underestimated the god of death."

"Pity," Saren said. "If you ask me, Superior Shralin doesn't need to know you found the book at all."

"He doesn't." She'd returned to the city with the intention of washing her hands of the Disciples, which would be an impossible feat. if the Disciples of the Flame kept sending intruders to her home. And if Viam knew she was home, the Disciples of the Flame would realise soon enough. "I'll go there today and get it over with."

Viam cleared her throat. "I'll go with you, if you like."

"I think I'll pass," said Saren, but without the biting tone she might have expected. "I'll be at home."

"I'll see you later."

———

By the time Viam and Yala reached the upper city, the parade had come to an end, though discordant cheers and claps continued to erupt in Ceremonial Square, and the gates were strewn with banners.

"It's strange," Viam murmured. "I didn't expect him to host a parade this soon. He's been showing his face in public more often, but this is far riskier than a walk on the palace grounds."

"Nobody threw a spear at him, did they?" asked Yala.

"Not that I'm aware of." She'd feared seven years was too long for the public to forgive his long absence, but they hadn't turned on him. A promising start. Viam had only seen part of the parade on her way to the paddock; it'd taken the better part of two days to get the war drake settled in and she'd have to put in extra time at the palace later to make up for it.

"People aren't going to see him like King Tharen," Yala said. "He knows that, doesn't he?"

"Yes, but…" Now it was Viam's turn to share the secrets she'd learned. "I found out that the books Melian used were originally the property of the Temple of the Flame."

Yala's steps halted. "Superior Datriem … *he* gave the king the books?"

"He did, I'm sure."

Yala gave a mirthless laugh. "I can see why it took them so long to have him murdered."

"Yala." Viam's insides squirmed like a nest of serpents. The way Yala had told her of the fate of the other Disciples of the Flame had awakened questions that would gnaw at her unless she voiced them aloud. "That Disciple, Mieren, who was involved in the conspiracy…"

"Is dead, yes."

Viam licked her lips. "Did she try to take the book from you?"

"Yes. By force." Yala's hand clenched on her cane. "I won't apologise for what I did."

Another secret added to the list within Viam's heart. "I don't expect you to."

"Good." Yala glanced sideways at her. "I don't envy you having to work in the palace."

"There are good people there." Viam felt compelled to defend them. "Even the king. I don't blame you for thinking otherwise, but he doesn't know, and really… how do you tell him that his father was murdered by the people he trusted?"

"If he learns the truth, he might not act," Yala ventured. "He didn't retaliate against Rafragoria, did he? If anything, he did the opposite."

"I suppose." Viam's lips compressed. She didn't think the king would declare war on the Disciples if he learned who had killed his predecessor, but there was a difference between his father dying to nameless assassins and his father being murdered by those he trusted.

This is a bad idea, she thought as they neared the Temple of the Flame. *They'll know Yala killed the others, or someone will guess.*

Yala slowed her pace. "What's he doing here?"

Viam's attention landed on the steps leading to the temple's door where a robed Disciple of the Sky waited for them. Kelan. Heat rushed to Viam's face at the memory of how she'd fled the temple during his last visit, though he might unwittingly have saved her life in the process. Kelan lifted a hand in greeting and glided down to meet them.

"This is unexpected." Yala walked up to the temple's stairs. "Did you have another mission already?"

"Yes." He hovered above the ground, preventing them from reaching the door. "It concerns a certain book, which I believe you were about to hand over to Superior Shralin."

Yala rested her cane on the bottom stair. "What of it?"

"Superior Sietra would like to request that you give it to me instead," he said. "She insists, in fact, on the reasonable grounds that it would be far safer to keep the book in Skytower than here in the capital."

"Unfortunately, my safety depends upon my keeping my word to Superior Shralin," Yala said. "I'd rather not risk my surviving squad members, too."

"I expect not, which is why I intended to have a word with Superior Shralin." Without preamble, he glided up to the door, raised a fist, and knocked. "He's welcome to return correspondence to my Superior."

A novice answered the door and ushered Kelan inside. Yala climbed the steps more slowly, and upon reaching the entryway, she reached into her pocket and pulled out the book. Seeing the worn drakeskin cover brought a rush of recognition, though Viam recalled this book being more of a historical journal than a guidebook. She hadn't had time to read every word in the limited time she'd held the books in her possession.

Superior Shralin dismissed the novice and surveyed Yala. "You made it back?"

"I did," Yala confirmed. "The threat is gone. Mekan was defeated."

"And you brought what we requested." He reached out a hand.

Kelan leaned over and plucked the tome from Yala's hand. "Superior Sietra wants the book, too, and I'm afraid she insisted upon me bringing it directly to her. She had some interesting stories to say about how texts were once shared among all the Disciples before certain individuals began hoarding that information for themselves."

"Give that to me," Superior Shralin ground out.

"I'm sorry to say I can't." Kelan pocketed the book inside his cloak. "You're welcome to visit Skytower if you want to read its contents."

"Kelan—" Yala broke off as he took flight in a single bound, leaving the three of them on the doorstep. Grimacing, she turned back to the Superior. "This was not my idea."

"No, I expect not." Superior Shralin scowled. "I will certainly have a word with Superior Sietra. What else have you to report? What of the fate of my Disciples?"

"Dead," Yala said. "Along with too many others, including Superior Dovial."

Worry flickered in the Superior's eyes. "He's dead. One by one, the older Disciples are falling."

"Not all of them," said Yala. "Only the ones who try to ignore what's right in front of them."

Superior Shralin's eyes narrowed. "You speak out of turn, Yala Palathar. I wonder if you would be quite so arrogant if you saw…?"

"Saw what?" Yala asked.

Superior Shralin's gaze flickered to Viam. "A body was delivered to us for cremation earlier today. It might interest you."

Yala, what are you doing? Viam thought, but her warning died in her throat when Yala followed the Superior into the entryway. Viam followed, and nobody stopped her. Viam might as well have been a ghost.

Through a door into a side room, Superior Shralin gestured towards a large rectangular table. A body lay upon its wooden surface, several days old, judging by its water-logged, bloated skin. The uniform the dead man wore wasn't Larian. He was a Rafragorian soldier.

Yala's sharp intake of breath told Viam she'd noticed the same. "Where did you find him?"

"He washed up in a small rowing boat," said Superior Shralin. "He was holding this."

He held out a scrap of paper. Words had been scrawled, both in Larian and in Rafragorian, and Viam's very bones shook to read them.

REMEMBER THE ISLAND.

ACKNOWLEDGMENTS

Firstly, I wanted to offer a huge thank you to everyone who supported *Death's Disciple* over the past few months. I've been floored and humbled by the way the SFF community has rallied around this series, and I want to give a particular shout-out to everyone involved with SPFBO (and especially Esmay for her glowing semi-finalist review). It means more than I can put into words.

I also wanted to thank my editor Sarah Chorn for being such a cheerleader for this series, my proofreader Trish Long, and my fantastic cover artists at Deranged Doctor Design for all the hard work they've put in behind the scenes. And of course my assistant Mary Fields has earned a special thanks for staying on top of promotion and social media while I'm hiding in my writing cave, scribbling away at my next book.

Lastly, I owe a huge thanks to my Patrons over at my Patreon and everyone who backed the Kickstarter campaigns for both Death's Disciple and Traitor's Tome. You're the reason I can keep doing what I love the most and creating dark and weird fantasy worlds to share with you all.

ABOUT THE AUTHOR

Emma spent her childhood creating imaginary worlds to compensate for a disappointingly average reality, so it was probably inevitable that she ended up writing fantasy novels. She has a BA in English Literature with Creative Writing from Lancaster University, where she spent three years exploring the Lake District and penning strange fantastical adventures.

Now, Emma lives in the middle of England and is the international bestselling author of over 30 novels, including the Death's Disciple series and the Relics of Power trilogy. When she's not immersed in her own fictional universes, Emma can be found with her head in a book or wandering around the world in search of adventure.

Find out more about Emma's books at
www.emmaladams.com.